SEA DRAGON HEIR

Storm Constantine

SEA DRAGON HEIR

Victor Gollancz
London

First published in Great Britain in 1999
by Victor Gollancz
An imprint of Orion Books Ltd
Wellington House, 125 Strand, London WC2R 0BB

A CIP catalogue record for this book
is available from the British Library.

Typeset by SetSystems Ltd, Saffron Walden, Essex
Printed and bound in Great Britain by
Clays Ltd, St Ives plc

ACKNOWLEDGEMENTS

I would like to thank the following:

My close friends, Eloise Coquio, and Debbie Benstead, for their late-night workshop sessions on the plot of this book, and for the informal editorials. Jo Fletcher, my editor, for her support, advice and enthusiasm. Robert Kirby, my agent, for being one in a million. My partner, Jim Hibbert, for his love, his culinary abilities, and his wicked sense of humour. Vikki Lee France and Steve Jeffery of my information service, Inception, for their unflagging support. Andy Collins for giving me ideas for the weird stuff. Anne Sudworth for the beautiful cover art. Yvan Cartwright for the wonderful job he did, and does, on my web site. My folks, John and Norma, for their love and support. All my other close friends, who have given me so much: Karen Townsend, Freda Warrington, Adele Stanley, Steve Chilton, Paul Kesterton, Mark Hewkin, Simon Beal, Adrian Mc-Laughlin and Phil Plumpton. The computer shamans, Mikey Clarke and Nick Thorndyke, for their cyber-hoodoo prowess.

Storm Constantine Information Service:
   Vikki Lee France and Steve Jeffery
   Inception
   44 White Way
   Kidlington
   Oxon OX5 2XA

   E-mail: Peverel@aol.com
   Web site: http://members.aol.com/peverel/inceptio.htm

Storm Constantine's official web site:
   http://members.aol.com/malaktawus/Storm.htm

*This book is dedicated to Deborah Jane Howlett,
my incomparable friend, whose humour and love
have brightened my life for many years*

Death

The lady of the castle huddled with her children in the shattered tower. The sky reached down in grey mist and bitter smoke, between the broken stones. Below the lowering clouds, the shadows of circling birds danced like demons, screeching with parched throats for carrion.

All around the castle, the sound of battle still crashed: the hoarse cries of desperate men, the ring of steel, the immaculate hiss of arrows. The lady's cheeks were dry, as were her eyes. Her arms were about her children, and she muttered in the ancient tongue an invocation. 'Come rise, come unto me, deepest dream, come from the foam, from the lost and lone. Come rise, come unto me, leaping heart, here to my sight, to my soul.' The children were silent among her dust-scored, ragged skirts. Their eyes were old and their faces grave and resigned. Grubby fingers clung to her, perhaps without hope.

The lady knew that below her, amidst the blood and the noise, history was being made. Her line, and her husband's line, would not end here, but change. When the men with the black and purple banners pierced the heart of Caradorc, came loping like wolves down the seared passages and, finally, beat down the last door of her sanctuary, they would no longer be fired with the lust of killing. Her invocation had made sure of that, even if she lacked the power for greater effect. Her body might suffer, as would the bodies of her older daughters, but they would survive. It was necessary. Had not her guides taught her the wisdom of patience? History was a tapestry long in the making, and through time the threads would change. She must protect the heir to this house, whatever it took. 'Come rise, come unto me . . .' Her voice cracked.

'Mama.' A single word.

'Hush, little one. Hush.' She rocked her body back and forth, waiting for the heart's pierce which would tell her that her husband was dead. There was a moment's stillness, and fragments of dust, ash and straw sifted down from the ruined ceiling. Then came the baying roar from the enemy, the irrepressible caw of triumph. She felt it in her heart, felt the light go out. It doesn't matter, she told herself, it doesn't matter.

The conqueror, the king of fire, was Cassilin, son of the great Magravandian house of Malagash. Now he held court in the place where once the banners of the Palindrakes had swung. The hall of old Caradore had been unsealed, its ceilings were embers. Rain came down now, turning the pungent ashes to a gruel of bone and earth. The grey blocks of the walls were blackened, bannered with bright blood; the smooth flagstones of the floor slick and dark, the crimson carpets soaked like moss, releasing an odour of must and meat fat. The Palindrakes and their rough army had fought with passion to defend their ancient domain, and the king of fire respected this. An entrenched code of honour nestled uncomfortably beside his ambition and lust for power. He had coveted this high, feral land, and now it was his. Caradore, and its guardian family, the Palindrakes, had once belonged to the sea. Their flags were adorned with the ocean's brutal, yet fragile, monsters: sea dragons; proud, attenuated and coral-frail. If the mournful cries of their shattered ghosts echoed from the ocean now, no one heard them. The flags had fallen and were burned. The elements had clashed and fire reigned triumphant.

The king of fire was omnipotent, drunk on his conquest. Wherever he moved in the world, crowns fell before him, and towers and banners. He was the spearhead of the new empire, filled with the energy of the god Madragore and his smoking eyes. This wind-sculpted corner of land was not far from the heart of his empire, but had proved resistant. The ancient families here knew the old wisdom and used it. They understood the language of the waves and the ocean's cold denizens. Ultimately Caradore had been no match for the hot, youthful zeal of Madragore.

When his men had finished with the women, the king, who would be emperor, had them brought unto him: the wife of his slain enemy, her cowering daughters veiled in blood. Boy children hung wide-eyed from their skirts. They could not swear fealty to Madragore, the god, because in their terror and despair they could not speak. He would be merciful.

Someone called out, 'All hail to Cassilin Malagash, divine king, emperor of Magravandias, the spiritual son of Madragore! All hail!'

The king of fire accepted this annunciation. It belonged to him. He had coveted this land for a long time; it was beautiful and wild, as were its people. He also needed its special power for his campaigns. Now he rose from the blackened throne and addressed the lady of the castle, whose husband was dead, his head impaled upon a rail somewhere in the outer courts.

'Madam, I grant you the clemency of Madragore. Give to me your eldest son.'

The lady did not cringe or falter. She remained silent, her body bent with pain and despair, yet somehow regal.

The king of fire stepped down to the floor of the court, his mailed feet firm upon the scum of drenched ash and blood. He inspected the brats pawing their mother's skirts, seeking a hiding place, finding nothing but rents and tears. One by one, he prised them away, held them up by their arms to inspect their faces. They dangled in his grip like puppies, wriggling feebly. Which was the one? She would try to hide the dragon heir. She had no doubt put a glamour on him. It was essential he was recognized, the mark of Madragore put upon him.

The king found an idiot boy who drooled, whose eyes rolled. He did not look like a son of the House of Palindrake. It must be the one, ensorcelled. The king knew he had made the right choice when the lady uttered a low, sad sound.

He hauled the boy across the floor and called for his mages. They came to him from the shadows, some drooping with age or dissipation, hidden by cowls, others fierce and upright with narrow eyes and lipless smiles. They bowed to the king of fire, their tall crowns of black and indigo inclined precariously. 'Do what has to be done,' said the king, dropping the boy at their feet.

The mages walked around the crawling child, their hands curled above their hearts. Their robes hissed along the damp floor, but otherwise they made no sound.

Presently, they began to hum, each chest expelling a different tone. It seemed the notes writhed together in the air somewhere above their heads and become another thing; dense and definite, yet invisible. The boy was caged by their voices, and the glamour that protected him decomposed. He crouched with terrified eyes, trying to appear staunch and resigned. The king of fire and his black sorcerers were not deceived.

At a signal from the mages, soldiers stepped forward and lifted the boy between them. He was carried out into the courtyard, where bodies lay like slaughterhouse rags and tatters of banners flapped soddenly in the sea wind. The rain had seethed away, but the wind itself was damp, tasting of salt. A fire now raged in a blackened brazier in the centre of the yard; its flames were a gout of colour in the rinsed world.

3

The boy knelt with bowed head, his hands between his knees, his black hair like a veil about his face. Only a short distance away, his father's head grimaced from its pike. The body lay somewhere among the others, discarded and unrecognizable, its centre of power hacked away.

The mages stripped the boy of his clothes and then bound his body with a net of indigo cords. They shaved off his thick black hair. All the while, they chanted in guttural, snarling voices. Their words seemed to leave smoke hanging in the air that the wind could not disperse. Once they had bound him, he was flung between them, spinning round, presented to each of the elemental corners, while his clothes burned on the spitting fire that leaned away from the wind.

The king of fire watched the ritual without expression. In his heart, the small thing that gave him grace empathized with the Palindrake heir. The boy looked so vulnerable, shaved and naked, stumbling as the mages pushed him cruelly around the courtyard. The cold must be biting into his young skin, seizing his bones. But it is necessary, thought the king. The dragon heir must bow to Madragore.

Now the mages held the boy firm beside the fire. A brand had been heating there, bearing the mark of the god. The boy did not struggle; perhaps he had become mindless with fear, for he was so young. He began to shudder uncontrollably once the brand had been pressed on to the back of his neck, but he did not cry out. The mark was livid against his pale skin, and an ephemeral reek of burned meat filled the hurrying wind.

They took him then down to the shore, where the waves pounced upon the rocks, destroying themselves in clouds of foam. Here, another fire was built, splashed with liquors to encourage the flames. The widow of Caradore and her remaining children were conducted there also, to watch the final ceremony. The sea was grey, implacable, and the sky full of tears that did not fall. Never had Caradore seemed so unwelcoming and stark.

The archmage, a tall, inhumanly pale and reptilian man, stood behind the boy and faced him out to sea. The dragon heir had been dressed in a robe of dark indigo, so that he looked like a neophyte priest, with his naked head and thin neck. The brand was crimson above the collar of his robe and glistened with pain-killing unguent. He must be in possession of his senses for this ultimate rite and pain robbed any man of such acuity.

The archmage's voice was soft, yet it rang out clearly above the crash of the waves, the complaint of the wind. 'Hear me, oh lords of the spiritual west, the realm of water. We take unto ourselves the rightful heir to the provinces of the sea, who is Valraven, son of Mestipen, son of Rualdon. We take unto ourselves the power of the dragon heir, so that he must pay fealty to the lord of fire, Madragore, father of the great mountain, of the flame of the soul. As the heir bears the mark of Madragore, we say unto you, should he not serve God's avatar in life, should he forsake the banner of Magravandias, the fire now within him will consume his body and all in his domain.'

The archmage's voice became quieter, confidential. 'Do you understand this, boy?'

The boy paused, then nodded his head once. He understood. His mother's words came back to him dimly, from a hundred years ago – yesterday – as the ground had shaken at the approach of the Magravandian horde. The sun had shone then, and the flags on the seven towers had cracked in the clean wind. Clouds had raced high across the sky as if in panic. 'Remember,' his mother had whispered, 'your life is safe. If your father lacks the power to protect himself, and the power passes on, the enemy will not kill you. You are only a boy and they will think you tractable, easier to control than your father. You must do as they direct and be patient. The line must not die with you, Valraven, but sleep. All things come to an end. Find the faith inside you, wrap it up carefully and lay it to rest. Never speak of what you know to your sons. The heritage must be forgotten. That will be its salvation. Others will come later and find it. It will be a secret gift to your own heirs.'

Now he bowed his head and felt the seared skin on the back of his neck stretch and burn. He knew what they would tell him to do next, and perhaps a more fearless person might refuse. His father would not have approved of his mother's advice. He would have told Valraven he should die rather than betray the power they served. Their line might die, yes, but the power would not go away. It would only wait for someone else. Valraven could not be that brave: he wanted to live.

'Repeat after me,' said the archmage, his fingers like clamps on the boy's shoulders, 'I, Valraven, heir of Caradore, swear fealty to Madragore and all his denizens.'

Haltingly, the boy spoke, his voice thin, hardly heard.

The archmage nodded approvingly and continued, 'I give unto my god all the power of my tribe, and of the sea, and of its creatures. Should I forsake my oath, may the fires of Madragore consume me and my domain.'

Further up the beach, cold tears ran down the face of the Lady of Caradore. Imperceptibly, she shook her head. Yet it was right that this should happen. Valraven must not die. There had been enough waste. Old Caradore was lost. She already knew that she and her family would be moved to the summer castle further south and here the new seat of the Palindrakes would be established. The Palindrakes as Madragore's servants. No one could fight Magravandias, not yet. It would take many lifetimes.

5

Her eldest daughter slipped her hand through the crook of her elbow. Together they watched the waves pulse up the shore, reaching for the fire that burned there. Presently Valraven was led away by the mages, and everyone began to climb back to the scene of battle. The lady paused at the cliff's foot. She saw the tide's return and the fire hiss to blackened ashes. The water dragged the embers into itself, until there was only a faint mark upon the sand. It was a message from time.

PART ONE

Life

CHAPTER ONE

Dream

Two hundred years later:

When Pharinet was only seven years old, she dreamed of the dragons. They danced in the sky for her, like moving pictures from a book, their wings of shell and bone fanned out against the piercing stars. She stood on the beach below them, jumping up and down, clapping her hands. They danced for her alone.

When she awoke, it was still dark, and she could hear the restless sea fretting at the shore below the castle. The dream had filled her up with strange sensations that felt like excitement, the sort of feeling she had when she was about to go out visiting her friends with her brother, Valraven. She still wanted to jump up and down.

Although she never mentioned the dream to anyone, she thought about it often, until it eventually became buried beneath layers of other dreams and experiences. In later years, she would realize that the dragon dream had marked the moment when she'd discovered there was more to life than what the senses beheld, and what others told her. Life was a secret, or a labyrinth of secrets. She had entered the outer chamber. Her father had still been alive then.

Pharinet's mother had died as she'd struggled to expel her daughter into the world. The girl child had followed the arrival of her twin brother, Valraven V, by scant minutes, setting the precedent for the haste in which she strove to keep up with him in later life. Pharinet knew her mother only from portraits which her grieving father had hung about the castle. In every room, dead Lerinie still held sway: gazing down her patrician nose, smiling privately upon her children. In some ways, the pictures were

9

rather sinister. Pharinet wondered what her mother had really been like. She was astute enough to recognize the gloss of her father's feelings over the portraits, since every one of them had been commissioned after her mother's death. When she asked Valraven what he thought, he seemed uncomfortable and would only mutter a stupid answer. Everna, her older sister, told her *that* was what boys were like. They couldn't talk about personal things, so Pharinet shouldn't be surprised or affronted. Everna was only too ready to relate stories of their mother. She had been nine when Lerinie had died, and despite the fact she had adored her mother, seemed not to resent the twins for their part in her demise. She had become their surrogate dam, and enjoyed the role. Memories were perhaps sweeter than reality. As far as Pharinet could gather, Lerinie seemed to have had little time for her elder daughter. She had been a busy woman, for ever gadding about Caradore visiting the estates of other noble families. Everna suggested that Lerinie had had a purpose for her, which she'd been keeping on hold until an appropriate time, such as the onset of womanhood. Unfortunately, her unexpected death had prevented her from revealing what this purpose might have been. No one had thought mere childbirth could have killed Lerinie. She'd been so strong.

Resigned and loyal, Everna had picked up the bloodied mantle of motherhood and wrapped it around her own small frame. Perhaps it had been that which had made her grow. By ten, she was tall enough to peer over the heads of several of the castle guards.

Valraven senior was sometimes away from home for months at a stretch, because he was held in high esteem by the emperor and was therefore required to spend time at court in Magrast, the capital city, or else direct campaigns for conquest and containment further afield. Everna told the twins that since their mother's death, the emperor, Leonid II, had allowed their father to spend more time at home. The emperor himself had visited Caradore on several occasions, each time claiming over dinner that the sea air did him good. He looked upon his visits as holidays, even though he brought with him a milling entourage of clerks, generals and attendants and spent most of the time closeted in Valraven senior's private office discussing politics and war.

Pharinet and her twin thought the emperor rather a ridiculous figure. He was neither tall nor fat, but seemed altogether too large to fit comfortably into any environment. His voice was not coarse, nor even particularly loud, but it carried far. His laughter was free and spontaneous, but somehow inappropriate. He was eager and bouncy, like an overfriendly lion cub, tawny and golden and laced with hidden claws. They supposed

10

he'd look more at home in the great city of Magrast, where everything was grand and organized. Caradore was sprawling and relaxed, and the emperor seemed like an irritant within its shell, getting bigger and bigger as his visit progressed, perhaps in the same way that a pearl forms in an oyster from a grain of sand. He singled the younger Palindrake children out for attention and, as they wriggled uncomfortably beneath his compelling gaze, told them about his own sons. The scions of the empire were paragons of male virtue, accomplished in every desired skill. The emperor never brought any of them with him to Caradore, however, and if there was a madam emperor, she might as well have not existed.

Sometimes, in her bed at night, Pharinet would think about how the greatest man in all the world sat drinking and chatting with her father somewhere below. The Palindrakes were the most privileged of families. She knew that her great-great-grandfather's sister had been married to an ancestor of the emperor's – his great-great-grandfather – and that the two families were therefore related. The emperor did not feel like a relative, though, despite his attempts at avuncular charm. If his sons were her distant cousins, why hadn't she met them?

'The man we see is not the man that is,' Everna said, during one of his visits. 'He is like a god in Magrast, yet here he can be a boy, perhaps the child he never was. We should not be deceived by appearances. In the capital, he would probably barely acknowledge us.'

Everyone in the castle knew that the emperor came to Caradore to escape the city. Perhaps, if he'd not had this refuge, he'd have gone mad. It must be difficult for one man to keep taut all the reins that controlled the empire.

Everna said that after their mother had died, the emperor had come straight away to Caradore, perhaps abandoning important business in Magrast. He cared for their father, and despite his elevated status, took charge of the household in the wake of grief, organizing an unusually grand funeral for Lerinie and making sure that the business of the estate ran smoothly.

After Lerinie died, Valraven senior should have taken another wife. Everna told Pharinet that he must have more male heirs in case anything should happen to Valraven junior. There had been two other boy children between the birth of Everna and the twins, but both had died. Pharinet was appalled by the idea her brother was not immortal, and did not want to think what life might be like without him. Still, whether their father had the intention of remarrying or not, he did not outlive his crushing grief. When the twins were ten, he was involved in a riding accident and died from his injuries. Afterwards, Pharinet had seen the grey stallion responsible, rolling his eyes and stamping in his stall. Later, the men of the castle had built a fire on the beach, and everyone had gone down there in the evening. One of the women from the kitchen had slit the throat of the horse and the blood had run down the sand to the sea.

No one questioned that Everna was now mistress of Caradore; Valraven's guardian and spiritual guide. She was only nineteen, but dressed and behaved like a much older woman.

Pharinet could not feel sorry for her father. She sensed his life had not been happy, grief had bowed his shoulders and greyed his hair. Dead wife, dead sons. It had pained her young heart to see him moving slowly around the castle alone, lost in his private thoughts. When he'd looked upon his surviving children, his eyes had been full of sadness. They'd never heard him laugh, yet he'd been kindly, if remote. He must have loved their mother so much. Now, his spirit was free. As the people of Caradore danced a slow, wistful pavanne upon the wide shore, Pharinet had felt a lightness inside her. It must be hope or freedom.

After their father's death, the emperor did not visit Caradore again, although he would send gifts to the children to mark various religious festivals. Sometimes Pharinet wondered how he was coping without his sanctuary. Had they all made him feel so unwelcome that he no longer felt he could visit? She could not say she liked the man particularly, but deep in her heart she felt sorry for him, realizing at the same time this solicitude might be misplaced. She discussed it with her sister, and Everna sent a letter to the emperor's steward, tactfully worded, but implying they hoped His Mightiness would still look upon their home as his. They received a formal reply, thanking them for their invitation, but making no mention of a visit, although there was a paragraph concerning Valraven junior's future training in the army. The letter was altogether disappointing, if not slightly threatening.

Throughout her childhood, Pharinet's best female friend was Ellony, the eldest daughter of the Leckery family, who lived a two-hour ride away at the family domain of Norgance. Montimer Leckery, Ellony's father, was hardly ever at home, because the emperor needed him in the army. Montimer was a great general, weighed down with medals. So Norgance, like Caradore, was a household devoid of a patriarch, a situation which prevailed in most of the noble houses of Caradore.

Valraven was always the one closest to Pharinet's heart, but she soon learned that there were some things only a female companion could provide or understand. While Valraven played boisterous games on the high moors above Norgance with Ellony's elder brother, Khaster, the girls sat nearby, the wind in their hair, wrapped in their own feminine pastimes. Usually, this involved planning out their future lives. They would act out fantasies of love, without fully understanding what this might entail. Are we in love with each other's brothers? they wondered, their sly young eyes peering through curtains of hair. The boys, ignorant of the intent inspection, slashed the heather with sticks to drive out snakes and lizards.

One day, when the girls were eleven, Ellony announced, 'I shall marry Valraven.' Pharinet stared at Khaster, to decide if she could echo this sentiment. They had climbed to one of the cloud forests high above Norgance, the boys carrying a picnic pannier between them. Much to Ellony's annoyance, her mother, Saska, had forced them to take Niska, her younger sister, with them.

Now the cakes and watered wine had been devoured and the boys were climbing trees. Ellony, Pharinet and Niska sat on the springy grass, making chains of flowers: red for blood and white for the sky. Sunlight came down in coins through the branches, making heat patches on their arms and hair. Khaster had jumped out of a tree and was looking up at Valraven, who was still clambering. Leaves showered down and dusty twigs. Squirrels fled in outrage through the high canopy. Khaster was certainly handsome, Pharinet decided. His heavy brown hair fell over his face all the time. She like the way he brushed it back, wrinkling up his nose and frowning.

'You will marry Khaster,' Ellony said, clearly thinking her friend had had more than enough time to respond.

Pharinet smiled. 'Yes, I shall wear a russet gown, decorated with sea pansies, and I shall twine coral in my hair.'

Ellony sighed, caught up in the image. 'On my wedding day, I shall ride in a carriage drawn by eight white horses and their hooves will be gilded.'

Pharinet was familiar with the picture book from which this image derived. One of her earliest tutors had shown it to her. It depicted a gleeful princess riding towards her prince. Why couldn't she share the dream? In her heart, the dark red of her wedding dress was the deep bloodied shade of mourning, heavy with lilies of the grave, and her hair was spiked with bleached bones. It must be Everna putting these thoughts into her head. She liked to talk about death, seeming to find it more romantic than love.

'I shall marry a man who comes out of the sea,' said Niska, broken petals spilling from her fingers.

Ellony made a scornful noise. 'Shut up. You're too young to think about such things. Why would anyone want to marry you? You're like a slimy fish.'

Niska shrugged resignedly. It was true she was strangely pale and her

13

almost colourless hair floated on the air like seaweed in water. Pharinet felt she ought to defend the girl. 'Perhaps she's right, Elly. Niska looks like a mermaid.' She patted Niska's unyielding shoulder. 'Maybe you'll find someone on the shore one day, a wounded merman needing help. He may be handsome.'

'We don't live next to the sea like you do,' Ellony said. 'That's the sort of thing that would happen to you.' She pulled a face at her sister.

Niska neither smiled nor frowned. She concentrated only on the blooms in her lap. Her placid nature seemed sometimes to verge on the abnormal.

For a couple of years after this, the girls' fantasies veered more towards heroes of legend. They decided that one day they would come across slumbering, ensorcelled knights in a cave deep in the forest. Their maidenly kisses would bring heat back to the marble flesh. They would be whisked away on stallions of thunder, up to castles in the clouds, where ranks of blind witches with coppery hair would sing eternally of their husbands' exploits.

Pharinet also liked to indulge these fantasies when she was alone. Sometimes, in a sea cave on the beach of Caradore, she'd imagine her faceless hero kissing her. She would feel his hands upon her back and the tickle of his hair on her face. The feelings these daydreams aroused were strange and powerful. They made her want to laugh and run.

Valraven found her once, giggling to herself and splashing her feet in a pool. Sunlight slanting through the cave mouth made watery patterns on the damp, black walls. 'Pharry, what's the matter with you?'

She froze, embarrassed, conscious of her skirts hitched up to her thighs, the heat in her flesh.

Valraven was framed in the entrance, the sea pounding behind him, his hair flapping in wet tendrils around his shoulders. 'What have you been doing? I've been looking for you.' Although his eyes were in shadow, she sensed he took in her wanton appearance and wondered about it.

She could not tell him what she'd been thinking. Not only were her thoughts private, she felt they might hurt him in some way.

'Race you!' she cried and launched herself past him out of the cave. He seemed at once to forget how he'd found her and charged up the beach behind her, overtook her and ran backwards, punching the air. His delight in beating her was so simple and pure, so *male*, as Everna would have said. Pharinet could have outrun him any time. She loved him so much it was like a stomach pain. Who needed heroes when she had Valraven? But he was her brother, and no one married their brother. Could she surrender him to Ellony? The idea was not entirely pleasant. She thought of the

14

future, when Ellony would sit across a table from him at breakfast time, accompany him on visits to friends and ride with him on eager horses across the wild cliffs. Where would Pharinet fit into this picture? There did not seem to be a space for her. Those are *my* things, she thought. Ellony can't have them.

CHAPTER TWO

Truth

When Pharinet was fifteen, Everna changed. Two important things happened. The first was that Everna fell in love. This in itself was a revelation, and the condition seemed to rest uneasily on Everna's gaunt frame. Love did not suit her. Her face was not made for dreamy expressions, and her long, restless body did not fit comfortably into postures of romantic languor. The object of her affections was the son of their late father's equerry. Pharinet failed to see the attraction. To her, Thomist was a plain, uninteresting man, who was always clutching at something: his hat in his hands, his jacket collar, the hem of his shirt. He blushed easily too, which made his scalp show through his rather thin blond hair. By this time, Ellony and Pharinet had discovered the mechanics of physical love from one of Ellony's maids – a worldly girl – and the thought of lustful feelings gusting through either Everna or Thomist, never mind together, seemed absurd, if not obscene. The subject provided hours of merriment, which clearly embarrassed Khaster and Valraven. They would always leave the room, or wander off, if the girls started discussing the supposed minutiae of Everna's impending sex life.

At first Pharinet thought that the other change in her sister was merely a result of the former. She seemed to become more aloof, almost secretive. At times, her eyes would shine with a private passion. She would gaze off into the distance and her lips would drop open, very slightly. It was only when Everna summoned her sister, in an unusually formal way, to accompany her on a walk upon the cliffs that Pharinet discovered the truth.

Dune grasses rattled along the path as they walked and the ceaseless wind mussed their clothes and hair. Everna seemed unnaturally serious, which, given that she was a serious person at the best of times, meant she had something extremely important to say.

'Pharry,' she said, the word like a shout in the wild air. 'There is something you must know.'

She is going to be married, Pharinet thought in wonder. She said nothing.

Everna stopped walking and turned her sister to face her. 'I have discovered our heritage.'

The words hung between them, and Pharinet supposed they meant something. 'What is it?'

Everna gazed above Pharinet's head, out at the ocean. 'We have been dispossessed!' she hissed.

An urge to laugh fought to express itself in Pharinet's narrow chest. Everna looked so dramatic, all wild eyes, hawk nose and flailing hair. 'In what way?' she managed to say.

Everna sighed. 'You are so young, and in some ways, I feel I shouldn't speak to you about this yet, but now that I know, I have to share it with my sister, whatever her age. You are a wise girl, Pharry, and even if this knowledge becomes a burden to you. I think you should know.'

The first seeds of unease began to sprout in Pharinet's mind. Everna wasn't going to tell her she was getting married. This was more serious. She had a dread it concerned Valraven. 'What have you found out?'

'Look at the sea,' Everna said. They both stood in silence, Pharinet tense with apprehension. What was she supposed to be seeing?

'How powerful it is,' Everna murmured. 'Such strength! It is around us all the time, pounding and pounding, yet we are so used to it, we do not hear it.'

For the first time in many years, an image of the dragon dream came back to Pharinet's mind, its flavour strong and intact. 'Sometimes we do,' she said. 'It does intrude – sometimes.'

Everna glanced down at her. 'That's true . . . Perhaps you feel it already – the truth, I mean.'

'I think so.' Did she? Pharinet had a feeling that whatever Everna said would not surprise her.

'It concerns the emperor,' Everna said.

Pharinet shuddered. Surely Valraven hadn't been summoned to court already? 'What have you heard? Has he written? Will Val have to leave?'

Everna closed her eyes briefly and shook her head, her hand reaching out for her sister's shoulder. 'No, no, not yet. I've heard nothing from Magrast. This news came from somewhere else.'

17

'Where? What news?' Pharinet's heart was beating fast now, as if a creature with frantic wings fluttered in her breast, trying to escape.

Everna took a deep breath, and simultaneously a fist of wind buffeted against them, muffling her words. 'We have not always been favourites of the empire. At one time, Caradore was an independent state.'

Pharinet did not think this particularly surprising. 'At one time, the whole of the empire must have been independent states.'

'Yes, I know. But remember that in order to be part of an empire, a country first has to be conquered.'

Because of their father's friendship with the emperor and their distant relatedness, Pharinet had always assumed her people had affiliated themselves willingly to Magravandias. She was chilled to think it might have happened a different way. 'Was there a war?' she asked, anticipating the answer with sinking heart. She did not want the history to be bloody; it would mean the Palindrakes weren't such a privileged family after all. Why hadn't her tutors ever told her of this?

Everna nodded briefly. 'Yes. There was a war. Our great-great-grandfather's sister was a spoil of it, to cement the alliance. And other things happened too . . .

'What other things?'

Everna took her lower lip between her teeth. Why was she finding this so difficult? It had happened so long ago. 'Pharry, something was taken from us, something very important and special.'

'Money? Land?'

'No! Our heritage. The old ways, the old beliefs. All gone. Our ancestor, Valraven I, was a boy when it happened. The Magravands came, led by the second emperor. They killed the Lord of Caradore and took the boy, Valraven, as their own. It is so terrible. They made him swear an oath to Madragore that bound his dynasty to the empire for eternity. If he, or his descendants, should forsake it, then Caradore will perish in flame.'

The story *was* terrible, Pharinet thought, but even if it was true, how could it affect them now? It had happened so long ago, and had no bearing on the present. Times change, things are forgotten. If anything, it was inconvenient to know these facts. What could they do about it now? The Magravands might originally have ridden into Caradore as conquerors, yet while their father was alive the emperor had looked upon it as a refuge, the abode of a beloved friend. 'It is nothing to do with us,' Pharinet said.

Everna glanced down at her. 'You are wrong. It has *everything* to do with us, not least Val. From the day of the conquest forward, every firstborn son of our house has been named Valraven. It is to help keep something

18

alive. They are kings, Pharry, but without a kingdom. I know you don't want to hear these things, but you must.'

'What else is there to know?'

'The dragons,' Everna said, gazing out at the ocean. She lifted a hand, pointed. 'The sea dragons.'

Pharinet took a moment to consider these words. So it had been no coincidence an image of her dream had come back to her. 'What of them?'

'The Palindrakes were the guardians of the sea power. The sea dragons danced for our ancestors, gave them knowledge of the ocean realm and its secrets. The women were their priestesses, and the dragon heir their spiritual son. The firstborn boy of every generation was a channel for the power. He was the lord of Caradore in more than one way. His presence ensured the vitality of the land, its security and fertility. The Magravands took this from us, because they wanted that power for themselves. That is why our father, and his father before him, was taken into the court at Magrast. Soon it will be the same for Val. The dragon heir is a symbol, almost like an insignia of war. Whatever army he leads will win their battles.'

'No wonder the emperor was so fond of Dada!' Pharinet exclaimed. *Could* this all be true?

Everna nodded. 'The dragons have sunk back into the sea. We cannot call them to us any more. The power is in the land and in our blood but we have lost that special connection with the sea. It has been severed.'

'Evvie, how do you know these things?'

Everna pursed her lips. 'Saska Leckery,' she said.

Pharinet experienced a wave of both disappointment and relief. It was only stories, then. Ellony's mother was like an unofficial aunt to the Palindrakes. She had helped Everna a lot since their mother had died, but despite many kind and noble qualities, had a busy tongue and an active imagination. It was well known in the district that gossip deriving from Saska was prone to rigorous exaggeration. 'How does Saska know this if we do not?'

'Don't you see?' Everna snapped. 'This is what our mother would have told me! Saska intimated as much. Apparently, Mama spoke to Saska about it a long time ago. She said that if anything were to happen to her, Saska should be the one to pass on the knowledge.'

'I'm not sure about all this,' Pharinet said, her eyes narrow. 'If it's true, I think other people would have told us.'

'Oh, Pharry, can't you just trust your instincts? I know you feel the truth of it inside. There is more. The women of this land have secretly preserved a lot of the ancient traditions. There is a cabal of priestesses, loyal to the dragons, who keep the old ways alive. It is like a tiny flame that cannot be stoked, for then it would be noticeable, but at least it keeps the death of belief at bay. And I . . .' She paused, frowned.

'Have become involved in it,' Pharinet finished.

Everna glanced down at her. 'I'm not supposed to speak of it. The tradition has to be secret because it opposes the law of Madragore.'

'Is Saska in it?'

'Yes.'

Pharinet sighed. She imagined a bunch of the local matriarchs dancing in secret to the legend of dragons. It seemed absurd. How could Everna be so taken in? She doubted there was harm in it, but it seemed ridiculous too. When she thought of the emperor, she could not imagine his ancestors involved in dark or magical deeds. He seemed so light and golden. And yet, there was the dragon dream. She remembered the feelings it had inspired within her, and suddenly the secret history seemed much more credible. 'You'll have to prove all this to me,' she said.

Everna smiled carefully. 'I anticipated as much. You are too young to join the sisterhood, but the evidence is there on Val, if you care to look.'

'What evidence?'

'On the back of his neck, you'll find the mark of Madragore. Our great-great-grandfather was branded there by the Magravand mages. The mark is passed on through the father and is part of what binds the dragon heir to Madragore. I want you to look for it. Once you've seen it, will you believe me?'

Pharinet thought she must have seen Val naked a thousand times since they were babies. She could not remember having seen a mark. 'What is it supposed to look like?'

'The hammer of the god.' Everna took her sister's shoulders in a strong grip. 'Pharry, I was driven to confide in you, even though it contravenes the laws of the sisterhood. I should have waited another few years before entrusting you with this knowledge, but some instinct has forced me to speak now. You must not reveal what I've told you to anyone. Do you understand? Not even Val.'

'Why not? Surely he should be told, too?'

Everna shook her head. 'No. This knowledge will only damage him. In a few years' time, he will be summoned to Magrast, and must go in innocence. The priestesses work constantly to undo the magic of the mages, and one day they will succeed. On that day, the dragons will rise from the sea, and the foundation of the empire will crack. Then we shall create change. But until that moment, the dragon heir must remain ignorant of his heritage. Our great-great-grandmother, Ilcretia, initiated the Sisterhood of the Dragon, and she decreed what must be so. We have to trust her judgement, even now. Promise me you'll keep silent. Swear on Val's life!'

Pharinet hesitated. Everna seemed panicked now, perhaps thinking she'd acted impulsively to unburden herself. Relenting, Pharinet softened. 'All right. I swear on Val's life to keep your secret.'

Everna's grip slackened on her shoulders. She bowed her head. 'Good. Good. Look for the mark, Pharry,'

It occurred to Pharinet that love might have driven Everna a little strange. After their walk, Pharinet wandered down to the beach alone. On the sand, she looked up and saw her sister strolling along the clifftop towards the castle, her gaunt body erect, but her head bent. There had been a kind of madness in Everna's urgency.

Pharinet went down to her sea-cave, the place where she always hid herself to think. The tide was coming in and soon the cave would be flooded. Pharinet clambered over the rocks, soaking her skirts. Further back, the floor sloped upwards and the cave narrowed to a tunnel. If she wriggled and struggled up the throat of stone, it would lead her out on to the clifftops. She had used it often when the tide had cut her off from the beach. She crouched on a high ledge, watching the water surge and coil beneath her.

Sea dragons. There was an echo of a feeling within her; some ancient memory had been prodded and had awoken. Valraven: the dragon heir. It made sense to her. There was a feyness about him, something tragic, which might be his stolen heritage. Was it this knowledge that had hung so heavily about their father? She had never known him before her mother had died, so she had no way of telling. Everna, presumably, had been too young to remember. But perhaps their grandfather had not known the truth. Perhaps their great-great-grandfather had never spoken of it to his sons, and only the women had carried the secret forward into the future. She experienced a moment of irritation that Everna's 'sisters' would not want her to know about this yet. The knowledge belonged to the Palindrakes, more so than anyone else. Everna had been right to tell her. Poor Val. So innocent, so beautiful, yet weirdly cursed. Emotion overcame her and she had to let the tears fall. Sadness welled up, threshing and lashing like the incoming tide. There was truth in the feeling. Perhaps she had known all along.

Later, as the sun set, she clambered out of the chimney of stone. Val would have missed her at dinner. What could she say to him? Now she had to see if the mark was there.

She found him at the stables, exercising his bay gelding in the yard. He looked so at home on the animal, his spine straight, his shoulders squared. His hair was tied in a cord at his neck, flowing like a horse's tail down his back. The moment he caught sight of her leaning against the fence, he began to perform, making the horse gambol and curvet. Pharinet smiled. Why did she feel so much older than him? He kindled a nurturing urge within her that made her feel melancholy. His beauty made him ephemeral, like a dragonfly.

She had an idea that she would offer to brush his hair for him, but realized that even this simple plan would take some manoeuvring. She had brushed his hair a thousand times, but now, because there was a purpose to it, she thought he would sense her intent, ask questions.

Presently he urged his horse over to the fence and there made it rear to a halt. Pharinet reached out to pat the sweating neck of the animal.

'Where've you been?' Valraven said. 'You missed dinner, and Everna didn't say a thing. What's going on?'

'I went for a walk,' she answered. 'Got lost in my thoughts.'

Valraven pulled a comical face and slipped down from the horse's back. 'You must be hungry, then. Let's go to the kitchens.'

He made to pull the cord from his hair, but Pharinet hurried to stay his hands. 'Let me,' she said. 'You know what you're like. You'll make a tangle.'

He laughed, turned his back to her and threw up his head, hands on hips. Her fingers shook as she fumbled with the knot. She hardly dared look. But then the mass of hair was free. She clutched it in one hand and lifted it, quickly pulled down the collar of his shirt.

'What is it?' he asked.

'Nothing,' she answered. 'A fly.' She reached out and touched his pale skin, registered his damp heat. Tiny black hairs curled beneath her hand, oily with sweat. There was a mark, and it looked like a mallet. Of course, she had seen it many times before, only now she saw it with new eyes. The mark was brownish-red, like a misshapen mole, and not very big.

Pharinet felt faint, disorientated, removed from the world. This is not the life I know, she thought, and stood on tiptoe to kiss her brother's neck, right on the place where the skin was stained.

'You are odd tonight,' he said, wriggling away. 'What's got into you? Haven't fallen in love yourself, I hope!'

She managed to laugh. 'No. Any man worth my love lives only in story books.'

He turned and put an arm about her waist, 'Good. I would be jealous.' Together they walked into the castle.

22

CHAPTER THREE

Love

Once Pharinet knew of the dragons, she searched for evidence. Each night before she slept, she would compose her mind to receive more strange dreams. None came that she could remember. After the talk on the clifftop, Everna did not mention the subject again, and Pharinet sensed it was now closed until she reached an age when she could be absorbed into her great-great-grandmother's sisterhood. It was easier to discover things about her. There was a statue of her in the solarium. Ilcretia Palindrake. Pharinet had previously ignored the statue as part of the surroundings; it peered whitely through spreading palms that came from warmer shores in the south. Now Pharinet decided she looked very much like this fabled ancestress herself. Because she looked at the piece with new eyes, she realized the pose was rather strange, not at all formal. Ilcretia stood erect with her head thrown back, her eyes staring, as if she beheld something marvellous in the sky. Her arms were rigid by her sides, fists clenched, and one toe peeped beneath her gown as if she was about to step forward off a cliff into the unknown. It was difficult to tell whether she was beautiful or not, because the whiteness of the stone seemed to blur her features, but her posture blazed with energy. She had lived in Old Caradore, which was nearly half a day's ride away up the coast. Pharinet had never been there. It was a ruin now, best forgotten. Too many terrible things had happened there. Ilcretia had come to New Caradore with her children, and had made it a home. She had clearly been a survivor of great inner resource. Here, she had built up her Sisterhood from the memory of pain. She had not succumbed to melancholy or despair. Pharinet imagined her commissioning this statue, leaving it as a reminder for all future generations: be strong and fearless.

23

On one occasion Valraven caught Pharinet meditating before the statue. She jumped when she realized he was there, felt strangely guilty. Valraven wrapped an arm about her shoulders. 'Mad granny!' he said with a laugh. 'Why are you staring at her like that?'

'She wasn't mad!' Pharinet blurted out before she could stem the words.

Valraven cast her a sidelong glance. 'But she *looks* mad. Can't you see it? The sculptor caught her grief in stone. She's contemplating throwing herself from the battlements, because her husband is dead.'

It occurred to Pharinet that Valraven's remarks suggested he knew something about their family history too. But from where? Everna had told her it was secret. 'How do you know that?'

'Dada told me a long time ago. The statue used to scare me, and he said that women's grief was scary.'

'Did he say how her husband died?'

Valraven shrugged. 'Can't remember. Perhaps it was a riding accident, like Dada's.'

Pharinet smiled. 'No. Perhaps she poisoned him and was driven mad by guilt.'

He grinned. 'You see? Scary!'

Pharinet yelped and hit out at him, and together they ran from the solarium, leaving the statue to continue her endless ultimate step.

Pharinet also began to view Ellony in a different light. Her family were involved in the sisterhood. Did Ellony know about it? Sometimes Pharinet was tempted to make a leading remark and see where it went, but something always stayed her tongue. She remembered the ferocity in Everna's eyes as she'd made her sister utter a vow of silence. She had sworn on Valraven's life and must not break it. Still, as the years progressed, it became ever more clear that Ellony thought of herself as Val's future wife. Pharinet became increasingly uncomfortable with the idea. She loved Ellony, but sometimes felt jealous.

Despite Montimer Leckery's scant home leaves, Saska continued to bear him children – after Niska, another daughter and two sons. Ellony began to talk more often of when she would have children of her own. Saska plainly encouraged her. She would often make light-hearted comments about how her daughter and Val should soon be talking of the future. Pharinet's face would burn on these occasions, prompting Saska to mention Khaster's name. She seemed to think Pharinet was embarrassed about adult relationships, and talk of Valraven and Ellony only made her think of her own marital destiny. Khaster could not have been unaware of the almost salacious currents that seemed to swirl about the two households as the youngsters all moved into their late teens, yet he never gave any indication of how he felt about it. Pharinet wavered between feeling relieved and outraged. She tried to imagine Khaster kissing her in the way that her imaginary heroes had done a few years before, but the image just wouldn't stick. She appreciated his looks and liked his company, yet he was always so distant from her, as if they never made a real connection.

One day, Pharinet said to her brother, 'Do you want to marry Ellony?'

It disturbed her that her question didn't make him look surprised. If anything, a certain furtiveness crept over his face. He looked away from her. 'Well, I'll have to marry somebody,' he said lamely.

'Do you love her?'

She saw the colour creep up his neck. 'Oh, Pharry, shut up! If I marry her, it won't be for a long time. I have to go to Magrast next spring. You know that.'

Yes, she knew that. The summons had come. The emperor cordially invited the heir of Caradore to the city, to take up the position of an officer in the imperial army. Khaster too would soon be gone, like his father before him. As Pharinet became older, she became more aware of what was going on in the world. Reality intruded into her dreams. Caradore was treated like a breeding ground for officers. The emperor regarded its inhabitants as good stock, and kept them plump and fertile in the corner of the empire. The empire had remained more or less static for forty years or so, with various problem areas on the borders, but now the emperor schemed to expand his territory. The official line was that Magravandias wanted to fill the world with the divine presence of Madragore and strip its barbaric corners of brutal overlords and oppressive governments. Perhaps that was true, and the Magravands acted upon purely noble instincts. But all about the world, there must be places like Caradore, whose own gods and magic had been suppressed and destroyed, whose sons were bred like horses to swell the ranks of the army: all in the name of the lord of fire. It was a holy war, and because of that, without pity.

Pharinet knew that sometimes men didn't come back from the campaigns and that all the noble families in the district were rent by gaping holes that grief couldn't fill. Valraven would be fairly safe, because he was marked to be a general, protected behind a horde of men who would soak up the arrows, the sword-thrusts, the poisonous steams. Khaster might reach a similar elevated position, but it would take longer.

On the night before Valraven was due to leave Caradore, all the local families gathered at the Palindrake domain for a melancholy, yet boisterous, celebration. Pharinet felt feverish, as if there was some business she hadn't concluded. Valraven looked radiant, as if he were pleased to be going away. Pharinet had to leave the party, and went out on to one of the terraces, where the spring breeze cut across her face. She realized her cheeks were wet; some tears had escaped without her noticing them. She heard footsteps and sensed a male presence. It would be him. What would she say? What was there to say? Then, something unfamiliar about the other's smell, or sound, made her go tense. It wasn't Val. She turned and saw it was Khaster, looking down at her shyly from beneath a mop of hair. He had grown so tall, so angular. He was leaving with Val and she'd forgotten about it. Now the proposal would come, she thought, because Saska would have bullied him into it. She wanted to say, 'Yes, all right, we might as well!' even before he spoke.

'Are you feeling all right?' he asked her.

She remembered the tears and brushed them away. 'No, not really. What do you expect?' She didn't want to be harsh, but something about the easiness of the situation annoyed her. 'Have you come to ask me to marry you?'

He laughed nervously. 'Pharinet, you are the daughter of the waves! Lashing and eroding the rocks of male resolve.'

His comment surprised her, and she softened towards him. 'I'm sorry. I just can't bear the thought of Val leaving – nor you, of course. It seems so unfair. Our life is here, in Caradore. Let the emperor do as he likes. He should just leave us alone.'

He took a step closer, ignoring her remarks. 'It would please our families if we were to be married, Pharry. I know this will be an alliance of convenience rather than passion, but is there anyone else you would rather have?' He did not ask that through arrogance, but practicality. There was no one else. The Leckerys and the Palindrakes had grown up together. They were already one unit.

'I know, Khaster. Yes, of course we shall marry. Perhaps when you have your first leave?'

He exhaled in what seemed to be relief. Had he thought she might refuse him? 'Yes. You might not believe me, but it is something I will look forward to.'

She laughed. 'I'm not sure I do believe you, Khaster. You have never struck me as a romantic type.'

He grinned. 'I just want a wife who's not afraid of getting her shoes dirty, that's all.'

'Ah, so the rock and tree climbing will continue, then?'

'Of course. It is a prerequisite.'

At this point, Pharinet realized that being married to Khaster wouldn't

26

be too much of a trial. Then she remembered Ellony, and some of her warmth fled. 'And your sister? Is she too happily betrothed?'

Khaster had the grace to look uncomfortable. He frowned. 'I thought you knew. Val asked for her hand a week or so ago. I can't believe he hasn't mentioned it.'

'Nor I,' Pharinet said lightly, although her insides had turned to ice. 'I would have imagined Ellony would want a big fanfare about it tonight.'

He shrugged. 'I don't know.'

Pharinet sighed. 'Oh well. It isn't something I hadn't expected.' He would think about how her tone suggested she'd just heard a lover of hers had announced he would marry another woman. Let him think what he liked. Wickedness stole into her. 'I suppose we must kiss now.' She faced him. 'Well, come on then.'

She expected him to cringe and mutter some excuse, but he merely rolled his eyes and took her in his arms. It was hard to imagine where he had learned this skill. Had he frolicked with maids and gypsy girls? Had Val, too? She closed her eyes, wondering if this was pleasant or rather disgusting. Was it invasion or sharing? A strange sound insinuated itself into her mind, like a mournful howl from far away. She pulled back. 'What was that?'

Khaster looked puzzled. 'What?'

She could still hear it. It was like a song, something unearthly and terrible, yet full of despair. She turned to the balustrade. 'It's coming from the sea. Could it be a bell or something?'

Khaster stood beside her. 'I can't hear anything.'

The sound had gone now, sobbing away on the wind. Pharinet shuddered. She felt desolate.

They went back into the castle, arm in arm. Now she belonged to him and the air between them had become charged. Strange how so great a change could happen so quickly. Pharinet saw Valraven standing beside one of the heavy columns that were garlanded with ivy and sea-moss. Ellony was a pale presence beside him, her colourless hair a cloud around her shoulders. She was dressed in white, like a bride, and her cheeks were flushed. Her sisters Niska and Ligrana stood close to her, proud and protective. Pharinet knew her own eyes did not sparkle as Ellony's did. She was a cool presence beside her future husband, no more than a friend to him.

'Val!' Pharinet exclaimed sweeping up to her brother and Ellony, and dragging Khaster behind. 'Wonderful news. I am to be a wife.'

Valraven's expression was unreadable, but she supposed he already knew

27

Khaster's intentions. Ellony uttered a delighted squeal and bounced forward to hug her friend.

Pharinet took a step back, fixed her brother with a stare. 'But I'm surprised you didn't tell me about your betrothal to Elly. Aren't you going to announce it tonight?' She could not be warm; it just wasn't in her. Ellony's face froze into an expression of alarm and confusion. Where was the girlish exchange of happiness she had expected?

'It will be announced,' Valraven answered stonily.

A wall had come between them, a soft wall of Ellony. How could it hurt this much?

'I want to dance,' Pharinet told Khaster, and hauled him on to the floor where enchanted couples whirled through the candlelight to the skirl of violins, the heartbeat of drums.

As the first guests began to leave, Pharinet wandered out of the castle and down to the beach. She could not think; she was numb. The sea crashed as hungrily as ever at the shore, the cresting waves like the curled spines of dragons. She knew that Valraven would come to find her and he did. She wanted to tell him what she knew about the sisterhood; shock him. But when she sensed his soft footfall on the sand behind her, the urge to speak faded away. He did not know what he was, but she did.

'Pharry,' he said. 'You are angry with me.'

She did not trust herself to speak.

'I would have told you, only I knew you wouldn't like it.' He paused. 'This is difficult; we both know how much.'

She turned round then. 'What are you saying, Val?'

His gaze slid away from hers. 'I don't know really.'

'Then let me tell you. I'm jealous of any other woman who shares your hearth, your life, your bed. I love you, Val, you are part of me, and if some aspect of that is impure, then let it be so. I will hate her for having you!' Even as she spoke, Pharinet knew Valraven harboured no such jealousy for Khaster. She turned away from him again, furious because her eyes were filling with tears. She shouldn't cry; it was weak.

'Pharry,' he said quietly, and put his hands on her shoulders.

She raised an arm, but would not face him. 'Go, Val. Go now. I pray Madragore will protect you in the army. My love will go with you.'

He squeezed her shoulders briefly. 'We shall speak when I return. Take care, Pharry.' Then he was gone.

Pharinet stared out at the ocean, seeing nothing. The splinter of the waves upon the sand was just a roar in her head, part of her hectic blood. What had she said?

CHAPTER FOUR

Rites

Pharinet was nineteen years old, alone and in love. Once Valraven had left her world, she realized this forbidden feeling had been within her for many years, disguised as something else. She was appalled: at herself, and at the strength of the emotion. This was the sea made manifest in her body, churning and heaving. Naturally, she could not speak of her feelings to anyone else. Everna would be disgusted and Ellony – well, Ellony was just out of the question. Pharinet knew the love would not fade with time, but would become deeper and harder, like a shard lodged in her breast. If Valraven had a dour legacy hanging over him, then perhaps so had she.

Once Khaster and Valraven had left Caradore, a heavy atmosphere of melancholy slipped over the land like a shroud. These were holes hacked from the bedrock that could never be filled nor healed. Ellony wanted to spend more time with Pharinet, which to Pharinet was like being tortured with blades. Far from feeling sympathetic, while Ellony moaned on about her loneliness, Pharinet wanted to slap her. Once she would have taken her friend in her arms, made her laugh. Ellony believed Pharinet's distance with her was caused by an unspeakable grief over Khaster's leaving. Pharinet let her think that.

In the autumn of that year, Everna would marry her Thomist. She expressed a desire to have her brother at the wedding, but Valraven's first leave would not commence until the following spring, and it seemed Everna could no longer do without a husband. She had waited long enough, and now that Valraven had left Caradore, she clearly felt comfortable moving her lover into the upper apartments as a spouse. Thomist had no lands of his own, no house to which to take his bride. But this didn't matter. He was a good, solid man, and Everna loved him. Pharinet tried to be cheerful for her sister's sake, despite having spent the summer beneath a pall of glumness.

'I feel almost guilty,' Everna said on one occasion, casting a wan glance at her sister. 'I am marrying, while you must wait.'

'You are older than me,' said Pharinet. 'It's only right you should wed first.'

Everna was too misty-eyed to view things so practically. 'Still, there is at least one compensation for you,' she said.

'And what is that?'

Everna touched Pharinet's hand. 'You are of an age to join the Sisterhood.'

This subject had not been mentioned since the talk on the cliffs some five years before. Pharinet wrinkled up her nose. 'Oh, I'm not sure, Evvie.'

Everna laughed. 'Don't be ridiculous! You can't spend your life mooning around over a distant lover. Fill your hours with something else.'

'With religion.'

'With magic,' said Everna.

Pharinet sighed grumpily. 'If it pleases you,' she said.

Everna hugged her.

Pharinet soon discovered that Ellony would share her initiation rite. This did nothing to inspire any enthusiasm in her for the event. Ellony, on the other hand, seemed transformed and uplifted by the prospect. Pharinet had to suffer an afternoon in Ellony's company while she twittered on rapturously about the implications of her initiation, how it would bring her closer to Valraven and meant she could actively do something for him. 'It is my duty as his wife,' she said, her hands clasped beneath her chin, while her eyes gazed off into some gilded fantasy.

'You are not yet his wife,' said Pharinet.

Ellony's expression clouded. 'Pharry,' she said. 'I have to ask. It seems to me that you are not entirely happy with this arrangement. Why? What have I done? Don't you think I'm suitable for your brother?' The tone of Ellony's voice suggested she expected only favourable answers to her questions.

'Val and I are twins,' Pharinet said. 'You have to understand that it feels strange to me he should have someone else so close in his life.'

Ellony nodded thoughtfully. 'I think I see.' She brightened. 'But Pharry, it will be me, not some stranger you neither know nor love. We shall have such fun together! I will live here! We will be sisters.'

'We shall swap places,' said Pharinet, 'for presumably Khaster will want me to live at Norgance.'

'Oh yes,' said Ellony, troubled again. 'Isn't it odd? I hadn't thought of that.'

Pharinet sighed and stood up. How would Valraven be satisfied by this woolly-headed creature? It would be a travesty. Now she found it hard to imagine how she and Ellony could ever have been close friends. They had grown apart, perhaps, or it might be that Pharinet had always been this different, only too young to realize it.

A date was set for the girls to undergo their rite of passage into the Sisterhood of the Dragon. It would take place on the eve of the Autumnal Equinox, known under Madragorian belief as the Feast of Corg, after one of Madragore's sons who was associated with harvest and death. Everna told Pharinet she should now look upon this day as Foymoriel. Under Dragon lore, this was a female day, when the mute priestesses of Foy, the Dragon Queen, came to reap the land of ripe souls, and take to their Bone Lady a youth of fair aspect as a sacrificial husband.

'Do we provide sacrificial husbands for the dragons?' Pharinet asked her sister.

'No,' Everna answered shortly. 'It could attract unwelcome attention to our activities.'

Pharinet smiled. In her present mood, the prospect of sacrifice would have livened up what she otherwise anticipated would be a bleak event.

'We make an effigy in sand,' said Everna. 'You'll see.'

On the eve of Foymoriel, while the villagers around Caradore celebrated the Feast of Corg with family meals, ritual dances and midnight weddings, Pharinet followed her sister on horseback to the wild moor beyond the castle. Both women wore hooded cloaks to conceal themselves, a precaution which seemed pointless in Pharinet's opinion, seeing as their horses would be well-known about the district. She had been ritually bathed by her sister, with a natural sponge soaked in a silver basin of sea-water where petals of frail sea-violets floated. She wanted to feel excited for Everna's sake, because it was clearly so important to her, but Pharinet felt simply dull inside.

A narrow track amid the wiry heather wound between stunted, wind-shrivelled trees, most of which were dead from salt, to a place that was generally shunned by the local populace: the rock village. Whether it had ever been a real village was debatable. The night was cool and breezy, the air filled with the smell of wood smoke from village bonfires, garnished with a perfume of brine from the sea below. After a couple of miles' riding, the track spilled over a rocky lip and led precipitously to a great crater in the ground. Several legends surrounded the formation of this phenomenon. Some said it was the result of a second moon crashing on to the world, others that one of Madragore's sons had killed a gargantuan demon in a heavenly battle, and the body had plummeted down to smash against the earth. Another, more ancient myth, spoke of a fire-drake who had breathed upon the ground to create a hiding place from the sea dragons for her kittens. Pharinet heard this particular story on the way there, amused at the way Everna wanted to invest this bit of fantasy with a gloss of truth. 'The fire-drakes were long ago banished from this realm by the sea dragons,' Everna said. 'If they still existed, they would be allied to Madragore.'

At the bottom of the crater, thick thorny shrubs and a litter of boulders made progress difficult. Around the sides, the knobbly dark cliffs were pocked with caves; allegedly abandoned dwellings. Other women had already arrived, for Pharinet saw a huddle of horses tethered to an ancient thorn near one of the cave mouths. Flickers of orange light illuminated the rock; a fire must have been lit inside.

'I would have thought you'd worship your dragons upon the shore,' Pharinet said, 'seeing as they're connected with the sea.'

Everna dismounted from her horse. 'You will learn soon enough what we do and do not do,' she replied.

Pharinet huffed an exaggerated sigh and jumped to the ground. Her horse whinnied softly, perhaps excited by the proximity of animals he did not know. 'Quiet, Kelpa, or you'll upset the mares. Your days for courtship were over the day they took the hot irons to you.'

Everna directed a stern glance at her sister, clearly wishing she could adopt a more sober mien.

Pharinet put her hands to the sides of her hood. 'Is it etiquette to enter the sacred cave with head covered or uncovered?'

'Do as you please,' Everna answered. 'Tether Kelpa. Be quick.'

Pharinet threw back her hood and tied her horse's reins to the branch of a thorn. 'No trouble, mind,' she said to him, wagging a finger before his placid nose, 'or the dames of the Order will be forced to skip out into the night and calm their mares, which would not be seemly under the circumstances.'

Everna ignored this comment.

The cave itself was unremarkable. There was enough room for twenty or so women to sit down in a circle, but the roof slanted so sharply, no more than five could stand up at one time. As Pharinet had antici- pated, a fire had been lit and sea-moss was crackling upon it, releasing its essential oil in a briny steam. Ellony was already there, sitting by her mother, her face pink in the glow of the flames. She's excited, Pharinet thought. She's thinking of Val. Pharinet tasted sourness in the back of her throat.

The High Priestess of the group stood up as Pharinet and Everna entered the circle. She was recognizable as a person of rank by the elaborate coral crown upon her head that was like a branch of bleached antlers, crusted with ancient weed. At first, Pharinet did not know her, but then, with some surprise, she realized it was Saska's sister, Dimara Corey. Dimara was often present at Norgance, but seemed a private person, who interacted little with others. She was a single woman, who lived alone in a crumbling old house on the outskirts of the Norgance estate.

'Welcome,' the priestess said in a voice that boomed – appropriately, Pharinet thought – like the sea. 'Do you come to us of your own desire, Pharinet Palindrake?'

'I would not be here under duress,' Pharinet answered lightly and sat down among the women.

Dimara did not look affronted as Pharinet had expected. A smile played around the corners of her mouth. She was middle-aged, large-boned and imposing. Her long brown hair was streaked with grey. Previously Pharinet had barely acknowledged the woman's existence.

'I am the Merante,' said Dimara, 'lady of this order, the Voice of the Deep. You have been recommended as a candidate by your sister, Everna, who speaks for you.'

Everna had not sat down. 'I petition my sisters that Pharinet Palindrake may be initiated into our secrets, to continue the sacred task, to work in the name of those whom we serve.'

'We hear your petition, sister,' said the Merante.

Pharinet had been prepared to mock and scorn. However, as she sat before the hungry flicker of the fire, a sense of solemnity stole over her. She could neither control it nor banish it. The women around her, many of whom she knew, were not showing her their everyday faces. They did know something, she could sense it. They hid their secret faces behind a screen, but now it was drawn back. There was Saska, looking wild-eyed and potentially fierce, her soft hands clawed upon her knees. Urendel Mafferitch, a timid female, appeared sorceress-sly. She recognized women of the families of Doomes, Ignitante and Galingale, people she met only very rarely, but who were clearly intimates of her sister. They all seemed to burn with a secret fire. Everna was a pole of concentrated purpose, a force waiting to be unleashed. Only Ellony appeared similar to how Pharinet normally knew her. Could Ellony feel the potential humming around her? She still stared moonily into the flames, no doubt dreaming of the days she thought would come.

33

The Merante raised her arms. 'Sisters, let us welcome these neophytes among us. Let us share our secrets.'

They all assented: 'Aye!'

'Brenka Galingale, our archivist, will instruct you in the lore,' said the Merante.

A woman stood up. She was small and thin, and when she spoke, her voice was high and soft. But despite this apparent fragility, her words made Pharinet tingle. 'There was a time when the Dragon Queen, Foy, ruled the ancient domain of Caradore. She was a creature of the sea, and a creature of the land, and was worshipped by all. When she spoke, the tides turned. When she roared, the waves devoured the cliffs. When she wept, the ocean poured up the mighty rivers and drowned villages and fields. Foy had three daughters, Jia, Misk and Thrope, who were dragon women, of neither the land nor the sea. Unto them, the people offered gifts and spoils, for they could be harsh in their nature. When the dragon women smiled upon you, you could be assured of good fortune, but their anger was swift and without remorse. People feared the daughters of Foy, yet loved them too, for they were the warriors of Caradore.

'The Palindrakes were the family with whom Foy had the strongest connection. Theirs was an ancient and spiritual link. The eldest son of the house was known as the dragon heir, who through his priestess, the sea wife, could conjure and speak with the dragons. He could petition them for boons, and inform them of injustice they should avenge. The presence of the dragons in the land ensured the health of the fields and the people who lived upon their fruits. Caradore was indeed a blessed domain.'

Brenka paused for a moment and gazed into the hungry flames before her. Had what she described ever been real? Pharinet wondered. It was like a fairy tale. She couldn't imagine these creatures of myth physically present in the land.

Brenka sighed and raised her gaze to the blackened roof of the cave. Now her voice was deeper. 'Fire came from the south. Fire led by its king, Casillin Malagash. With the might of his hordes, he conquered fair Caradore. He took the castle, its heart, and subjugated the Palindrakes. He took the dragon heir and marked him with the sigil of the fire god, Madragore. The first Valraven was forced to take an oath, so that his connection with the dragons was severed. Casillin wanted the power of the sea, but he feared it. Ilcretia, the lady of Caradore, made a secret of the ancient ways. She would not let them fall into the hands of fire. She initiated the Sisterhood of the Dragon, so that we, her descendants, should keep the old ways alive. Though the dragon heir leads the armies of Madragore, and has done so since that terrible day, we, the women of the land, work to restore all that was lost to us. A time will come when great Foy and her daughters will rise once more, and extinguish the fire that burns the spirit of Caradore. This is our legacy. To this, you must now pledge your oath.'

Pharinet was conscious of Ellony breathing heavily nearby. She was ready to say anything that was asked of her. Pharinet thought of the strange sound she had heard from the sea on the night when Khaster had first spoken of marriage. Had that been the voice of Foy?

Brenka sat down, and the Merante spoke once more, fixing first Pharinet, then Ellony with a steady gaze. 'Do you pledge yourselves to the dragons, sisters?'

Pharinet nodded, while Ellony breathed, 'Yes!'

'Then repeat these words after me. Pharinet, you shall speak first. "I, Pharinet Palindrake, do swear fealty to great Foy, the dragon queen. and her daughters, Jia, Misk and Thrope."'

Pharinet repeated the oath. She had to offer them her heart and her body, her intention and her will. As she spoke, she wondered what effect this night would have upon her life. Would it change in some way? A dull ache in her breast was the invading presence of her love for Valraven. She could not speak these words without thinking of him. He was the sea inside her.

By the time it was Ellony's turn to speak, tears had filled Pharinet's eyes and her chest was full of the pain of repressed weeping. The moment was wonderful and terrible. In this agony was a sweet, pure feeling. Ellony would never experience it.

After the oaths, the Merante said, 'We welcome you among us, Pharinet Palindrake, Ellony Leckery. Keep close the secrets of the Sisterhood. Attend the rites with faith and courage.'

A young woman sitting beside the Merante uncoiled to stand erect. She lifted a silver basin from the floor in the shadows. This she presented to the Merante with a respectful bow. The priestess dipped her fingers into the bowl. Water dripped from her pincered hands. 'We all affirm our pledge,' she murmured and flicked droplets over the fire, which shouldered to the side a little and hissed in warning.

'As this brine, which we have blessed with our spirit, has the power to douse these feeble flames, so we, the Sisterhood of the Dragon, call upon the powers of the ocean to douse the flames of Madragore.'

The bowl was passed around the circle, while the Merante still stood among them. Each woman dipped her fingers in the bowl and flicked droplets on to the fire, murmuring, 'To the great extinguishing.'

Everna passed the bowl to Pharinet, nodding her head in encouragement.

As Pharinet lifted it in her hands, an image of Val's face came to her, as he'd been as a young boy, carefree and happy. This was why she was here. As they spoke the ritual words, she could feel her own voice vibrating with feeling.

The bowl returned to the Merante via Ellony, who stumbled over the words. She appeared to be quite overcome by the significance of the occasion. Pharinet was glad Ellony had been unable to mimic her own determination.

The Merante lifted the bowl on high, uttered a few more phrases, then tossed the remainder of the water on to the fire.

Pharinet jumped. Blackness filled the cave in an instant, while the embers gasped their last upon the sandy floor. The smoke smelled acrid now. Pharinet felt as shocked as if she'd witnessed an execution. She could not explain the strength of her feelings. The splash, the ending of the fire, had been sudden and unexpected. Her face was wet and she had no doubt that it was stippled with moist black ashes.

The air rustled around her and Pharinet realized the women were getting to their feet. She reached for Everna, unnerved by the darkness. Everna's dry hand groped out for her. Together, they ventured towards the blue-grey crack that was the mouth of the cave.

Outside, a sea-soaked wind moaned through the shrubs and trees. Pharinet heard the distant honk of a perigort, a native seabird that was elusive and rare. She felt very cold now; the cloak was not enough to protect her from the wind. Something had happened to her. She had been marked. She felt different to how she had before. Her teeth were chattering as Everna took her arm once more. 'To the beach now.'

'More ceremonies,' said Pharinet. 'Was that not it?'

Everna shook her head, a strange smile upon her lips that was hardly a smile at all.

The women walked in silence, leaving their horses in the valley. As they rose up on to the sea moor, the wind abraded their exposed faces with salt. It had come up hard, the wind, fierce and cruel.

'Air is the nearest element to water,' said Everna close to Pharinet's ear. 'You might say the denizens of that element are allies of ours.'

'And Earth?' Pharinet asked.

'Earth harbours fire, hides it deep within.'

'But water too . . .'

'Earth is a subtle element in this conflict.'

A winding path led to the edge of the cliffs, where skeletal bushes of dune rosemary, looking more dead than alive, rattled in the wind, releasing a pungent scent that was at once antiseptic and redolent of cooking. Here a perilous path was revealed leading down in great jagged leaps. The wind would be a harsh examiner upon that path, Pharinet thought.

The Merante led the way, and as she descended, she began to sing. Other women joined in the harmony, creating a weird and haunting melody that was the essence of longing and resolve. Pharinet had ridden along the clifftop a thousand times, yet had never seen this path. The cove below was like all the other bays that bit into the coast; sheltered with a high fortress of cliffs, its rocks below sculpted thoughtfully by the tides. It could have been the same cove where her own sea-cave was hidden. The sea was dark, dreaming far away from the land, for the tide was out, though Pharinet sensed it was returning. It was almost as if it felt the presence of the women and was drawn to them. Pharinet heard again the forlorn honking cry of a perigort. The birds nested in deep holes in the cliffs, their big bodies stuffed into a bed of grass and feathers, only their eyes glinting in the darkness.

At the bottom of the path, the sand was death-white. There was no moon, though the stars were hard and brilliant above. Everna pointed overhead and said, 'Look.'

Pharinet saw a sliver of light scratch down the sky. 'A shooting star,' she said, and in her heart, wished. She wished for what would happen to be something incredible and life-changing. She wished for it to be important.

The Merante led the way on to the beach. Now she carried a long staff of white wood, whose tip was carved into lifted wings that cupped a gem. They walked far out, where the sand was damp and sucking.

We must be walking to the edge of the surf, Pharinet thought. A ritual will be conducted there. We will be doused in seawater.

Ellony was some way behind her. Pharinet supposed that Ellony would be frightened, thinking of the ghosts of sailors and cruel mermaidens with necklaces of finger-bones.

Presently Pharinet made out the shape of a tall thumb of rock that rose from the sand. As the group drew closer, she could see that it was a black island, crowned by a natural standing stone that grew up out of the rock. She sensed that her companions had become tense, it was not just excitement. Something would happen at that rock. It must be sacred.

'What is it?' she asked Everna.

'The place where the dragons may be summoned,' Everna answered. Her voice was tight.

The women climbed on to the slick jagged stones of the island and arranged themselves in a circle about the stone. Wind plucked at their robes, and within it was concealed a faint stink of rot. Two priestesses unwrapped a sheet of red silk, which they threw over the top of the stone. Its edges were tattered, silk strands unravelling into the wind.

The Merante raised her arms and spoke, starlight glinting in the depths of the gem that tipped her staff. 'In the days of the Dragon, on this night of Foymoriel, the people brought to this rock the fairest of youths. Here his blood was spilled and cast over the stone. Our silken cloth represents this blood. As the youth lay swooning against the rock, so the women called to the great Foy. She smelled the boy's blood and came up from the deep to accept the offering.'

They said it was a husband, Pharinet thought. It was a sacrifice. At that moment, she realized that Valraven too was a sacrifice. Not one of blood, but of something else, perhaps spirit. He had been sacrificed to Madragore.

The Merante fixed Pharinet with her gaze, her hair whipping around her head like crazed sea serpents. 'Pharinet Palindrake, Ellony Leckery, this is the night of your initiation. To be absorbed into our sacred Sisterhood, you must first be accepted by those we serve. The dragons can no longer rise as they used to do, but their spirit is strong in this place. This night, you undergo a rite of passage, which is not without danger. Do you accept this with trust?'

The sea was creeping closer now and Pharinet intuited some of what must come. She and Ellony would be left here for the waves to paw at. Ellony nodded. She looked afraid but exultant, prepared to do whatever was necessary to help the man she loved. Pharinet choked back her anger. 'I accept,' she said in a clear voice.

The Merante inclined her head, and at this signal the rest of the women began to grub around in the sand, to mould it into a shape. It was the figure of a man, a symbolic husband perhaps, for the hungry dragon bride. There was nothing beautiful or fair about this hastily constructed golem. It was merely the rough symbol of a man, only its genitalia carefully formed, so that the dragon queen would be in no doubt as to its gender. As the priestesses put the finishing touches to their sand sculpture, the edge of the waves was only feet from where they stood.

'We shall leave you here until the tide recedes,' said the Merante. 'This is your trial, your rite of passage. If you survive, the dragons have acknowledged you.'

Ellony expelled a short, high-pitched sound. She had not expected anything like this. Pharinet thought to herself, but I have braved the voracious swirl of the tide in my own sea-cave. This will be no different. We will climb to stand against the standing stone and hang on. Once the waves have broken over us and surged to shore, it will not be too bad.

38

'We could die,' said Ellony.

Her mother reached out to embrace her. 'You must have faith, daughter,' she said. 'We have never lost a soul in this rite. Intention is enough to sustain you. The denizens of the deep respect our contract.'

Pharinet could see that Ellony had little faith. She believed in pretty words and pretty rituals, poetry for the soul. She did not trust in experience, in fear, in courage. Pharinet could see why this rite must be as it was. What was the point of pledging yourself to something that meant little? You had to face the fear to be worthy of acceptance.

Now the Merante spoke a blessing over the two young women, and the rest of the group embraced and kissed them in turn. Everna held on to Pharinet for several moments, and whispered, 'Are you afraid?'

'I am, but then I am not,' said Pharinet. 'This is more than I had hoped for.'

'A sentinel will be left upon the cliff,' said the Merante, 'to observe what takes place.' Pharinet felt there was a concealed threat in those words. She and Ellony could not run away and lie to the Sisterhood that they had undergone the trial.

The women retreated up the beach in an undulating line, leaving Ellony and Pharinet alone. Wavelets were feeling their way closer to the island, while just a few yards away the waves threw themselves upon the land. The girls' hair was already wet and sticky with spray carried on the wind. All they had were their cloaks to protect them, and these would presently be sodden, cold and heavy against their bodies.

Ellony leaned against Pharinet's side, clearly seeking comfort. 'Will we die, Pharry?' she asked. 'Are we safe?'

'We may die,' said Pharinet soberly, with inner glee, 'or we may not. We are certainly not safe. But isn't that the point of what we're doing?'

Ellony huddled closer against her. 'I don't know. Hold me, Pharry. I'm afraid. Look at the sea. It knows we're here. It's coming forward like a cat on its belly, waiting to pounce.'

Pharinet relented and put her arm around Ellony. She laughed. 'We are part of the sea, aren't we? How long have we lived here, breathed in its scent, eaten the produce soaked in its salt? Think how we used to play in it as children.'

'That was your domain,' Ellony said. 'Remember we live further inland.'

'That does not seem to bother your mother,' said Pharinet. 'Oh, come now, Ellie. You want to help Val, don't you? Aren't you prepared to sacrifice anything for that? You must gamble for your own survival, for once you have survived, you will have become something more than what you were.'

Ellony only whimpered and buried her face against Pharinet's shoulder. How strange that the roles have reversed, Pharinet thought. In the cave, Ellony was the one with face aglow, eager for the ceremony. Now she was afraid, yet Pharinet was filled with excitement. One action with intent was worth a thousand beautiful words.

The waves seemed to grow bigger as they approached. Pharinet realized that Ellony was right; there was something feline about them. They reared up and hung playfully in the air, dangling paws of surf, then leapt forward, sinuously hurling themselves on to the sand. 'The sea is alive,' Pharinet said. 'Haven't you ever felt that, Ellie? When you stand in it, it tugs at you like living hands.'

'I know,' said Ellony. Pharinet felt her swallow hard. 'Give me some of your strength, Pharry. I want to be as strong.'

The first wave crashed against their legs. Pharinet was concerned they might be plucked from the rock to be smashed to pieces in the roiling surf below. 'We must hold on to the stone,' she said. 'Put your arms around it, Ellie. Grip my arms.' Facing each other, they embraced the stone. Pharinet pressed her cheek against it and closed her eyes. She thought she could detect a faint heat and a low humming sound, as if echoes of a deep ocean song were reverberating through it.

There was a moment's respite, when all fell quiet. The sea was merely a cold murmur. Then what felt like tons of water fell over Pharinet's body. The weight of it pushed the air from her lungs, bruised her skin. It tore at her clothes, slapped and pounded at her body, as if intent on breaking every bone. It wanted to pluck her from the stone. She could sense its playful yet wicked intent. Pharinet could not open her eyes. She could feel Ellony's fingernails digging into her arms through her drenched sleeves. For this time, they were united. The sea must not have them.

Ellony uttered a strange laugh, which Pharinet was impelled to mimic. This was wild, but it was also ridiculous. What must they look like, clinging here, with the waves thrashing over them? We are mad, Pharinet thought, a clear cool current in her mind. Why are we doing this?

It seemed to take an eternity for the van of the tide to pass them, but eventually Pharinet felt a stillness around her. The crash of the tide had receded. Water no longer pawed and pounded at her body. She opened her eyes, and found her sight was obscured by matted tassels of hair. Her arms were rigid. She could not let go of Ellony, whom she could barely see. Ellony's hands were like ancient coral, white and hard.

'Elly, are you all right?'

After a few moments, Ellony raised her head and peered round the stone. She looked like a drowned mermaid.

Pharinet laughed, but it came out of her in a sob. 'We're alive,' she said.

They both looked towards the shore. The tide seethed towards the beach, punctuated by crashing breakers. The sand was shining. Night birds arced over it, casting no shadow.

'How long will it take before it recedes?' Ellony asked.

'A few hours, probably,' Pharinet said. 'We're not that far from the sea line.'

Ellony pulled her arms away and tottered on her feet. 'Is that it?'

'Until it returns,' said Pharinet. She tried to pull her hair from her face with stiff, numb fingers. 'It seems worse than it is. Look, the water doesn't even come to our feet.'

Ellony enfolded herself with stiff arms. 'I'm so cold.'

'We were lucky, the waves weren't that high.'

Ellony sat down upon the rock, her back against the standing stone. 'Come here,' she said. 'We can warm each other.'

Pharinet sat down beside her and accepted Ellony's embrace. Not far from their feet, the black water rolled and muttered at the rock. 'There is something I want you to tell me, Ellony said.

'What?' Pharinet said, thinking, please don't.

'I want to know why you're so angry about Val and me. Don't deny it, Pharry, because I know you are. You can't hide it. Don't you think I'm good enough for him?'

This is part of it, Pharinet thought, part of our rite. 'Of course I don't think that,' she said. 'I did try to explain the last time you mentioned it. There's nothing I can add to that.'

'I think there is,' Ellony said. 'You must tell me, Pharry. I will marry Val, nothing can prevent that, but if there's something I should know, you must tell me. I have to understand, and I have to be aware of the truth.'

Pharinet realized she had underestimated Ellony. The words hung unspoken between them. There was no other time when they could be voiced. Out here, isolated from the life they knew, it was possible to speak the truth. 'Tell me what you think the reason is,' Pharinet said.

Ellony drew in her breath, pulled her saturated cloak closer round her shoulders. 'That you and Val have experienced things together that Khaster and I have not.'

Pharinet expelled a nervous laugh. 'Such as?'

Ellony uttered a sound of annoyance. 'Oh, Pharry, don't dance around this. Tell me I'm not mad, then. Tell me I'm imagining things when I think that you and Val are, or have been, lovers.'

Pharinet was silent. All that could be heard was the hiss and thunder of the sea. After a while, she said, 'You're not imagining things.'

Ellony released a sad sigh; her head drooped. 'I knew,' she said. 'I suppose I've always known. Your relationship with Val is special, because you are twins. I suppose it seems only natural to you to love him in that way. How close you must have been in the womb. I think you need to recapture that intimacy in some way.'

'You have been thinking about this a lot,' said Pharinet.

Ellony slumped against her. 'Of course I have. I don't hate you for it, Pharry. How can I? But I don't want it to be a barrier between us. Tell me, is it still going on?'

'No,' said Pharinet, unable to keep the bitterness from her voice. 'It was just something that happened once.'

The lightness that came into Ellony's voice was almost unendurable. 'When did it happen?'

'I'd rather not talk about it.'

'I understand,' said Ellony gently. 'But you must know how much I love Val. I don't think I could bear it if he really wanted to be with you, his sister. Can you promise me it won't happen again?'

'What did happen will never happen again,' said Pharinet. 'Of this you can be sure.'

Ellony hugged her. 'Thank you. In some ways, I feel I have no right to ask this of you, but I will be his wife, Pharry. I hope you understand.'

'Completely,' said Pharinet.

A silence fell between them. Pharinet was now numb both on the outside and the inside. Had she lied? She wasn't sure. She knew her feelings for Val, but could not tell if they were returned. If Ellony wanted to think they'd already consummated their relationship, let her do so. 'There is a promise I want from you,' said Pharinet. 'You must never mention this subject to Val. Never.'

'I promise,' said Ellony. 'We have a contract between us now.'

I have promised you nothing, Pharinet thought, and a fierce, cruel joy filled her heart. It cast out the numbness.

Ellony sighed, her head resting on Phannet's shoulder. 'Look out there,' she said softly. 'The ocean seems to glow.'

'It is the light of the stars.'

Ellony sat up a little. 'No, I don't think it is. Look, Pharry, the sea is glowing. Just out there. Do you see it?'

Pharinet peered into the darkness. Ellony was right. A greeny-white radiance shifted beneath the surface. 'It must be a mat of luminous weed,' she said. 'I've seen something like that before. It absorbs sunlight during the day and expels it at night.'

'Perhaps,' said Ellony doubtfully, but she did not lean back against the rock. 'It's coming closer.'

Pharinet realized she was not looking at anything of vegetable origin. The light was approaching quickly now, more like a fish than floating plants.

'Pharry,' Ellony breathed, reaching out to grip her friend's cloak.

'By Madragore,' Pharinet murmured.

It was coming towards them, unbelievably fast, then suddenly the sea spumed up before them in a violent spire, as if some immense aquatic creature had exhaled it. Could it be a whale of some kind? It was as if a thousand frenzied fish were threshing in the sea around them, surrounding the island. The water churned and heaved.

Pharinet was afterwards unsure of what she saw in the waves. It could have been a strange, equine reptile head, or a mass of tangled weeds and broken spars from drowned ships. It could have been her imagination. But she remembered the eye, the pupil vertical like a serpent or a cat. The eye saw her, knew her. An immense formless shape hung over her, dripping ocean bed detritus. The head swooped towards her, enveloping her in an odour of brine and rot. She winced against the rock, against Ellony, her mind struggling both to deny and accept what was before her. Ellony was stiff like a corpse at her side. Pharinet could not close her eyes and seconds seemed to bleed into eternity. Then she was staring at the calm ocean, and there was nothing there, nothing there at all.

'Elly,' she murmured, and her friend expelled a whimper.

'I hurt,' she said.

They were completely soaked in cold water, but when Pharinet's arm snaked around Ellony to comfort her, the wetness against Ellony's left side was warm.

At dawn Everna and two other members of the Sisterhood returned to assist the new initiates back to warmth and shelter. Pharinet was virtually frozen against the rock. She had spent the rest of the night in a fevered delirium, Ellony clamped against her side. She had dreamed, she remembered that. She remembered the flavour of the dreams, the wet stark fear of them, but the images eluded her. For that she was grateful.

When Pharinet opened her eyes to the sound of Everna's voice, the sea was far out – she could not recall the tide's retreat. For a horrifying moment, she thought that Ellony was dead, the girl's body was so stiff and cold against her, but when she moved her arm, Ellony uttered a feeble groan.

Everna marched towards her, cloak flapping. 'Pharry, are you all right?'

'Yes,' Pharinet murmured. Her lips were cracked and crusted with salt. She tried to move Ellony's weight from her body. 'But Elly's hurt.' She could see that the hand and arm she'd pressed against Ellony's side were rusty with dried blood.

'What happened?' Everna asked, as the other women lifted Ellony between them.

'Something came,' Pharinet said. She reached out for Everna's hand, unable to stand by herself. 'Something from the sea. It was monstrous. It attacked Elly.'

'Hush now, let's get you home,' Everna said.

'It happened,' said Pharinet.

'You are exhausted,' Everna replied.

A covered wagon waited at the top of the cliff path, laden with furs and blankets. By the time Pharinet crawled in among them, she could barely function. Her head pounded with pain, and her body felt boneless, atrophied. Someone pressed a vessel containing hot milk to Pharinet's lips. The smell made her feel nauseous, but she drank, taking in the warmth. Then she was lying among the musty furs, snuggled inside them like a swaddled child, and the wagon lumbered back towards Caradore. Ellony's body lay limply beside her, but at least she was snoring. What had come up from the sea? Had they dreamed it? Pharinet experienced a pang of anger. Everna and the others had almost killed them. What stupidity was it that decided anyone should lie exposed upon that rock for the duration of a night? They were lucky to be alive. The cold alone could have frozen them to death. And yet, they had survived. The experience could not fail to touch them in some way. They would be changed by it.

Pharinet suffered a mild fever after her initiation, but it was of short duration. Everna nursed her assiduously, as she had done many times before, whenever Pharinet had been ill as a child. Once the fever had passed, and Pharinet lay pale but lucid in her bed, Everna said, 'You are one of us now.'

'At what cost?' Pharinet asked. 'It was terrible, Evvie. Have you lived through that?'

Everna appeared uncertain. 'I have spent my night at the rock, yes. Of course I have. Like you, I felt very drained by the experience.'

'But the other thing . . . Did you see that?'

'No,' Everna said.

'What *did* I see?' Pharinet asked.

Everna sat down on the bed. She smiled, but seemed troubled. 'Some would say the dragons came to you.'

'Would you say that?'

Everna plucked at the thick coverlet. 'I don't know. I've always believed they can no longer come to us in that way.'

'How is Ellony?'

'She suffered a wound to her side. We found splinters of wood in it. Perhaps some flotsam was hurled against the rock.'

'Perhaps,' said Pharinet, but she did not believe it.

'The Sisterhood have done all that they can,' Everna said. 'Ellony's wounds have been drizzled with fresh seawater. If anything can cure her hurt, it will be that. She has been wrapped in poultices of gulfweed to take out the poison.'

'It was the sea that injured her. Why should its produce heal her?'

Everna made a sound of irritation. 'I don't think you understand,' she said, but could offer no further explanation.

Left alone, Pharinet thought, 'Ellony is marked. They marked her,' but could not decide whether this signified a blessing or a curse.

A week later, Pharinet went down to the sea again, to her private cave. It felt as if she'd been absent from it for years. The swell of the water there was benign, contained. Since the initiation night, she had felt melancholy and detached from the world. She had not seen Ellony. Pharinet sat in her cave and watched the water. She could not help feeling that she and Ellony had experienced something none of the other Sisters had ever come close to. Why? Did that presage an imminent change? Were they different to the others in some way? In her heart, she felt she was caught in the lull between the tides. The waves had crashed over her on their journey to the land, but they had not yet receded. The ebbing tide had slithered past her on the dragon rock, silently, without waking her. In this way, her soul was still surrounded by water. She was stranded on the island, with no safe passage to the shore.

Her feelings towards Ellony hadn't changed, but Pharinet felt a need to talk to her. The following day, she rode out to Norgance, where Saska greeted her with exaggerated warmth. 'My dear, you are such brave girls!' she declared, herding Pharinet into a salon where a fire burned high. 'Drink this after your journey.' Into Pharinet's hands, she thrust a goblet containing an aperitif that was as full of heat as the hearth. Dimara Corey sat beside the fire. Pharinet had no doubt she hadn't left the house since Ellony's illness.

Pharinet sat down on a couch. 'How is Ellony? May I see her?'

'Of course,' Saska said. 'She is still not completely well, but that is only to be expected. Something wondrous happened that night, Pharry. I have no doubt in my heart that the dragons have chosen Ellony. You, of course, were there as her guardian, which is only pertinent for a Palindrake woman.' She turned to her sister, who seemed unnaturally quiet. 'Is this not so, Mara?'

Dimara inclined her head. 'It would seem to be.'

Pharinet took a sip of her drink. 'Everna thinks that some sea-born wreckage caused Ellie's injury.'

Saska laughed. 'It is Everna's function to be the bell of rationality. She would naturally say that. But we know differently, I'm sure.'

'Why would the dragons mark Ellony with a wound?' Pharinet asked, addressing her question to Dimara. 'It does not seem an act of favour.'

Dimara gave Pharinet a shrewd glance. 'Ellony is Valraven's betrothed. We must accept it is a role that sets her apart from all of us, whatever we would like for ourselves. We each have our part to play, but for most of us, that part will be of supporter and hand-maiden to the bride of Caradore.'

'Ellony is our hope,' Saska said. 'Pharry, you must see that.'

Pharinet put down her goblet. 'I would like to see Ellony now, if that's possible.'

'She will be delighted,' said Saska, recovering her excitement. 'She is aware your warmth protected her through the night.'

Saska rose from her seat to accompany her guest, but Pharinet said, 'I would like to see Elly alone. We have things to discuss.'

Saska's face creased into a mask of empathetic concern. 'Of course. You will stay for lunch, won't you? I will instruct the kitchens.'

'You are kind,' said Pharinet, and left the room.

Her jaws ached from the suppression of angry words. She mounted the curling blackwood staircase to Ellony's room, fighting down a threshing tide of rage. Ellony was half the woman she was. Saska was an ignorant fool. If the dragons had marked Ellony, it was to doom her, not favour her. They knew the forthcoming marriage would be a travesty. If the power of Palindrake was ever to ascend once more, then she and Valraven should be united in purpose and in love. They had grown together from the tiniest seeds. They were part of each other. Ellony was an invading irritant.

Pharinet found Ellony draped languidly and gracefully beneath her blankets. Her pale hair, fanned out over the high starched pillows, was only slightly darker in colour than her face. Her lips were as white at the sheets. She looked drowned, bleached by brine.

'Pharry,' she murmured, weakly lifting a hand.

Pharinet came into the room, feeling like a riot of colour and energy. Rays of light would splash off her, fill in the pastel corners of the chamber. 'How are you feeling?'

Ellony smiled faintly, bravely. 'A lot better. I'm just very tired. And you?'

'I'm fine. I have a robust constitution.'

Ellony smiled. 'I know. Oh, Pharry, what happened to us that night? Did we dream it?'

'I would say it was unlikely we would have the same dream, but tell me, what do you think we saw?'

Ellony's head moved slowly from side to side upon her pillow. Her brow furrowed. 'I can only remember the lights and the wildness of the sea. Then there was a great eye hanging over me, and what seemed like huge shards of broken coral. It came for me . . .' Her head ceased its restless movement. 'Was it a dragon, Pharry? Is that possible?' Her eyes were dark like deep pools. There was a hint of madness in them.

Pharinet reached out to touch one of Ellony's cool white hands. 'I don't know. Don't upset yourself.'

'The wound, though,' Ellony said. 'Mother thinks it is a boon, but I am afraid. It wasn't like that – it was something else, an omen. Oh Pharry!' Ellony lifted herself from the bed and pressed herself into Pharinet's arms. Her hands might be cold, but her body was hot and seemed too fragile in Pharinet's hold. 'Keep me safe. You are the one. Hold me.'

Pharinet curled her arms tightly around Ellony's back. She could feel the knobs of spine through her friend's nightgown. I am vile, she thought, vile and contemptible. 'Perhaps my sister is right,' she said, stroking Ellony's shoulder. 'She says that some flotsam was flung against us. We were in a strange state, expecting anything to happen.'

Ellony pulled away from her. 'That's true, but in that situation, I don't think anything happens as coincidence. If it was only flotsam, then it came to that place with a purpose. It still marked me, and made me think of dragons. The Sisterhood say the dragons can no longer rise, and maybe that's the truth of it. They have to use other means to communicate their plans to the world.'

'Your mother has no fear for you,' Pharinet said. 'Neither has your aunt. You should trust them. They think you've been chosen as special.'

Ellony lay back down again, slowly. 'I wish I could share their feelings. I can't. What are your thoughts, Pharry?'

'If we have a destiny, it will be revealed to us. I think we must conquer our fears, because they'll be our weakness.'

'Then maybe it's a test,' Ellony said. 'Something I have to learn about myself.'

'I'm sure that's it,' said Pharinet.

Ellony expelled a long, but shallow sigh. 'I want to do what's right for Val. You do believe that, don't you?'

Pharinet reached out to stroke Ellony's hair. 'Of course I do.'

'I trust you more than anyone,' Ellony said, 'because I know you love him as much as I do, and – ' she risked a tremulous smile ' – in much the same way.'

Drive a knife into my heart, Pharinet thought. Yet Ellony was innocent. Hating and envying her would only shrink Pharinet's soul. She must fight to overcome those unworthy feelings. She leaned down and kissed Ellony's brow. 'Come spring, we shall be sisters,' she said, 'and both Val and I will be there to keep you safe.'

CHAPTER FIVE

Brides

Three weeks after the initiation rite, the marriage of Thomist and Everna took place in the small chapel of Madragore on the estate of Caradore. Wind gusted in under the scoured wooden doors and made the guests shiver in their seats. Candleflames leaned hectically to one side then the other, and tapestries portraying the exploits of the gods flapped against the walls. Pharinet stood behind her sister at the altar, holding a tall red candle in frozen fingers. Ellony sat with her family on the first row of pews, wrapped in a gigantic coat of black fox fur. Pharinet had seen her on the way in. She still looked frail.

The guests were all dressed in the traditional wedding colours of the god, dark reds, scarlet, the occasional slash of royal purple and cyclamen. Pharinet wore a long-sleeved crimson gown which was cuffed and collared with black ermine. Everna wore a more fiery colour, her bodice adorned with rubies and beads of jet, patterned into the sacred glyphs of the god. Her mother's jewellery looped across her chest, clasped round her neck and wrists, dripped from her ears. At her side, Thomist was in black, sporting only a red sash. Banners overhead swung back and forth, distributing a cloud of slightly acrid incense around the building. The officiating priest was kind enough to instil the rather severe vows and pledges with human warmth. It was clear he liked a wedding.

Pharinet knew that Everna hated having to speak her vows in the name of Madragore, because her sister had complained about it ceaselessly for days. 'How will it mean anything to me?' she snapped. 'That beast of war knows nothing of love.' Still, she had no choice.

Traditionally, marriages between the nobility took place at the home of the bride, but for Pharinet and Ellony the doors of the larger place of worship, The Church of His Holy Fire, would be opened. This was a large chapel a couple of miles from Caradore, where high-ranking families observed life's rites of passage: the offering of children to the church, marriages and funerals. Everna could have made her wedding vows there, but chose the more intimate surroundings of the family chapel.

Standing there, shivering in the network of draughts, Pharinet tried to imagine the day of her own wedding. It seemed impossible that it would ever happen. But come spring she too would stand before a similar, if grander, altar, vowing to become Khaster's property. How would she feel on that day, knowing Val was behind her, the candle of faith tall in his hands? Would he be a married man by then, his wife standing two paces behind him? Pharinet felt guilty about Ellony now. She felt as if she'd cursed her friend with her sour, jealous thoughts. Ellony was slow in recovering from her ordeal at the dragon rock. The wound in her side had become infected, and still pained her. It leaked a viscous fluid. She tried to be cheerful, for that was her nature, but Pharinet knew Ellony was still haunted by fears. She would not speak of them, but they lived in her eyes.

The ceremony concluded with the sharing of wine, and the company went out into the blustery day. Clouds surged massively across the grey sky and the trees, this close to the coast, were already stripped bare of their leaves. Winter had come early to Caradore. There had been snow, but it had been sucked away in the night by the wet sea wind.

Ellony came to Pharinet's side, while some distance away Everna and Thomist lapped up the compliments and well wishes of their guests. 'I hope the wind has dropped a little by tomorrow,' Ellony said. 'I don't relish a ride to the rock village in this weather.'

The Sisterhood had planned a private ceremony for the following day, so that Everna's nuptials could be blessed by the Merante.

'I think we can anticipate an uncomfortable ride,' said Pharinet. 'Still, I hear the ceremony is a short one.'

Ellony nodded glumly. It was clear she had no real affinity for the rites of the Sisterhood. Pharinet felt the same. They had undergone something beyond mere words and genuflections, and the rituals seemed empty in comparison. 'I had a letter from Val today,' Ellony said.

Pharinet squashed the green barb in her heart before it could wound her properly. 'What did he say?' She had received a letter from Khaster also. Perhaps officers in training were required to write home at specific times.

'Not much,' Ellony said. 'He described some more of Magrast. Life is so different there.'

'Khaster wrote to me and said they had befriended certain of the emperor's sons,' Pharinet said.

50

'Val didn't mention that,' said Ellony. 'Has he written to you, Pharry?'

'A couple of times,' Pharinet said. He hadn't written at all. His silence seemed deliberate. She was already bracing herself for a cooling of their relationship when he came home. In a contrary manner, this gave her unspeakable hope. If he did not share her feelings, why would he consider coolness necessary?

The winter was hard that year. Animals froze upon the moors and a child went missing in the snow, not to be found until the thaw of spring, crouched up like an ancient sacrifice in a rocky crevice. The midwinter festival, with its ox roasts, torchlit processions and beacon fires, came and went. Everna and Thomist held court at Caradore, and the Leckerys came over for a few days to celebrate with the Palindrakes. Montimer Leckery, Saska's husband, made a rare visit home from the army. Saska fussed around this comparative stranger like a panicking hen. He looked tired and would not speak of his life in the army. Pharinet saw an echo of horror in his eyes. He was a frightening thing, like the animated corpse of a torture victim.

The Sisterhood sang sad songs upon the beach of their isolated cove, battered by wind that was clawed with sand and salt. Pharinet saw no sign of dragons. She would walk upon the beach alone at night, wrapped in her dark cloak, gazing out to sea. Sometimes, on calm nights, when the moon sailed high, she would catch sight of a ship ghosting across the horizon, an imperial patrol perhaps, or a stray memory. Valraven did not write to her, although there were many letters from Khaster. It seemed that distance from home made him think more fondly of her. He spoke to her in a tone they had never used together before. 'My beloved . . .' he would begin. Since when? thought Pharinet. She wrote back saying she had little to say. 'Everything is the same.'

Ellony coughed her way through the cold months, although with the return of spring, she seemed to bloom once more. The memory of the night on the rock had faded, and with it, perhaps, her symptoms of illness. She looked forward to seeing Valraven and talked of it often. As tight pink buds appeared on the trees around Caradore, Pharinet felt a sense of ending creeping towards her. Soon her home would be at Norgance. This she did not relish. She liked the sea, and Norgance was further inland. She liked the draughty, airy complexity of Caradore, whereas Norgance had smaller, lower rooms. It wasn't a castle, but a house. Its valley was pretty, and high on the hills behind it stood the Ronduel, a circle of ancient menhirs, but Pharinet doubted it would ever feel like home. She also suspected that Saska would grate on her nerves.

A letter came from Valraven, addressed to Everna, informing her that he would be returning to Caradore in two weeks' time. He trusted his sister had already finalized with the Leckerys the arrangements for his marriage. In fact, this topic had engrossed the women of both families since midwinter. Everyone was excited, but for Pharinet. She tried not to feel gloomy and practised imagining Khaster as a romantic figure, but all she could see in her mind was the lanky twelve-year-old who had followed Valraven around, grinning crookedly and shyly whenever the girls had poked fun. Gowns had been made, and guests invited. Khaster and Valraven would be home for a scant two weeks, so the weddings were scheduled to take place at the same time, only three days after the men's return.

As the inevitable day approached, Pharinet felt sick with nerves. She dreaded seeing her brother again, while at the same time it was something she yearned for more than anything. The marriages were convenient because everyone could put her distraction down to pre-nuptial jitters. 'You are so pale,' Everna said. Her face took on a serious cast. 'Am I right in thinking you fear the bridal night?'

Pharinet had, in fact, refused to think about it. She shrugged.

'There is nothing to fear,' Everna said, and no doubt would have said far more, but Pharinet couldn't bear to hear it.

'It's just that I'll miss Caradore,' she said quickly.

Everna frowned in concern. 'But you won't be far away. You can come home whenever you like.' She laughed. 'What I mean is, of course, you can come to your *old* home. You'll learn to love Norgance as much, I'm sure. It's already a second home to you.'

On the day of Valraven's return, Pharinet went to hide on the beach. A green mist covered the trees, and beneath them fragile white snow poppies shivered in the wind. The air was still chill, yet perfumed with the smells of fresh growth and early flowers. Calves, lambs and foals wobbled in the fields. Life moved on, inexorable.

'I am your priestess,' Pharinet muttered at the sea. 'Aid me now.' But what did she want to happen? For Ellony not to marry Val? For Khaster not to marry her? What were the alternatives? The only way those things wouldn't happen was if something terrible occurred – deaths.

She went to sit in her sea-cave, and there watched the waves lick round the rocks. He might already be at Caradore, taking off his cloak in the great hall, greeting Everna and the staff. Would he say, 'Where's Pharry?' Would he come to look for her? She would be cold with him; he had not written. But then, neither had she.

The sun sank into the sea in a great sulky glow. He wasn't coming.

Stiffly, Pharinet got to her feet and climbed up through the chimney of stone to the clifftop. She saw a horse cantering towards her, and her heart clenched in terror and longing. Then she saw the rider was Khaster. He pulled his horse to a halt beside her and dismounted. By the Spines of Foy, he looks different, she thought. Magrast had turned him into a man, but perhaps she should have intuited this before. 'Khaster,' she said, inadequately. She was pleased to see him, she realized. He was an old friend she'd not seen for a long time. He could tell her things about Valraven.

'You look like you were expecting someone else,' he said, in a tone that suggested he thought no such thing.

'No, I was just lost in my thoughts. I didn't think you'd be here.' She held out her arms. 'I'm sorry. This is no welcome. Come here, Khas. I'm pleased to see you.'

He embraced her and she noticed his arms trembled slightly. 'You are the most beautiful sight on this world,' he said. 'It's good to be back.' They kissed without passion, like friends, then he drew away. His face was leaner, the muscles corded down his cheeks. There were fine lines around his eyes. Pharinet hooked an arm through one of his, and they strolled back to Caradore, Khaster leading the horse.

'Has life been hard?' Pharinet asked. 'You seem tired – and sad.'

He sighed. 'I'm not sad, Pharry. I'm glad to be home, even if it will be such a small handful of time. I've looked forward to this since I set foot in Magrast.'

Pharinet noted this phrase. She had been right; homesickness had probably increased his love for her, but was that real? 'How's Val?'

Khaster paused almost imperceptibly before answering. 'He is well. Soon you'll see for yourself. He should be back from Norgance for dinner.'

Pharinet was both relieved and disappointed that Val was not already at Caradore. She had difficulty imagining him paying court to Ellony. What were they saying to one another? Were they simply in each other's arms? That would be easier, because then they wouldn't have to talk particularly. The thought made her shudder.

'Have you missed me?' Khaster asked. 'I thought of you every day. You were the light that sustained me.'

Pharinet laughed. 'Khas! Don't speak to me that way. It doesn't sound like you, and we know each other too well. Since when have we been simpering lovers? We are betrothed and we are friends. Of course, I missed you, as I missed Val.' She paused and he did not respond. 'I don't mean to sound cruel. What happened in Magrast, Khas?'

He shook his head. 'Nothing much – yet.'

53

Pharinet made him stop. She put her hands on his shoulders and he lurched towards her as his horse rubbed its nose against his back. What she saw in his face disturbed her. 'You must tell me,' she said. 'If you want the poetry and sham of romantic love, you are mistaken in me, but what you can have is loyalty and understanding. Speak to me. Tell me your heart. You are upset, I can see it in you.'

For a moment, she thought he might speak, then he rubbed his hands over his face and fixed a smile there. 'We'll talk of it another time. I want to forget Magrast for now.' He laughed, but it was a sorrowful sound. 'Dear Pharry, you and this land have been like a dream for me. That is why it was destined we should become betrothed before I left. It was an anchor to the past, to the gold of it.'

Had the military training been so hard, or were the Magravands vile people? Had Khaster been bullied and scorned for being foreign? Pharinet was curious to know. The Khaster she had known had been an imperturbable creature, shy only of women. Something fundamental had changed in him. Did this mean that Val had changed also?

At Caradore, a Leckery carriage stood in the courtyard. Pharinet's heart sank. Val must have brought Ellony back with him, and probably Saska too. 'Looks like your family are here,' she said.

'My father returns tomorrow,' Khaster said. 'In a few weeks' time, they are sending him to the east of Cos. There's trouble there.'

'What kind of trouble?'

Khaster looked at her keenly. 'Do you really want to know?'

She frowned. 'Yes.'

'Cos has been part of the empire for thirty years, but recently a resistance movement has sprung up. Terrorists are attacking the garrisons. It's a nuisance and a potential threat if it gathers momentum, so Leonid and his generals have to deal with it. They do this by ordering disguised Magravand military to slaughter whole villages. Then they claim the terrorists were responsible. They say that the rebels will kill anyone who has knelt before an altar of Madragore. It's a lie, of course, but it induces people to betray the rebels to the authorities, whether they're friends, family or neighbours. Fear makes people do anything you want them to.'

Pharinet was silent for a moment. 'Are you being sent there, too? Is Val?'

Khaster sighed. 'There are other places for us, Pharry. We don't know where yet.'

'How can you . . .?' Pharinet began hotly, but Khaster silenced her by placing his fingers gently over her mouth.

54

'We do what we have to, to keep you and everyone else in Caradore safe. You must not question or judge, just accept what is.'

They had reached the steps of the castle. From inside, a scent of spiced wine drifted out. Pharinet could hear excited female voices. For a moment, she just wanted to be outside, in the wind, and embraced Khaster hard. 'I will be your wife,' she said. 'You must always talk to me. My ears will hear, and my heart will heal you.'

He kissed the top of her head. 'Let's go inside.'

The families had gathered in a room on the second floor that overlooked the sea. Fragrant logs spat amid flames in the hearth, and steaming flagons of mulled wine stood on trivets before them. Most of the castle staff were present, allowed the privilege of a cup of wine with their employers. This usually occurred only at the major seasonal festivals. The Leckerys were all there, including Saska's sister and senior members of their own staff. Khaster's younger sisters and his brother, Merlan, dominated the company with their high-pitched laughter. Nobody chastised them for their raucous games. Thomist stood awkward yet jovial at Everna's side, clearly unsure how to behave in front of Valraven.

And there *he* was, standing with his back to the door, instantly recognizable; not just for his presence, but for the fact that Ellony was attached to him like ivy. Her pale face was pink along the cheekbones. The light in her eyes quivered and flickered like the flames in the hearth.

Ellony noticed Pharinet and Khaster before anyone else did. Pharinet saw a fleeting expression of complete awareness cross her friend's face, then Ellony disengaged herself from Val and said, 'Here they are.'

Valraven turned round.

Pharinet felt sick. His gaze met hers as if their eyes were joined by a cord. The room seemed to go still, people to freeze. A second passed, another.

Then Pharinet stepped forward and kissed her brother lightly on the cheek. The tension in the room was released. 'Val, welcome home.' She hooked an arm through one of Ellony's elbows. 'Well, here they are, our men the wanderers, safe and sound.'

Ellony gave her a shrewd glance. The fire in her eyes had dampened a little. 'You've been out grubbing on the beach again, haven't you? Really, Pharry, I believe you'd have forgotten to come home if Khas hadn't ridden out for you.'

Pharinet managed a laugh. 'I was just on my way back, actually. You know what I'm like. I forget about time.'

She glanced again at her brother. He was looking at his betrothed, and trying to smile, but Pharinet could perceive a bitterness beneath it. Like Khaster, his face had aged. He seemed harder somehow, held in. Perhaps it was because of the flame that danced between them.

Thomist held up his wine cup. 'Replenish your drinks, everybody. We must propose another toast.'

From the glow in everyone's cheeks, Pharinet guessed a lot of toasting had been going on already. She accepted a warm cup from a maidservant. The liquid within it was dark and cloudy. She could not perceive its colour. How could she drink from it and wish her brother well?

The fervour of the family and their guests was a tide that caught Pharinet up in its swell. It carried her to the dining hall, and after a meal, it swept her back to the family salon, where more wine flagons appeared from the kitchens, puffing steam like breath. She found she could smile and converse merrily, almost as if she had borrowed a ghost to talk for her and installed it in her body, where she could watch it from the inside. Occasionally she caught Valraven looking at her, his gaze speculative. He seemed like a stranger. Only months before, they had been close, yet now they watched one another as if over a vast distance, like wary animals.

Ellony was unbearable in her fawning delight at having Valraven beside her. She giggled and pulled faces, encouraged by her mother, who looked on with radiant pride. Saska had her youngest child in her arms: Foylen, a boy. Pharinet was not blind to the way Ellony gazed upon this robust baby: she was thinking of the children that she would have herself. Everna made regular sentimental sounds, her hands clasped beneath her chin. Everyone was happy, their mood underscored by a sense of stalwart courage, for they knew Khaster and Valraven would not be home for long. Pharinet felt like a black, wizened thing amid this joyful company. Khaster, sitting beside her, whispered at one point, 'I should not have told you what I did. Please don't dwell on it.'

Pharinet raised a hand in a dismissive gesture. 'It's not that. I just can't put out of my mind the fact that you and Val will soon be gone again.'

'It'll get easier,' Khaster said. 'Once we're out of training, we should get more leave.'

'It will never get easier,' Pharinet said, and lightly pressed one of Khaster's wrists with her fingers. 'But it'll be harder for you than for us, I'm sure.' She smiled tightly.

The celebrations continued well into the night. There was no question of the Leckerys returning home. 'Let me share your bed, Pharry,' said Ellony.

'Mine?' asked Pharinet archly.

Ellony shrieked with laughter. 'Pharry, what are you suggesting? Don't be so wicked!'

Pharinet sighed.

Fortunately, whatever hours of girlish discussion Ellony had planned were curtailed by the fact that she fell asleep as soon as she crawled into bed. Wine made her snore. Pharinet stood brushing her hair at the end of the bed, watching her friend twitch and turn beneath the covers. She felt immensely tall and remote, as if she were a goddess temporarily sent to earth to observe the antics of humans.

The following morning, the Leckerys travelled back to Norgance and would not return until the wedding day. Leckery staff would remain in attendance at Caradore to help with the preparations. The castle felt alive, like an anthill full of ants. Pharinet found it unnerving, being used to echoing, empty rooms and comparative silence. Khaster embraced her warmly before he left. The next time she saw him would be in the church. So close now: the end of one life, the beginning of another. Would she forget her useless passion for Valraven then?

Everna wanted her to try on her wedding gown yet again, so that the seamstresses could make any final adjustments. Pharinet submitted to this passively. She caught Everna looking at her contemplatively on a couple of occasions, but she did not speak. Pharinet had learned how to freeze her sister's questions and concern, so that Everna now knew the folly of trying to reach her. She no longer said things like 'Why aren't you happy?' Now it was, 'Try to be happy, Pharry.'

Pharinet longed only for the comfort of the sea, the sigh and hiss of waves upon the sand, but there were so many things Everna wanted her to do. Presents had begun to arrive from neighbouring estates, and also from further afield. Although the emperor's family would not be represented at the marriage, he was sending a couple of court dignitaries instead. The best chambers were being refurbished for them. Already crates of gifts had been delivered from Magrast. Their contents had been unpacked in one of the ground floor rooms, from where the furniture had been removed. Pharinet managed to escape Everna's gaze for a few minutes and went to examine the haul. The city gifts looked inappropriate for Caradore; over-fussy ornaments and tapestries, elaborate decanters and glasses of crystal, golden figurines. They would suit Norgance better, with its dark cluttered chambers, but no doubt Ellony would love them. Because Khaster was regarded as less important than Valraven, he and his bride were not accorded such rich gifts, but Pharinet was pleased to discover she preferred what had been sent for them: a set of embroidered cushions, pewter goblets and suchlike.

Pharinet wandered the labyrinth of gifts, many of which still stood stacked upon the floor or leaned against the walls. Several paintings had been sent, and these were covered with linen. Curious, Pharinet went to examine them. She saw from their labels they were destined to remain at Caradore, but perhaps they would show scenes of Magrast. She pulled away the linen on the largest frame to see. For a moment, she was shocked and stepped back with a gasp. It was as if she'd uncovered a window, and someone was there on the other side looking in at her. She saw a pale, sardonic yet voluptuous male face; the mouth set in a smile that bordered on sneering. Thick yellow hair tumbled around his shoulders like the mane of a lion. He sat upon a golden throne, situated somewhat bizarrely in a tamed and ornamented garden, beneath an ancient oak. The painting was beautifully crafted, almost as if the subject could step from the canvas at any moment. Sunlight coming down through the branches of the tree glanced off his golden hair and illumined his eyes. Was it a portrait of the emperor Leonid as a young man? Pharinet took another step back, her head on one side. She was drawn to stare at the picture. There was something repellent about the face before her, yet also seductive.

She heard movement behind her, then a low curse. Turning, she saw Valraven had come into the room, and was also looking at the picture. Pharinet forgot about the awkwardness that had shivered between them the previous evening. 'This is yours,' she said, pointing at the portrait. 'Who is it?'

'Prince Bayard,' Valraven said dryly. 'He will have sent it to me himself.'

'One of the emperor's sons? How exciting. Is he now a friend of yours?'

Valraven made a disparaging sound. 'Bayard is not exactly the sort of person anyone could describe as a friend,' he said. 'He exists in a universe populated solely by himself.'

Pharinet looked back at the picture. 'Well, he is the son of the emperor, so I expect he thinks himself unique. Is he the heir?'

'No. He is a minor son. As you know, the emperor has many.'

'No daughters?'

'Only one. A child.'

Pharinet shook her head, smiling. 'I should know this. We really are so isolated out here.'

Valraven shrugged. 'Well, when has it ever been our business?'

'Even so . . .'

Valraven stepped forward and flicked the linen cover back over the painting. 'I want nothing to remind me of Magrast for now.' He smiled at Pharinet. 'I was hoping I'd find you here. Fancy a gallop along the cliffs?'

Pharinet frowned. 'Everna will not be pleased. She has a mountain of trivia for me to attend to.'

'So what? Come on.' Valraven offered her his arm, and Pharinet could believe, for a short time, that the brother she had grown up with and loved had not changed at all.

They walked to the stables, both remaining silent on the subject of the forthcoming weddings. 'Khaster does not seem happy,' Pharinet said. 'Is life hard at Magrast?'

Valraven shrugged. 'It is not the sort of life Khas would have chosen for himself. He wants to run his father's estate, breed horses, grow corn. Empire-building has no attraction for him.'

'And does it for you?'

'I shut myself off, do what I have to do.'

Pharinet narrowed her eyes. 'They treat you better than him, don't they.'

'Not really. Khaster makes his own life. He is like an old woman at times, full of tutting disapproval for everything.'

'He told me some things about the empire that can only inspire disapproval – the incidents in Cos, for example.'

Valraven laughed. 'He told you that, did he? There are two sides to every story, Pharry, and each of those sides can argue that they are right.'

Pharinet felt a worm of discomfort at Valraven's words. Surely he did not condone what had happened – could he have changed that much? Had the luxury and privileges of Magrast corrupted him?

He was marked by Madragore at birth, she thought. Perhaps corruption is what happens to the Palindrake men. That could be our curse.

The air was full of a misty rain, gentle as the creeping arrival of spring itself. They rode along the narrow path that hugged the cliff, but in the opposite direction to the rock village. Further south, there was a forest that leaned right towards the lip of the land. It was very ancient, the trees bulbous and crooked, full of secret hollows. Valraven rode ahead, as he always had, his hair flying out behind him. It was as if they had somehow gone back in time. For these few short moments, Pharinet could believe that nothing had changed. There were no impending weddings, and Valraven did not live in Magrast. They would go home together, play crack-bones with Everna, and then retire to bed. Not separately, but together.

Pharinet attempted to banish these thoughts from her mind, but the effort was half-hearted. Her hands yearned to touch Valraven; her throat was full of words waiting to be spoken.

By midday the rain had been burned away by the strengthening sun. Pharinet and Valraven were far from the castle now, only an hour's ride from Mariglen, the nearest town. The forest still huddled close to the sea, and here the trees appeared strangely warped. Their leaves and bark were covered in an ashy dust. A winding path led off the main cliff back into the trees. Instinctively, perhaps, Valraven swung his horse's head towards it. 'I thirst for a cup of Granny's posset,' said Valraven. 'Shall we?' He did not wait for Pharinet's reply.

A short way down the path, surrounded by soaring elms, was a wooden cottage, where pyramids of logs were stacked outside. This was the home of Grandma Plutchen, a woman who habitually provided refreshments for walkers, travellers and traders. As children, Valraven and Pharinet had often visited the old woman. They had been amused by the way she'd treated them as if they were ordinary. It meant nothing to her that they were members of the Palindrake family. Grandma Plutchen had always seemed old, yet, bizarrely, never seemed to age any further. Valraven would tease her and the woman would tut and box his ears. She was considered to be something of a witch. Valraven and Pharinet used to try and make her read their fortunes for them in the flight of birds across the sky, but Grandma Plutchen would never do it. Perhaps she was afraid of what she'd see.

They hadn't visited the old woman together for some years. Seeing her now might augment the sweet illusion that things hadn't changed. But when Pharinet and Valraven emerged from the trees into Grandma Plutchen's glade, they found the cottage was closed up, the shutters locked. The old woman was not at home, although it was clear she was still very much in residence.

'She'll be at Mariglen,' Pharinet said, with an irritated sigh. 'I forgot. It's market day there. She always goes to the market.' Disappointed, she dismounted from her horse and sat down on a sagging wooden bench beside the wide uneven veranda. Around the cottage, the garden was a riot of rampant greenery that seemed to bulge with almost unnatural fecundity from the soil: Here, Grandma Plutchen grew her herbs and teas.

Valraven joined Pharinet on the bench. 'You want to wait for her?'

Pharinet shrugged. 'There seems little point. She probably won't be back for hours.' Still, Pharinet had no urge to leave. She was conscious of every contour of her brother's body beside her. She could smell his hair, the thick dark waves of it. The weight of the forest was oppressive here, its scent thick and intoxicating. Pharinet had no doubt Grandma Plutchen worked magic, although she sensed it was very different from anything the Sisterhood did. The sun drew heat and moisture from the earth and in the quiet the shuffle and rustle of greenery could be heard. A single linnet sang. Here I could stay for ever, Pharinet thought.

There was a silence between them, then Valraven said, 'Everna wants me to talk to you.'

Pharinet shifted uneasily. 'So that's why we're out here. Strange, I thought it was a gallop for old time's sake. Something that won't ever happen again.'

'She says she fears you're unhappy about the wedding.'

Pharinet glanced at him from beneath her lashes. 'Whose?'

Valraven did not flinch. 'Yours, of course. Is it true?'

Pharinet shrugged. 'When you left, it didn't seem real, all this talk of marriages and so on. Now I know that in a couple of days' time, Caradore will no longer be my home. I'll have responsibilities and duties I do not welcome.'

'Do you not love Khaster?'

Pharinet threw back her head and laughed. 'Oh, was it ever about love?'

Valraven frowned. 'You did not have to give him your consent. If you don't love him, and don't want this, why did you agree to marry him?'

'Shall I renege now?'

'Pharry! Would you do such a thing?'

She sighed. 'No. It would cause too much trouble, and I'd never be forgiven. I suppose I'll get used to it.' She looked at him directly. At that moment, nothing seemed further from reality than the impending weddings. 'And you? How do you feel about Ellony? Is it a grand passion?'

'Ellony will make a good wife. You know that. Whom else could I marry around here?'

Pharinet clasped her knees, although one foot swung restlessly. 'Oh, I don't know. You could have brought home a little countess from Magrast or something.'

'You know very well I could never marry into a Magravandian bloodline.'

'Why not? We of Caradore *are* Magravandian, aren't we? We're part of the empire.' She studied him carefully. Was he referring to his heritage? How much did he know about it?

'In one sense, we are Magravands,' Valraven said, 'but not in all. We have our traditions. Perhaps it is to do with pride. Once, the Palindrakes were forced to meld with the Magravandian aristocracy. We complied with the emperor's desires, for we had no choice, but now we do.'

'You are a contradiction,' Pharinet said. 'I was sure you'd embraced the

61

culture of Magrast whole-heartedly, now you speak of a secret patriotism for our little land. What is the truth of you, brother?'

He gave her a look which seemed very young and told her he did not know the answer to that himself. 'It is not patriotism,' he said at last. 'I respect what our people want, that's all.'

'But what do *you* want?' Pharinet stood up and marched up and down before him, hands on hips, apparently examining the wild garden around them.

'They are our closest friends,' Valraven said quietly

Pharinet paused, one foot tapping the grass. 'Circumstance,' she said. 'They are our nearest neighbours.'

'We have to marry someone, Pharry. Why not these people whom we love as brother and sister?'

Pharinet raised one eyebrow, but did not speak. The silence was absolute. Even the forest was quiet around them. She stared unblinkingly at her brother, allowing the significant moment to continue. Then, judging the time right, she spoke to fracture it. 'We are our own people.' Her voice was low and fierce. 'Yes, perhaps we should marry the Leckerys for the sake of Everna and Saska, and the families of Caradore who still think the Palindrakes are their great lords, and the folk of the villages and farms who need a spectacle. But marry them for ourselves, no. We marry in name, and perhaps in body, but never in spirit. We are different, Val; you don't know how much.'

He pressed the fingers of one hand against his eyes. 'We are not free. We cannot have everything that we want. That is one of the costs of our position.'

Pharinet growled in her throat. 'No, we are not free. If we were, who do you think the people of Caradore would want to rule them? We could be who we are – together.'

He looked at her unsteadily, the expression in his face so like that of the ingenuous boy he once had been. She knew he'd always been aware she was cleverer than he was, and had sought to hide it. 'That would be unthinkable,' he said. 'If you believe anyone would condone that, you are mad or stupid.'

Pharinet leaned over him. 'What are we talking about, Val? What are we really talking about? Do you know? Will you say it?'

'Stop it,' he said, but seemed paralysed by her presence.

'No,' she answered. 'I won't. Before you left for Magrast, I accepted a simple truth in my heart. I am your sister, yet I should also be your wife. Whatever anyone else makes us think or do will never change that. We are the last flickering remnants of a once-mighty heritage, Val. We should keep that flame alive.'

He stared at her for a moment, then said, 'I know.'

Pharinet dropped to her knees before him, grabbed his hands in her own, shook them. 'Say it, Val. Say you recognize what lies between us! I have waited so long for this moment, longing for it, dreading it, afraid you did not feel the same.'

He closed his eyes and turned his head to the side. 'What we feel is wrong. We should not give into it.' Yet despite his words, Pharinet felt his fingers curl about her own. She was filled with a mad joy. Nothing else mattered now. Nothing.

'Wrong?' she snapped. 'Why? Who decrees such things? The Magravands intermarry, you know they do. And did you not say we were Magravands?'

Valraven turned back to her. 'The Caradoreans do not hold the same beliefs. We are different. Intermarriage weakens the blood. You know brothers and sisters cannot bring forth healthy children. I have seen the pallid, sickly creatures spawned by incest at court, Pharry.' He shook her hands within his own. 'I do know what I'm talking about.'

'But Val . . .'

He shook his head. 'Listen to me. Don't believe I haven't been thinking about this dilemma, because I have. Sometimes, at the beginning, when I was missing you so much, I even considered asking permission for you to come to court. I am quite sure Leonid would have given it. The Magravands do not forbid incestuous marriages, we both know that. I could not write to you, because everything I wanted to say was forbidden. You haunted my dreams, my every waking moment. I cannot tell you how many times I thought I caught sight of you in Magrast. Khaster and Ellony meant nothing to me then. But what I saw around me was sour evidence. It seemed to me that Magravandians marry blood relatives to one another when they desire them *not* to have a healthy heir. We could never have children, Pharry, and you know that I, at least, must do so.'

Pharinet was silenced by this, and pulled her hands away from his. She stood up, once more tapping her foot in agitation on the forest lawn, staring out through the trees. Then she drew in her breath and faced him again. 'Ellony will bear you children,' she said.

Valraven stared at her, said nothing.

Pharinet nodded. 'Yes. We will marry our Norgance neighbours. That is our duty, I suppose, as you have pointed out. But that does not mean we cannot experience that which our souls know is right.'

'And if we don't, you will hate Elly for ever, won't you,' Valraven said in a tone that was a mix of bitterness and relish. 'You will punish Khaster for it.'

'While you will punish only yourself.'

Valraven stood up beside her and took hold of her hands once more. 'You don't know me, not all of me,' he said grimly. 'All the time, I feel myself changing, pushing against a barrier or resistance, like a creature trying to break out of a shell. When that shell is broken, I will be different, and I have no way of knowing how. That creature will be a stranger to you. Pharry, I know it. I feel it. I cannot be sure of your enduring love.'

'No.'

'Listen!' he snapped. 'I see myself at the head of armies, and can feel a bloodlust within me. It's like a dream of battle, but I feel I've lived it before. Some part of me hungers for it. Some part of me is like Prince Bayard and his brothers. If you haunt me as a beautiful ghost, he is the demon of my nightmares. But part of me somehow resonates with what he is. I'm a wolf, a wolf of the fire. Once that wolf within me has tasted blood, he will take me over completely.'

'Bayard or the wolf?' Pharinet asked carefully. The wild look in Valraven's eyes made her feel breathless.

He shook his head, his eyes screwed tightly shut. 'The wolf, the wolf. Bayard is its master.'

'You're afraid,' Pharinet said, half in wonderment.

'No, I am not. That is the worst of it.' He stroked her face with his long fingers, suddenly calm again. 'When I think of you, I know you belong with that part of me, Pharry. The wolf couples with his sister, regardless. What will we be together but savage? That is what makes me balk at what my body and heart desires. That more than anything.'

'I do not fear it,' Pharinet said. 'If that is what you will become, then so be it. It is what you are. Ellony would never understand.'

Valraven uttered a smothered cry and pressed his palms against either side of her face. When he kissed her, it was nothing like Khaster's chaste, soft caresses. This was passion, not fiery, but the inexorable surge of a tide. It was as if they were trying to eat into one another's bodies, absorb a part of them that would be for ever outside.

Valraven pulled away from her, breathing hard. He wiped his mouth.

'I will not go to Khaster's bed a virgin,' Pharinet said. 'You must take what is yours.' She felt dizzy, powerful and fierce, full of resolve.

They stared at one another, like animals ready for combat, stooped and wary. Then a sound came through the trees, Grandma Plutchen wheeling her cart back from the market. They could hear her singing.

'Meet me on the beach tonight,' Pharinet said in a low voice. 'At the sea-cave. Just after midnight.' She turned to the approaching old woman before Valraven could utter a reply.

Grandma Plutchen was tramping sure-footedly along the path from the forest, dragging a cart behind her. Her body was swathed in a voluminous purple shawl with tangled fringes. A confusion of green and red glass beads adorned her neck and tumbled over her pillowy bosom.

'Granny, you've made us wait!' Pharinet called. 'And on the eve of our weddings, too!'

'Valraven and Pharinet,' said Grandma Plutchen, as if she'd seen them only the day before. She was a wide, short woman, with a mass of thick grey hair, which she wore in an unruly bundle on top of her head. Valraven had once said to her that it looked like a disreputable old tom cat, who was covering up the fact that she was bald. Grandma had been used to these cheeky remarks. Pharinet had always sensed she'd harboured a deep regard for Valraven. Now, she felt she knew why. It was because of what he was: the dragon heir. To a common Caradorean like Grandma Plutchen, that must mean a lot. She, and others like her, were excluded from the Sisterhood because they were not of noble birth, but Pharinet had no doubt Grandma understood far more about the dragons than any woman like Saska Leckery could. I should have come here before, she thought. Of course.

Grandma drew her cart up before the veranda and began to unload produce: hams, cheese, vegetables she did not grow herself and a bolt of beautiful crimson cloth. Pharinet winced when she saw the bloody spillage of fabric between the cabbages: the wedding colour.

Valraven went to help the old woman.

'Oh, found some manners now, have you?' she said.

'I could never stand by and see a lady exert herself unnecessarily,' he replied.

Grandma snorted. 'Oh, and found a glib tongue too, it seems.'

Pharinet went to join them. 'You will come to the church tomorrow, won't you, Granny? Everyone local is invited to the garden party at the castle afterwards.'

'I know that, child. It's been the news of the land for months.' Grandma Plutchen gave her a penetrating and disturbing glance. 'A grand new life for you,' she said, only the expression in her eyes suggested she could see the truth of the matter in Pharinet's heart. 'I'll be there with my cart. Might sell a few simples.'

'I shall look out for you.'

Grandma nodded.

Valraven and Pharinet took the old woman's purchases into the cottage. She had never invited them in before. Despite outward appearances, it was very tidy within and smelled exotically of pungent herbs. 'I'll make you some tea, on the house,' said Grandma. 'It'll be a special wedding gift.'

Pharinet felt slightly disorientated. It was difficult to believe the conversation she'd had with Valraven had ever happened. The only proof she had was the lightheadedness, and a faint yet oddly delicious sense of nausea. She and Valraven sat down at the kitchen table, which was bleached with age and constant scrubbing. Valraven tried to make the joky, light-hearted remarks Grandma would expect of him, but Pharinet could tell his heart wasn't in it. He was trying to remember a part he'd ceased to play.

Grandma put water in a black kettle on the range to boil. 'Come with me, child,' she said to Pharinet. 'You should cut your own ramage for a wedding pot.'

Valraven glanced at Pharinet sharply as she stood up. She could tell he was afraid Grandma Plutchen had heard them speaking and would mention it once she got Pharinet alone. Pharinet shook her head briefly to show he should not worry.

Outside, Grandma led the way purposefully to the herb garden, and there indicated which bush Pharinet should cut some leaves from. 'It's furry,' Pharinet said. 'Like animal ears.'

'Brings strength to a home,' Grandma said.

Pharinet did not comment, but cut the leaves. 'There, is that enough?'

'Plenty.' Grandma pointed to another bush, where delicate lilac flowers nestled in a mist of ferny foliage. 'Now, go and fetch me a sprig of that hazeflower for your brother. He needs strength for more than just the home.'

'What will it do?'

'It is the breath of Caradore, its fragrance. He needs to carry that with him.'

Pharinet grinned. 'That explains it nicely, thank you.' She leaned over the bush and a wash of pure, slightly salty perfume filled her nose. She cut the flowers carefully, slowly, playing for time. Eventually, she said, 'Granny, one day I would like to talk to you about something.'

There was no reply, so Pharinet looked round. Grandma's face remained impassive.

'About Caradore, about the land and its history,' Pharinet said. 'About magic.'

Grandma pointed at the hazeflower. 'Not too much. Don't strip my plant.'

Pharinet straightened up, her hands full of frail blooms. 'Will you talk to me? Not now, but another time. I could ride down from Norgance.'

Grandma studied her for a moment. 'I can't tell you anything, child. We come from different sides of the shore. You have your rock, I have mine. When the beach is clear and the tide is low, we can talk across the sand. But we cannot leave our rocks, and sometimes the waves make it impossible for us to hear one another.'

Pharinet was stung by this refusal. She'd thought Grandma would welcome her suggestion and be happy to teach a willing younger woman the lore of her craft, especially a Palindrake. 'I don't feel as if my rock is that far from yours,' she said.

Grandma reached out and pinched Pharinet's left arm. 'Sorry, child. I know what you want, but I'm not the one. You must follow your own heart.'

'Why won't you talk to me? Is it because of who I am?'

'I revere the blood of the Palindrakes,' Grandma said. 'It is the blood of this land, but I know my place. One day, you will know it too – both mine and yours.' She patted Pharinet's arm. 'Come now, we've tea to make.'

Pharinet hesitated, but could not find the words to express her thoughts.

Grandma, who was already on her way back to the cottage, turned round. 'It will happen regardless of what you say or do, or anyone else, for that matter.'

'What will happen?' Pharinet asked. She felt a flush rise up her neck.

But Grandma was already near the veranda, whistling through her teeth.

CHAPTER SIX

Magic

The tide was only a distant moan. Pharinet crouched upon a damp ledge at the back of the cave. At home, over dinner, she couldn't have imagined this moment. She'd believed she wouldn't come down to the sea at midnight. But she was here, so she must have.

It was convenient for Pharinet to believe she was gripped by the coils of some ancient tradition, that what she would do with her brother was preordained, dynastic and right. The dragons were to blame, roiling in their lightless depths. They influenced what the Palindrakes did.

Pharinet's toes curled over the cold stone. Her skirts were wet about the hem and heavy with sand. That afternoon, she'd felt so different, alive in an adult, female way. She and Valraven had drunk Grandma Plutchen's special tea, then had ridden home. There had been a silence between, but it had not been uncomfortable. Pharinet had no doubt both of them had been thinking about the night to come. At home, in the stableyard, Valraven had kissed her cheek. He'd said nothing aloud, but his eyes had said, 'I will see you later. I will be there.'

At dinner, Everna had kept the conversation going, preoccupied as she was with the forthcoming marriages. Pharinet could barely speak, which prompted Thomist to offer her a series of ever more fiery liqueurs. He obviously thought she was nervous about the following day. Right after the meal was over, Pharinet had escaped the room, knowing she left Everna disappointed. Her sister had wanted to spend the rest of the evening finalizing plans. Pharinet thought that if she heard one more word about the weddings, she'd be overtaken by a red mist and would come to her senses, only to find her hands locked around someone's throat, probably Everna's. She'd gone to her rooms, where she'd taken a bath. By ten o'clock she was down on the beach, unable to stand the feeling of walls around her any longer.

Now she felt like a child again, but a wicked, primal child. Her eyes stared unblinking at the pale hole of the cave mouth. Her hair was stuck to her face like ribbons of kelp.

She remembered the time when Valraven had found her in this very place, kicking her feet in the brackish pools left by the tide, dreaming of men to come. The girl she had been would never have dreamed of this moment. Everything had been right then. There'd been no need. She'd spoken of not wanting to go to Khaster a virgin, but what was uppermost in her mind was the fact she did not want Valraven to go to Ellony as a husband without his sister's mark upon him. She would do something cruel, like leaving a bruise.

The outline of a man imposed itself across the cave mouth. It was not immediately recognizable as Valraven, because Pharinet was remembering the shape of him as she'd known him in childhood. He came forward softly, saying her name. She could remain still now, and silent, and perhaps he'd not see her and go away. Sea-foam gripped his ankles as he made his way into the darkness. He was blind and vulnerable. Pharinet shifted upon the rock.

'Pharry . . .'

'I'm here.' He felt his way to where she sat and stood over her.

'It was difficult to get away,' he said. 'Everna would not go to bed. She's like an excited child.' He paused. 'She asked where you were. I think she went to your room.'

Pharinet could sense his nervousness. Only she knew Valraven like this. He allowed her to see he could be vulnerable. 'She is our sister. Perhaps, in her heart, she knows the way things are with us.'

'I hope not.' He sat down beside her, his thigh laid alongside hers. She took his hand. 'For now, we are alone. We can forget anyone else exists.' She could not go on. She could not initiate this. It was all too prearranged. They should have come together more naturally. The weddings had forced this, made it difficult. She wanted to cry.

For a while neither of them spoke nor moved. Pharinet felt that her hand had melded to Valraven's. Her arm was numb.

Eventually, he cleared his throat and said awkwardly, 'Pharry, we could go home now. If you want to.'

She could not see his face properly in the darkness, but from the tone of his voice, she could tell he'd been thinking about this all night. He was worried she might have changed her mind.

'It should not have been like this,' she said. 'But we can't go back.' She stood up. 'Come with me.'

She led him further into the cave, where the sand was damp and firm beneath their feet. It would make a more comfortable bed than the rock. She sat down again and Valraven settled beside her. This was so clumsy. Perhaps, when they started, it would get easier.

'Who was the last person you kissed?' she asked him.

He would not respond for a while, then said, 'It must be Ellony.'

'Do you enjoy it? I can't imagine she's much of a woman in that way.'

She heard him sigh. 'Forget her. Forget Khaster. They're not why we're here.'

'Oh, they are,' Pharinet said. 'Otherwise we would have danced our dance in our own time.'

He reached out and touched her face, his fingers gritty with wet sand. 'Hush now. Remember what you said. No one else exists.'

Then it was happening. He'd pulled her towards him and his mouth was against her own. Gradually, he pushed her back on to the sand. His expertise unnerved her. He must have done this so many times before. He had a secret life of which she knew nothing. Did he have a lover in Magrast? Would he tell her about this?

The kiss became deeper, its message reaching into the core of her body. Of its own accord, her flesh hungered for him. It was as if she had nothing to do with it.

He lifted her skirts and slid his hand against her skin. His fingers explored her, gently probing. He pressed his face against her hair and expelled a soft moan. She could tell he could not believe he was doing this. She opened her legs a little wider. 'Will it hurt me?' she murmured.

'As little as possible,' he answered and slowly pushed into her with a finger.

She arched her back. 'Don't, don't . . .'

He withdrew. 'Relax, Pharry.' She lay on the sand, quivering, while he took off his clothes. Then he bent to unlace her bodice. The cold sea air hit her skin. He cupped her breasts with his hands, leaned down to kiss them.

'You are beautiful,' he said. She could feel this hard, alien thing bobbing against her thigh. It seemed inconceivable it could go inside her. But it had obviously been inside other women, and soon Ellony would own it. Hesitantly, she reached down to touch it and found it hot beneath her hand, the skin softly pliable. The muscles in her belly clenched.

'Now,' she said.

He laughed softly. 'Don't be afraid.'

'I'm not. I want to see.'

'Not yet.'

He was like a sculptor, shaping flesh. His hands, his lips, travelled her body, conjuring sensation. When his mouth touched her between the legs, she lifted her knees, half shocked, half swooning. The tongue was more pleasant than the finger. It didn't feel so invasive. She couldn't bear the thought of him doing this to Ellony. Get out of my mind, she thought. Go away. She did not want Ellony to be there with them.

He rose up and knelt between her splayed legs. Then he pulled her towards him. She felt the pressure, then a giving way. It wasn't pain exactly, but it felt so strange.

'Don't move,' she said. 'Please don't move.'

But he couldn't contain himself. He lay down upon her, thrusting into her deeply. She clutched him to her. The power of him, the energy. 'My lover,' she murmured. 'My brother.'

At dawn, Pharinet rose like a drowned thing from their bed of weed and sand. They had only fallen asleep once the cave had filled with dawn light. Now Valraven lay at peace, gently snoring, his maleness flaccid against his thigh. Pharinet studied him for some minutes. He looked so young, so beautiful and fragile. His black hair was spread out over the sand, full of its pale grains. In the night, she thought their lovemaking would never end. They'd be together for eternity. But now it was morning, and wedding bells would soon be ringing. She must leave him.

Numb, Pharinet left the cave through her secret route, and dragged herself up the cliff path, seeking handholds of spiky dune grass: the child of a seaborn resurrection. She had come back from the dead, her lungs full of brine, her eyes like the pearly shells of oysters. The flags on Caradore's towers cracked mournfully. Overnight, it seemed, the land had unfurled itself. What had been a mist of green was now a carpet, banners, streamers of verdure.

Everna was already in her sister's chamber, her face pale with concern, perhaps terror. 'Where have you been?' she demanded, as Pharinet poured through the door, dragging her drenched gown across the floorboards.

'Doing what you would have me do: communing with the sea,' Pharinet replied. She began to strip off her ruined clothes.

Everna eyed her with disapproval and worry. 'You look disgusting. Pharry, this is your wedding day. You look as if you haven't even slept.'

Pharinet shrugged and stepped out of a pool of sodden fabric. Her body felt scored with salt and sand. Perhaps there were suspicious marks for Everna to see and think about. 'Is Val awake yet?' she asked.

Everna bent to pick up her sister's discarded clothes, then straightened up again without touching them. 'I have no idea. My first concern is you, and has been for some months.'

'There's nothing for you to worry about, I'm fine.' Pharinet drifted listlessly towards her bathroom. She would have to wash off the smell of him, and the smell of the sea.

Everna came to stand in the doorway. 'You shouldn't be bathing yourself. This is an important day. I'll call for a couple of the girls.'

'No,' said Pharinet, turning the creaking faucet. Water chugged down into the bath, steaming.

'Pharry . . .' Everna began, taking a hesitant step over the threshold.

Pharinet straightened up quickly and saw her sister flinch away instinctively. 'Leave me,' she said in a croak, then softened her voice. 'Evvie, I had to think. This is a changing time for me. I'm losing my home, all that I know. I just wanted a night on the beach for the last time.'

This seemed to mollify Everna a little, but Pharinet was not blind to the shadow of suspicion in her sister's eyes. 'I'll fetch you something to eat,' Everna said. 'Something warm.'

Lying in her bath, which she'd deliberately left unscented, Pharinet squeezed water from a sponge over her breasts. She would not be sorry to leave Caradore after all. How could she live here with Ellony ensconced in the chambers of the bride, twittering about the place, shining with repletion? Better to escape to Norgance, where she could indulge her pain in exile.

Everna allowed her only half an hour before returning with an army of women. The dress was brought forth from the wardrobe, an execution robe, stained with blood. Pharinet eyed it with loathing. She thought of the bolt of red cloth in Grandma Plutchen's hand-cart. Even yesterday, in that enchanted time out of time, the wedding had been hanging over her like a curse.

The women pawed at her body, clothing it, preening it. They tugged at her hair, wound it with flowers. There was something greedy about their attentions. It made Pharinet's flesh crawl.

By nine o'clock, the Leckerys had arrived and poured into Pharinet's chambers like a horde of drunken bees. The loud voices and hysterical laughter were poison-tipped stings down Pharinet's spine. She fixed a smile on her mouth and pretended to concentrate on making up her face. In the mirror, she saw the bride of death. She ached between the legs. Flashes of what had occurred the previous night kept coming back to her. She could still smell Valraven, feel his hands upon her, his body enclosed by hers. It had felt like being consumed by a fire that did not burn, but imparted a fierce energy. It still buzzed through her blood. Ellony pranced about the room, her pale face flushed with excitement and expectation. Pharinet watched her in the mirror, her mind full of murder.

'You are so in love,' Saska said to her daughter, her eyes damp with sentiment.

'We both are,' Ellony said, and Pharinet gritted her teeth, waiting for the next remark, which would undoubtedly be addressed to her. But no. 'Valraven loves me too,' Ellony trilled. 'I cannot believe I own such happiness.'

Pharinet sucked in her breath through her teeth. Ellony was hardly even aware that she was there. 'Dragons take you,' Pharinet hissed at the mirror.

Most of the year, The Church of His Holy Fire was closed, but on special religious occasions, a priest came from Talabrake, the nearest town. The interior of the church was decked in flowers and incense soaked the air. Outside, the local population clustered round the entrance, decked out in their finest costumes. It was a festival day for them, when the Palindrake family would allow them into the castle gardens for roast ox and ale. Pharinet rode up to the church in an open carriage, accompanied by Ellony, Saska and Everna. Khaster and Valraven would make an appearance later, accompanied by their groom escorts; local men from other noble families to whom they probably hadn't spoken for years. The younger Leckery girls followed behind the main carriage. They were accompanied by their aunt, Dimara. Not for the first time, Pharinet thought about how Saska's sister rarely spoke to her. At Sisterhood gatherings, Dimara became the Merante, their priestess, a woman who shrugged off her everyday mask of maiden aunt. But even then, she paid scant attention to Pharinet. Perhaps she knew the truth. Pharinet glanced behind herself in the carriage, determined to catch Dimara's eye, but the woman was engrossed in conversation with her nieces. Pharinet had expected a dour countenance to look back at her, full of knowledge, but all she saw was a face full of excitement and laughter. Maybe she doesn't have any real power, Pharinet thought. If she did, she'd know about me.

At the entrance to the ceremonial gardens of the church, Pharinet scanned the crowd as she alighted from the carriage. She was looking for Grandma Plutchen, unsure of why it was so important to her that the old woman was there. Everyone was dressed in shades of red, pink and purple, as was the custom, but then Pharinet noticed a particularly vivid shade of crimson. There was Grandma, swathed in a shawl that looked as if it had been fashioned from the cloth she'd bought in Mariglen the day before. She was not smiling, but neither did she frown. Pharinet raised a hand to her, and Grandma nodded once. Then the crowd surged around her and hid her from Pharinet's sight. Thomist came forward with Montimer Leckery from the door of the church, to accompany the brides inside.

The building was filled to capacity with rustling human presences, shapes that Pharinet could barely make out as she trod the cold flagstones to the altar. Thomist and Everna bore the candles for her – Valraven was yet to enter. Ellony was surrounded by a clutch of grinning female relatives. She looked pale yet feverish about the cheekbones. Pharinet could not bear to look at her.

The brides were sprinkled with a dust of ashes from the sacred censor, while the priest intoned archaic phrases over their heads. The words had no meaning. Pharinet felt light-headed and removed from reality. She heard the murmur start up around the fane when Khaster and Valraven arrived, escorted by their companions. The men were loud and jovial at the door, while Ellony shivered and giggled softly beneath her veil of red voile. Pharinet stood straight-backed and silent. She did not resent Khaster – she liked him. Khaster was not a part of all that was important to her. She would marry him willingly, for he could not affect the bond between her and Valraven. The other marriage was a different matter. She supposed, distantly, that her feelings were unfair.

The ceremony itself was a blur. Later, she remembered Khaster's face the first time he looked at her, the weariness in it, but also the affection. She felt that he knew her secret and sympathized, although of course he was in ignorance. Valraven, she could not turn her face to. She could feel his presence so close, like a black fire roaring towards the vaulted ceiling. If their auras should touch, they would both burst into flames. She must have spoken vows, declared her love for this man she would marry, but could not recall the actual moments. At one point the priest put her hand into her husband's. Her flesh looked like sallow coral, wizened in Khaster's elegant fingers. From one side of her came the warm energy of Khaster's relief and love, from the other a painful raw blast of force that was Valraven's feelings. He was not thinking of Ellony at all. He was in agony, but all the while building a cold, impenetrable wall about himself. Pharinet sensed the bricks going up, one by one, bricks of ice. But we did what we had to do, Pharinet thought. They couldn't stop us. It's done now. Nothing can undo it. Not all the love in the world.

The wedding feast was held at Caradore. A joyous multitude surged towards it, scattering petals and singing. Children clapped their hands against each other's, and spun round in spiralling circles, chanting marriage rhymes. As the company walked back to the castle, followed by a horde of guests and locals alike, Pharinet made herself smile widely until her face ached. She waved to people, clasped hands, kissed cheeks and uttered soft words of thanks for the presents she'd received and the wishes of good luck. There was no sign of Grandma Plutchen. Now that the ceremony was over, a strange calm had crept into Pharinet's mind. The Valraven who walked some distance ahead of her, with Ellony clinging to his arm, was not the man she had loved the previous night. That man was like a ghost or a god that only she could invoke. He was in hiding. Would a time come when she could conjure him up again? She had a husband now, tall at her side. He looked beautiful, his soft brown hair tied behind his neck, tendrils of it falling loose. His angular face was smoothed of care. She might even be able to say to him later, 'Khaster, my beloved.'

Once they entered the castle, the brides were allowed to retire for some minutes to refresh themselves. They were escorted by a fluttering flock of women, all squawking and cheeping like hysterical birds, up to Pharinet's rooms. Ellony's new apartments, as yet, remained unviolated.

'Oh, but you looked lovely, my dear,' the women said to Ellony, 'so lovely, the perfect quintessence of a young bride.'

Pharinet they tended to mutter to briefly, before turning back to Ellony with relief. Pharinet applied a fresh layer of pale powder to her already white cheeks. She was conscious of Everna's scrutiny behind her in the mirror and couldn't resist curling her lips into a secret smile. She saw from her reflection what this did to her face. She looked like an imp of fire about to pinch and burn.

At last, Ellony broke free of her admirers and swooped to Pharinet's side. 'I almost envy you,' she said, laughing. 'Khaster looks divine today. I could fall in love with him myself.'

Pharinet smiled back meaningfully, perhaps with a touch of she-wolf, and for a moment, a cloud crossed Ellony's face, as she realized the implications of what she'd said. Pharinet let her suffer for a second, then squeezed her friend's arm. 'You are right. I'm very happy to be his wife, Elly, I can assure you of that.'

Ellony's smile returned and she engulfed Pharinet in a warm embrace. 'I'm so glad,' she murmured against Pharinet's ear, and there was a promise of tears in her voice.

The flock descended the stairs to the main banqueting hall, which was rarely used. It was teeming with jabbering guests. Sound did not echo there, like it should. Pharinet was accustomed to seeing the hall in dim light, with all the shutters closed, but now it was a great light, airy space, filled with the scent of spring flowers. An arrangement of long tables of blond wood skirted the room. In the middle was a huge trestle, where the smaller of the wedding gifts were displayed. Everything was pastel and virginal, but for the clothes of the gathering. Pharinet considered that the marriage colours of Madragore were really more suited to sombre affairs in dingy, musty halls. The dark crimsons and hectic scarlets seemed out of place amid the soft green of the abundant decorative foliage, the limpid white of the flowers. She supposed that weddings in Magrast were stately and joyless. The brides would be meek and pale and frightened, and huge bells would clang over them, threatening to shatter their fragile bodies.

She met Valraven's eyes across the room. His expression was unreadable, but she suspected that so was hers. She inclined her head and he smiled slightly. The sound of flames crackled inside her head. Would they congratulate one another? The idea was absurd. They should grab each other's hands and run out of the castle, laughing, down to the beach with the wind in their hair, leaving everyone surprised and speechless.

Pharinet sat down between Khaster and her brother. Khaster took her hand and examined her face with concern. But he did not speak. She was grateful for that.

The first course was brought in, amid great ceremony: the feast was about to begin. I don't want to be this isolated thing, she thought. Let me be normal for a while. She forced her heart into her smile and leaned over to kiss Khaster's cheek. He looked momentarily surprised, then returned her kiss. The way he looked at her as he drew away kindled a slow but insistent beat of lust in Pharinet's body, a distorted memory of the previous night. She had experienced sex and already wanted more. This man was hers. She could have him whenever she wanted to. Would she derive pleasure from him after Valraven? She glanced briefly at her brother. Tonight, he would deflower his bride, but Pharinet would not be alone. She must not think about what might take place in the bride of Caradore's chambers.

Course after course was brought into the hall. Every time the servants appeared, the company cheered and clapped, as if they'd never eaten such wondrous fare before. People made speeches, or stood up and made impromptu toasts. Montimer Leckery delivered a speech. Enlivened by wine, he spoke warmly about his children, both those of his loins and those who had come to the family through love. Pharinet and Valraven exchanged a glance, a hot needle between them.

The crescendo of the occasion was the marriage wine. This was not just a drink, but a dessert, soaked in herbal essences and thick with dumplings of rich cake. Pharinet supposed it was an extravagant version of the pot Grandma Plutchen had made for them the previous day. Good luck charms would be concealed within it. It was customary for the bride and groom to take the first ladle of this confection, and considered fortunate if they should draw out one of the charms. This was hardly unlikely as every cook who ever made a marriage wine made sure the charms were plentiful enough to be included in every spoonful. This made consumption of the wine hazardous and tortuous. Many a drunken wedding guest had broken a tooth on such occasions. Therefore, tiny spoons had been devised with which to eat the dessert, which made identification of hard objects easier.

The wine, contained in a massive silver tureen, was brought in on a high trolley, guided by two servants. Everyone fell silent and got to their feet. The brides and their husbands came out from their seats and went to the middle of the room. Here, a servant lifted the lid of the bowl with reverence. Valraven indicated that Pharinet should take the first cup. She was surprised by this, as everyone would expect him to make that offer to his wife. Pharinet dipped the ladle into the steaming cauldron. The mixture within looked disgusting, like entrails floating in blood. She poured a measure into one of the miniature bowls arranged beside the tureen. Taking up one of the ridiculous spoons, she fed herself with a minuscule portion. Everyone released their breath and cheered, banging the table tops with their hands. Why? thought Pharinet. The process was embarrassing. She handed the ladle to Khaster. This too was perhaps short of etiquette, as she should really have passed it to Ellony. She couldn't. Khaster could do that. Khaster, however, seemed to think that Valraven, as highest-ranking male, should perhaps have gone first, for he handed the ladle to him. By this time, Pharinet was aware that the company were somewhat bemused by the order of this ritual. Still, what did that matter? Soon, everyone could get back to drinking and congratulating the couples. Valraven handed the ladle to his new wife.

Ellony smiled up at him like a devoted puppy then leaned forward to take her wine. For a moment, she hesitated, hanging stooped over the tureen as if time had stopped for her. Everyone just stared, unsure of what was happening. Then Ellony expelled a deep, animal groan, a sound that seemed impossible to have come from her modest lips. Valraven put out a hand to her, murmured a brief enquiry. Ellony staggered away from him, her palm pressed against her side. The ladle clattered to the floor. Everyone began murmuring, and Saska leapt up from her seat. 'Ellony!' she cried, trying to fight a way through the guests.

Ellony straightened up for a moment. She looked directly at Pharinet with silent, yet open-mouthed, appeal. She raised the hand that was pressed to her side.

The colour of the gown has come off on her, Pharinet thought. Or is it wine?

But then Ellony slumped to the ground in a graceful heap, and Pharinet realized that what she'd seen was blood.

The whole hall erupted into activity as people swept towards Ellony. Valraven lifted her in his arms and shouted at people to get out of his way. Khaster went after him, then realized Pharinet was not following. He paused and looked back at her. She had no choice but to accompany him.

They took Ellony to the bride's chambers, which were laid out in readiness for her occupation. Flowers and ribbons hung from every available source. The coverlet of the bed was folded back, waiting for the virgin bride's nervous arrival. She had come there too early. The feast was not yet finished, and Ellony was in no state to be anxiously awaiting the advent of her husband. Valraven laid her on the bed, where she moaned and writhed. Blood came off on the white covers.

'The wound has opened up again!' Saska cried, pushing Valraven out of the way in her concern. She was closely followed by Everna and Dimara. Ligrana and Niska stood at the threshold, their eyes wide in their pale faces.

'What wound?' Valraven demanded.

Saska searched the group who'd entered the room, clearly needing her sister's support.

Dimara came forward, oddly glacial. 'She had an accident some months back,' she said.

'What kind of accident?'

Dimara did not answer his question.

'I have already sent for the physician,' Everna said.

Dimara nodded. 'Saska, Evvie, help me undress her. Everyone else: out!'

'She's my wife,' Valraven protested.

'Get out,' said Everna. 'Leave her to us. Let us make her decent and comfortable, then you may return.'

Those who had come into the room obeyed Everna's request. Pharinet hooked her arm through Khaster's but Everna said, without looking round, 'Not you, sister. You remain here.'

'Of course,' said Khaster, and pressed his lips briefly against the top of Pharinet's head.

Pharinet was incapable of speech. She looked at the door and saw Valraven standing there, one hand against the frame. She shook her head at him and he departed.

'Don't stand there like a dumb mare,' Everna snapped at her. 'Help us.'

Pharinet went towards the bed. Her steps were too slow. Dimara and Everna were bent over Ellony, their fingers tearing at the ties to her gown.

Saska didn't appear to know what to do with herself. She kept making small movements over her daughter, only to straighten up, wringing her hands.

'What's happening?' Pharinet murmured. Tears had gathered in her eyes; she was crying.

'Stop dithering!' Everna said. 'Help us undress her. Saska, fetch hot water from the bathroom.'

Saska pushed blindly past Pharinet, her face white. Pharinet reeled a little on her feet, then murmured, 'Why are you angry with me, Evvie?' She almost said, 'It's not my fault', but stopped herself in time.

'I'm not angry, this is an emergency,' Everna answered, in a softer tone. 'Please help, Pharry. Saska's very upset. We all have to do this together.'

They pulled away the scarlet wedding gown. Beneath it, Ellony's pale torso was equally red. The wound itself looked old and festering, as if it had never healed. A stale stench rose from it. 'How could this happen?' Pharinet said. 'She was better, wasn't she?'

Everna's lips were clamped tightly together. She shook her head, helping Dimara to steady Ellony's writhing body. 'I don't know,' she said. 'The infection must have gone deeper than we thought.'

'The hanging head!' Ellony cried.

'Hush.' Dimara stroked her face, which turned this way and that upon the pillow.

'Deepest, darkest place,' gasped Ellony. 'In the dark, coming up in a froth.'

'She's raving,' Pharinet pointed out needlessly.

Saska had returned with a basin of water and some cloths. She bathed her daughter's wound, her face set in a strange expression of mingled calm concern and terrified hysteria. 'She was marked,' Saska said. 'Blessed. What does this mean?'

Dimara and Everna exchanged a glance. 'It's quite possible something was lodged in the wound,' Dimara said briskly, 'and an infection has been building up.'

'But what a time to happen.' Saska's face crumpled. 'Great Foy, on her wedding day, and to the dragon heir! How can this be?'

A small, voice whispered in Pharinet's mind: 'Because she's not the one. Never was and never will be.' She hated herself for that thought.

The physician arrived, trailing a couple of young male assistants, and ordered the wound to be drained. As Everna had suspected, an infection still lingered beneath the skin.

Pharinet went back down to the banqueting hall, where guests milled uncertainly. The marriage wine stood cold in its tureen, collared with a thin rind of grease. No one had dared to taste it, perhaps believing that by doing so they would only seal Ellony's doom. They did not want that she alone, the most fêted of brides, would not partake of its luck.

Pharinet soon realized that Valraven had already spoken to everyone, assuring them that Ellony was not gravely ill. She wondered whether her brother believed this himself. Did he care? He did not appear to be overly anxious, but of course the new Valraven, groomed in Magrast, had learned how to contain his feelings in public.

Khaster came to Pharinet's side as he saw her picking at a plate of food. 'How is she?'

'They are draining the wound,' Pharinet said. 'I'm sure she will be fine.'

Khaster frowned. 'How did she sustain such an injury? It was like something you'd get in battle, from a spear thrust or a sword.'

'Actually, it was from some sea wreckage. Ellony and I were down at the beach one day, and she fell. A spar pierced her side.'

Khaster looked at Pharinet doubtfully. It was a ridiculous excuse. If she were him, she would not believe it either. 'Pharinet,' he murmured, close to her ear. 'Tell me now. Did a man inflict the injury?'

'A man?' Pharinet tried not to smile and failed. 'No, Khas. I can assure you of that; I was there.'

He stared at her.

'And *I* didn't inflict it, either. How could you think such a thing?'

Khaster smiled grimly. 'I have learned there is more to the Palindrakes than meets the eye.'

She answered lightly, 'Yet only yesterday you loved me passionately. I am affronted.'

He shook his head. 'Pharinet, despite what I know of Val and whatever I might suspect of you, I will always love you both. You are strange creatures, and always have been. That is no doubt part of the attraction. All I can say is that my sister's wound does not look like the result of an accident, certainly not an accident incurred while young ladies walk along the beach together.'

'I would agree with you, but that is what happened, however unlikely it might seem.'

'And there were no wild games involved?'

'Khaster, I am too old for games.'

'Human beings are never too old for games.'

She put her arms about his neck and kissed his mouth. 'This is our wedding day too, Khas. Ellony is being taken care of. We should snatch back whatever happiness we can of this celebration.'

'You are different today,' Khaster said.

'I am your wife today,' Pharinet answered.

That night, Valraven went alone to his private chambers and did not visit those of his new wife. She was too ill, muttering, and writhing upon her bed. Pharinet and Khaster should have returned to Norgance that evening, but as none of the Leckerys felt they could leave while Ellony was so ill, Pharinet's wedding night would pass in her own room. She felt it prudent to look in on her friend before retiring. Everna, Dimara and Saska were still in attendance, with one of the physician's assistants nearby. Ellony was snarling, fighting with the single sheet that covered her, her body slick with sweat. Her wound had not yet been closed, in order for any poison remaining to drain away. A sweet, rotten smell hung in the air.

'This was to be her night,' Saska said. 'How is Valraven, Pharinet? Does he understand why he cannot come to her?'

'I think so,' Pharinet answered, 'although I had little chance to speak with him this evening.' She paused. 'Is there anything I can do?'

'Go and await your own husband,' Everna said. 'It would be ill indeed if none of you consummated your nuptials this eve.'

Pharinet felt pricked by Everna's tone and choice of words. She left without another word and went back to her own room.

All of her possessions had been packed in trunks and stood in her salon awaiting transport to Norgance. Her bedroom seemed cold and echoing, as if her presence had already left the castle. She sat down on the bed and wept silent tears. Her body was perfectly still. Presently, she took off her wedding gown and her underwear and let down her hair. The shutters were closed, so she opened them and stood in the beams of moonlight that came down though the clouds. What she could see of the beach looked white and distant. No shadows covered the moon. Last night seemed like a dream now. She wanted to go to Valraven, press her flesh against his. She wanted to know his thoughts. It was not Khaster's imminent advent that prevented her. She was afraid that Everna would know.

Pharinet paced in the moonlight. She felt full of energy, glad that Ellony could not have her wedding night. In just a short time, Khaster and Valraven would leave Caradore once more, and Ellony would still be virgin. Who directed the fate of the Palindrakes but the dragons? It was Foy's will that this should happen. Pharient recalled her bitter words, which earlier she had spoken into the mirror. *Dragons take you.* Had she cursed Ellony? Her anger and resentment dissipated a little. She saw Ellony twisting on her bed, poison oozing from an injury that would never heal. It must surely be Pharinet's own venom that leaked from the wound.

Have you come to this? Pharinet asked herself. Are you simply a spiteful, cruel creature? Ellony is your oldest friend. Circumstances have decreed she must be Valraven's bride. Why punish her for it?

Guilt tortured the fibres of Pharinet's body. She used the power of the dragons for harm. Yet there was something else moving within her, something fiery and fierce. Was this the presence of Madragore, who had presided over the weddings, and who might, in some lofty spiritual realm, be condemning Pharinet for her viciousness? Pharinet did not think so. It felt too elemental and wild, too delicious.

Khaster broke her thoughts by opening the door. She wondered what his first impression was of his young wife standing naked and unashamed by the window. She hoped he'd been expecting a demure, nervous girl. She padded towards him on silent feet, not daring to look behind for fear she would see the floor smoking where she'd trodden.

'Pharinet,' he said and she pressed her body against him, winding her arms about his neck.

'Here I am,' she said. His lips felt cold beneath hers, but she could feel his heart beating fast, as if he were afraid. He had been drinking with the men, with Valraven and Montimer. They would have been laughing together, or perhaps not. Perhaps Ellony's illness had bled all happiness from the gathering. What would Khaster say if he knew the truth about it? Pharinet put her hands in his hair, raked his scalp with her nails. He gasped and broke away from her, then lifted her in his arms and carried her to their bed.

'I don't know you,' he said, kneeling over her. 'What are you?'

She laughed and reached to up to undo his shirt. 'I am yours, my husband.'

He must have known she was no virgin but did not comment. Perhaps he could also tell how recently she'd been deflowered. Her body ached, yet she hungered for him. It was a fire that Valraven had kindled within her.

Afterwards, he lay like a dead thing beside her, breathing heavily. Pharinet felt languorous and replete. He had proved himself to her; she was not disappointed in him. His thoughts, however, remained unknown to her. She leaned over him, draping him with a shawl of tangled hair. 'Are you happy?' she asked him.

He reached up and twisted a lock of her hair in his fingers. His expression was introspective. 'You are a sorceress,' he said in a low voice, 'I am enchanted.'

'But happy?'

He nodded. 'Yes. Will you save that fire for me?' His voice did not sound happy.

'Once you are gone, there will be no other to ignite me.'

He pulled her down into his arms. 'You have shaken me,' he said and laughed softly. 'I had always believed marriage to be as my parents portrayed it, something safe and staid. With you, that will not be so.'

'I will be faithful to you, Khas. You must not fear.'

He stroked her face. 'I feel I have no right to demand your fidelity. You are apart from me, as Val is apart from Ellony. It is by circumstance alone that I now share your bed.'

'Don't be gloomy,' Pharinet said. 'Perhaps you will get me with child, and there will a son or daughter to greet your next leave.'

He smiled, but with sadness. 'That would please me. Do you think it's likely?'

'Possible,' she answered.

He sighed. 'But what of my sister?'

'You must not worry. I'm sure she will be well by the next time you come home.'

'That's not what I mean,' he said. He rolled Pharinet on to her back, holding down her arms with his hands. 'I'm not sure this marriage will be good for her.'

'How?' Pharinet murmured.

Khaster released her and sat up. 'Val has changed, Pharry. I didn't want to speak to you of this, but I must.'

'Of course you must. Your concerns are now mine.' Her heart pulsed painfully beneath her ribs.

'You must not speak of this to Val.'

'I won't. You have my word.' She knelt up behind him and circled his waist with her arms, laying her cheek against his smooth back. 'Tell me your heart.'

'Ellony is an innocent,' he said. 'I don't think she can understand or cope with the man she has married.'

'It was her choice. She longed for it.'

'She longed for a dream,' Khaster said, 'like something out of a story.'

'She has married Valraven; she has her dream.'

'Has she? Listen.'

CHAPTER SEVEN

Prince

Magrast, so huge and busy, had unnerved Khaster and Valraven at first. They were used to the wild, free air of Caradore. Here they found enclosed spaces, areas of decay and poverty where the air was almost unbreathable. High walls enclosed them, and a forest of bleak turrets, immense domes, elegant spires.

The military training establishment where the new officers had been given quarters was situated close to the palace. They were accorded many privileges, but still the regime was hard. Prince Almorante, the second son of the emperor, was the general responsible for supervising their training. Caradoreans were valued in Magrast. They were seen as lucky, as if they carried a special magic in their blood. Valraven and Khaster were reunited with several Caradoreans they had not seen for years, but the majority of the crop were far from the empire's heart, mostly in Cos where trouble was rife.

On the first day, Almorante presented himself in the new recruits' quarters. The Caradoreans had already been made familiar with the list of names that comprised the offspring of the emperor, because they'd had to swear fealty to the royal family upon arrival in Magrast. Almorante was a tall, severe man, accompanied by six young knights, who eyed Valraven and Khaster with a strange blend of curiosity and indifference. 'My father will see you immediately,' Almorante said to Valraven. 'He is pleased that you are here.'

Khaster was not invited to the audience. He sat in his new quarters, wishing he was at home. The few Magravandians they'd seen since their arrival had been aloof and disdainful. Khaster could not see how they would make friends here. Caradoreans might be considered valuable, but he sensed that the esteem in which Leonid held them bred resentment too.

Valraven returned from his audience with the emperor clearly impressed, a reaction that Khaster found disappointing. Valraven had been quiet and surly during the journey south, and Khaster had interpreted this as indicating how much he loathed having to leave home. Like himself, Valraven must be nervous and apprehensive too. But now he seemed quite at ease.

'What did Leonid say to you?' Khaster asked. 'Who was there?'

Valraven sat down, exuding an uncharacteristic nonchalance. 'He told me of his plans for the future, how important I am to them,' he said and laughed to show how this struck him as absurd. 'Prince Gastern was there, Almorante, of course, and Leonid's vizier, Khort. He's a mage, a sly creature. He watched me all the time.'

'And what are the emperor's plans?'

'To bring the divine fire of Madragore to every cold corner of the world. He speaks with passion, Khas. He is a man fired by zeal.'

'And this zeal has warmed you?'

Valraven looked slightly uncomfortable. 'I cannot help it if he wants to speak to me. It's because of my father. He and Leonid had a close friendship.'

'Are you implying I'm jealous?'

'You don't seem very happy about it.'

Khaster expelled a snort. 'I'm not jealous of you, Val. I just wonder how you can be so taken in.'

'We always knew this future was waiting for us. We cannot fight it, so why make life difficult for ourselves?'

From that first day, Khaster perceived a small but significant change in his friend. He believed Valraven was flattered by the emperor's attention. For all Magrast's unsavoury corners, the palace and its surrounding environs were opulent beyond anything the Caradoreans could previously have imagined. Food, weapons, animals and every other conceivable produce poured into it from the furthest reaches of the empire. Every luxury was to hand. Magrast could beguile with her perfumes, her liquors and her beautiful exotic foreign slaves. It seemed to Khaster that Valraven was gullibly seduced by it all. They might have to rise before dawn and train with their warmasters for most of the day in the use of weapons and discipline of the body. They might have to endure lengthy evening lectures on the history of the empire, on strategy and politics. They might have little free time, but those luscious moments were enough to capture a weak heart. Khaster did not want to think of Valraven as weak. Perhaps he himself was too austere.

Very quickly, over the next couple of days, the emperor's retinue of sons became more than mere names. Prince Gastern, the eldest, clearly considered himself above court intrigue, and the new recruits learned that he spent most of his time with the emperor and his generals. Valraven and Khaster were told they'd barely catch sight of him. More in evidence were Almorante and the next three in line, Eremore, Celetian and Pormitre. The four youngest sons were away from the city, at a mage college in the south. Of those who remained, only Prince Bayard, who seemed to have quite a reputation for wildness, was yet to be seen.

From the second day, Valraven was required to attend certain rituals in the great cathedral of Madragore. As a Palindrake, he was automatically affiliated to a holy order of knights known as the Splendifers. All of the emperor's own sons belonged to this order. Again Khaster was excluded from the proceedings, which effectively widened the increasing gap between himself and Valraven.

It was at the cathedral that Valraven first came into contact with Prince Bayard. Bayard was only two years younger than Valraven himself, and unlikely ever to attain the throne. Therefore, he had to struggle constantly to maintain a position of status and prestige within the family. The royal brothers both adored and loathed one another, each aware that the others were continually trying to usurp them in their father's favour. The royal women were unseen, living like nuns within their own cloistered environment in the palace, but it was well known in Magrast that Bayard was the Empress Tatrini's favourite son. He was certainly the most handsome, having a deceptively effeminate appearance. But other than that, it was said he was as hard and unyielding as steel.

For some reason, Bayard picked Valraven out for sport. He challenged him whenever the opportunity arose, insulted him for his rustic background, and made constant cruel allusions to the Palindrakes' conquest by the empire. Khaster saw danger in this behaviour. The young blades of the palace were wild and competitive, and their relationships were complex. Each had their coterie of admirers and followers, and intrigue and betrayal were rife. Prince Almorante had seemed to favour the Caradoreans, but withdrew his fragile support once Bayard took an interest in Valraven. Almorante was the most level-headed of the emperor's sons, but for his elder brother, Gastern. Khaster had come to respect Almorante, and had found him to be a fair man. His withdrawal was worrying. What did he expect to happen?

The first altercation between Bayard and Valraven occurred when the Caradoreans had been in the city for only five days. They had already established the routine of rising early, before the dawn. After a simple yet nourishing breakfast, they would go to their masters for instruction in the arts of war. Most Caradorean youths would receive this training from a young age at home; Khaster was no exception. But Valraven was different. No one had trained him to fight, although he was proficient with a bow, a legacy of learning to hunt deer with his father. As for the modern weapons, such as the pistol and the musket, neither Khaster nor Valraven had ever seen one before. Valraven's training was just a gesture. He would never really have to fight. He was the dragon heir. He would lead an army with his divine luck. Strategy would be more important to him than how to hack down an enemy in hand-to-hand combat. Or so the Magravandians thought.

The exercise yard for officers was in the heart of the military complex, which in itself was annexed to the imperial palace. The yard comprised a wide expanse of sand – replenished, raked and swept daily – surrounded by a colonnaded walkway. In the centre was an immense old millstone, which Master Rezien, Valraven's mentor, explained covered a deep pit into which recalcitrant officers in training had once been flung for days at a stretch. Valraven and Khaster would sit on its sun-warmed, pitted surface to eat their lunch. Khaster wondered if any bones were concealed far below. The Magravandians, however, did not appear disposed to hide their atrocities, but displayed them in public places. Cages on the outer walls of the palace contained the remains of miscreants, traitors and heretics. They looked as if they'd hung there for centuries. So far, Khaster had observed no fresh corpses.

At noon, the recruits always paused to refresh themselves, and on the fifth day, Prince Bayard chose this hour to saunter into the collonnaded yard, accompanied by a half dozen of his cronies. They were all spectacularly handsome young men, fit yet pampered, believing themselves to be among the best Magrast had to offer, which of course they were. As Valraven and Khaster ate their meagre lunch, Bayard and his companions lounged beneath the walkway that surrounded the yard, murmuring and laughing together. Presently Valraven began once more to exercise with his master, using the sword. It was then that Bayard, who had clearly been awaiting the right moment, got to his feet and sauntered out on to the sand.

'Master Rezien,' he said, 'allow me to spar with your pupil.'

Rezien could hardly refuse, although he must have known Valraven was far from ready to fight with someone who'd trained in swordsmanship since childhood.

Khaster and his own master had ceased their activities to watch what happened, Khaster's heart filled with misgiving. He had already heard rumours of Bayard's escapades; he had a reputation for unpredictable, grudge-bearing behaviour.

Bayard danced lightly around Valraven for a few moments, dextrously flashing his blade. Valraven's movements seemed clumsy and sluggish in comparison. The prince allowed Valraven a few moments' uncertain parrying, then with a combination of swordplay and kicks sent Valraven to the sand. Blood flowed from a precise razor cut on his throat. 'You have much to learn,' Bayard said, while his followers laughed with unnecessary volume behind him.

Valraven appeared to accept this humiliation philosophically. In his place, Khaster would have burned with fury.

A couple of weeks later, Valraven was taken to the great temple for a grand initiatory rite into the Splendifers. He confessed to Khaster beforehand that he had no great enthusiasm for this. Valraven was not a religious person and the idea of an order of holy knights held little appeal for him. Standing in the cathedral with other knights watching incomprehensible rites was one thing, taking oaths and performing ritual acts himself, another.

It was clear to Khaster that the Magravandians, the emperor and his immediate staff in particular, had high hopes for Valraven. They wanted to rush him into this holy order with a haste that seemed almost reckless. Valraven had barely glanced at the thick books of prayers and sacred stories the priest-mages had given to him. He was clearly not prepared. Surely an initiate should have a heartfelt, irrepressible desire to join the Splendifers. It should be a vocation. Nothing called to Valraven.

The ceremony took place one evening, and Khaster waited up for Valraven to return. He felt uneasy about the whole thing, scenting hidden agendas and secrets. The whole city sometimes made his skin itch with discomfort, as if conspiracies were incubating in every dark corner. Whispers would sometimes seem to follow him down twisting alleys that were like canyons between the high narrow buildings. Valraven was being led into this labyrinth. A monster was waiting for him. Khaster could sense it strongly. He feared the monster, because he thought its name was 'traitor'.

When Valraven returned from the cathedral and came into Khaster's room, he appeared thoughtful.

'Don't tell me it touched your soul,' said Khaster.

'It taught me something,' Valraven said. 'I have an enemy.'

'Who?'

'Bayard.'

'We knew that before.'

'No, this is more.' Valraven frowned. 'He wants something, or to prove something.'

Bayard had challenged Valraven's initiation. He had said, 'The last Lord Palindrake proved himself in battle and achieved many glorious victories for Magravandias. He was initiated into the Splendifers after his first successful campaign in Astinnia. Valraven, his son, has won no victories. He cannot even lift a sword correctly, and still stinks of mother's milk. He is not ready to join the Order.'

Gastern, presiding over the ceremony in a rare appearance with his siblings, had spoken of tradition, how the Palindrake heir was always affiliated with the Splendifers, and that the timing of his initiation was irrelevant. Almorante had also spoken in Valraven's favour. The other brothers, perhaps because of an ingrained envy of their privileged elders, had taken Bayard's stance. Valraven must undergo a trial to prove his worth.

'And what did they make you do?' Khaster asked.

'I have yet to learn,' Valraven answered dryly, 'though I fear my great friend, Prince Bayard, will make sure it is not an occasion for joy.'

Some days later, a message was brought to Valraven in the training yard. It was delivered by a beautiful yellow-haired boy who did not wait for a reply. Valraven scanned its contents. The message was from Almorante, who informed him that his trial would be by fire, as only appropriate for a future general of Madragore's army. In careful terms, Almorante seemed to apologize for this circumstance.

'Trial by fire,' Khaster said, his voice dry. 'What does that mean exactly?'

'It will not be too bad,' Valraven said. 'I have only to spend a night in the fire pits beyond the city. It's a place sacred to the Splendifers.'

'Only . . .' Khaster said with meaning. 'If it were a case of "only", surely Bayard would not have suggested it. Come on, tell me, what will this involve exactly?'

Valraven shrugged. 'Apparently, the mineral fumes from the ground at that place induce an euphoric state. It is supposed I shall hallucinate and rave, to everyone else's amusement, no doubt.' Valraven screwed up the message and threw it on to the sand. 'He thinks he can break me. He can't. I may not yet be a swordsman, but I am something Bayard will never be.'

Khaster put his head one side. 'And that is?'

Valraven smiled. 'Very flexible. Like a serpent. I will slither from his grasp. I will be like the Caradorean mist. If someone punches me, they will hit only air. I cannot be broken by force. I will bend and twist and float away. If he cuts me with a sword, I will laugh. If he cuts me with words, I will simply shrug. He will laugh at what happens to me at the fire pits and I will smile and shrug. It doesn't matter.'

It occurred to Khaster that Valraven's stream of words, which were quite uncharacteristic, had meant he'd thought about this deeply. He must have lain awake at night perfecting that little statement.

However, Khaster was pricked by a presentiment about the trial and made careful enquiries of his master about it. He learned that the effect of the fire pits was not simply delirium. The fumes that rose from the earth there were toxic. Sometimes the madness incurred in their foul breath never faded.

Khaster related this fact to Valraven. 'You must not do it. Appeal to the emperor.'

'Don't be ridiculous,' Valraven said. 'If I do that, Bayard and his supporters will never give me peace. They are testing me, that's all. It's only to be expected.'

Concerned, Khaster combed the narrow, twisting streets of Magrast until he found the shed of an old fire witch. Within its gloom, he asked her for advice concerning Valraven's trial.

'Fire-drakes dwell in the pits,' she told him. 'Sometimes they demand sacrifice.'

'What are fire-drakes?'

'Elemental creatures, like dragons. They breathe the fire and feast on the minerals found in its wake.' The woman made a strange, enveloping gesture with her arms. 'Some may guard against the breath of the fire-drake, but some will succumb, whatever precautions they take. I have treated many bravos of the court for this condition. Some I have had to send into the land of eternal sleep to end their pain.' She sighed. 'Such is the folly of the youthful male.'

'And how may my friend guard against the madness?'

The old woman handed Khaster a herbal mixture wrapped in a stained purse of leather. 'Make him a tisane of this. That's all I can offer. If he has any sense, he'll pray to Madragore to be spared.'

Valraven was not impressed by Khaster's suggestion. He looked into the leather bag and sniffed its contents. 'If I put this into my body, I shall risk a poisoning,' he said. 'You can't trust what you find on the streets, Khas.'

Khaster did not comment, but on the evening of Valraven's trial, he mixed the tisane himself, and disguised it by pouring it into a glass of merlac, the potent liqueur favoured by the court. 'Drink this,' he said. 'It will at least give you courage.'

Merlac's arresting mélange of sweet and bitter flavours was still a novelty to Valraven. He drank from his glass without hesitation, shuddering afterwards. 'Will we ever get a taste for that? It is like sugar and spice mixed with bile.'

Khaster perceived a smothered excitement in his friend, and realized that Valraven actually welcomed the trial to come. Over the last few days, Bayard had been a constant irritant lurking at the edges of the Caradoreans' routines. It plagued Khaster, filled him with fury, to hear the prince's sarcastic laugh, and the sycophantic responses of his cronies Valraven did not seem to mind. Khaster wondered whether he was in fact playing willingly to an audience.

That night, Khaster thought of Pharinet and wished that she were there. She alone might be able to persuade her brother not to go along with Bayard's games. Khaster was not sure what the point of the game was, nor how it could be won, but he was deeply uneasy about it.

Khaster could not sleep while Valraven was away. He left his own room and went into his friend's, lay down on the bed there. The window was open, and a bloody sunset filled the room with burning light. Khaster felt drenched in it. Magrast was like someone's vision of hell; there was opulence and luxury, but a dark, rotten heart to it. So far, Khaster had only glimpsed hints of this other Magrast, but he sensed it was there. The eyes of the whores, both male and female, who haunted the maze-like streets, oozed a knowledge that was not just sexual. Khaster perceived a veiled invitation: I can show you things beyond your dreams or night mares. Come with me, succumb. Learn. Then pay.

Often Khaster heard noises in the night that he could not identify. They were the sounds made by animals, but they had a human resonance to them. Sometimes, gouts of light would spurt into the sky – red, turquoise, gold – and some moments later thunder would come, but from beneath the earth rather than the heavens. Strange smells, bitter yet musky and sweet, would occasionally come in through an open window to haunt a room. Khaster knew that the priest-mages of Madragore employed a regiment of alchemists who worked in a shuttered citadel on the east of the city. Its huge domed roof, which was covered in flaky verdigris scales, rose up from an area of factories and tanning shops. Stories leaked out of the citadel along with the fumes. Creatures were made there, homunculi, golems, beasts of war. Sometimes these creatures escaped, or else were let out to roam the city by their keepers. That accounted for the strange nocturnal noises. But perhaps these were only stories after all. Perhaps the citadel hid secrets of a more mundane yet more brutal nature. Prisoners could be interrogated there, tortured with corrosive steams. The alchemists made killing perfumes for use on the battlefield. Khaster had heard tales of a liquid that, when released into the air, corroded all the flesh from anyone who smelled its delicate aroma. The alchemists made weapons; if not magical beasts, then mordant potions and poisons. They had to test them on someone.

Khaster shuddered. The priest-mages and their underlings were demons, muttering in shadows. Bayard and his brothers were demon princes, and the emperor was the archdemon, an incarnation of depravity: gilded and beautiful and terrible. Over this hideous hierarchy, Madragore held sway. A black and crimson overlord, lit by flames, his eyes pits of darkness. Now Valraven was being sucked into one of the cabals closest to the fire god's purpose. Splendifers. The fire pits would change Valraven. There was nothing Khaster could do.

Valraven did not return at dawn. Khaster breakfasted alone and went down to the training yard to meet his master. Rezien, waiting nearby, was not impressed to find Valraven absent, and perhaps later, if Valraven survived at all, he would be punished. Khaster had to say, 'It is Prince Bayard's will,' and Rezien made it clear that he could not view that as an excuse. Valraven might have no choice in what he'd done, but he would still be chastised.

That morning Khaster could not concentrate. He earned the rebuke of his master and the scorn of other young officers on the field. One of them said, 'He fears for his lover,' and laughed. Another said, 'You have lost him, get used to it.'

As he paused to eat the bread and meat that comprised his lunch, Khaster thought about these comments. The young men of the court seemed to despise women, and treated them carelessly, yet the love they often had for each other was fierce and enduring. Could the officer have uttered a truth? Could Bayard's behaviour be some kind of courtship ritual? Surely Valraven could not be interested in the prince?

In the evening, Khaster returned to his quarters and looked into Valraven's chamber, hardly hoping to find him there, But there he was, slumped face down on the bed, snoring loudly. Khaster was torn about whether to go and wake him or just walk away. He felt oddly betrayed. Ultimately, he closed the door and went to find his dinner.

Later, Valraven made an appearance at the door to Khaster's chamber as he was preparing to retire. 'You are in trouble,' Khaster said. 'Rezien is angry with you.'

Valraven sauntered into the room. 'Better to risk Rezien's wrath than lose face with the snapping puppies of Magrast.'

'You wanted to do it,' Khaster said. 'What happened?'

'It was informative,' Valraven replied. 'I lay down among the rocks, and they were gold and crimson like a royal tomb. I saw wondrous shapes rise in the fumes, twisting and curling like cats about me. They breathed upon me and filled me with fire. I saw myself leading armies. I saw myself killing men, and in my heart I felt a fierce glee. I saw myself ridding the world of all that was worthless.'

'You were delirious.'

'I felt power there, and knowledge. I think the Splendifers know more than we give them credit for.'

'And now you will be one of them.' Khaster faced Valraven. 'One of the lads on the field today suggested Bayard has an interest in you.'

'We both know that already, otherwise this situation wouldn't have occurred. I think we fascinate him because we are foreign.'

Khaster made a disparaging sound. 'We? He is barely aware I exist, and the interest I was referring to was rather more than simple curiosity.'

Valraven shrugged. 'Their ways are different to ours.'

'And you condone them?'

Valraven sat down on the bed. 'It does not affect me. Why should I make judgement?'

'Make sure it does not affect you,' Khaster said stiffly. 'Remember my sister.'

He was stung by Valraven's laughter. 'Your sister? What has she to do with this? You sound like a fussing old woman, Khas.' He lay back on the bed, his arms behind his head.

'Don't lose yourself to them,' Khaster said softly. 'Remember where we come from and whom we love.'

'Do you know who I love?' Valraven asked, his eyes hooded. 'We are old friends, Khas, but you hardly know me.'

'I know that, I've always known that, but I know you love your family and Elly. Don't forget them, Val. Think of when we must return home, and how at that time you must live with whatever you do here.'

'Home is home and here is here,' Valraven said. 'We have two lives now, Khas.' With these words, he got to his feet and left the room. At the doorway he paused and turned. 'That little potion you fed to me was quite unnecessary. I was never in danger.'

'How did you know about that?'

Valraven fixed him with a steady, shadowed gaze. 'I knew because I felt it in my blood before I ever reached the fire pits.'

'Were you alone there last night?' Khaster asked.

'No one is ever alone there,' Valraven answered and closed the door behind him.

After this, Khaster had to suffer Valraven's slow withdrawal. Everything that he saw and heard about the city filled him with distaste, yet Valraven seemed to embrace it. News from the frontiers was often horrifying, yet Valraven viewed it with indifference. Almorante gave him a magnificent horse, which would be trained to strike at enemies.

The training moved on from the sword to the gun. Khaster had never seen one before, but soon learned what it could do when it was demonstrated on a condemned prisoner. Bayard executed the man. He handed the gun to Valraven and said, 'Shall I fetch another peasant so you may try it?'

Khaster was alert for a change in the relationship between Valraven and Bayard, but mostly it seemed as before. Bayard still made sniping comments and often tried to make Valraven look a fool. Khaster, he ignored completely.

News of their forthcoming weddings got out a few days before they left for home. Both Valraven and Khaster had kept quiet about this, knowing it would only provide food for ridicule. On the night before they left, Bayard accosted Valraven in the lounge where the officers could be served food and drink in the evenings, or acquire the services of whores.

'Back home to your women-folk, tomorrow, Palindrake,' Bayard said. 'And of course to your little bride. Will you cry to see them?'

Valraven did not even look at him. 'I look forward to the peace of Caradore and the clean air.'

Bayard took this, rightly, as a covert insult and sneered. 'You Caradoreans are like simpering girls. What's wrong with you? Is it so vital you beget an heir? Are you afraid you'll die in battle?'

'It is the custom in our land for men to marry before they fight for Magrast,' Valraven said. 'We all have customs. I am not afraid to die in battle, but you cannot deny it is a distinct possibility.'

'You are not yet a man,' Bayard said. 'Only old men marry.'

Khaster's tongue itched to point out the lack of substance in Bayard's argument, but Valraven only said, 'In our country, it is different.'

Valraven's calm seemed only to irritate Bayard. 'You are just peasants. I can't understand why my father values your stock so much. You should be foot soldiers. They say that even your father died for the love of a woman. How can such a man lead an army? Perhaps we should have your little wife here, or your sister, to lead our men into battle. They might have more balls than you. I've a mind to taste Caradorean woman meat. What about it, Palindrake? You go home to be a housekeeper and send your women here!' He laughed and turned to his friends, adding more insults and salacious remarks.

Valraven put down his drink and stood up. Bayard turned back to him, his face set into an expression of challenge. For a moment, the two of them faced each other motionlessly, then Valraven threw a punch. Khaster was on his feet in an instant, expecting a full scale brawl. Around a dozen of Bayard's cronies were present. It seemed he and Valraven would get thrashed. But even as Bayard crashed back into a table, no one else moved to intervene. The prince picked himself up, glaring at Valraven. Then, with a snarl, he leapt forward. This was clearly sport for the onlookers. The only action they took was to cheer Bayard on. He and Valraven reeled about the room, tearing at one another. Khaster stood helplessly, unsure of what to do. He saw Almorante appear at the door, but the older prince only lingered at the threshold, observing the altercation with an unreadable expression.

Bayard had the fighting instincts of an animal. He attacked mindlessly and beat Valraven to the floor. Once he had his adversary pinned there, he took out a small dagger from his belt and drew the blade across Valraven's left cheek. It was only a light wound, but blood sprang quickly from it. 'Do not presume to take liberties with me,' he said. 'You will always come off the worst.'

Valraven growled in his throat, his head tossing from side to side. Bayard's followers cheered and roared, stamping the floor and clapping their hands.

'Now, my spoils,' Bayard said. He took Valraven's face between his hands, licked the blood from his face and then kissed him on the mouth.

Valraven spluttered and struggled, but his shoulders were pinned beneath Bayard's knees. Khaster could not stop himself from stepping forward and grabbing hold of Bayard's arm.

'Leave him, you've had your fun.'

Bayard did not lift his head immediately, but when he did, he fixed Khaster with a look of utter contempt. 'Jealous, are you?'

'Of course not. You sicken me.'

Bayard laughed and jumped up, while Valraven rolled on to his side. He seemed dazed, stricken. Bayard flicked Khaster's face with his fingertips. 'Accept defeat, peasant.'

He signalled to his followers and led the way out, saying without turning, 'Enjoy your wedding, Palindrake. I have sent you a gift for it.'

After he'd gone, everyone in the room fell back into their conversations, as if nothing had happened. Khaster helped Valraven to his feet. 'That creature is despicable,' he said. 'Must we endure this treatment?'

Valraven wiped his mouth and went back to his seat. He walked carefully, as if his body pained him. He would not speak.

Khaster sat down again, opposite him. 'He sought to humiliate you,' he said. 'You must forget it, Val. Don't let him win.'

Valraven lifted his drink, and Khaster saw that his hand was shaking. He didn't know what to say, although in one way he felt relieved by what had occurred. Bayard's behaviour could only turn Valraven more surely against him. Whatever he'd planned would not work on a man from Caradore.

'Tomorrow we leave for home, thank Madragore,' Khaster said. 'I cannot wait to breathe its air once more. Your sister shines in my head like a goddess. How I need her healing touch.'

Still Valraven did not speak. Perhaps he was in shock.

'Shall we return to our chambers?' Khaster asked.

Valraven remained silent.

'Val,' Khaster said softly, 'what can I do?'

Valraven shook his head. Perplexed, Khaster signalled to a potboy to bring more drinks. He ordered a stimulating aperitif for Valraven.

'If Madragore ever gives me the chance, I shall kill that leering prince in battle,' Khaster said. 'I shall wait for that moment, Val. He is scum and should be destroyed.'

'You don't understand them,' Valraven said. He cleared his throat, for his voice was husky.

'What don't I understand?' Khaster demanded. 'Val, don't try to explain away what happened.'

Valraven downed his drink in a single swallow. 'We should get some sleep, Khas. We have a long journey ahead of us tomorrow.'

CHAPTER EIGHT

Fate

'And was that the last he said on the subject?' Pharinet asked. Her eyes felt hot in their sockets, her heart was beating so heavily it felt twice its normal size.

Khaster nodded. 'Yes. Val would not speak of it again.' He turned to Pharinet for the first time since he'd begun the story. 'I am concerned for him, Pharry. A taint has put itself upon him. I fear he will end up like the royal filth of Magrast, disdainful of life itself, cruel and selfish.'

'I can't believe that,' Pharinet said. 'I know him, Khas. It's not in him.'

'There may be many things in him of which we're not aware.'

Pharinet turned away. She climbed off the bed and went to the window. She didn't know whether to laugh or cry. Khaster clearly knew nothing of the sea dragons, but surely the emperor's family did. It was the prime reason the Palindrakes had been subjugated in the first place. Now they had placed the dragon heir in the heart of the realm of the fire-drakes. Everna and the others of the Sisterhood maintained these beings of fire had been banished by the sea dragons thousands of years before. Pharinet was not so sure. If they had been banished, maybe Valraven, delivered to them upon a plate, his heart carved away, would be suitable inducement for them to risk a return. Then what might happen? More than a battle of arms. The sky might bleed for it.

Pharinet rested her head against the cool stone of the window casement. By Foy, she had felt the fire-drakes' burn the previous night. She had summoned it. Entities of the elements moved beyond human understanding. Had she, and Valraven, unwittingly catalysed a new drama? Had Ellony been a casualty of this? Maybe the emperor's family had planned it all along. They had sent Valraven back to Caradore, full of the fire-drakes' breath, and he had exhaled it over a priestess of Foy, contaminated her with its smoke. She shuddered.

Khaster's hands curled around her shoulders. 'I have distressed you. I'm sorry. Perhaps I was too frank in my story.'

Pharinet curled her hands over his. 'No, no, it's not that. Really. I just fear that the empire has somehow become closer to us, more real, since you and Val went to Magrast. It's touching us now, Khas, and I don't like it.'

Khaster sighed and rested his chin on the crown of her head, staring out into the night, where the waves heaved restlessly about the sea-caves. Lances of spray were thrown high. The sea was wild that night. Enraged? 'We have lived in a dream,' he said. 'This was waiting for us always. Our parents lived through it, and their parents before them. It is our curse.'

The following morning, Ellony was no better. The physician feared that her body would burn away in its fever. Khaster and Pharinet could not yet go to Norgance. Once again, Ellony was the centre of attention, as servants rushed back and forth with steaming basins of herbal water, with delicate soups and milky drinks. Ellony herself could not bask in this treatment, as her mind wandered a realm far from reality.

Pharinet forced herself to visit the sick room every day. Ellony was wasting away. Her skin was no longer pale, but sallow, as if a jaundice ate at her from within. Standing at the end of the bed, Pharinet struggled to understand her conflicting feelings. A dark, cruel part of her hoped that Ellony would not get well, while another part, that which she hoped represented her true self, was aghast at what had happened. Khaster was right: Ellony *was* innocent.

One evening, Pharinet went down to the beach. The waves were low, but heavy and watchful. She tried to conjure up feelings of empathy and worry for Ellony, but it felt as if the place inside her where these emotions should be was only an empty hole, with a wind blowing through it. What has happened to me? Pharinet wondered. How can I be so cold inside? I don't want to be. Then, an insidious voice whispered in her mind. *Perhaps it is because the sea dragons are cold. You need fire to warm you.*

But Ellony is a warm creature, Pharinet thought. And she is probably more devoted to the old beliefs than I am.

She sighed, and stood at the nibbling lip of the tide, holding back her hair with both hands against the wind that blew from the sea. 'If I cursed her, I did not mean to,' Pharinet said aloud. 'I want her to be well. Make her so, I beseech you.'

She wanted a response, some kind of sign, but none came. The elements seemed to be preoccupied. Clouds hurried across the sky, the sea wrestled with its own anxieties.

You are like the waves yourself, Pharinet thought. Your feelings of anger and jealousy ebb and flow. At high tide, you could kill. At low tide, you repent. If you did curse Ellony, you alone are responsible. You alone can lift it.

So she went back to Ellony's room, and found her sleeping there. The room was lit only by a flickering night-light. A nurse dozed in a chair nearby, but did not wake at Pharinet's soft intrusion. She lifted a cold, white hand from the counterpane and murmured, 'I give to you my strength. Come back to us, Elly. Be well again.'

Ellony's lips moved slightly and her eyes opened. 'Pharry,' she said in a husky voice. 'I dreamed of you.'

'Hush now,' Pharinet said, leaning down to smooth the hair from Ellony's face. 'Sleep deep and find your strength.'

'Pray for me.'

'I have. I will.'

Ellony smiled a little and closed her eyes once more. Her fingers gripped Pharinet's hand quite tightly. She could not pull away. Only when Khaster came looking for her could she bring herself to prise Ellony's hand from her own.

Despite visiting Ellony several times a day, Pharinet was always glad when the cloying air of the sickroom released her. Her steps would lighten as she hurried away. Downstairs, her husband and brother would await her. What else could they do during these terrible days but console one another?

Every day until Khaster and Valraven went back to Magrast, they would ride out with Pharinet into the countryside. They were drawn to visit sites where they had played as children, and these times were both joyous and poignant. The tension between Valraven and Pharinet vibrated like a plucked harp string. They could touch and embrace in front of Khaster, for he would think nothing of it, but they resisted. The ache of longing was sweeter if its gratification was denied. On one occasion, Pharinet was in the stableyard alone with her brother, while Khaster searched for his boots indoors. Pharinet resolved to make good use of this time. 'Khas has told me many things about you,' she said.

Valraven, standing beside his horse to adjust the saddle girth, gave her a brief pointed glance. 'Has he?'

Pharinet smoothed the horse's neck. 'He has indeed. Are you considering an affair with a royal prince, Val?'

Valraven laughed. 'Khaster *has* been talking. The Magravands upset him because he can't understand their ways. I just go along with them. It's easier.'

'And how far are you prepared to go in this course of action?'

Valraven's hands became still upon the leather strap. He took a breath. 'Bayard just likes playing games with people. Khaster is over-reacting. He saw something he found uncomfortable and thinks the worst.'

'He is also concerned about your connection with the Splendifers. He thinks the odour of the fire-drakes ill-becomes you.'

'Khaster is too loose with his tongue. He is dangerously close to becoming what Bayard accuses us of. He should not go whining to his wife in that way.'

Pharinet expelled a gasp of shocked laughter. 'Val! How dare you say such a thing. I won't have you adopting the Magravand view of women with me.'

'I didn't intend to.'

'I don't want secrets between us. Khaster was right to tell me his thoughts. I can see that you certainly won't.'

Valraven swung himself up on to the horse's back. 'Didn't I warn you of what I am becoming? A day or so ago, you said you accepted that.'

Pharinet looked up at him. He was a dark stranger. She could almost see the smoke of the fire-drakes hanging around him. Why then did she want him more than ever?

'Don't treat me as anything less than yourself. and I will accept it. That is one change I will not tolerate.'

'You are part of me, Pharry.'

He might have said more, but at that moment Khaster came into the yard. They rode down to the shore and galloped through the spume at the edge of the tide. Am I betraying my heritage? Pharinet thought. The sky was overcast, and the green of spring insanely bright against it. They came upon a drowned seabird, spread out like an angel in the sand. Tomorrow, the men would leave. Ellony remained a virgin in her damp, troubled bed, but Valraven seemed unconcerned. Like Pharinet, he dutifully visited his wife several times a day, but once free of Caradore it was as if Ellony did not exist.

Pharinet brought her horse up alongside her brother's; Khaster was some distance behind. 'We must be together once more before you go,' Pharinet said.

Valraven turned his head to her. 'How? Will you drug the attentive Khaster?'

'No. I will tell him I need some time alone in the shrine tonight, to offer the proper prayers for his and your safety. He will respect this. He is most superstitious at this time.'

'As you wish,' Valraven said, and spurred his horse forward.

That evening, Ellony regained her senses. She asked for Pharinet to visit her, and Pharinet had no choice but to comply. 'Sit with me this evening,' Ellony said, frail upon her pillows.

Pharinet sat upon the bed. 'I will, for some time.' She took Ellony's hand. 'You will be well soon. I can feel it.'

Ellony smiled weakly. 'Have you been to the sea for me? Have you spoken to the dragons on my behalf? Only you can do it, Pharry. You and I have knowledge the Sisterhood does not.'

'I have been to the sea,' Pharinet said.

'I need to know why this has happened to me. You'll have to help me find out.'

'Of course. We'll commune with the dragons together, once our men have gone.'

Ellony's brow puckered and she turned her head to the side. 'Oh Pharry, I have been a useless wife for Val so far. I have given him nothing a man requires.' She looked back at her friend with feverish eyes. 'Do something for me. Speak to Val, and have him visit me late tonight. My mother and Everna must not know, for they would prevent it, but Pharry, I know you will understand. My weak body will bear his love, for it is not right he should return to Magrast and leave me still an untouched maid.'

Pharinet swallowed with difficulty. 'I will do what I can.'

Ellony squeezed her hand. 'Thank you. I love you, Pharry. You are closer to me even than my mother.' She smiled. 'Tell me what it is like, this love between man and woman. Did Khaster please you? Did it hurt you?'

'Khaster did not hurt me,' Pharinet replied. 'I find the act altogether agreeable, but not everyone is the same, of course.' Ellony seemed to have forgotten the conversation they'd had during their initiation rite, when Pharinet had implied she had already made love with Valraven. She must have blanked it from her mind.

Ellony sighed. 'I yearn for a man's love, yet I am afraid. It seems grotesque and unimaginable, but at the same time so exciting. I long to share Val's body, to feel him within me, but I'm so worried I might faint when I see him naked before me.'

Pharinet pulled her hand from Ellony's and stood up. 'Shall I read to you now?'

Ellony blinked dampness from her red-rimmed eyes. 'Yes. That would please me. Your voice is beautiful. It soothes me.'

Pharinet walked blindly to where she knew the bookcase was. A selection of freshly printed volumes had been placed there for the new bride's pleasure. Pharinet picked one at random from the shelf. She burned with fury and anxiety. At the tenth hour, she would leave this room to visit the shrine.

Red candles, burning low, cast shadows upon the walls. Pharinet stepped in through the door and pulled it closed behind her. The air was still, as if some alert presence observed from the darkness high above. Pharinet stepped up to the altar. The stern countenance of Madragore glared down at her. He had no love of women; she would not pray to him. He seemed like a man who long ago had decided to make himself a god. There was nothing ethereal or spiritual about him. Perhaps he kept his sons from women because he feared them. Human life was not sacred to him, only conquest. And the conquest itself meant only running away from all that was human within. She closed her eyes and for a moment was assaulted by a clear yet fleeting image of her brother. He was naked, standing with his back to her, his pale buttocks pumping like those of a rutting dog. She could not see who he was with and opened her eyes quickly. She did not want to see herself.

The door opened behind her and closed again quickly. She did not turn round. What if some other family member or a servant had come in? She heard footsteps and then arms enfolded her, lips were against her neck. She tilted her head to the side and reached back to pull him closer. He pulled up her skirts and grabbed at her between the legs. She turned then, haunted by the brief image she'd glimpsed. His face looked gaunt yet hungry. 'I watched you walk in here,' he said. 'You floated like a wraith. I could smell you.' He pushed her back against the altar.

'Not here,' she said. 'Anyone might come in.'

For a moment, it looked as if he was going to say he didn't care about that, but then he nodded.

She took him by the hand and led him among the columns, where darkness reigned. Her body burned with need. She lay down, looking up at him, dragging her skirts up to her waist. 'Come to me, Val. Fill me.'

He smiled and knelt down. Then with a lunge his face was between her legs. She uttered a smothered shriek as he bit and sucked at her. She tried to pull him up by his hair, but he would not relent. He must taste Khaster in her, for only that afternoon she and her husband had made love. Her whole body throbbed with pain and pleasure. At the moment of release, he reared up and thrust into her, pushing her head sharply against one of the stone columns. What if Khaster should see them now, or Ellony, or Everna? Pharinet laughed aloud and curled her legs around his back, her flesh pulsing with waves of orgasm from the top of her head to her toes. Valraven climaxed with a wordless shout that echoed throughout the shrine. She pulled his head to her breast and he lay upon her panting. They did not speak for some time. Pharinet thought about what Ellony had asked of her. She could comply with that now, give back some of what she'd taken. But the words wouldn't come.

Valraven got to his feet and began to rearrange his clothes. 'Will you go to Khaster now, sister?'

'Naturally. I am his wife, and we happen to share a chamber here.'

'Will you tell him what you've done?'

'No, of course not. He would be devastated. Do you want him to know?'

Valraven shrugged. 'He will never own you. You are mine.'

'You don't own me, Val.'

He laughed. 'No. Own is not the right word. I *am* you.'

Pharinet sat up and pulled down her skirts. He was wrong. He couldn't see into her head. 'Will you write to me this time?'

'I could not say the things I mean in a letter.'

'You could tell me what happens to you.'

He nodded shortly. 'I'll write.' He extended a hand to her and she took it, pulling herself to her feet. They embraced.

'Take care in Magrast,' she said. 'Play the games by all means, but learn the rules first.'

'I will.' He kissed her. 'Remember me.'

'Have no fear.' She pulled away from him. 'I must go. I don't want to risk Khas coming looking for me. What will you do now?'

He smiled. 'Perhaps I should visit my poor, ailing wife. How is she today?'

Pharinet brushed back her hair from her face. 'Oh, the same. I think she'll be a long time healing. I would not disturb her.'

'It is a strange business.'

'Yes, but perhaps fate.'

He gave her speculative look. 'You are me,' he said.

The following day, Pharinet stood on the steps of Caradore and watched the men in her life ride away from her. She tried to dismiss a pervasive feeling of gloom that she would see neither of them again. Ellony was not quite well enough to come downstairs, although she did receive Valraven in her room before he left. Pharinet accompanied him there and stayed with them. Ellony did not seem to mind.

Two days later, Everna persuaded Saska that Ellony was well on the mend, and the Leckery women rode home to Norgance. A cart followed their carriage, laden with Pharinet's wedding gifts. On impulse, Pharinet had removed the label from the portrait of Prince Bayard and commanded the servants to load it into the cart. There were so many presents for Valraven and his bride; it was unlikely Ellony would miss one.

Saska had redecorated a small suite of rooms for Pharinet, which were not like the lofty chambers of Caradore, but filled with light for the better part of the day. They had a comfortable atmosphere. Resigned, Pharinet arranged her belongings around the rooms. She hung the painting of Prince Bayard in her bedroom. At night, while summer coiled around the valley, she would lie awake in moonlight, wondering what her brother was doing now. Bayard stared back at her, inscrutable. Sometimes, he was in her dreams.

On the rare occasions when Khaster came home on leave, Pharinet would put the painting in her sitting room. She could tell he disapproved of its presence in Norgance, but since Valraven had never mentioned it and Pharinet herself said she just liked the composition, he clearly shrank from complaining.

Pharinet spent most of her time with Ligrana, who, like Pharinet herself at a younger age, liked to explore the ancient sites on the moors above Norgance and the shadowed forests beyond. Pharinet knew that Ligrana admired her greatly and tried to emulate her expressions and opinions. Niska was not so effusive, but then she was a peculiar creature anyway. Dimara spent nearly every day at Norgance, only going home to her lodge in the grounds at night. Pharinet shrank from trying to initiate a friendship with the woman. There was definitely a reserve between them, but Dimara clearly did not intend to try and transcend it.

Merlan Leckery's tutor, impressed with his student's work, advised Saska to send him to college in Magrast. She resisted this suggestion at first, but eventually, because Merlan himself was keen to go, wrote to Montimer and asked him to arrange it. Merlan was young to be leaving home, but his tutor believed he had a great future in front of him. His intellect might save him from joining the army, and this very soon proved to be correct. Now Norgance was a house of women, but for the boy child, Foylen.

Every couple of weeks, Pharinet rode over to the rock village with Saska and Dimara to attend the rites of the Sisterhood. Usually, she would spend the night at Caradore on these occasions. It still felt painfully like her real home. Ellony had not made a mark on it, although her own chambers had been garnished with flounces that Pharinet did not like. Ellony now possessed a strangely serene, yet melancholy mien. Sometimes, she and Pharinet went down to the sea-cave together, which Pharinet felt sure must still pulse with the echoes of her incestuous lovemaking. Here, Ellony attempted to divine information about what had happened to her. Her pleas to the dragons were heartrending in their simplicity, but neither Foy nor her daughters deigned to make any kind of contact. Not even the wing of an omenic bird crossed the sky.

Superficially, Ellony was healed of her injury, yet Pharinet perceived a lingering odour of sickness about her. She was sure it would never go away. Perhaps it was that which affected her relationship with Valraven. No matter how much Ellony looked forward to her husband coming home on leave, his arrival always made her ill. It became noticeable after the second leave since the wedding. This did not prevent her finally consummating her marriage, a time during which Pharinet seethed and paced alone at Norgance. Khaster's leave had not coincided with Valraven's and rarely did. It was easy for Pharinet to meet her brother on the wild moor above Norgance's valley. They would ride out to sheltered locations, and there consummate their forbidden passion, time and again.

Pharinet asked Valraven about Bayard, but received very little information in response. With every leave, he seemed to become more distant and self-contained. He grew taller, harder. His eyes were like those of a predatory bird's. Khaster was pining for Caradore. Valraven made it clear he disapproved of, and even despised, these sentiments.

'Don't leave me for ever,' Pharinet said.

'There is no chance of that,' Valraven replied. 'One day, I shall send for you.'

Pharinet knew that would never happen, no matter how much her brother might like to imagine it. They occupied different worlds now. Only when they were naked together did some of their old closeness return. But it was too brief.

Two months after Valraven's first leave following his marriage, Pharinet stopped menstruating. She realized with a thrill of both dread and wonder that she could be pregnant. It must be Valraven's child, although no one would ever guess that. Khaster had come home only two weeks following Valraven's visit. She was safe.

One day, obeying an inner compulsion, Pharinet saddled her horse and galloped madly to Caradore. She did not visit the castle straight away, but rode down towards the cliff path, where the forest leaned towards the sea. She wanted to see Grandma Plutchen. The old woman would be able to confirm whether or not she was with child. As yet, Pharinet had no desire to speak to any of her female relatives about her condition.

Grandma was sitting outside her cottage, polishing apples on her apron. She looked up without apparent surprise when Pharinet pulled her sweating, excited horse to a standstill beside her. 'You can do me a service,' Pharinet said.

'Aye.' The old woman got nimbly to her feet and without another word walked into her cottage.

Pharinet followed her. 'There is something I need to know.'

The cottage was in golden gloom, its air filled with the aroma of the apples that simmered in a great black pot on the range. Grandma wiped her hands on her apron. 'I know, child,' she said. 'Your face says it all. Slip into my bedroom and make yourself ready. I'll wager you're six or seven weeks gone already, but a quick check should tell you all you want to know.'

Pharinet felt her face burn. She had not expected so direct a response.

When she hesitated, Grandma said, 'That is what you want of me, isn't it?'

Pharinet nodded and went into the small dark room where Grandma slept. She removed her undergarments and sat on the lumpy bed. Grandma came in and subjected her to swift but thorough examination. 'Yes, as I thought. But you knew this yourself, didn't you?'

'In a way,' Pharinet said.

Grandma nodded. Pharinet found it difficult to meet her gaze, sure that she knew what was on her mind.

'Take heart,' said the old woman gently. 'It is not your privilege. This you must accept. Don't force the hand of Lady Fate up behind her back.'

'What do you mean?'

Grandma put a hand on her shoulder. 'Dress yourself, child. I'll make us a drink.'

Pharinet grabbed hold of her arm. 'Please, tell me what you mean.'

'You'll know soon enough. But not this moon.' She turned away and left the room.

Pharinet sat alone in the silence, feeling it press down upon her. A darkness filled her heart, made her ache. She wanted to cry.

When she went back into the kitchen, Grandma Plutchen chattered on about her garden, her neighbours and gossip of the town concerning people Pharinet did not know. She felt as dazed as if she'd received a blow to the head. A child was in her womb, Valraven's child, yet it no longer felt real.

After she'd ridden home, Pharinet fought against this feeling of doom.

Defiantly, she told Saska that she was pregnant, which predictably sent the households of both Caradore and Norgance into a fever of excitement. Only Dimara's reaction seemed muted, but Pharinet would expect nothing else from her. Pharinet spoke to her baby, willed it to demand life from the elements. She told it how special it was, how much she loved it.

Four weeks later, while walking with Ligrana in the gardens at Norgance, Pharinet fell to her knees with a searing pain in her belly. Blood came out of her, soaking her gown. She expelled a single, despairing moan, while Ligrana cried out in horror. Their cries brought servants running, then Saska. They bore Pharinet away to her bed, and there the new life inside her flowed out and died. Pharinet's love, her desire and her will had not been enough. The child had never been hers. What had she been thinking of? It would never happen.

CHAPTER NINE

Persuasion

Life progressed through the seasons without remarkable changes. Pharinet saw a few grey hairs appear on her head, even though she was young. She believed this was because she had to grit her teeth so often, dealing with Saska on a daily basis. This changed somewhat when the news came back to Norgance that Montimer Leckery had been killed in action. The imperial army had suffered a rout in Cos, and although it had been contained Montimer had been one of the casualties. Pharinet imagined him on horseback, waving a sword and being taken by an enemy bullet. The truth was he'd been murdered in his bed by Cossic terrorists. Valraven told her this when he and Khaster brought the body back to Caradore for the funeral. Everyone dressed in purple and Khaster supported his drooping mother at the graveside. Ellony, pale of cheek and nursing a virulent stomach ailment, clung grimly to her husband's arm. Valraven and Pharinet exchanged smoking looks across the opened ground.

Some of Saska's buoyancy diminished as she assumed the role of widow. Pharinet saw bitterness harden the lines around her mother-in-law's mouth and her eyes became pouched with unspent tears. Perhaps she'd believed that being a priestess of Foy would protect her from life's hardships. It hadn't. Pharinet now thought that if there ever was to be a deliverance for the Palindrakes and Caradore, it would not happen in her lifetime. Both Valraven and Khaster, in their separate ways, showed her how powerful the empire was. Whatever the Caradoreans might think, enacting their melancholy rituals beside the sea, they could change nothing. The sea dragons remained a tantalizing myth and if they had risen from the deep to touch the hearts and minds of two young initiates, they had once again sunk into dreams. All that remained of that time was a livid scar on Ellony's side and a tendency to contract whatever ailments and diseases smoked their way across the land. She did not conceive a child.

A year after Montimer's death, Khaster wrote to his wife and told her that the houses of Norgance and Caradore should prepare for a grand event. For the first time since his father's death, he and Valraven were to be given leave at the same time. They would have a companion with them: Prince Bayard.

Pharinet read the letter aloud to Saska over breakfast. Once, Saska would have been thrown into a giddy turmoil of excitement. Now, having developed a hatred of all things imperial, she merely lifted her lip. 'He no doubt intends to continue where his father left off, having the run of Caradore as if it were his own home.'

'That makes sense, I suppose,' Pharinet replied. 'It must be a tradition.'

'Intriguing that the eldest son, who is heir to the empire, has not taken the role,' Saska remarked, pouring herself more tea.

Pharinet had noticed that Saska had ambivalent feelings about Valraven, that sometimes manifested in subtle snipes. It was no secret that his marriage to Ellony had not been the romantic grand passion of dynasty-building significance that the Leckery women had imagined or hoped. Ellony confided in Pharinet only with care, for obvious reasons, but Pharinet had gathered her friend had no taste for sex. If anything, she seemed bewildered by it, almost betrayed. Everna had told Pharinet how Ellony would wander about Caradore at night, like some mad ghost, dragging the hem of her nightgown across the flagstones. 'It is as if she is looking for something,' Everna said, 'but Foy knows what.'

She is looking for the future she lost, Pharinet thought. She walks in the great hall searching for the wedding feast that faded away like a dream. She is looking for herself as she was.

One aspect of Ellony's behaviour was a certain feyness that manifested itself at Sisterhood gatherings. Sometimes she would go into a trance and say strange things. She told of underwater realms of disturbing beauty, where creatures she could not describe writhed like eels among fallen marble columns. She spoke of the dragons, and then she would become agitated and flecks of foam would gather at the corners of her mouth. Pharinet thought that for Ellony the sea dragons had become a personal horror; a haunting she both welcomed and feared. No wonder she walked at night.

Pharinet felt distanced from the dragons now. She lived further from the sea. Sometimes, lacking her sea-cave as a refuge from Saska's abrasive moods, she would climb to the Ronduel, the stone circle perched high

109

above Norgance. Here she would imagine dead kings and queens parading before her, but she never saw anything with her eyes. The wind blew a mournful lament, while the grasses hissed an accompaniment, and Pharinet wondered if this was how the rest of her life would progress.

Therefore, the prospect of meeting Prince Bayard was an exciting distraction. Saska resisted being drawn into it at first, but eventually had to give in. Everna, naturally, was thrown into a frenzy of activity, which Saska could not avoid without being rude. Ellony too became roused from her usual dreamlike state. In private, the Sisterhood might revile the emperors of Madragore, but the presence of a royal male on Caradorean soil still provoked a feeling of occasion. Thus it had been in Pharinet's father's day.

A feast would be thrown at Caradore, and many of the local noble families would be invited. Everna confided to Pharinet, 'Perhaps the old days are returning.'

Pharinet was astonished her sister could say such a thing.

The day dawned when the men were due to arrive. Pharinet, Dimara, Saska and her children converged on Caradore, while Everna whisked about the castle issuing orders to her staff. Noon passed and there was no sign of the visitors. 'Perhaps delayed on the road,' said Everna, frowning, although Pharinet thought this unlikely. Khaster had described the itinerary of their journey in his letter, and had said the party would be breaking their travels overnight at a hostelry which lay only three hours' ride from Caradore. Perhaps they were late risers.

They clattered into the castle yard late in the afternoon, trailing a retinue of boisterous young men whom Pharinet assumed must be Bayard's entourage. The women had gathered quickly on the castle steps once the call had come from the battlements that a company of riders approached. The prince was instantly recognizable from his portrait, a shining presence whose charisma seemed to eclipse everyone else present.

Ellony was the first to glide down to the prancing horses, no doubt keen to make a good impression. Khaster looked surly and Valraven bemused.

Bayard dismounted from his horse and surveyed the waiting women. Pharinet noticed his gaze skimming briefly over every one until it fell upon her. He came towards her. 'You must be the Lady Pharinet,' he said.

'I am,' she replied.

Ellony hovered at Valraven's side looking puzzled. She had clearly expected a royal greeting before everyone else. Khaster jumped down from his horse, his lips tight. He walked purposefully to Pharinet's side, who leaned towards him for a kiss.

Everna came down the steps and curtsied to the prince. 'I am Everna

Palindrake, Valraven's elder sister,' she said. 'I welcome you to our home and trust your journey was pleasant.'

Bayard bowed to her. 'Tolerable,' he said. 'I am pleased to be here, my lady. Valraven is always extolling Caradore's virtues to me.'

Pharinet eyed the prince with suspicion. He seemed very much his father's son – polite and gracious. Where was the sneering sullen creature described to her by Khaster?

After light refreshments in the castle, Bayard insisted on visiting the family shrine. Everna explained that there was no priest in residence at Caradore. He lived beside the great church in the town of Tarabrake, some miles to the south. 'We can summon him, of course,' Everna said, 'but he may not be able to come immediately.'

Bayard placed a hand upon Everna's shoulder; a gesture Pharinet found to be amusingly familiar. 'Fear not,' he said. 'Enough of my father's god resides in me that I can stutter a prayer or two.' He turned slowly before the assembled company of Palindrakes and Leckerys. 'You must all come. We should pray together.'

This apparent piety was another thing neither Khaster nor Valraven had mentioned before. Pharinet suspected Bayard was being ironic. He seemed the epitome of the golden prince, but she could smell a danger in him, something that moved slowly and purposefully beneath the surface.

Rather self-consciously, the company went out through the castle yard to the shrine. Inside, it felt cold and damp. No candles were lit and no incense filled the air. Everna hurried to correct these deficiencies, and presently the half-burned red candles flickered upon their tall sconces and a heavy waft of peppery smoke curled out of the burnished censor that hung above the altar.

Nothing lives in here, Pharinet thought as Bayard took his place before the altar and raised his arms. Why is he bothering?

Bayard called upon Madragore and, as the emperor's son, made a personal royal request that the god should bless the families of Caradore.

Watching him, Pharinet was suddenly filled with the impression that the fire Bayard worshipped did not reside in the dour countenance of Madragore. It lay somewhere else, and where it lay, it coiled and writhed, puffing out ribbons of acrid smoke. It was waiting. She was sure that Bayard himself was aware of this. He was invoking something there, in their little shrine, calling something into being in Caradore.

After the brief ritual, everyone went back into the castle, and Bayard was shown to the guest apartments Everna and Thomist had made ready for him. They were the same rooms once used regularly by his father, in the days when the emperor had been a frequent visitor.

Everna suggested that the prince and his companions should rest for a couple of hours before dinner, which, that night, was to be a fairly private affair, with only the Leckerys and the Palindrakes, and two local squires and their wives. The following evening, the rest of the local nobility would arrive, intent on viewing this new royal. Some would attempt to curry favour, while others would judge him in silence.

Khaster told Pharinet he felt tired and in need of a bath. Without actually saying so, he implied they should retire together to the room they usually occupied while staying at Caradore. Pharinet was not tired, and felt far from in the mood for physical intimacy. Because Khaster would not be forthright in his request, she was equally vague at side-stepping it. 'You take a bath and a rest,' she said. 'The windows will be open, and the sea breeze will soothe you. I'll just be a fidget, for I'm wide awake. I think I'll walk in the gardens for a while.'

Khaster, though clearly disappointed, did not argue. As she watched his retreating form, Pharinet felt slightly guilty. He did not know her at all. She deceived him constantly.

The gardens stretched away from the castle. The lichened pale stone of their enclosing walls rose high and muffled the crash of the waves, though the ground vibrated beneath Pharinet's feet as if water gushed and foamed into rocky caves beneath them. As a child, Pharinet had spent little time among the cultivated arbours and cropped lawns, preferring the wild open spaces beyond the castle walls. Now the gardens seemed peaceful and welcoming. Whatever wind teased the grasses on the cliffs was kept out; the air was still and fragrant. Pharinet sat down on a stone bench before a fountain. The sun was pleasantly warm on her skin and the distant cry of seabirds lulled her mind. She missed her home.

She wondered whether Valraven was making love to Ellony now. The image disgusted her. She dreaded some plaintive sounds drifting out from the open windows behind her. Some time during the men's brief visit, she and Valraven would find the opportunity to be together. It always happened, as if it was meant to. Then she would imprint her own strong sensuality over the memory of Ellony's feeble frame. Valraven would return to Magrast with his skin redolent of her own scent. She wondered then what Bayard thought of Ellony. The fact that he had ignored her when he'd first arrived perhaps indicated the depth of his feelings for Valraven. He'd sought Pharinet out straight away. Did he know about her? Perhaps she and Bayard had an affinity in the forbidden nature of the love they both felt for Valraven.

Pharinet heard footsteps behind her on the gravel path that led to the fountain and her skin prickled. It was Valraven; he was coming to her already, risking exposure of their secret. At the last moment, she turned on her seat, her face set into an expression they reserved for one another; wicked desire. Therefore she was shocked to find that it was Prince Bayard who had sought her out. Or perhaps it was coincidence.

'You are supposed to be resting,' she said, in a tone she would usually reserve for someone of lesser status than herself.

Bayard only smiled, apparently ignorant of the insult. 'You were not expecting *me*, that is clear.'

Pharinet made no comment. She knew this man; he had stared down at her from his portrait a thousand times. She smiled. 'I'm sorry, my lord. That sounded rude of me. I was expecting my husband.'

Bayard sat down beside her. 'Were you? That look on your face did not seem to me to be one ever worn by a wife. If it was, I might even be induced to marry someone.'

Pharinet felt herself redden. 'I have not seen Khaster for some time. You must understand . . .'

'I have no wish for pretences between us, Lady Pharinet. I know for whom you were waiting.'

She paused. 'Really?'

He grinned at her lasciviously. 'Of course. You and Valraven are lovers.'

Pharinet was so astonished, she could not deny it. 'He told you this?' She was horrified to think her brother might discuss their relationship with someone else.

Bayard raised a languid hand dismissively. 'Not in so many words. He is too much a gentleman where you're concerned. That alone alerted my suspicions.'

It was clear he thought his words would please her. Pharinet despised herself for the gratification they invoked in her heart. As a kind of self-defence, she was impelled to say, 'I might say that certain aspects of Val's behaviour have alerted me to other clandestine relationships he might be conducting.'

The moment the words had left her mouth, she regretted them. How could she say such a thing? But Bayard did not seem offended, or even surprised. 'Oh? The dalliance he enjoys with me? I didn't realize it was a secret.'

Pharinet swallowed thickly. Then it was true. She felt slightly faint, unable to imagine her brother ever making love to a man. Could Bayard be lying? She did not think so. 'How long have you . . .?' She could not continue.

Bayard glanced at her with amusement. It was clear he understood his remark had come as a shock. 'We became close shortly after he returned to Magrast following his wedding. It was inevitable. Some things are just meant to be. You should know that.'

Pharinet looked away from him. 'I would prefer it if this matter was mentioned to no one but me. Our ways are different here, my lord. My family would not understand.'

Bayard shrugged, leaned back against the ancient stone of the seat and stretched out his legs. 'Whatever you wish. Anyway, that was not what I wanted to talk to you about. I looked out of my window just now and saw you sitting here alone. It was too good an opportunity to miss, although I confess it took me some minutes to fight my way out of the maze of your castle.'

'Are you looking for gossip? Val has said nothing to me about you.'

Bayard wrinkled his nose fastidiously. 'Didn't you hear me? I'm not interested in anything like that. I know where I stand with him, and what he gets up to in these domestic sojourns holds no fascination for me at all. There are more important things for us to talk about.'

Pharinet studied him for a few moments, then said, 'I'm intrigued. What?'

Bayard did not reply immediately. He returned her stare, seeming to exude a searing golden light from his eyes. Pharinet could not see it, but she felt it. Eventually she had to drop her eyes from his gaze. He could wither her. 'It is a pity you cannot come to Magrast,' he said. 'I am sure you would find much to stimulate you there.'

Pharinet felt slightly confused now. Eloquence had fled, leaving her with the tongue of a simpering girl, someone like Ellony. 'You don't know me, my lord. I cannot see how you could reach such a conclusion.'

Bayard laughed. 'I know more about you than you think. Your mind, your soul, is like an overturned jug. Everything pours out. Your magic is not the only kind.'

'My magic?' It seemed that walls were closing around her, walls of fire.

'Yes. You know what I mean. The emperor is not ignorant of the fact that his subjects here attempt to keep alive the old beliefs. But there are many old beliefs. It might seem we stand opposed, but in reality this is not the case. Many years ago, the emperor of Magravandias took for himself the power of the seas from the Palindrake heir. It has never been quenched, that power, merely contained. I know, as does my father, how strongly it resides inside Valraven. But he is ignorant of it, isn't he?'

'I don't know what to say. Your words are astounding.'

Bayard tipped back his head and grinned at the sky. 'Don't try to fool me. You are a sea priestess or some such thing. It will be in your blood, and the women-folk in this godforsaken place will expect it of you. Are you an oracle of the oceans, sweet Pharinet? Come now, you can tell me. I would expect it of you also. There is nothing for you to fear in being honest.'

Pharinet hesitated. 'I am aware of the old traditions, of course. It is folklore, but means a lot to people who live so near the sea.'

Bayard sucked his upper lip thoughtfully. 'I am surprised you people have not tried to rekindle that ancient power. Are you really so afraid of Madragore?'

Pharinet laughed uneasily. 'This is not a conversation I would have expected to have with you, my lord. As you know, the mages of Madragore stipulate clearly that all countries of the empire should adhere to the beliefs of their church.'

'Things become changed over the years, though. Once my ancestors were tribal lords who worshipped fire. In those days, the fire-drakes held power, and the dragons of the sea, the earth, the air. Where are they now?' He raised his hand expressively. 'My father knows the old legends, but has never thought to investigate their claims. Fortunately, my mother is not nearly so short-sighted.'

'The empress? What did she tell you?'

'Just the truth of what happened in the past, and how the power of fire was shaped into the god Madragore. He is a much more civilized face for our beliefs than the wild, free spirit of the raw element.'

'You mean the fire-drakes?'

He studied her. 'I feel them,' he said, 'as you feel the creatures of your own element. There should be fusion, not estrangement between them. That is the way to true power.'

'Does your eldest brother share these beliefs?'

He smiled, slowly and lazily, like the sun coming out from beneath the veil of a cloud. 'You see, we each have our own secrets.'

Pharinet blinked at him as she came to a sure realization: Bayard wanted to be emperor one day. 'You believe that the power of the sea dragons, combined with that of the fire-drakes, will give you ascendancy over your brothers?'

'I would not say so exactly,' Bayard said, 'as you would not admit to sleeping with your brother or trying to conjure sea dragons. But I think we understand one another.'

'What do you want of me?' she asked. 'That, at least, you can spell out.'

'I believe in you,' he said, 'that's all you need to know for now. You are not in ignorance like your brother. The deep tides live in you.' He stood up. 'We shall speak again. I want something to be done before I leave here.'

'What?'

'You must work your magic for me. All that you reserve jealously for yourself you must share with Val.'

'It's not like that. You don't understand.' She stopped herself saying any more. Already she had revealed too much, no matter how candid Bayard appeared to be.

'I am still confused as to why you have spoken to me in this way,' she said. 'How can you trust me?'

He shrugged. 'In all the world, there is only one woman I respect, and that is Tatrini, my mother. She spoke your name to me. She sees all.'

'If you have no respect for me, then why honour the powers you imagine I have?'

'My opinions can be changed,' he answered. 'You are very much like your brother.'

'We are twins. That is hardly surprising.'

Bayard looked away from her, up at the soaring walls of the castle. 'One day, I shall bring together all the elemental creatures: the sea dragons, the fire-drakes, the winged serpents of air and the basilisks of the earth's deepest chasms. Only then can power be brought into balance and the empire secured. I believe you and your brother have a place in this future that I see.'

Pharinet shook her head in amazement. 'Again, I do not know what to say to you.'

'Say nothing. Think on what I've said.' He stood up. 'Now I had better withdraw lest some vigilant member of your family observe our conversation from the castle.' He bowed to her. 'Until later, dear lady. Thank you for such a stimulating conversation.'

She watched him go, feeling completely disorientated. Her head spun as if he'd buffeted her with his fists. But his words made sense of the strange sensations she'd experienced over the last few years, the insidious presence of fire in her world. She had not imagined what he'd been doing earlier in the shrine. He was bringing the fire-drakes to the water.

Over dinner, Bayard made a great effort to entertain. Pharinet could see that he'd won over nearly everybody, except for some of the Leckery women. Ligrana was different, but then she was a little flirt to the bone. Ellony looked fretful and red along the cheekbone, toying with her food. Saska and Dimara were both stern and unsmiling, while Niska seemed hardly to be there at all. Everna, however, bloomed beneath the attention. Pharinet found it hard to believe her sister, who was such a devout priestess of the dragons, could be so taken in. How would she react if Pharinet should tell her of her conversation with Bayard? The most disturbing thing to Pharinet was that she knew she would never reveal what had transpired. Some part of her, perhaps her darker side, was already a confederate of the Magravandian prince. She told herself she wanted to know what was in his mind. She told herself she was intrigued by him because of his relationship with Valraven. But in her heart she knew the truth: there was power in him that he could show her, that she could learn about, power that Ellony could never have. Also, he was very attractive.

Poor Ellony; she seemed to writhe upon her seat, unsure whether to look modest and coy or outrightly annoyed. Whenever Bayard spoke to her – which he now made a point of doing – her words came out in a confused mumble. Perhaps she had guessed, from something in one of Valraven's letters, the extent of the prince's relationship with her husband. This too, despite Pharinet's earlier request, Bayard seemed quite prepared to make public. Fortunately, the gathering thought nothing of the blatant caresses and shoulder hugging. They probably just believed that Valraven was fortunate to be favoured by so prestigious a man. The emperor had once brought glamour to Caradore; perhaps his son would do the same. Pharinet despised this fickle loyalty. On the one hand the Caradoreans reviled the emperor's line, while on another they were prepared to fawn over his son.

After dinner, the company retired to a salon where a village girl sang folk songs, accompanied by a troupe of three musicians. Bayard murmured about how charming it all was, then managed to isolate Pharinet from the group for a few moments. 'The wife,' he said. 'What about her?'

'Excuse me?' Pharinet had no idea what he meant.

'The little fair one. Is she the sea wife?'

'The sea wife? I don't know. What's that?'

Bayard rolled his eyes. 'Do you know so little? We must speak later.'

'That will be difficult.'

He raised an eyebrow. 'Is that so? I'd have thought you'd be adept at engineering private moments.'

'I'll speak to you tomorrow,' Pharinet said. 'If you like, I'll take you down to the sea. I'm sure it can be arranged.'

'That sounds most agreeable.' He held out an elbow for her. 'Would you care to dance? Let's liven up the company.'

Pharinet glanced uncertainly at the guests. 'Oh, very well, why not?' Together she and Bayard pranced to the middle of the room. Bayard was a good dancer; he made a great show. People began to clap and tap their feet, and then join in. Bayard took Pharinet in his arms and swooped up and down the length of the salon. Her skirts whirled around her and tendrils of hair escaped confinement. It was like being carried along by a wind. She caught glimpses of face, in particular, Ellony, Valraven, and Khaster. Ellony looked glum, perhaps thinking she could never dance like that. Valraven was speculative, perhaps amused. Khaster's expression, predictably, was dark.

Later, once the party was over and everyone had retired to their chambers, Khaster lost no time in making some disparaging remarks about how the prince appeared to have favoured Pharinet's company. 'Don't be fooled,' he said. 'He has venom in his veins, not blood.'

'That much is obvious to me,' Pharinet said, pulling a chemise over her head. 'Please don't be nettled if he speaks to me, Khas. I can hardly ignore him.'

'His behaviour towards Elly was intolerable.'

'Was it? What did he do? I didn't notice.'

Khaster sat down on the bed fully dressed, looking at her with a hard expression. 'Sometimes, Pharry, I see things in you I don't like.'

She tried to soften and padded over to him, her hair hanging loose over her naked breasts. 'This is most unfair of you, Khas. What have I done?'

He sighed and pulled her down into his arms. 'I'm too affected by what my life has become. Forgive me. It is just that I fear for you.'

'I'm quite capable of looking after myself,' Pharinet said. 'Tomorrow I shall show our prince to the sea. I want to observe his reaction.'

Khaster looked disapproving, so Pharinet put her lips against his own, using all her skill to divert him from his concerns. 'I am here for you. I am your wife,' she said.

In the morning, Pharinet slipped from her bed early. Although she took care to dress quietly, she had a feeling Khaster woke up, but he did not stir or speak to her. Attired in her riding gear of soft leather, she went directly to Bayard's chamber and knocked on the door. One of his entourage opened it and told her to wait. He did not invite her within, and closed the door again, virtually in her face. Bayard emerged only a couple of minutes later.

Before the dawn had fully fallen across the land, they were riding on the clifftops. At first, Pharinet had imagined she would take him down to the beach and perhaps even into her sea-cave, but now she decided to show him the rock village instead. She would not, however, reveal to him the cove where the dragon stone reared from the sand. It would be taking her betrayal of the Sisterhood too far. And it was betrayal, she felt sure of that. She had never spoken of the sea dragons to anyone but a member of the Sisterhood before. She knew they would not approve of what she was doing. Even though she was curious about what Bayard would say to her, she sensed danger approaching. Her control of the situation was fragile at best.

Where the cliff path narrowed, they slowed their horses to a walk. 'There is a legend associated with the place we're going,' Pharinet said. 'A legend concerning the fire-drakes.'

Bayard raised his eyebrows. 'Really? Tell me.' He looked beautiful, his hair flying on the wind like golden banners.

She laughed. 'You may not wholly approve. A female drake created a great hole in the ground to hide her kittens from the sea dragons. She was not successful. People believe the dragons banished the drakes thousands of years ago.'

'Perhaps an elemental battle did take place there,' Bayard said, 'but it might have been between opposing factions of fire and sea worshippers. Myths are made of such events. Perhaps a presence of the fire-drakes still remains.'

They rode to the lip of rock and down into the crater's depths, then continued down. At the bottom they dismounted. Bayard was silent, looking around himself.

'Can you feel anything of your fire-drakes here?' Pharinet asked.

He shook his head slowly. 'I'm not sure. There is a flavour of magic to the air, but no doubt that comes from you.'

'From me personally?' Pharinet uttered a laugh.

'From your coven and you,' he said.

'I like the image you have of me, though I fear it is exaggerated from truth.' Pharinet hooked her reins over a thorn branch. 'Come, look into one of the caves. They say people lived in them once.'

She did not take him into the cave used by the Sisterhood for their rites, but another close by. Bayard examined the walls. 'Human hands helped to shape this place,' he said.

'No fiery breath?'

He turned to her with a thin smile. 'I can't dispel the feeling you're mocking me, Lady Pharinet.'

'Not at all. I am simply in the mood for levity.' She sat down on a boulder. 'Well, now we can speak. There are no prying ears and eyes, but for those of the dragons themselves.'

He studied her thoughtfully. 'I will come straight to the point. It is my wish for you to summon the sea dragons. I know you can do this, especially with the help of the sea wife. Is she an acolyte of yours?'

Pharinet laughed again. 'You are mistaken about us, my lord. I cannot summon dragons, for if they existed at all, they no longer roam this realm. Also, Ellony is no acolyte of mine.'

He leaned towards her so swiftly, she could not resist the impulse to recoil. 'You are wrong, about yourself and the sea wife.'

'What do you mean by "sea wife" exactly?'

He drew away from her again. 'Only what my mother told me of the relationship between the Palindrakes and the dragons in ages past. The wife of the Dragon Lord was accorded certain powers. His female relatives had their function, but she had her own. All elemental creatures communicate with humanity and bestow their powers through women. The Dragon Lord would send his wife to the shore and the priestesses of his family would conjure up the dragons. Then the wife, who without the assistance of Palindrake women could not invoke them herself, would channel their energy and knowledge to her husband. It was a position of great responsibility.'

Pharinet frowned. 'It sounds to me as if the sea wife should be a woman of strength, in both mind and body.'

'Yes, though appearances can be deceptive.'

'Not in Ellony's case they can't.' Pharinet stood up and went to the cave mouth, knowing that he followed. 'Even if I say I am not a priestess and know nothing of the things you describe, would you still believe I can do what you ask?' She turned to look at him. He was very close to her.

He nodded. 'I have no doubt.'

'Why should I, though? There is a curse over us. And you are a son of Madragore.'

Bayard shook his head. 'You should do it for yourself. The curse will not fall on anyone who works magic in the empire's name.'

Pharinet turned away from him again. She felt breathless, and chewed into her lower lip until she could taste the metal of blood. 'If I were a priestess of the sea, wouldn't working with you be a heresy against my beliefs?'

'The sea is but one element,' Bayard said gently. 'There are others. It is a mistake to separate them. Only good can come from my suggestion, for Valraven, and for Caradore itself. Ally yourself with me, Pharinet. Be what you should be.'

Pharinet sighed. She felt guilty for wanting to believe him. Yet ever since Caradore had been conquered, the women of the land had worked to keep the old ways alive. Bayard was offering them permission to revive them without fear. How could that be bad? Because of what he is, a cold voice whispered in Pharinet's mind. You should not trust him.

'We have the means to make Valraven more than just a man,' Bayard said. 'Very soon he will be sent from Magrast to fight for my father. Would you let him leave as he is, knowing you could have given him more protection and strength?'

'No,' Pharinet said. 'But how can I be sure you speak the truth?'

'Truth resides in your own heart,' Bayard said. 'Look into it, Pharinet. Look deep.'

'All I see is a murky fog,' Pharinet replied. 'It is the fog that comes from the ocean, smothering everything.'

'Then burn that fog away.'

She turned to face him. 'You said you needed Ellony's participation?'

He nodded, his expression guarded. She could sense his thoughts. He could tell he nearly had her, and was afraid of letting her slip away again.

'Then all I can say is this. Even if we could persuade Ellony to assume this role, which I doubt, because she is a fearful creature, I cannot see how we could get the privacy we'd need to enact any kind of ritual.'

He smiled in obvious relief. 'I have convinced you. You are considering my suggestion. Good.'

'I'm pleased to gratify you, but you haven't offered a solution to the problem.'

Bayard smiled. 'You forget who I am. If I order that certain people should be present on the shore to conduct a rite of Madragore, my word will be obeyed. My companions will be posted as look-outs to ensure no curious eyes observe the proceedings.'

Pharinet nodded slowly 'That seems feasible. It must be heady to own such power as yours.'

He reached out to touch a lock of her hair. 'Yes, it can be.'

She was unsure whether to move away from him or not. His gaze was compelling, although she sensed something almost repulsive in it. 'I hope you have an idea of what you wish me to do in this rite of yours, because I have none.'

His hand snaked beneath her hair to caress her neck. 'I am quite conversant with what is necessary. When my mother came to my father as a girl, she acquired a book from my grandmother. It was taken from your family at the time of the conquest. Perhaps it was a book of secrets even then. But now it is in my mother's hands. She has instructed me from it.'

'I feel I have quite a picture of your mother,' Pharinet said. 'She is ambitious for you.'

Both of his hands were on her now, slightly squeezing her throat. He was not a golden lion like his father, but a golden serpent, who might coil about her and constrict her life away. 'My mother loves all her sons, but in me, she senses something different. I am an organ of power for her, in a country where women have little.'

'I am surprised, given your upbringing, that you conspire in her plans.'

'I am not so blind,' he said, and leaned forward to kiss her.

The kiss was an enchantment; oddly chaste, yet steaming with repressed desire. Pharinet came out of it dazed, limp in his arms. 'Tell me everything,' he said. 'I know you have knowledge, Pharinet. I can sense it in you. Share it with me now. Tell me what the dragons have taught you.'

'I will tell you about Ellony,' Pharinet said. She could not resist. She had to offer him something, so without mentioning the Sisterhood she related how she and Ellony had spent a night at the dragon rock, and what had happened there. 'She was marked,' Pharinet said, 'but I'm not sure in what way.'

'This is good,' Bayard said. 'A connection has already been made. I thought it had.' He smiled and plunged his fingers into her hair. 'We will go back to Caradore now. You have work to do.'

That evening, Caradore was a beacon to all the countryside. Light blazed out of it, music filled the air. The courtyard was thronged with carriages that bore the emblems of all the old Caradorean families. Ellony, who loved a party, was in her element, sweeping about the place, trilling greetings, dispensing orders to the harassed servants. Pharinet knew that at some point she would have to speak to Ellony alone. How could she be persuaded to take part in Bayard's ritual? Ultimately, it was not that difficult for Pharinet to find a way.

A huge feast had been laid out in the main hall of Caradore, where guests could take their pick of the food on offer. Some wandered out into the gardens to consume it, while others stood around in groups, conversing loudly. Ellony flitted from group to group, making sure everyone was content.

Pharinet chose her moment, just a few minutes before the dancing began, to home in on her sister-in-law. 'Elly, for Foy's sake, take the weight off your feet for a moment. Come and have a plate of food. You look very flushed.'

Ellony laughed. 'I'm not sure whether I feel exhausted or full of energy. But tonight is a success, isn't it, Pharry? It's brought Caradore to life.'

'Very much so. You've done splendidly.' Pharinet took Ellony's arm and steered her towards one of the tables. Here, she poured them both large goblets of wine, while Ellony filled two plates with shellfish and salads. Then Pharinet propelled Ellony out into the garden. The trees had been strung with tiny lanterns and plates of incense smouldered among the flowers. 'Look, there's a private spot, over by the pool,' Pharinet said. 'Let's escape the throng for a few minutes.'

'Oh, this is like being girls again,' Ellony said.

'Yes,' Pharinet replied. 'Come on.'

They sat down together, and began to eat, their goblets set on the flagstones beside them. 'Let's have a toast,' Pharinet said.

Ellony put down her plate and picked up her wine. 'Oh yes! To what?'

Pharinet thought of enough toasts for them to drain their goblets: Valraven, Khaster, the dragons, family, land, ocean and sky. The wine went to Ellony's head very quickly, as Pharinet thought it might. 'Elly, I have something very important to say,' she said.

'What?' Ellony hiccuped, then giggled.

'As you know, Val will leave Magrast very soon. What would you say if I told you there is a way we could give back to him the power of the dragons?'

Ellony frowned a little. 'How can we? No one knows how, and if we did, the whole of Caradore might burn.'

'Not necessarily,' Pharinet said. 'I have a secret to tell you. We have an unexpected friend, who knows all about what we believe and desire. This friend is very powerful, and is willing to help us.'

'Who?' Ellony asked. 'Does Dimara know them?'

Pharinet shook her head. 'Not exactly.' She turned and took Ellony's hands in her own. 'Elly, it is the prince..It is Bayard!'

Ellony's mouth dropped open. 'No! Pharry, what is this? Has he spoken to you?'

'Yes! And he has told me wonderful things about you, what you should be. He has knowledge that has been lost to us, Elly. Listen, I'll tell you.'

Frowns and smiles rippled across Ellony's face as Pharinet told her an edited version of what had transpired with Bayard. Like Pharinet, it was clear she wanted to believe, yet part of her was unsure. 'But why, Pharry?' she asked when Pharinet finished speaking. 'Why should the prince care what happens to Val?'

'He is very fond of Val,' Pharinet said. 'And he understands magic. He understands *us*, Elly. He wants to help us.' Pharinet raised her hands. 'Oh, I know he must have selfish reasons, too. He wants to experience the sea dragons' power for himself. But he is willing to share that experience.'

Ellony was not yet smiling again. 'It would be dangerous. The Merante would never approve. None of our Sisters would.'

Pharinet paused. 'They won't know.'

Ellony's hands shot to her face. 'Oh Pharry, we can't do that! We can't!'

'Why not?' Pharinet asked softly.

Ellony shook her head. 'It would just be wrong. Bayard is the emperor's son. It would be a betrayal of all we hold dear.'

'No it wouldn't.' Pharinet paused again. 'Elly, we have the means to make Valraven more than just a man. Very soon, he will be sent from Magrast to fight for the empire. Would you let him leave as he is, knowing you could have given him more protection and strength?'

Ellony stared at Pharinet beseechingly. There were tears in her eyes now. 'No,' she said faintly, shaking her head. 'I couldn't.'

Pharinet touched Ellony's white hands, which were clasped tightly in her lap. 'Then you'll do this thing?'

'Oh Pharry!' Ellony collapsed against her. 'I would do anything for Val, you know that. But I am afraid. The dragons marked me. I'm not sure I'm the person you want me to be.'

Pharinet put her arms about her friend's warm body, felt her shuddering, silent sobs. She kissed Ellony's hair. 'You are,' she murmured. 'Have no fear. We will be doing the right thing. Trust me.' Her spine prickled. Someone was watching them. Quickly, she turned to look back at the open windows of the castle and saw Bayard standing there, looking out at her. She had a feeling that, in some arcane way, he had heard every word of their conversation.

Later, Bayard cornered Pharinet at the side of the main hall. Her feet ached because she had danced for over two hours with Khaster and Valraven. Everyone seemed to be in a strangely euphoric mood, as if a battle was to start in the morning, its outcome unsure. Bayard bowed to her. 'I have yet to experience the pleasure of a dance with you,' he said. 'Shall we?'

Pharinet inclined her head and got painfully to her feet. She staggered a little and Bayard put an arm around her for support. 'You have been over-taxing yourself.'

She laughed. 'I rarely get the chance to dance.'

He led her out on to the floor, where they spun round for a few moments. Then Bayard steered her back towards the gardens. 'We must speak,' he said.

Pharinet glanced around her. No one of significance appeared to be watching them. 'Very well. Just for a moment.'

She took him to a secluded arbour surrounded by ancient yews. Pharinet sat down upon the trunk of a fallen tree. Bayard stood before her, looking like a fierce angel in the radiance of the moon. His hair was white gold. 'Stand up,' he said.

'My feet pain me. I'd rather sit.'

He held out a hand. 'Please stand, Pharinet.'

Sighing, she did so. 'Why? What do you—' Her words were cut off as he pulled her swiftly towards him and covered her mouth with his own.

She managed to break away. 'Stop! Anyone could come looking for us.'

'Oh, and don't you like such risks?' He pulled her towards him again, his hand clawing her voluminous skirts up her thighs.

Pharinet could not help but think of the snatched moments of illicit lust she enjoyed with her brother. It was always like this, in some secluded spot, groping, fumbling, haste and anxiety. But desire too, strong desire. She could feel it now, igniting in her belly. Bayard pushed her back against one of the yews. He tore the lace of her undergarments in his impetuosity and took her standing up against the tree. The bark scored her shoulders, ripped into the fabric of her gown. She welcomed the savagery of it, and curled her thighs around his waist. He was so strong, holding her there, thrusting into her. She couldn't help but cry out when the moment of climax came. His whole body went rigid. She felt him empty his seed into her, strong pulses of scalding ichor. Then he shuddered and lowered her gently to the ground. 'There, I am now part of both of you,' he said.

Pharinet pushed tendrils of tangled hair from her face. She was still panting. 'You are a beast of fire. How can I return to the party now? Look what you have done to me.' She began to laugh.

He pulled her to him, kissed her briefly but deeply. 'You smell like him,' he said and pressed his nose into her hair, inhaling slowly.

'We must talk now,' Pharinet said. 'Quickly. It is why we are here.'

Bayard laughed. 'There's no need. I know you've accomplished what you set out to do.'

Pharinet pulled away from him and folded her arms. 'I see.'

He grinned. 'I wanted you, Pharinet. Is that so terrible? I love your brother. It often frightens me how much. I have to possess what he possesses.' He pulled her to him once more. 'We should be together, all of us. Would you like that?'

'Don't!' Pharinet said, but a wild, fleeting image splashed across her mind. She could imagine it easily.

'After tomorrow,' he said, cupping one of her breasts with a hand and squeezing it. 'Before Val and I leave. I shall request both of you to dine in my chamber. How about that?'

'What will Val say?'

Bayard grinned. 'What will Val say? Do you really have to ask?'

Yes, Pharinet thought. I do. The Valraven I knew would never do anything like that. 'You've changed him,' she said.

Pharinet had to creep into the castle through a turret door and run with prickling flesh to her room, terrified she'd be discovered in a dishevelled state, which clearly advertised what she'd been doing. She'd have to make an excuse about spilling wine on her gown, anything. Her underwear was ruined, her legs slick with Bayard's seed.

Once she'd gained the sanctuary of her room, she leaned against the door with relief. In a mirror opposite she could see what a wanton spectacle she presented. Khaster could never do for her what she'd just experienced, nor could he approximate the intensity and fire of Valraven's lovemaking. Pharinet felt weak to think that within a day she might be with Bayard and Valraven at the same time. It was beyond her wildest fantasies.

When she went back down to the main hall, everyone commented on the fact that she'd changed her gown, and seemed to find it hilarious she'd ruined it with wine. No one suspected the truth. Pharinet felt drunk with power. Guests were leaving now, and servants had begun to clear away the remains of the feast. Bayard stood with Everna, Thomist, Valraven and Ellony near the great fireplace, in which no fire burned. Pharinet went to join them. She saw Khaster sitting alone at the edge of the hall. He watched her intently. A pang of remorse stabbed through her body. Khaster looked vulnerable and beautiful. He looked pure. She smiled at him and forced the thought from her mind. They would all be gone soon. She must do what she had to do.

'I've explained to your family I'd like to enact a Madragorian rite at the beach tomorrow at dawn,' Bayard said. He turned to the others. 'I have already mentioned this to Lady Pharinet.'

Pharinet could tell Everna was not at all happy about the suggestion. Ellony looked stricken, hanging on to Valraven's arm and staring at the floor. 'Of course we must indulge your request,' Everna said, 'but why the beach?' She risked a stern smile. 'It is rather too similar to a rite that took place a long time ago, when Caradore fell to the empire.'

Pharinet was surprised Everna said that. Her earlier sycophantic behaviour with Bayard appeared to have vanished.

Bayard, however, remained gallant, which was no surprise at all. 'I can understand why you would think that, but please believe I have nothing sinister in mind.' He put a hand on Valraven's shoulder. 'I wish only to bless my friend before he leaves for Cos. It is only fitting that his twin sister and his wife should be there. I want males and females to be equally represented.'

'Perhaps Thomist and I should take part,' Everna said in a hard voice.

Bayard laughed lightly. 'It's very kind of you to suggest that, but I prefer to conduct this rite with a limited number. It's personal to me.'

Everna shrugged in a stiff manner. 'You do not have to ask for permission from me, my lord. You are the emperor's son. We are merely your servants.'

'Never that,' Bayard said. He glanced at Pharinet with hooded eyes. 'I look upon the Palindrakes as friends.'

CHAPTER TEN

Dragon Daughters

The dawn came heavily, muffled in fog, which hung over the sea some miles out from the shore. It seemed to be waiting. By the time Pharinet went down the beach, the others were already there. Along the clifftop, the prince's guards were a line of immobile silhouettes. Khaster had barely spoken to Pharinet since the previous evening. Again she knew he'd been awake as she'd quietly dressed, but his back was turned to her. At that moment, she'd despised him. He seemed weak and ineffectual. The men upon the beach were very different: powerful, charismatic and slightly dangerous. Ellony did not look at all comfortable, but Pharinet expected nothing else. Valraven appeared to be the most cheerful. Pharinet studied him. Who was this man? How could someone be so familiar, yet a complete stranger?

Bayard's people had built a fire, which leaned away from the soft wind coming off the sea. The tide itself was tranquil, perhaps unusually so. Small wavelets fanned over the sand, barely on the retreat.

Bayard wore a belted robe of dark red fabric. He was confident, in control and clearly stimulated by what they were about to do. Pharinet was still astounded that Bayard dared to meddle with the sea dragons, and yet he appeared to have knowledge she did not, through the book of her ancestors that his mother had kept hidden. Bayard's own ancestors had once instigated the banishing of the dragons. Perhaps only a person of his tribe could reverse the process.

'Is everyone ready?' Bayard asked.

'Just get on with it, Bay,' Valraven said. 'It's cold out here.' He seemed to be faintly amused by the proceedings, but not entirely at ease.

Bayard glanced at Pharinet. 'I will instruct you in what to do. Are you happy with this?'

She shrugged. 'You know more than I do.'

Ellony coughed quietly into a handkerchief, shivering in her cloak.

Bayard stood before the fire and raised his arms. The wind caught in the folds of his sleeves, made wings of them. 'We meet here to recall the ancient covenant,' he said. His voice was not loud, but carried far above the sounds of wave and flame.

'Lady Pharinet,' he said, and held out his hand to her. She went to stand before him and he put his hands upon her shoulders. She was conscious of his body behind her, its male heat. 'Call to them,' Bayard said in a whisper. 'Summon the Dragon Daughters of Foy, the Three, Jia, Misk and Thrope.'

'How?' she murmured back.

'With your body, with your blood, with your energy,' he answered. 'I will direct into you the breath of the dragons, the life force, which is in all things.'

His hands were hot upon Pharinet's shoulders. Her flesh began to tingle as if an unheard tone resonated through it.

'I want you to make a journey in your mind,' Bayard said. 'Close your eyes.'

Pharinet did so. She could hear the crackle of the flames, the slow heave of the sea, and somewhere, a bell was tolling mournfully through the sea-mist.

'You are travelling out of your body,' Bayard said. 'You are entering the water. Feel it swirl about you. Feel its power.'

Bayard's lilting voice was hypnotic. Pharinet found it easy to follow his instructions. He told her what to see, what to feel, and the sensations in her mind were so acute, it was as if she was experiencing them physically. She became oblivious of the presence of Valraven and Ellony. Her mind was drawn out over the gentle tide and plunged down beneath it. She rushed downwards, streaming a trail of bright bubbles. There was only chilly murk beneath her, yet dim glows pulsed through it. She imagined stately jellyfish, with trains of deadly rags and spines. She thought she saw great sinuous fishy tails undulating beneath her. She hung in this night water like a jellyfish herself, faintly pulsing.

'Call to them,' Bayard said, his voice a plash of water hitting a heated rock. 'Call to the creatures who attend the dragons' court. They dwell in the great abyss, where the black steam of the earth rises from vents encrusted with grey barnacles. They sleep among the darkened coral. They breed in caves. They are the anointers of the old ones, and sing secret songs to appease great Foy in her repose. Their fingernails are daggers of ivory, and their teeth are the teeth of sharks. Their blood is black. Their voices have the sweetness of death, yet they sing of life. They hate those who walk the land, yet are subject to them, for their souls are smaller. See their pearly eyes. See their waving hair. They are Ustredi, the merfolk, and they will hear you. As you call to them, so their city will appear before you. I want you to see them swimming in their dark, ruined temples in the deepest abyss of the ocean floor. See them become aware of your presence. My voice will aid you, but you must be the channel.'

He began to croon a wordless chant which gradually rose in timbre. The sound blended with the soft cry of the wind and the susurrus of the waves.

Pharinet leaned back against Bayard's body. In her mind, she could see the milky eyes glowing through the dark ocean. They watched her with apprehensive hostility. Pharinet opened her mouth and expelled a sound which derived from the song that Bayard sang around her. This agitated the Ustredi, who began to swim around her swiftly. Some were fish-tailed, while others had what appeared to be boneless legs equipped with fins. Some did not have arms, but great flippers. Some had beautiful faces and hideous bodies, while in others these aspects were reversed. A few were too lovely to gaze upon, and these Pharinet sensed were the most dangerous.

The murk cleared, or perhaps her inner eye had become accustomed to the darkness. She hung above a vast range of cliffs. Buildings were set into their faces, constructed of cyclopean stones. All the entrances were triangular, and the lines of the buildings were stark and symmetrical. Pharinet sensed immediately that they were deserted. The thousands of Ustredi, of countless variety, who swam in and around these edifices were not the people who'd built them. Pharinet wondered if this part of the ocean floor had once been above sea level, and what she looked upon now was the remnants of a sunken civilization. There was little time to ponder this. The Ustredi had begun to swim closer to her, brushing her with their fins. A couple peered into her face, their mouths hanging open like fishes', displaying combs and coronets of spiked fangs. They raked her with their claws, but applied no pressure. They wanted to tear her limb from limb, but could not. Sailors who fell from ships were their prey, and those who dared to swim in the great ocean, but a daughter of the Palindrakes was safe from them. They could smell her warm blood and recognized it.

'Ustredi,' she cried in her mind, and the sound of it flowed out into the ocean she imagined. 'Ustredi, hear me. I am Pharinet Palindrake, and I am your mistress. I command you now to bring forth your dark sisters, the Dragon Daughters. Bring to me Jia, Misk and Thrope. They must awaken Foy, the ancient queen. It is time for her to rise. It is time for her to shake off the coral that encases her. Her daughters must swim beneath her belly

130

and bring her forth from her black sleep. Oh Ustredi, do not ignore my command.'

Pharinet did not expect the response to be so swift and violent. As soon as the summoning left her mind, the sea began to boil. The Ustredi swirled in confusion around her. She could hear their voices. Some hurt her ears, while others were sweet beyond imagining. The towering underwater mountains around her seemed to shake and huge oily bubbles rose up from the ocean floor. Something immense and powerful stirred beneath the rock, behind the façades of one of the buildings. 'Foy!' Pharinet cried. Where were the daughters? A cry fluted out, like the call of a whale and a thousand seabirds combined. Waves of force erupted out of the abyss and hurled Pharinet's body backwards. She was caught in a wild swell, tossed helplessly among the tangled limbs and fins of the mewing Ustredi. Then, with a gasp, she opened her eyes and found herself standing on the seashore, Bayard's hands cold upon her shoulders. He was breathing heavily and she had no doubt he had shared her visualization. The appearance of the sea had not changed, but Pharinet sensed a difference in the atmosphere. The air was still, as if a storm was coming. The sea fog seemed nearer to the land. Valraven and Ellony stood apart some feet away. Valraven looked slightly disapproving, but puzzled. Ellony's eyes were staring wildly, as if she too had caught a glimpse of Pharinet's vision.

'They are coming,' murmured Bayard. 'Take their force into yourself and pass it to the sea wife.'

'Will she be safe?' Pharinet asked. Whatever conflicting feelings she had for Ellony, the sight of her friend looking so vulnerable and afraid pulled at her heart. Doubts wriggled through her, terrible doubts.

'It is her true function,' Bayard murmured. 'And as you told me, she was marked.'

But for what? Pharinet wondered. She sensed something immense and invisible rushing towards her, like a tornado. It was a formless energy that could tear her body to fragments. It rolled over the ocean, twisting and spiralling. Had she called this? Was it the spirit of Foy? How could she tell?

Bayard had not released his grip on her shoulders. His fingers felt like nails driving against her bones. 'Bring the sea wife to you,' he said.

Pharinet shivered and turned her head. Her eyes met Ellony's gaze and she held out her hand. 'Come here, Elly.'

Ellony frowned. 'Why, Pharry? What's happening? I can feel something. What are you doing?'

'Trust me,' said Pharinet and waggled her fingers.

Valraven merely watched, saying nothing. The strange light had taken on a greenish quality, which Ellony's pale face reflected. She looked inhuman.

'Come to me,' said Pharinet, and as if entranced, Ellony finally obeyed. She slipped her cold, slim hand into Pharinet's strong fingers. When this is done, Pharinet thought, we will all be stronger, and Val will know his heritage. At that moment, she felt no jealousy for Ellony at all.

'What's coming?' Ellony asked.

'Don't you know?' Pharinet murmured. 'Can't you sense it?'

Ellony frowned. 'I don't know what it is I sense.'

'It is Foy,' Pharinet said.

Ellony stared at her with wide eyes. 'It can't be.'

'It is, and she's coming to you.'

'No!' Ellony tried to take her hand from Pharinet's grip, but Pharinet only closed her fingers around her with greater strength.

'Don't be afraid,' she said. 'This is your moment, Elly. You are the sea wife.'

Ellony twisted in Pharinet's hold. She turned her head and appealed to her husband. 'Val, stop them. Please stop them.'

Valraven's face looked almost black. He did not move. Pharinet could see the fire in him, a smoky shadow all around him. He might not know what was happening, but something inside him did.

'Prepare yourself,' Bayard said to Pharinet. 'They are upon us.'

Pharinet looked out at the sea. She could see nothing, but could sense an immense boiling energy that hovered close by. It was terrible, an utterly impartial force with the potential for complete destruction. Filled with Bayard's strength, she willed this force to enter her and to stream from her body to Ellony's. She closed her eyes and waited. But no energy came. Her body remained unmoved.

Ellony uttered a shriek. Pharinet opened her eyes. Her right hand, which had been holding Ellony's, was completely numb. She had not felt Ellony break away from her. Now the girl staggered and reeled on the spot, beating at her head. Hideous sounds came from her lips, sounds of pain and terror. Pharinet glanced at Bayard. 'It's gone straight to her.'

'Yes.' He released her.

'Do something,' Pharinet said. 'She can't take it.'

Bayard strode over to her and tried to take hold of her, but Ellony slithered away. 'Take control!' he shouted. 'This is not Foy, but the presence of her daughters. They are yours to command.'

Ellony suddenly raised her face to him and her features were set in an ugly snarl. She looked like an Ustredi, green-skinned, with milky eyes.

The sight of her appeared to shake Valraven from his stasis. 'What's

132

happening to her?' he demanded. 'She's having a fit.' He went to his wife's side, tried to embrace her.

Ellony fought off all attempts to constrain her. She struck out fiercely with her hands, uttering guttural snarls.

This isn't going right, Pharinet thought. Bayard did not expect this. She glanced back at the sea and saw that the thick fog was now an impenetrable wall only a few feet from the shoreline. It was not natural. Something was inside it. Something of immense power and hunger. She saw movement within the fog, vague darting shapes. 'Bayard,' she said. He was still helping Valraven with Ellony. He did not hear her.

Shadows oozed out of the fog like black oil, slithered across the dirty foam at the water's edge. 'Bayard!' Pharinet's voice was a desperate cry. The men turned towards her. She could not see properly. She was enveloped by a pulsing darkness that felt hot and cold at the same time. It was seeping into her, running fingers through her thoughts. She could hear laughter, cruel and low. Valraven and Bayard were surrounded by spinning columns of darkness that Pharinet saw with her mind rather than her eyes. She could not warn them. Whatever held her in its grip had frozen her tongue.

Ellony's body was lunging where she stood, as if she was underwater, fighting a powerful current. Coarse, brutal sounds came from her throat, from somewhere deep inside her. She began to straighten up, and her eyes glowed with a faint green light.

Then someone was running across the hard sand towards them, from the direction of the cliffs. At first, Pharinet didn't recognize who it was, but quickly realized it was Thomist. Behind him, Everna was clambering over the rocks outside the sea cave. She appeared to be shouting, but the thick still air muffled her voice. Her fists were bunched and raised in anger. Whatever precautions Bayard's men had taken, they had not known about the secret cliff entrance to the sea-cave. Everna must have been watching the whole procedure from the shadows of the cave.

Pharinet felt filled with relief, a reaction she had not expected. Everna knew how to deal with Ellony. She'd calm her down. Everna would make all this strangeness go away.

Thomist had reached Ellony and wrapped a heavy cloak around her. She was moaning and sobbing now, while he offered words of comfort.

Everna marched with purpose towards them all. 'Are you insane? she snapped, looking at Pharinet. 'Can't you see that Elly isn't up to whatever it is you're doing? I'm surprised at you, Pharinet, I really am. She turned on Valraven, 'And you, you know how ill she's been. I can't believe you'd condone this!'

While Everna continued to rail at her brother and sister, Pharinet saw Ellony's head lolling against Thomist's shoulder. Her face still looked green and the expression on it was one of cruelty and cunning. She was no longer moaning piteously. She was silent and smiling. It looked as if her teeth were broken and pointed. Her hair had come adrift from its confinement and hung in tendrils over her face, like mermaid's hair, like weed.

Pharinet experienced a stab of dire premonition, but then Ellony expelled a gust of evil laughter. With inhuman strength, she began to drag Thomist towards the waves. Everna shrieked out a warning, Bayard and Valraven rushed forward, but in the next moment, Ellony had disappeared into the sea. Completely, without leaving a ripple. She had taken Thomist with her. Valraven ran into the waves, until they reached his waist. He called her name. Everna stood in mute shock, her hands to her face.

'Do something!' Pharinet gasped at Bayard. 'Dispel the power. Bring her back!'

Bayard looked dazed. A dark mist still hung around him. The air smelled strongly of rotten seaweed.

'It's not possible,' he said, and Pharinet was unsure of what he meant. She still felt strange in her body, but whatever alien thing had gripped her flesh seemed to have fled. Perhaps she had imagined it. She ran down to the sea. 'Val, come back. Don't go into the fog!'

He was standing in front of it, splashing his hands in the water, as if he hoped to draw Ellony out of it. Everna stood screaming out Thomist's name. Bayard's men, alerted by the commotion, were now running across the sand towards them.

'Val!' Pharinet grabbed hold of his arm. The sea sucked at her skirts, tried to drag her towards the fog. 'Come back.'

'We have to find them,' he said. 'Pharry, they'll drown. We have to find them.'

Pharinet looked around herself frantically. There was no sign of Thomist or Ellony at the edge of the waves, and beyond that was the greeny-white wall of mist. 'We can't. Let the men look. We must go back to Caradore, get help.'

He looked up at her, his face that of total vulnerability. He was a boy again, confused because the world had acted against him. 'Pharry, what did we do? What was it all about? I felt something.' He rubbed his wet hands against his face. 'It was so cold. It took Ellony, didn't it? It went into her. We made it come.' He looked back at Bayard. '*He* did.'

Pharinet took hold of his arm. 'Come on, Val.' She felt sick now, and disorientated. Gradually, the implications of what had just happened were sinking in. Ellony had gone. You wished it, a spiteful inner voice murmured. Isn't this what you want?

'No,' Pharinet said aloud. 'No!'

People came from all the local villages and farms to help with the search. Caradore was busy again as the castle staff provided hot soup for the volunteers. The entrance hall was full of people. Valraven went out again, with Khaster, who barely acknowledged Pharinet as he swept past her in the hall. Everna and Saska had to be restrained from going back to the beach themselves. They were inconsolable. The fog had come right in now, and swirled in damp tendrils about the castle. It made the search virtually impossible.

Pharinet stayed in the hall, helping the servants dish out soup. She saw Dimara coming down the stairs and hoped the woman would not confront her. Dimara, however, strode straight to her. 'What have you done?' she hissed.

Pharinet looked up at her. 'Nothing. Are you here to help?'

Dimara looked so angry, Pharinet had to force herself not to wince away. She expected a blow at any moment. The servants nearest to her had gone quiet. She could feel their tension.

'You are a liar,' Dimara said, in a low, vehement voice. 'You can't hide what you are from me.'

'Ellony has been ill,' Pharinet said uncertainly. 'I agree we were wrong to take her out there this morning, but it was nobody's fault she reacted the way she did. We could not foresee that. We meant only to bless Valraven.'

Dimara raised her hand and pointed at Pharinet with a rigid finger. 'Your time will come,' she said. 'Have no doubt of it. You'll derive no happiness from this.'

'Happiness?' Pharinet threw the ladle she held into the great cauldron before her. Soup splashed out over her gown. 'How dare you!'

The entire hall had gone quiet now. Servants stole away. Dimara held Pharinet's gaze for a few moments longer, then spat at her and marched back upstairs.

The search continued all day. Fishermen dared the fog to sail around the coast, looking for signs. Nothing was found. Ellony and Thomist had disappeared without a trace. In the afternoon, Pharinet went to Bayard in his chamber, where he'd stayed all day. His face was sallow. He looked ill.

'What happened?' Pharinet asked him. 'Did you anticipate these events?'

135

He shook his head, sipping from a goblet of warmed wine. 'Of course not. The daughters came, and would have co-operated, if the sea wife had been stronger. I should have listened to you. You were right about her.'

Pharinet expelled a snort of derision. 'How can you say that? It's not enough. Ellony and Thomist are probably dead. It's our fault.'

'She was marked,' Bayard said. 'They took her. It was necessary. We did what we had to do.'

Pharinet narrowed her eyes. 'You knew.'

'No. But I've thought about it.' He put down his wine and took Pharinet's hands in his own. 'They came to us. Didn't you feel it? We succeeded.'

She pulled away from him. 'At what cost?'

'Sacrifices are necessary.'

'I would never have agreed to it if I'd known. You used me.'

He laughed softly. 'Oh, Pharinet, guilt ill becomes you. Don't torture yourself. Do you really care about that girl?'

'You're disgusting,' Pharinet said. 'Thomist was my brother-in-law. What did he do to deserve this? Ellony was an innocent, who only wanted to please. Their lives were not ours to play with.'

'Too late for such sentiment,' Bayard said. 'When Valraven returns to the castle, bring him here.'

'What?'

'We have an arrangement.'

Pharinet shook her head and backed towards the door. 'No,' she said. 'Not any more.'

Pharinet lay alone in her wide, cold bed. Khaster had not come up to her. Her mind and body felt so tortured she did not know whether she wanted to cry hysterically or succumb to a mindless lethargy. She could not bear to think about what she'd done, yet her thoughts were filled with a constantly replaying image of her conversation with Ellony the previous night. She heard the words 'It's like we're girls again', full of affection and trust. She saw Ellony's radiant face, looking healthier than it had for a long time. Pharinet despised herself utterly. She thought about her brother too, how the events on the beach had invoked an earlier form of himself. He was less hard, bewildered, more vulnerable than ever. Was Bayard with him now? She wanted to protect Valraven, but shrank from going to find him. She was afraid. Something dark and without compassion had seeped into her that day. Its chill still coiled around her bones. Was she strong enough to expel it?

She closed her eyes, willing a dreamless sleep to come, but there was a voice in the darkness telling her, 'I am Jia, you are Jia. Rise up and find our sisters.'

Pharinet turned restlessly in the bed, but opened her eyes to find herself standing at the entrance to her room, with one hand on the doorknob. Something twisted inside her, sighing and languorous. Lustful. Pharinet uttered one short grief-stricken cry and then the door was open, and her feet were padding along the cold floor to the guest wing.

'Misk! Thrope!'

She could not resist. She could feel the dragon daughters writhing in their beds of flesh, enjoying the sensation of it. *Sometimes, we envy the living.*

Another cry reverberated through the castle, low, male and hoarse. It was Valraven. It was the cry of someone who'd looked in the abyss, someone who previously had not even known the abyss existed. It was the sound of a soul tearing.

PART TWO

Rebirth

CHAPTER ONE

The Bride

Six Years Later: Magrast

On the eve of Varencienne's wedding, there was red lightning in the sky, high up among the curdling clouds.

'Madragore smiles upon you,' said Carmia, pointing out through the juddering curtains.

Varencienne stared at the ominous forks, her body stiff. Surely Madragore rarely smiled, preoccupied as he was with war, but his presence was a good omen, wasn't it? She still felt numb.

Around her, her friends feasted on soft fruits imported from a warmer land. The imperial chambers were decked with the first of the spring flowers: heavy tulips of the royal purple and delicate narcissi with tight hearts. Girls sprawled on the floor and across the couches. A sickly scent of plundered fruit flesh filled the humid air. Wine had been drunk and spilled; goblets stood upon the table and lay upon the floor. Young faces were flushed with pleasure and vicarious excitement. Gowns were rumpled and stained, slippers cast off. The fire burned loudly and fiercely. Wood cracked in the flames. There was little other light, for the candles had burned nearly all away.

Varencienne felt removed from it all; as if she were just a spirit in the room observing the hot, frenzied antics of the living. She herself – dead and blue – could barely comprehend their movements, their chatter. Who am I? she thought.

Mavenna, dressed in red, her hair a wanton, brazen mop falling from its net, came to sit beside her. 'Ren, cheer up,' she said, squeezing her friend's shoulders too tightly. 'You're bound to be nervous, but don't worry. You are about to receive the greatest prize in all the empire.'

Varencienne smiled as best she could, although she knew her friend was wrong. It was she who was the prize, delivered into the hands of the man who had won her. Her friends were envious simply because they were not her. It would not be them who'd walk the long, cold avenue of the cathedral to the faceless victor at the altar. She was not afraid; she felt nothing.

On the day she'd heard the news, her mother, the Empress Tatrini, had summoned her daughter to her morning room, where she'd sat among her women working on the tapestry of the life of the emperor. Varencienne had come into the room, seen the winter sunlight falling in through the narrow windows to shine upon the ermine of her mother's collar as her fingers worked slowly and carefully with the thread. There were baskets upon the floor, spilling an exuberance of coloured yarns. The women spoke together quietly, content in their position as companions of the empress: a robust and handsome woman, with thick dark gold hair. It seemed inconceivable that her firm, powerful body had born fourteen children for the emperor. Twelve of them still lived and Varencienne, at eighteen, was the only girl.

'Ah, my daughter,' said the empress, looking up. Her voice, as always, was oddly formal. She did not know this young woman who stood before her. Although Varencienne had daily spent time in Tatrini's company, she'd had no more impact than the various cats who lolled aloofly around the royal chambers. Varencienne thought that the empress had lost interest in her children after her third son, Clavelly, had died, aged six. She had continued to bear them, as was her duty, but probably cared for her tapestries more. Now Varencienne knew that her mother was probably thinking something like, 'Just a few short years ago, she was crawling among my yarns on the carpet. Now look at her.' The empress smiled with her mouth, while her eyes remained faintly puzzled.

Varencienne dropped a polite curtsey. 'Mama.'

'Good news,' said the empress. 'You are to be married.' She was not a woman to temporize.

Varencienne's mouth dropped open, but no sound came out.

If her mother divined her daughter's shock, she did not show it. 'You are a fortunate young woman. Your father has devised a contract with Valraven, Lord Palindrake. He is, as you are no doubt aware, the most favoured of our generals and a distant cousin of yours.'

Everyone had heard of Palindrake. Favoured he was: yes. But feared too. 'Why?' asked Varencienne. 'Why now?'

The empress seemed surprised by these squeaky questions, and a little put out. Surely the answer was obvious? 'You are of an age, and it is our wish that the links between Palindrake and your father's dynasty be made more formal.'

Keep the fiercest of the beasts close to the hearth. No beast ravages its own hearth. No sane beast.

The empress's fingers stilled for a moment in their industry. 'It is your duty, my daughter.' She had perhaps forgotten Varencienne's name.

Varencienne dropped another curtsey. 'Yes, Mama.'

'The wedding is arranged to take place at the cusp of spring. I will send my women to you to arrange about the dress. The fabric must be red, of course, but you may choose the design yourself. I have at least half a dozen for you to choose from.'

The room swam before Varencienne's eyes: thin winter sunlight on dark old wood and red plush. The window casement, where a queen would sit, pricking her fingers with a needle, watching blood fall on snow. She shook herself inwardly to dispel this strange image. Her life was about to change. Six short weeks away. She would leave her home, her friends, her pets. She was to be put away tidily in a different drawer. Panic welled up within her, but it quickly stagnated. Before she even left her mother's room, the numbness came, and it had not left her since.

She had met her future husband only once, in a cold cloister, with one of her mother's women as chaperone. It had been snowing and the courtyard was covered with a white frosting. The black spires of the palace rose severely against the pearly sky. Bright winter sunlight failed to soften them or warm the air. Crows flung themselves from spire to spire, venting their spite in coarse cries. On the tallest tower, cages hung, filled with bones. No one had died there for five years. Executions took place further afield nowadays.

Varencienne's feet were rigid in her flimsy slippers. Later, they had ached. The woman led her out from a door for inspection and Varencienne saw him standing there, tall and dark, at the end of the walkway. She sensed his impatience immediately, also a faint embarrassment. This was an inconvenience to him. No doubt he trusted her father's word that she would be comely, quiet and obedient. He did not need to view the merchandise himself. He had a hundred better things to do.

She had been led up to him, and could not look him in the face. Even now, she was unsure of what he looked like. His garments were black and deep purple. Dark red jewels winked among the folds. She saw his hands, loose by his sides; long and dark-skinned and strong.

'The princess,' announced her companion, and she'd heard him make a noise of assent, a grunt. How long had he looked at her? Five seconds, perhaps, just to make sure she wasn't ill-favoured. Out of habit, she dropped a curtsey, a reflex action that always covered a silence.

'I am greatly pleased by our betrothal, Your Highness,' he said, his voice like black silk ripping.

And she, the girl, felt her numbness crack a little, and all manner of warmer, electric emotions crackle through. Just a moment of it. He took her hand in his cool-skinned palm, rubbed the back of it with his thumb, then lifted her fingers briefly to his dry mouth and imprinted upon them an arid kiss. Without further words, he walked away, across the courtyard.

Varencienne was able to look up then and saw his cloak lift about him like wings, heard the crows above grow momentarily hysterical as if their king walked below them. His hair was loose, a cloak of dark feathers. She was afraid of him, and also hungry. She could not understand these feelings and, swiftly, buried them beneath the grey ice of her resolve. She knew her marriage to this man would not be happy, for he could not see her as a person. She would be a possession, like all his other things. Perhaps once a month, he would come to her bed and she would bear for him a series of children, some of whom might die. He would be away from home a lot, securing the empire for her father, and when he was at home, she would rarely see him, for he'd be busy about the estate. She would have women as companions, who would be married to Palindrake's minions. They would bring their children up together in the stark castle among the star-flowered crags of distant Caradore, talking of their absent husbands as if they knew them well.

In the cold air she shuddered, and her mother's woman fussed and cooed over her, drawing her back into the humid warmth of the over-heated palace.

Now the six weeks had passed and her crimson bridal robe hung in tissues of silk in her dressing room. Her friends had gathered about her to keep the vigil until midnight, when she would be led to her lonely bed for the last time by women of her mother's who would, at this final hour, instruct her in the duties of a wife. The girls around her giggled about the marriage night, and flashed their eyes at her in envy. Varencienne did not care about it. She knew what would happen, and it did not disturb her detached calm. He would not kill her, and if she were quiet and well-behaved, any discomfort might only be brief. Varencienne had always been adept at facing pain. She dealt with things as quickly as she could and then moved on to the next experience. As a child, she had once almost lost a finger as she played. The walls of the palace were scythed with metal, its gardens clawed with traps, to injure intruders. The game had been boisterous and she had fallen into a bed of blue periwinkle. Blades hidden among the fragile blooms had cushioned her fall and although her robe had been slashed, only one vulnerable white hand had taken the full cruel impact. While her friends had shrieked and fainted, she had repositioned her dangling bloody finger as best she could, held on to it tightly and walked deliberately to the chambers of her nurse, who had done what had to be done. Varencienne had not cried, and her shock had been invisible. The wound did not become infected, and had left only a muddled, white scar. She presumed all life's accidents to have the same results.

She looked at Mavenna and Carmia critically. They really were silly geese, incapable of reason, but they were kind and had grown up with her; she would miss them. Perhaps, after a year or two, she might send a message to her husband, and ask if he could arrange weddings for them also, with a couple of his squires, so that they could come to Caradore and be her friends once more. She knew these things happened. It was the kind of favour a husband could indulge for his wife. Her own mother had childhood friends about her and Varencienne's own companions were the daughters of these women, kept neatly in their own female quarters of the palace.

Earlier that day, her brother Bayard had visited her. He was her favourite, the rest of his tribe had scant interest in girls. She and Bayard had seen little of each other for some time, because he had been away with the army. Once, they had been close, even though there were ten years between their births. Unlike his siblings, Bayard had always maintained a close relationship with his mother, and visited her chambers every day. He alone of Varencienne's brothers had witnessed her childhood and growth to womanhood. As the years had passed, they'd inevitably been unable to spend as much time as they wanted in each other's company, but their bond had been strong and had survived enforced separation. Now Bayard was like a stranger, tall and somehow troubled, his sleek dark gold hair plaited severely down his back, his clothes stiff and formal, a soldier's garb. 'Are you happy?' he'd asked her.

Varencienne shrugged. 'I'm not anything. I just have to do this. We both know that.'

He had taken her hands in his then, his dark eyes looking down upon her. 'If ever . . .' His voice was cold and fierce, but words seem to fail him. He shook his head, held her fingers tightly.

'If ever what?'

'Little Ren,' he'd murmured, and kissed the top of her head. 'Try to be happy. He is rich and they say Caradore is a marvel.'

'You will visit me, of course. It should be easier for us now.'

He smiled bleakly. 'Yes.' A pause. 'Palindrake is a singular man, Ren. He is unique. Myths are made about him.'

'Are they? Tell me some.'

'In battle, he is savage and merciless, and his justice is cold. His men fear him but adore him too. He lives austerely on campaign, never takes ale or wine, nor enjoys the company of concubines. They say he has black days, when he hides away from light, and cuts himself with his own blade. This may not be true. I cannot imagine him as a husband to someone like you. I can't imagine him being any woman's husband. I hope he treats you well.'

Bayard's worry, the things he could not say, hung as a tension in the air. Varencienne stood on tiptoe to kiss her brother's cheek. 'Please don't fret for me, Bay. You should know I can take care of myself quite adequately.'

He nodded, but would not smile. 'I will pray for you,' he said.

Rumours and tales. Because Lord Palindrake was so self-contained and disciplined, and let no one know his inner self, it was only natural the stories would arise. Varencienne thought she knew entirely what kind of man he was. She listened to the women talk. She knew about the commerce of men and women. He was like all the others in her father's court and army, only more so, bigger than them, more adept, and therefore more visible. She had no fear that he would ill-treat her. Bayard would be sharp-tongued about whomever it was decided she must marry. He would happily have wed her himself, but there would have been no political advantage for her father in that and sometimes the union of siblings produced monsters as children. She must be sent outside, to secure alliances and strengthen them.

That night she dreamed about her father's empire. She saw the world looking like a flat map that was spread out on a table. The land belonging to her family was coloured dark blue, like storm-clouds. At the edges, it lightened to a strange pinky-purple. These were the weak areas, the places where men like Palindrake led their armies. In the dream, she heard cries and smelled smoke and burning flesh. Red lightning flashed across the boiling sky. And in the wreckage below, amid the rubble of fallen buildings, something white moved feebly like a child's hand.

The wedding morn dawned bright and clear, the storm clouds had blown away to other lands. Varencienne was roused early by a gang of eager women, who doused her in a scented bath and brushed her long green-gold hair until her scalp burned. At eight o'clock, Carmia and Mavenna came tumbling into the room, already dressed in their wedding gowns. They seemed so happy, as if it was they who were to be wed.

'Ren, you seem so glum,' said Mavenna as Varencienne stood before the long glass, her arms held out stiffly. Women fussed with her gown. It was heavy upon her body, and did not move the way she moved.

'I shall miss you,' said Varencienne.

Tears sprang immediately to Mavenna's wide eyes. Her face puckered and she reached over the seamstresses to hug her friend at arm's length. 'Oh, my dear, my darling Ren, I shall miss you too. But I'm glad for you. I shall visit Caradore, and you will be lady of the castle, high up by the sky. I look forward to the day we shall meet again, and walk arm in arm along the turret wall.'

Varencienne smiled. 'You have thought of this a lot.'

Mavenna nodded, her eyes still damp. 'Yes.' She turned away, dabbed at her drenched lashes.

'He is the dark angel of Madragore,' announced Carmia, who had clearly been immersed in private thoughts.

Mavenna and Varencienne both looked at her.

'Valraven,' Carmia said, somewhat embarrassed. 'Your husband, Ren. I saw him last night as I went back to my room.'

Mavenna laughed; a brittle sound. 'A dream, my dear. Valraven Palindrake would not come near this wing.'

Carmia frowned and flushed. 'No. It was him. He stood out on a terrace, beyond a wall of coloured windows. I.have seen him before at court. I knew it was him. He was looking at the clouds.'

Mavenna's and Varencienne's eyes met. Varencienne shook her head to silence any further remarks from her friend. 'I do not feel quite real today. How quickly things can change.'

'But you are happy, really,' said Mavenna firmly, then less confidently, 'aren't you?'

Varencienne stepped away from the seamstresses, who had finished arranging the dress. She put her hands upon Mavenna's shoulders. 'Of course.' She did not want her friend to worry.

At ten o'clock, Varencienne was taken to her mother's quarters. It seemed all the women of the court were there, dressed splendidly. A concoction of conflicting perfumes soaked the air. White flowers, big and fleshy, were strewn everywhere; some standing in vases, others discarded upon the floor. The empress was a dark flower herself, dressed not in red, as all the other women, but resplendent in a gold so muted it seemed almost black. Varencienne wondered if any emotion struggled through Tatrini's closed heart. Was she thinking of her own wedding day, all those years before, when her husband had been only a prince and the empire a smaller collection of lands? Had she been happy then, dizzy with girlish anticipation, or had she felt as Varencienne did now: resigned and cold?

'My dear, you are beautiful,' said the empress, and Varencienne curtsied. After this judgement had been made, all the other women twittered flatteringly about Varencienne's dress and hair, her figure and her face. Mother and daughter exchanged a single, poignant glance. She knows, thought Varencienne, but this did not comfort her, as she'd imagined it might.

The cavalcade of women walked slowly through the palace, streaming fragrance and rustling. Voices were whispers. Along the high, vaulted corridors, past the stern statues of Varencienne's ancestors, across perilous galleries, down cascades of basalt stairs. Varencienne walked behind her mother, her gown trailing out behind her, hissing over the rugs and the polished flagstones. She held an immensity of white flowers in her arms. They erupted about her, already dying. Servants, drawn to witness the procession, bowed as they passed, as if they were blades of grass and the sight of the royal women was a scythe passing over their field.

Then, finally, the procession descended the grand staircase, down into the hall of the palace, and here the men of the family were gathered: Varencienne's father, who was so distant a presence in her life as to be almost mythical, her eleven brothers, and numerous cousins and uncles. The men clapped politely as the women descended, and for the first time in her life, Varencienne touched her father. He was like a statue come to life; gilded and perfect. He smiled at her kindly and offered her his right elbow, through which she slipped her thin hand. The great doors to the palace were thrown wide. Beyond, the sunlight seared, and trees put forth a mist of green in her honour. The company walked down the steps to the waiting carriages, and the whole of the palace staff, who were gathered in the driveway, began cheering and clapping, throwing flowers and coins for good luck. Bells were being rung all over the city. It was a celebration. This is not wholly mine, Varencienne thought. This day is everyone's day.

White horses pranced madly before the glossy black and purple carriage of the emperor. He climbed into it with his daughter and his wife and his eldest son, Prince Gastern, a dour man Varencienne did not like. Then the whips were flying and the horses leapt forward with crazy eyes and foamy breakers of manes and tails. The cheers were a roar, faintly threatening. Varencienne felt her eyes water. Were these tears?

'Be as your mother,' said the emperor, smiling down at his daughter as if they were close in spirit. 'Be a good wife, and Madragore will shine upon you with blessings.'

Perhaps that was a ritual phrase, part of it all. 'I will, Your Mightiness,' murmured Varencienne.

The carriages rumbled down through the palace gardens, the whole driveway lined with people. At the griffin gates, a multitude waited, merchants and doctors and teachers who lived in this area, the hill where the rich bred; it dominated the city. The further into the city they went, so the crowd changed. Now it was commoners, washerwomen and fish-wives, potmen and farriers. Each face was delirious; Varencienne saw no one frowning or sad, not even in the shadowed corners. Her eyes moved rapidly beneath downcast lashes. The faces were a blur, but it was as if her mind froze certain images into pictures. She knew she would never forget them.

Then the cathedral, as big as a small town itself, reared before them. The bells were so loud, Varencienne could feel their clamour reverberating in her chest. The army was here – some of it, the ceremonial part. The soldiers were gleaming and perfect like her father's horses. They stared straight ahead in their purple livery.

Inside, the cathedral was full of foreign dignitaries. Some were friends, others representatives from subjugated realms, and therefore not wholly participating in the celebratory mood. Varencienne felt weak. It would take so long to walk down that long, indigo-carpeted aisle. She was like a feather on her father's arm. He might forget what she was and accidentally brush her away, or the wind would come and she'd be blown, high, high, up into the ancient arches, where a colony of gargoyles were frozen against the walls. She'd hang there, watching herself walk towards her fate, and then she'd just fly away, out into the endless sky, turning and turning.

Was she going to faint? Her father's fingers, unexpectedly, patted her own. She was moving, somehow, although the bells had filled her with sound and stolen her breath.

Valraven Palindrake was a looming shadow at the end of the aisle. Priests were ranged about him like crows. The immense statue of the god Madragore dominated the space behind the altar. The god wore armour, for he was a warrior and the patron of the empire. Palindrake was the most blessed of His disciples.

I am already his, Varencienne thought. Am I going to run away? I can see myself doing it, any moment now, but where would I run?

Then she was delivered into his hands. She saw his face properly for the first time. It wasn't cruel, but it wasn't kind either. It was dark and terrible and beautiful. This can never happen, Varencienne thought, but it did. The words were being spoken over her head, the incense waved, the flowers scattered. Presently there was a ring upon her finger and she had sipped the holy wine, her lips touching the place on the goblet that Palindrake's lips had touched. Her hand was a piece of white lace in his strong, long-fingered grip. He looked so stern, not smiling at all. He did not want to do this, and yet he knew he must, as she did. Does it always happen this way? Soon I must call him Valraven to his face, or Val. Do people ever call him Val? It seemed unlikely. She could say, 'my husband' when she addressed him. That might be better.

Now they walked back down the aisle together and people were singing a hymn to Madragore. The god had no wife; his sons had sprung from the blood of a wound he had received warring with some other god. There were goddesses in the empire, but they belonged to the women and had no churches of their own. If Varencienne felt frightened enough to pray to someone, it was Mivian, a minor, almost faceless female deity, whose father was one of Madragore's sons. If Madragore had had a daughter, she would have been given away to a dark god of war, spirited away to a distant land where no one knew her and she had no worshippers.

The sunlight was harsh upon Varencienne's eyes as she stepped out of the cathedral with her husband. So many bells, so many flowers. Flocks of black and white doves had been released into the sky and the voice of the city was a lamenting howl. In those moments, Varencienne looked forward to Caradore, where the voice of the wind would be the only sound, and the crack of flag cables against their poles. She would find her own happiness there in the loneliness of the world. She would be a mother, a lady, with her own tapestry to fashion. Her husband's life. What dark threads she must use; so many battles. Were there scars upon his body?

After the celebrations, at which she could eat or drink nothing, the women took her to a different part of the palace, where guests were stowed. Here she was dressed in a nightgown and put into a strange bed. They said things to her, advice and so on, but she could not remember it. She was still full of the clamour of bells; it deafened her. Finally she was left alone, only half herself now. Some of her must have stayed in the cathedral, flown up into the vaults as she'd imagined. Perhaps that part of her was free for ever.

The door opened and he came into the room. She was glad he hadn't made her wait too long, but then Bayard had told her he didn't drink, so probably the party downstairs didn't hold much interest for him. He looked like a demon, something that might be carved into the cathedral walls. Those hands that would touch her: they had taken lives.

He undressed behind a screen and came out wearing a long, dark robe. When he looked at her, sitting there so small and white in the big dark bed, she could tell he felt pity for her. 'Do you know what to expect?' he asked. He wasn't nervous, but not altogether at ease either.

She nodded. 'Yes, my lord.' Would he tell her what to call him now?

'It is the custom,' he said, seemingly to explain the need for this physical act they must endure.

'I understand.' She arranged her hair about her shoulders.

'They will come and check you afterwards.'

She blinked at him for a moment. That, she had not heard. 'I see.'

He drew back the covers and, looking into her eyes, lifted her nightdress. She turned her head to the side. His hands were cool upon her, almost like a physician's hands, probing expertly, seeing if all was right. He parted her legs and she closed her eyes. He did not lie upon her, but knelt between her thighs. He spat on to his hand to lubricate her shrinking, parched sex. Then he lifted her hips towards him and entered her, like a surgeon excising a wound, carefully but quickly. It was too much for her mind to take in. She felt him moving in her, the hot scald of his alien presence stretching her virgin body. It was soon over. He made no sound. The only evidence she had that he'd found repletion was the wetness that oozed out of her once he'd risen from the bed.

'Tomorrow we leave for Caradore,' he told her, standing beside her, looking down. She stared at him dazedly, and he reached down to rearrange her nightdress. 'Are you well?'

She could not speak. He paused and then said, 'I will send one of the women to you.'

Then he was gone. The door had closed behind him. Cold tears leaked out of Varencienne's eyes. Her body shuddered and burned. She dared not move. It hurt too much, and yet she knew he had been gentle with her. If there were scars upon his body, she did not know. He had simply come and stabbed her, sealed the contract of their marriage. She felt now that she knew less of him than before.

CHAPTER TWO

The Domain

There were mountains in Caradore, rearing into a purple haze, but the castle itself dominated a high, flat tongue of land that licked out into the crashing northern ocean. Varencienne leaned out of her carriage as her company made the final approach, up a wide, winding road of yellow gravel. The vehicles and horses emerged from a tunnel of ancient, gnarled trees whose leaves seemed almost silver, and ahead of them, Caradore: a fairytale edifice of turrets and battlements, rose pale against the white sky, coroneted with undulating flags. Varencienne shivered: she thought again of the crack of flag-cables in the wind. The wind here was so pungent and so fierce, like sea-soaked hands in her hair.

'Be careful, Your Highness,' warned Oltefney, the woman who'd been appointed as her handmaid. 'Don't get dust in your throat, and watch out for those straggling branches.'

Stout, opinionated and seeming older than her years – which was probably only mid-thirties – Oltefney had grated upon Varencienne's nerves for the entire, long journey: just the two of them in a carriage, surrounded by wagons and a clutch of cavalry as escort. Valraven Palindrake had ridden on ahead. Varencienne had not seen him since her wedding night, an experience upon which she did not dwell. Already, she missed her friends; the fiery presence of Mavenna and the more glacial calm of Carrnia. They should be here now, sharing these new sights, this hidden future.

Ignoring Oltefney's warning, Varencienne leaned out further into the wind. The horses' hooves threw up gravel; the road beneath was a blur of dust. Caradore, fine Caradore; the name itself – which belonged not just to the castle but to the entire region – conjured images of mystery and magic. It stood upon a clifftop plateau of sandy stone and spiky dune grass. A cluster of buildings huddled around its walls: Caradore's own townlet, where the hard mountain berries were conjured into tart heady liquor, and the dune-grasses were woven into rope, and the sea harvested of its meat-filled shells. Skeins of smoke rose up from its chimneys into the blustery spring air. Varencienne could hear the sound of metal being hammered and smell the warm earthy-sweet aroma of animal dung and straw, the scent of sea which was both fresh and rank and the spiced-fruity scent from the liquor sheds. She wanted to leap from the jolting carriage and run the rest of the way; her limbs felt starved of movement. She imagined herself saying 'Stop the carriage!' and descending with dignity. She would arrive in the village and all would cease their labours to view the new wife of their master. 'I am mistress here now,' she would say.

Varencienne smiled to herself, her hair wriggling free of its jewelled net, but she did not call out to the carriage driver.

People did stop their work as the carriage rolled past, but by that time, Varencienne had withdrawn behind the modesty curtains, through which she observed a watery view of the world. She knew much could be learned about her husband from the condition of his serfs, was alert for signs of discontent, maluourishment or misery, but all seemed ordinary in the extreme.

Oltefney grumbled about everything; she was a woman of the city and begrudged being exiled to this lonely spot with someone she no doubt considered to be a 'strip of a girl', for all her royal breeding. The woman would make enemies at the castle first, Varencienne decided, then a host of gossiping friends, over whom she'd hold sway, having once worked in the imperial palace itself.

'Smells of fish and weed!' announced Oltefney.

'Salt and wind,' said Varencienne dreamily.

'Scavenging birds to keep us awake till all hours with horrible screams.'

'The lament of mermaids in coral caves,' said Varencienne, aware of how her comments needled the older woman.

'Tch!' said Oltefney, arranging her capacious carpet bag more firmly upon her wide knees.

Varencienne was excited about her new environment, but nervous too. Oltefney had relished telling her that Lord Palindrake had two sisters at home, who would no doubt object to the arrival of a new female in their domain. 'The Palindrakes were nothing more than barbarians until a few generations ago,' she'd said, in that confiding, greedy tone Varencienne loathed.

'Perhaps they still are,' she'd answered coldly. 'They'll come running from the castle with bones in their hair, shrieking maledictions.'

If Mavenna was with her now, she would not feel so nervous. Mavenna could outwit any other female, having the sharpest, quickest tongue Varencienne knew. She would also defend her close friends to the death. Oltefney, on the other hand, would no doubt enjoy any occasions of social discomfort her young mistress might have to endure.

The carriage rumbled beneath a great yellow arch and halted in the courtyard of Caradore. Even before she climbed out, Varencienne was overwhelmed by the cold rushing voice of the wind and the irresistible heave of the sea. Was it ever warm here?

The castle appeared neat and scoured, constructed of wind-sculpted creamy stone. Servants had gathered outside on the steps to the main entrance in a sharply defined semicircle. A tall, dour-faced man, dressed in livery of soft green cloth, stepped forward briskly to greet the new bride.

'Good day to you, ma'am,' he said, bowing stiffly from the waist. 'I am Methlin Goldvane, steward of Caradore. May I welcome you to Lord Palindrake's estate. The staff are ready for your inspection.'

'Thank you,' Varencienne answered, covertly eyeing the curious faces around her. As far as she could gather, there were no Palindrake sisters in evidence. But for Goldvane, all the staff were dressed in the black and purple of the Palindrake crest. They were tidy and appeared contented; surely a good sign. Varencienne passed along the line, smiling in what she hoped was a dignified fashion. These people did not hide their interest in her; some were rosy-cheeked and dewy-eyed to behold the young bride, others more speculative. The men appeared scrubbed and awkward, bowing too low. None of them could know anything about her, other than her age and that she was the daughter of the emperor. Perhaps they'd thought she'd be haughty and cruel. What was their opinion now after this brief inspection? Varencienne felt small and young before them, a stranger in this high, gusting place. She accepted posies of sea-violets from a couple of the younger maids and made a mental note to request certain girls to be added her personal staff. She did not want to feel so alone.

The castle was not dark inside like the imperial palace, but neither was it very warm. The flagstones in the main hall were gritty with sand, and the great tapestries upon the walls were never still. The wind found its way in continually, snaking up corridors and passageways like a restless ghost.

Goldvane clicked his fingers and a maid glided forward, carrying a silver tray upon which stood two stone goblets. These were offered to Varencienne and her woman; a blood-reviving aperitif that went immediately to Varencienne's head. The castle did not feel lived in; no fire crackled in the cavernous hearth, but perhaps the family did not use the main hall much. Still, a fire would have been a sign of welcome. Varencienne felt like a guest whose stay was to be discouraged. Had the sisters made sure she would feel that way?

'Lady Everna and Lady Pharinet will be home shortly,' announced Goldvane, apparently divining her thoughts.

Where had they been? They must have known she was arriving that afternoon. Varencienne placed her goblet back on the tray and did not speak.

'You will be taken to your chambers at once,' said Goldvane. He clapped his hands, and men scuttled in from other rooms, to see about the women's hand luggage.

'Is my husband here?' asked Varencienne.

The steward's face did not flinch. 'Lord Palindrake is out inspecting the estate.' He paused, and then softened the information. 'He has been absent from home for many months, and there was much for him to attend to.'

'Of course.' Varencienne smiled weakly. She felt relieved. The Palindrake women, however, should have arranged a formal greeting party, such as was protocol in the city. Was this a slight against her, or just the alien ways of a family who, despite being Magravandian, lived in so remote a region as to be considered foreign? Perhaps the Palindrakes were not a tribe for formalities and niceties. She imagined the sisters; women like their brother, with purple-black hair, out among the crags, riding muscly stallions astride like men, using the whip.

Varencienne approved of her chambers, although they were very different to those she had left behind. The main door opened on to a short corridor, filled with pale light from overhead windows. From there, Goldvane conducted the women to a large sitting-room and then withdrew. Here the walls were of stone rather than the wood panelling Varencienne was used to, and adorned with tapestries that shivered in a breeze she could not feel. The windows were high and narrow and had folding wooden shutters rather than curtains. In the creamy stone hearth, a fire burned, and utensils were set out ready to prepare refreshment. Varencienne went to inspect these alien implements. A black metal trivet was set into the surround of the hearth and could be swung out over the flames. Hot beverages at home always appeared on a tray and she had never witnessed them being prepared. Stone was always polished to a gloss and wood varnished. Here, stone was rough as in nature and wood pale and full of sap.

'Doesn't appear to be a housekeeper,' Oltefney said, with suspicion.

'Perhaps she was busy,' Varencienne suggested lamely.

Oltefney shook her head. 'I doubt it. What kind of an establishment has no housekeeper, and only a man to see to all?'

A maid was found loitering in the bathroom polishing taps, and Oltefney took charge of her at once. Presently a kettle was boiling on the trivet and pungent tea had been measured out into a clay pot. Varencienne took off her cloak and gloves and went to explore her new home. The bedroom was hardly grand, but with a wall of the tall, deeply set narrow windows, where gauzy drapes of coarse-spun linen scraped against the floor. The bed was low and devoid of posts, but when Varencienne sat on it, it was pleasingly firm. She was surprised to find she had her own kitchen and laundry – just small rooms, but obviously for her use. There were also two chambers clearly intended for the accommodation of servants – so close to her, it seemed strange. They would be like their own small household within the larger domain of the castle. The bathroom was functional and, again, hardly palatial, but here the flagstones were covered in fleeces, upon which Varencienne's damp feet would be able to pad in comfort after bathing. Chunks of grey soap lay in earthenware dishes on a shelf. They looked repulsive, but when Varencienne sniffed them, she inhaled a wonderful salty aroma, like the sea, spiced with tart herbs. Perhaps it was made in the village below, or even in the castle kitchens. Caradore seemed very rustic – living there might be like staying on a farm – but its simplicity appealed to Varencienne. She realized then she had never felt completely comfortable in the stuffy, regulated atmosphere of the imperial palace. Here she might move more freely and her dreams would seem more real.

Back in the sitting-room, Oltefney was in full complaint. 'Never seen the like!' she exclaimed, hands on hips. 'It's like a ruin – all draughts and cold spots!'

Varencienne smiled at the maid, who was kneeling by the hearth. 'I like it.' The maid risked a tiny smile back, then returned her concentration to her tasks.

'But Your Highness,' protested Oltefney loudly, 'the least *they* could have done was been here to meet us. I shall write to your mother about it immediately. It's an affront.'

Varencienne flopped down into a chair. 'Oh, don't bother about it. What could my mother do, anyway? We're here now.' Her mother would not care. Varencienne was out of her sphere of influence now. She imagined that already the space she had occupied in the palace had been filled by other people, other dreams. Sighing, she gazed around the room. It had a presence all its own; restful, but also secretive. There was a basket on the wide windowsill, filled with shells. Someone had gathered them and put them there. Someone.

After drinking her tea – which was far stronger than any she was used to – Varencienne changed her clothes and let her hair out of its net. She would have liked to let its perfumed mass fall free down her back, but Oltefney protested and then insisted on plaiting it for her. 'You are not a farm girl, Your Highness, but a representative of your father's house.' Oltefney, no doubt, considered her rather wild. From the top layer of one of her clothes trunks Varencienne chose a plain, sand-coloured gown, which she knew defined her figure flatteringly and swept loosely around her ankles. Its hem was decorated in gold motifs.

'Not very fancy,' criticized Oltefney, frowning as her mistress wriggled into the dress, refusing assistance.

'Perhaps not, but it was very expensive indeed – a gift from my brother, Bayard. He brought it back with him from Pepherus.' Varencienne guessed Oltefney was thinking only of the Palindrake sisters, and that perhaps the new bride should be dressed more splendidly, to impress. Varencienne just wanted to feel comfortable.

Someone knocked on the door, and opened it before Oltefney could reach it. Varencienne stood up quickly. She saw a woman in the doorway, perhaps the missing housekeeper. She appeared to be of middle years, very tall and thin. Her nose was over-large for her face, yet she still managed to look handsome. Grey-streaked brown hair was coiled up on her head, as neat and immobile as the hair of a statue.

'Good afternoon,' this woman announced. 'I am Everna Palindrake.'

Varencienne's fantasies of wild, black-haired beauties broke up into fragments and blew away. Everna was possibly the exact opposite of such a vision. She ignored Oltefney and marched purposefully into the room, her hands laced before her, eyes fixed upon her brother's new bride. Varencienne noticed Everna's white knuckles; was she nervous too? Out of courtesy, she bobbed a curtsey, which made Everna smile. They weren't formal at all here. Everna had walked into the room without ceremony or escort. Varencienne had expected to be presented to the two sisters later, in a formal reception room, where they would sit at a polite distance from one another and discuss trivialities, all the time sizing each other up.

'I apologize that no one was here to greet you,' said Everna, thrusting out a hand.

Varencienne stared at it in perplexity for a few moments before realizing she was expected to shake it. Men greeted one another that way. She had never shaken anybody's hand. Everna's grip was strong, brief and business-like, the palms dry and gritty as if dusted with sand. 'It's quite all right,' Varencienne managed to say. 'We've had some tea, and have been settling in.'

'Good. We shall all dine together this evening, of course. Val has had an ox slaughtered, so I hope you have an appetite.'

'Yes, yes.' Varencienne felt like a child. This woman must be older than her mother. She realized she could never be mistress here.

'I hope you have everything you need.'

'Yes. Everything.'

Everna nodded in apparent satisfaction. 'Good. I run the household for my brother, so if you should need anything, send word to me at once.'

No housekeeper then, but a maiden sister. Everna had an air which suggested she was no man's wife. 'That's very kind of you.' Varencienne said. 'My rooms are lovely.'

Everna smiled, rather tightly. 'I'm glad you like them. They are but a small example of Caradore's splendours. Are you tired, or would you like to be shown around?'

'Yes please, I mean, I'm not tired.'

'Well, come along, then. Caradore must be very different to the palace in Magrast.'

Oltefney appeared silenced by shock. 'You can finish unpacking,' Varencienne told her and swept past her out of the door.

Everna walked very quickly, her dark gown puffing out around her ankles as she thrust out her feet. Varencienne hurried to keep up.

'We hope you'll be happy here,' Everna said. 'I must confess it was a shock to us that Val had married.'

Of course, his sisters had not been at the wedding. He hadn't even told them. They were so isolated out here, in this corner of the world, that no news had come to them. Varencienne felt momentarily chilled. 'I'm sorry,' she said. She wanted to say that it had been a shock to her too, but thought that might be considered importunate.

'Not your fault,' said Everna briskly. 'I can't imagine you had much say in the matter.'

'No. Not at all.'

'We don't see much of him nowadays,' Everna continued, 'and I don't expect that to change.' She paused. 'You are a poor little thing, aren't you.'

No, I am a princess. I am not poor, or even that little. Varencienne found her voice. 'Actually, I've been looking forward to coming here. I like the sea, and I'm used to the company of women. At home, the ladies of the palace rarely see their husbands.'

Everna smiled in an approving, if tight, fashion. 'Well, I'm glad to hear you know some of what to expect. If you like the sea, you will have your senses indulged to repletion here. We have rather a lot of it.'

'I noticed.' Varencienne returned the smile. I have done something right, she thought.

There was a turret walk, a place where the wind tried to take captives. Varencienne could barely breathe out there. Her robe was flattened to her legs, and she felt chilled to the core. Everna didn't seem to notice the cold. Perhaps a person would become used to it, living here.

Varencienne told Everna about Mavenna, and how she had pictured them one day walking together in a place like this. 'I would like her to come here some day,' she said.

Everna frowned slightly. 'I don't know about that.'

'But why?' Varencienne could not keep the surprise from her voice.

Everna cast a shrewd look in her direction. 'Well, we are all set in our ways here,' she explained. 'We don't want Caradore filled with twittering girls running about the corridors. Also, the sea air does not always agree with city folk.'

'Mavenna was very much looking forward to coming here. Will none of my friends be welcome?'

'Don't misunderstand me,' Everna said smoothly. 'I don't wish to sound authoritarian. I expect you'll forget your old life very soon, and the memory of those childhood friends will fade. You'll find much to do, and perhaps soon you'll have children of your own, which will of course fill your time to capacity.'

Children, in Varencienne's experience, did very little to fill the time of royal women, but it was clear that life was very different in Caradore. Would she be expected to look after her children herself? The prospect did not please her. She had imagined childbearing to be an inevitable conse-quence of being married, but hoped she could cope with it in the same way she'd coped with other sicknesses. She'd assumed that once it was over, the child would be handed to someone else and she could get on with her life. But what was her life going to be? What had it been? A dream, a long pageant of dreams.

'I'm not sure I like children,' she said.

Everna wrinkled her nose, which made her look younger. 'I *certainly* don't like children, which is why I live here, unencumbered by a husband. As a girl, I just couldn't stomach the thought of spawning some man's offspring year after year, lumbering round like a broodmare. It drains a woman, you know, uses up her blood and makes her bones fragile.' She glanced sideways at Varencienne. 'I hope your children won't be a nuisance.'

'To any of us,' Varencienne couldn't help adding. Her numbness was coming back. She could feel it slipping over her like a shroud.

Everna put a hand upon her shoulder. 'Val must want heirs, otherwise he wouldn't have married you. At least you shouldn't be shelling them once a year, like most women. As I said, Val rarely comes home now. Your father keeps him busy. And you're young. I expect your body will recover very quickly from the first one.'

This is terrible, Varencienne thought. Her fond imaginings of rearing Valraven Palindrake's children had not involved the actual bearing of them herself, nor any subsequent mothering. She had been so stupid. She had not realized. One of her dreams was to become reality, but not in any way she'd thought. She could be pregnant already. There could be something growing inside her, preparing to suck the marrow from her bones and feast on her blood. Varencienne stumbled to the battlement wall and leaned into the wind, gulping the salty air. She felt faint.

Everna glided up behind her. 'Oh dear, I'm sorry. I shouldn't have spoken in that way. My views are hardly feminine and must have frightened you. Please ignore my ramblings. I'm sure your own mother – or indeed most other women – would tell you what a rewarding experience motherhood can be.'

But not you, Varencienne thought. She could not contest Everna's feelings; they were similar to her own.

At sundown, a maidservant with narrow eyes came to tell Varencienne and Oltefney that dinner was ready to be served on the first floor, in the grand family dining room, which they called the Carving Hall. Varencienne thought of whole oxen roasted over an open fire, of male laughter and the sinister glimmer of flames, of sly-eyed women and spilled wine. Would Valraven's slaughtered ox be turning slowly in the great hearth, dripping hissing gobbets of fat and blood? She felt half nauseated, half starved.

The Carving Hall was situated at the back of the castle. As Varencienne and Oltefney followed the maid through the corridors and down stairs, all Varencienne could think of was that *he* would be present at dinner; the one who could infect her, dominate her body, make it do things over which she had no control. Why had her father made her get married? She could have remained a virgin, and lived in her brother's house. She could have been the one saying those terrible things to a young bride as they walked the battlements. It would never happen now.

Oltefney was already speculating greedily on the forthcoming feast, but Varencienne ignored her comments. They had reached the Carving Hall, and the doors were opening before her. She stepped through.

The room was long and lit by soft candlelight. A stoked fire chewed enormous, gnarled logs, dwarfed by the size of the hearth. Above, on the wall, was the crest of the Palindrakes in carved, painted wood: a fishtailed dragon rising from a nest of foam and surrounded by a court of hideous merpeople. The table, which could have comfortably seated thirty people was, like all the furniture in Caradore, of a blond unvarnished pine. High-backed chairs surmounted by swooping wooden gargoyles were ranged along its length, but only two were occupied. The air smelled heavily of flowers and furniture wax. A bowl of spring blooms dominated the centre of the table; tiny flowers that had come adrift lay wilting on the wood.

Valraven Palindrake's presence flowed out into the room, hanging around him like a dark miasma. Varencienne imagined that he drew energy from the candle flames, made them grow dim. She could not believe he had once touched her so intimately; it was a stranger sitting there, his inky hair cataracting over his shoulders, his hawk eyes deep and shadowed. Handsome, yes, but not classically. There was a brutality to his face, and his eyes were cold, like a predator's. Hardly a surprise; how many had been his prey? Near him, at the head of the table, sat a woman who could only be his twin – undoubtedly Pharinet. She was leaning towards him and laughing conspiratorially, her strong dark arms lying with pan-ther's ease on the tabletop. Here was a black-haired enchantress, who could have stepped from Varencienne's own fantasies; a charismatic crea-ture who shared her brother's aloof mien.

Varencienne could tell that Pharinet was aware of her presence immedi-ately, even though she did not look up in either politeness or welcome. Perhaps she had already made up her mind to despise the young bride. She was not slim, but muscular, dressed in a pale cream gown that seemed almost too feminine for her and made features of her dark-skinned shoulders and masses of coiling hair. Her brows were arched for wicked-ness, her eyes black and heavy-lidded beneath them. She could not be termed beautiful, being too angular and aggressive-looking, but her pres-ence was arresting. She possessed a quality Varencienne could not name, but knew she did not have herself.

Outside, behind Valraven, the sky seemed almost mauve, full of clouds. The sea's presence was very strong in the room, threshing against the

161

cliffs. Through the windows Varencienne could see the wild spray around the bay and sensed the inexorable strength of the waves. Valraven seemed the focus of this energy.

'Ah, the little princess!' Pharinet said at last, once Varencienne had made the seemingly endless journey from one end of the table to the other.

Valraven Palindrake got to his feet, his long fingers pressing lightly on the table. 'Good evening, Varencienne,' he said.

The only other time she'd heard him speak her name was during the wedding ceremony, when he'd had to repeat it after the priest. It sounded strange coming out of his mouth, as if it wasn't her name at all.

'My family call me Ren,' she said. She would not call him anything.

Pharinet laughed. 'Ren. A little wren. How *sweet*!'

Valraven gave her a stern look and she shrugged her shoulders. Still, Varencienne could tell the unspoken censure had stung Pharinet. The atmosphere in the room changed; became charged with tension.

Valraven indicated that his wife should sit next to him, opposite his sister. 'I welcome you to my home,' he said formally, bowing his head. His home – not hers, or theirs.

As Varencienne took her place, she studied Pharinet's face while she turned a crystal goblet of wine in her fingers, gazing into the ruby fluid. I would prefer to be liked by a woman who looks like her, Varencienne thought. She looks interesting, yet she is jealous of me, perhaps in the same way Bayard is jealous of Palindrake. How will this end? Will I win her over, or will she destroy me, push me from the battlements, poison me, or have me killed by a brigand? Perhaps we will always be enemies until we are old, or perhaps she will marry and move away.

'Everna has shown you the castle,' Valraven said, breaking Varencienne's reverie. 'What do you think of the place?'

'Very nice,' Varencienne replied, without thinking, regretting the facile remark at once. Pharinet made a small sound of amusement. Varencienne forced the blood from her face; she would not blush in front of a potential enemy. She shook out a linen napkin that smelled of flowers and spread it on her lap. Insouciance itself. 'Tomorrow, I think I shall walk upon the beach.'

'Not alone,' said Valraven. 'The cliff paths are unsafe.'

Pharinet looked up then. 'I will take you.' Her expression was inscrutable, her voice without inflection.

'Perhaps not,' murmured Valraven. 'I am sure Varencienne would prefer a more measured tour with Everna. She is not used to your gallivanting, Pharinet.'

'No, no,' Varencienne said, looking Pharinet directly in the eye. 'I would love to walk with you.' Don't think me a mouse, she thought, or even a little wren. I am yet to discover myself what kind of animal I am. She glanced at her husband with assumed docility. 'I'm sure Everna will not mind.'

'That's settled, then,' said Pharinet.

Valraven pulled a wry face, but did not intervene. Perhaps this was because it was the business of women; a territory strange and unwelcoming to him.

Everna made an entrance, accompanied by women carrying the soup. She stood by Valraven's chair and leaned stiffly from the waist to kiss his brow. 'I missed you earlier. How were the Leckerys?' Her voice indicated a ruffled disappointment.

Valraven suffered the kiss, but seemed impatient with it. 'They are all in good health.'

'I would have liked to have ridden out with you, but never mind, perhaps next time.'

Valraven took a sip of wine. 'Saska sent her regards.'

Everna sat down beside Varencienne. 'It is impossible to pin my brother down. Once you have made friends around here, my dear, don't expect him to take you with him when he goes visiting. He will temporarily forget you exist.'

'It was a fleeting visit,' Valraven said mildly. 'I did take the liberty of inviting the family over soon to meet Varencienne.'

Varencienne found the exchange embarrassing. She herself would never betray such pique before someone she didn't know, but then she had already learned that formalities did not appear to exist in Caradore.

The soup was exquisite, thick with fruits of the sea. Everna took a long time to finish hers, as she sniped at her brother continually, to remind him how much he neglected both her and his home. Pharinet remained silent, but smiling. Once she caught Varencienne's eye and appeared to deliver a conspiratorial glance. Varencienne smiled back, but Pharinet looked back to her soup plate.

After the soup came the promised meat, slabs of rare beef, swimming in blood and served with young scallions, potatoes and leeks. It was simple fare, devoid of the rich sauces favoured in the capital. Varencienne had never seen meat that so much resembled living flesh and at first balked from cutting into it. Once she had dared to taste a morsel, she had to finish it all.

'You eat well for one so small,' Everna remarked. 'Perhaps your shape will change dramatically as you age.'

163

'I always eat a lot,' Varencienne said. 'My nurse used to tell me I have to graze like a horse – all the time – otherwise I'd die from starvation.'

'So much energy to burn,' Pharinet drawled, and raised her brows slowly, making the remark immediately salacious.

The family discussed people Varencienne did not know and both of the women spoke with authority about the running of the estate. It seemed that Valraven's presence was not really needed, and his inspection over the last few days had merely involved catching up with friends. The sisters deferred to him, made him feel important, but his role must involve something other than day-to-day administration. Perhaps he had more of a spiritual function, riding over the landscape proclaiming his ownership, and thus his protection of it. It was clear the sisters managed quite well without him, but now that he was back, however briefly, they would be reluctant to let him leave again.

Oltefney seemed to fit in well. Despite Everna's initial snubbing, she now seemed content to converse with Oltefney about domestic matters. Oltefney spent the entire meal praising anything her eyes fell upon, which seemed to please Everna.

Valraven spoke only as much as he needed to; his mind seemed elsewhere, but Varencienne did not flatter herself he was thinking about her. He barely glanced at her. It seemed inconceivable that she belonged to this man.

As a platter of cheese was being circulated at the end of the meal, Everna asked the question that was on the mind of every woman present. 'How long are you staying this time, Val? Are you going to run off in a day or two and leave your poor little bride alone?'

'The emperor has cordially granted me leave,' Valraven answered carefully. 'I shall be home for some weeks.'

'That is marvellous!' Everna exclaimed, while Varencienne's heart sank.

He will not leave until he's sure I am with child, she thought. There were hands of steel around her head.

'Everyone in the area will want to meet you,' Everna told Varencienne, 'and of course we should indulge them. It might look as if we live in a lonely wilderness, but several large estates border our own, and there are also two towns nearby, not to mention all the farms and villages.'

'Quite a community, aren't we,' Pharinet said. 'You will be busy, Evvy.' She reached out and touched her brother's arm. 'And you, of course, will hate it. All that small talk, Val. How will you manage?'

'Everna will do everything she can to make sure events run smoothly,' he answered.

'I enjoy entertaining,' Everna said. 'It brings life and energy to Caradore.'

She is too easily pleased, Varencienne thought, as she observed how Everna's face shone with a private happiness. She craves his attention, and the least morsel of it gives her satisfaction.

'Perhaps we could all go into the evening room and play crack-bones after dinner,' Everna said.

Valraven shook his head. 'Varencienne will be tired. There will be plenty of other occasions for games.'

'I'll play with you for a while,' Pharinet said, and Everna agreed readily.

Varencienne wondered whether she should say she wasn't tired at all and would like to participate in the game, but realized Valraven might have a particular reason for getting her upstairs so quickly and dared not speak, afraid of what he might say in return.

Varencienne lay awake, listening to the moaning whistle of the wind and the distant thunder of the sea. The tide was far out, and fierce white moonlight fell into her bedroom through cracks in the shutters at the long windows. The air smelled strongly of a salty perfume; she felt drunk with it. She had wondered when her husband would make an appearance, and for some time had lain in a fit of dread, but as the moon arced across the sky and he did not come, the feeling left her. She sensed that tonight he would leave her alone. Was this through compassion, or simply because he was tired himself or had something better to do? Whatever the reason, she was grateful for his absence.

Restless, she got out of bed and went to the window, where she opened the shutters. Immediately a thread of wind found its way in and the thin drapes started shivering. The world was black and white outside. She could look down upon the beach, where the sand seemed to glow with its own light. Someone was walking there; she could see a dark figure. Perhaps it was her husband, thinking of his girl-wife alone in the high castle, or perhaps it was Pharinet, eating her heart out for a forbidden love. Would Everna walk there, lost in her own dry thoughts? I would like to be on the beach now, Varencienne thought. I would glide across the damp sand with bare feet, so that anyone who saw me from the castle would think me a ghost. I would not leave footprints. I would not feel the wind, nor the sting of sand and salt. I would be walking out towards the water, and there would be a silver ship, or a city of crystal rising from the waves. I would leave this world, and no one would know where I'd gone, but there would be legends left behind, of a girl who walked along the beach to a magical place, and whose shadow could still be seen on moonlit nights . . .

Her thoughts were broken by a noise from outside that made her jump. It was a strange sound; a honking howl, like a great pig, or a bird of some kind. Sea-owls must roost in the cliffs. Was it that? There; it came again. Varencienne shuddered. The sound did not seem natural, but she knew how her own imagination liked to romanticize. It was just an owl, its cry amplified by the empty night, and the distance of the waves. She saw that the shadowy figure on the beach had stopped walking and now stood straight and still, perhaps staring out at the ocean – or back at the castle? Instinctively she ducked behind the shutter, even though it was unlikely she could be seen in an unlit window from so far away.

The howl came again, but more distant. It had a mournful quality. Something answered it, in a rasping screech. Varencienne risked a glance round the shutters. It seemed the sea, a distant wrinkle of foam, was shining with a weird light. Shadows rose up from it and crossed the moon, monstrous shadows. There was a gracefulness to their movement, and looking at them, Varencienne became aware of strange feelings twisting in her heart. She was at once filled with melancholy and excitement. When the howls came again, she wanted to open the window and answer with her own wild voice. She wanted to be up there, eclipsing the stars with wide wings. Her body was trembling. She had to pull away from the window and lean back against the wall. Her face felt hot, her eyes were watering. What was happening? Her heart was going mad.

The next howl seemed to be almost in the room with her, it was so loud. It pinned her to the cool stones of the wall. She was filled with it, like the clamour of the bells on her wedding day. It has found me, she thought. Sweet Mivian, it saw me watching. She was afraid, yet did not feel threatened. The fear came from knowing that something might manifest before her, that her mind could neither comprehend nor cope with; she would be driven insane. Only blind priests could invoke the presence of Madragore, for if he decided to manifest in the incense smoke, whoever saw him lost their eyes. It would be like this, she thought and squeezed her eyelids shut. Go away! Go away!

The presence vanished with such immediacy, Varencienne doubted her own heart's cry had been responsible. It had been called away from its distraction, that's all. For a while, she stood motionless against the wall, waiting for her racing heart to calm down.

What have I come in to? she wondered. All her life, she had dreamed of excitement and enchantment. Had it found her at last?

After some minutes, she closed the shutters over the windows without looking outside, and went back to bed. The darkness did not frighten her. As she lay between the cool sheets that slowly warmed around her body, she became aware of a yearning within her. It was a simple hunger, but for what?

CHAPTER THREE

Meeting the Sea

At daybreak, Varencienne was awaken by the maid who brought her a cup of strong tea. It was too early; Varencienne was used to rising late. When she voiced a complaint, the maid informed her that Lady Pharinet was expecting her company at eight o'clock. Varencienne groaned. Outside, it was raining. She had forgotten about the walk. 'What is your name, girl?' she asked the maid, who was clearly ten years older than her at least.

'Twissaly, ma'am.' She was laying out a set of clothes for Varencienne, without asking for her preference. It seemed an importunate act for a servant. The ways of Caradore would take some getting used to.

'And you have been appointed to my staff?'

Twissaly smoothed a length of fabric with apparent affection. 'This is my place, ma'am, in these rooms. I have always serviced them.'

'Even before anyone lived here?'

'These are bride's chambers. I have always worked here.'

Deciding to come back to this eccentric custom later, Varencienne launched into another topic that puzzled her. 'What manner of creature is it that makes such a racket at night?'

'Beg your pardon, ma'am?' Twissaly frowned at her, in puzzlement or distress?

'I was woken last night by howls,' Varencienne replied lightly. 'What was it?'

'Seabirds, ma'am.'

'They seemed very big, then.'

'Seabirds are big in Caradore, ma'am. They're called perigorts. We eat them at festival times. Very tasty. You'll like them.'

'They squawk like pigs.'

Twissaly laughed. 'They do. Taste better though. Once you've had some on your plate, it will be your favourite meat. Don't mind their rumpus. A body soon gets used to their screeching, until you don't hear it at all.'

'I am relieved. My night was much disturbed.' Varencienne was disappointed. She remembered how she'd felt the previous night. Was there a secret here, or just her imagination working busily as usual? If it had only been birds screeching, why had she felt an unearthly presence in the room? She wasn't yet sure how she felt about the informality of the staff in Caradore either. Oltefney was allowed certain privileges of expression because she was a woman of fairly high birth herself, but the maids in the palace at home would never have dared to offer opinions or suggestions. Twissaly did not appear nervous or seem particularly eager to please. She just got on with her work and said what she liked. Should I change this or not? Varencienne wondered. Do I like it?

Twissaly prepared her a breakfast of eggs and fish in the small kitchen, and after consuming it, Varencienne dressed herself in the clothes her maid had laid out for her. Rain hurled itself at the windows in great splashes, as if a lazy servant of the gods overhead was emptying divine bathwater over the castle. The wind virtually screamed its way about the turrets; this was not the day for a walk. As she dressed, Varencienne considered whether Pharinet would cancel their outing; perhaps they could explore more of the castle instead. But when Pharinet arrived at her rooms, it was clear she intended to take Varencienne outside. She wore what appeared to be men's clothes beneath a thick leather cape. 'You will see the best of the ocean in this weather,' she said, 'but make sure you wear a thick cloak.' She eyed the flimsy article Varencienne was inspecting. 'Hmm. Perhaps you should borrow something of mine. Run to my rooms, Twiss, and see to it, will you?'

Twissaly left the room, and Varencienne was alone with Pharinet. Oltefney must still be in bed. For once, Varencienne would have welcomed her presence. She did not know what to say.

'You are so young,' Pharinet said, her voice frighteningly clear and strong. 'It seems almost a crime Val has married you. Perverse, even. But then, I understand your family has always married its female stock off as soon as they're capable of breeding.'

Again, mention of the hated topic. 'Given the choice, I would be your sister,' Varencienne replied, unable to keep the ice from her voice. She wasn't *that* young either. Some girls at home were married off at fifteen.

Pharinet laughed. 'You should prefer to be me. I am, after all, somewhat better favoured.'

'I don't want men to like me,' Varencienne said vehemently.

'That might change,' Pharinet said, her voice milder. 'Actually, I do sympathize, but don't think badly of Val. I think you should know that he had little choice about marrying you.'

'I had guessed as much. I could tell.'

'You should learn to be friends.'

Varencienne could not help laughing – the prospect of that seemed so unlikely. She could not be friends with a man like Valraven Palindrake.

Pharinet sighed, perhaps mistaking the reason for Varencienne's response. 'You are right to laugh. There'll be no time for it. Val will soon be away again, and in his line of business there's always a risk he'll not return.'

'Surely that's his choice,' Varencienne said, involuntarily heartened by the thought she might one day be a widow rather than a wife.

Pharinet did not answer.

Outside, the wind shook Varencienne's body as if she were a child in the grip of a murderous adult. It stole her breath, so that she had to walk with her head turned to the side. She had never been out in such fierce elements before; it made her realize how puny humans were in comparison. An emperor might command an entire world, but one inadvertent stroll across a windy cliff and he might be no more. Pharinet seemed invigorated by the foul weather. She marched along a clifftop path, the sodden dune-grass soaking her trousers. Varencienne's own woollen gown was soon heavy; cold and wet about her knees. Her hair hung in dripping tendrils out of her hood, whipping her face with painful stings whenever the wind caught them in its playful fingers. Conversation was impossible. Pharinet walked slightly ahead, glancing back every few minutes as if to make sure she still had a companion.

To the right, the ocean thrashed in a frenzy of hellish joy, waves breaking against the rocks in a chaos of foam that must have been nearly forty feet high. The tide was well in now, and they were walking down towards it. Varencienne experienced a gut-deep fear of the maddened water, but also a great excitement. She could imagine how easily those waves could smash helpless flesh to bloody fragments, and could not help visualizing what it would be like to have them fall down upon her with their inexorable weight. She could sense the way they would grab hold of her and send her into a mad spin, throwing her against the rocks again and again, until she was nothing but bleached meat.

Pharinet led her to a place where, upon finer days, it would be pleasant to sit and watch the ocean. The path widened into a small platform that had been cobbled with stones and wide shells from the beach. A wall of blue rocks provided a waist-high barrier against a drop down to the sand, some sixty feet below.

I do not want to be here, Varencienne thought. We must go back. It is terrible.

Here the sea roared at her, and seemed too close. Pharinet took her arm and pulled her to the wall, so that her thighs were pressed against it.

'Feel the power of it!' Pharinet yelled.

Varencienne saw a wave forming out in the dark turbulent waters. It rose and rose. That one is big, she thought, so big. Then she was looking up and the water was hanging over her head. She screamed and threw her arms around Pharinet, who laughed aloud as the water broke on to them. Varencienne had felt the power, sensed its weight and casual authority. She felt more wet than if she'd immersed herself in a bath. Salt stung her cheeks and eyes. She had been claimed by the sea, yet not devoured. It had marked her.

Pharinet did not push her away, and curled an arm around Varencienne's shoulders. 'Listen to this,' she said. 'It is a traditional rhyme of these parts. "Come rise, come unto me, deepest dream, come from the foam, from the lost and lone. Come rise, come unto me, leaping heart, here to my sight, to my soul."'

'What does it mean? Who does it call?' Varencienne was thinking of drowned lovers, perhaps of mermaids.

Pharinet let her go and raised her arms. She began to murmur words that Varencienne could not quite catch. They seemed almost to make sense to her, but then were only gibberish.

'Is that part of the rhyme?'

Pharinet glanced down at her. 'Yes. It is very old. It is a song to the sea. Does it hear me, do you suppose?'

Varencienne gripped her cloak firmly at her throat and narrowed her eyes against the spray to stare out at the ocean. Beside her, Pharinet's voice was a suggestive whisper, guttural and intense. Varencienne wanted to share the words, to say them. She felt their history in her bones. Surely they summoned something? The ocean seemed to have grown quieter, as if listening to Pharinet's voice. The waves continued to break against the rocks, but now, it seemed, with less intensity.

There is something moving there, far out, beyond the furthest rocks, Varencienne thought. There is a dark core pushing upwards, rising towards the air.

For a moment, her sight blurred and it really seemed as if she could see something. Her heart was beating fast now. She heard a sound, a deep echoing howl that was like water booming through subaquatic caves. How could she have felt afraid of the sea? It demonstrated its power because it was the primal form of all female power; she had always been kin to it. Now, it called to her.

Without thinking, Varencienne began to walk away from Pharinet, down the path towards the threshing water. The only sound in the world was the voice of the ocean; its roar and moan, a melancholy song. Waves came over the low wall that flanked the path. Several times, she was thrown to her knees, but every time, she used the wall on her left to lift herself up, pressing herself against it as she crawled slowly downwards.

I will come into you. Show me your treasures.

She could barely walk now. Wild water, threaded with foam, whirled around her ankles, her knees, dragging at her skirts. Soon, she must let herself go.

Then Pharinet's hands were on her arms, pulling her back. She did not speak, but hauled Varencienne back up the path, until they were again on the clifftop. Varencienne felt numb and drowsy, not cold at all. She was shivering, but her soaked clothes seemed sensual against her body. Her hair and face were stiff with salt.

'Little Ren,' said Pharinet in an arch voice. 'What were you thinking of?'

'It called to me,' Varencienne answered sluggishly, pushing her hair, unsuccessfully, from her mouth. It was like weed all over her face, already drying in the ferocious wind.

'Some calls it is unwise to heed,' Pharinet said. 'Let's go home.'

In the imperial palace, she would have hurried off to bed with possets and hot-bottles, but Pharinet did not seem particularly concerned for Varencienne's health. She took her to a parlour on the first floor, which seemed to be the family's living quarters. It was a strange room; high and narrow and wooden, with tall narrow furniture and a high narrow hearth. It should have seemed uncomfortable, yet was not. This was the personal space of the Palindrake women. Here they whispered together, and they had marked it as their own. The air smelled strongly of woody resin, and the light fluctuating against the walls seemed full of the sea, as if the sun was shining on water outside, although Varencienne could see through the window that it was still raining heavily. Pharinet made her sit down on a chaise longue, covered in plush the colour of seaweed. Presently she thrust a large goblet of liquor into Varencienne's hands. 'That is liquid warmth,' she said. 'Distilled and blended at the castle's feet. Drink it down quickly and I'll pour you another.'

Varencienne did so and, swallowing repeatedly to assuage the spicy burn in her throat, lay back in her chair. A fire raged in the hearth, sending out a wall of heat to her face. She knew she should change out of her wet clothes, go to bed, take a bath, let Oltefney fuss over her full of censure. What had happened out there? She remembered the urge to walk into the sea, the surety that something other than death waited there for her.

She closed her eyes and dozed in the chair, lulled by the cracking of the logs in the fire. She could hear Pharinet moving around, sometimes humming softly beneath her breath. Doors opened and closed somewhere else. There were footsteps. She felt as if people were leaning over her, but lacked the strength to open her eyes.

'You fool, she's drunk!' Everna's voice.

Pharinet, when she answered, sounded excited. 'But it was more than I could have believed, Evvie. The charm. She more than saw something, she went to join it!'

'Hush!' Everna snapped. 'She might be tipsy, but not asleep.'

'She is the one,' said Pharinet.

'She could be,' Everna answered, 'but then you always think that.'

That night, Valraven came to her. The storms had passed, and beyond the windows in Varencienne's bedroom, only vigilant moonlight held sway. He did not knock upon her door, or speak, merely manifested soundlessly at her side, standing there, looking down. She still felt languorously tranquil, an effect of her morning's adventure that had stayed with her throughout the day. As on their wedding night, he lifted aside her bed covers and set about the business of copulating with his wife; a soulless function. And yet, despite her decision to remain unmoved and patiently await the act's conclusion, it seemed that the air beyond her windows was full of moving shadows, and echoing howls, as if lamenting from a far distance, filled her head. She became aware of the hissing of the waves on the shingle far below. It made her thirsty for water, to be immersed in it. Her whole body was fluid, her sex a molten sea creature. Valraven's hard flesh stabbing into it awoke it, made it want to seize and contract. She did not yearn to hold him close, nor for any whisperings of love. She wanted only what he was capable of giving, that simple connection, groin to groin. Curling her legs around his hips, she pulled him deeper, refusing to allow him leave until her body had finished its convulsions of delight.

There was an intense silence between them, then came his voice, low and cold. 'They have got to you already, with their meddling.' He expelled a kind of hissing noise and pulled away from her. She watched him, filled with an utter calm and repletion. The air was cool against her flesh now. Before he'd even left the room, she turned on to her side and slept.

CHAPTER FOUR

Other Women

In the week before Valraven Palindrake was due to return to his command in the east of the empire, the Leckerys came to visit. They arrived in the balmy spring evening, alighting from a low, open carriage drawn by four blond horses. Varencienne, self-conscious of being on display, had dressed herself in dark green and wore her hair in a single plait down her back, much to Oltefney's disgust, although they had decorated it with tiny white flowers. She sat demurely in the great hall, her hands folded in her lap, while the Leckerys made noisy greetings to the Palindrakes. Servants flitted unobtrusively about the room, bearing aperitifs on trays. Varencienne sipped hers too hungrily. She craved light-headedness. She felt nervous.

Saska Leckery, the matriarch, swept towards her and peered down her long nose at Varencienne, emitting silent judgements and opinions. Varencienne felt scorched, laid bare. 'How do you find life beyond Magrast, my dear? Is country living to your taste?' She spoke with the authority of someone who had once lived in the Magravandian city herself, who could tell the difference.

'I like it very much,' Varencienne answered, conscious she might be thought a liar.

The party moved in to the dining room to eat.

Saska had brought two daughters with her, a maiden sister, and a young son of around ten years. The rest of her men, she explained to Varencienne, had been sent to the capital, and the one who'd survived was an administrator for the empire in Mewt.

As Caradore's servants glided silently through the candlelight, dispensing fragrant soup, Saska said, 'I have already lost one son and a husband to Madragore, and pray that my other boy, Merlan, returns.' She glanced with cold eyes at Valraven. 'Have you spoken to the emperor on my behalf?'

'Saska,' Valraven responded in a soft, even tone, 'you know as well as I do that the decision is more in the hands of your son than any other. He believes in his country, and his emperor. He enjoys his work in Mewt. Now, please, enjoy your soup. We have had our people scouring the rock pools for miggions for it since dawn.'

Varencienne noticed that Saska Leckery continued to look at Valraven for several seconds after he had dismissed her from his attention. He had an enemy of sorts in her.

As for Saska's sister, Dimara, Varencienne found her hard to fathom. At one moment, she seemed relaxed and amiable, at others dark-eyed and watchful. She was striking in appearance for an older woman who clearly did little to augment nature's gifts. Varencienne discerned a coolness between Pharinet and Dimara, simply because they were incredibly polite to one another. It was the kind of politeness Varencienne had often seen at court; insincere and concealing snarls. Sometimes she found Dimara looking at her. It was unnerving, although once Varencienne caught her eye, Dimara always softened her examination with a smile.

The daughters were equally intriguing. Ligrana seemed like a younger version of Pharinet, vivacious and flashing, with dark skin and hair. She spent most of the meal laughing too loudly at Pharinet's quiet, sharp remarks. Varencienne, crumbling bread on her plate, wondered if Ligrana was Pharinet's protégé, and whether they had discussed her. Ligrana's attempts to ignore her bordered on rudeness. In an arch and affected voice, she reminded the whole company continually of Pharinet's accomplishments and escapades. Niska was different. She seemed fragile and fey, quite dark of skin but with strange water-coloured hair that had little hue at all. Waterweed. She was a mermaid come to land, mute and desiccating. She did not speak at all, but ate with the focused concentration of a cat, neat and with small movements. Her brow was clear, yet it seemed that deep inside she was frowning in bewilderment. Her veil of pale hair obscured her face for most of the time. If she was not a mercreature, then she would have been brought up by wild animals and had only recently learned the manners of being human. The boy child, Foylen, was a soldier in the making; respectful and courteous, speaking only when addressed. His mother, Saska herself, gave the impression of being large, although she was not, and had the neat waist of a woman much younger than she was. She should have been striking to look at, but smothered tears had made pouches around her eyes, which destroyed her beauty. Her mouth also had soured. We wear our troubles on our faces, Varencienne thought, then imagined herself with frozen agony etched into the set of her mouth. It wouldn't happen. She was too young to believe that life would ever treat her that cruelly.

These people were the Palindrakes' closest friends. No men, of course, for the emperor's campaigns had taken them all. Varencienne had already learned this was the case with all the noble families of Caradore. Men had been a small part of the lives of women in Magrast, but here it was different and their absence left a hole.

Saska turned her vivisecting gaze upon Varencienne. 'How much have you seen of the countryside, my dear? Have you been taken to the Chair and the rock village?'

Varencienne shook her head. 'I have spent much time at the beach; there is so much to see.'

'Pharinet, Everna, you are neglecting your duties. A newcomer should be shown the sights of Caradore.'

'There is plenty of time,' drawled Pharinet.

For two weeks, Varencienne had been exploring the coves below the castle. Pharinet had not offered to accompany her again, and Valraven seemed to have forgotten his concern about the danger of cliff paths. Perhaps the family hoped she would again feel compelled to walk into the waves, and thus be rid of her. That had not happened, however. Sometimes she thought of the fragments of conversation she had heard between Everna and Pharinet after their visit to the sea wall. Afterwards, she had wondered whether she'd dreamed it. She had returned to the seawall alone, but it seemed different now that the weather had changed and the mild spring currents slipped up the coast. There was no repetition of that strange compulsion to enter the waves. However, the experience had been important. After it, her love for the sea had been instant and overwhelming. She woke each morning desperate to get back to it, to commune with it in silence, let it watch her. She knew she had been altered in some way; the sea had touched her at a vulnerable time, but it had not called to her so strongly again.

She wondered too whether the experience had altered her in other ways. Sometimes she caught sight of strange smoky black shadows on the edge of her vision. When she turned to look, there was never anything there. Often she smelled burning in odd places around the castle, as if clothes were on fire, or curtains, but when she investigated, she could never find any evidence of it.

'You must, of course, visit us at Norgance,' Saska said. 'You will find the castles in Caradore all so different, representing the characteristics of their respective families. "Our homes are our faces" – that is an old saying.'

'I would love to come,' Varencienne said. It was the truth. The women of Caradore had not become close to her in any way, and her husband was an impenetrable void, yet Varencienne felt very much at home in the area. Even Ligrana's obvious manoeuvres to discomfort her could not distress her. It no longer mattered what people thought.

After the meal, the company walked slowly into one of the drawing-rooms. Outside, shingle hissed beneath the raking caress of the waves and the sky was clear, full of stars. Varencienne had to fight a compulsion to go and stand by the window, stare out. She was always looking for shadows across the stars, although she had experienced no strange phenomena since her first night in the castle, and if the perigorts had screamed, she had slept through it.

Valraven stood before the hearth, removed from his companions, while still their focus. He was a prize to them, to be admired, as if looking at him was a blessing. Varencienne experienced no sense of ownership. She had never stroked his hair, or even pressed her hand against his warm flesh. He had come to her bed three times, and since the night when she had offered him her hunger, his body had not affected her. He did what had to be done; she endured it. They did not speak like friends. Perhaps her closeness with Bayard had misled her as to how men and women might interact. As a younger girl, she had read the old stories of love and chivalry, and had believed a man would come to his wife in love and adoration. Perhaps this was the truth of it: cold commerce. It did not matter. Soon he would be gone and Varencienne would surrender herself to her dreams; walk along the empty beaches, making pictures in her mind of circumstances she could barely imagine. Men are made for war, she thought, for without it, we might have them round us all the time. It is the comfort of women. Briefly, she imagined a world without men, and it seemed a place of light and freedom.

'Varencienne.' Her name had been spoken, and she found she'd wandered to the window without realizing it. There was a presence hovering nearby that felt barely human. Varencienne looked into Niska's grey-green eyes, but Niska hadn't called her. That was Saska, sitting with Everna, Dimara and Oltefney. 'Come here, my dear.'

They had been plotting, Varencienne thought. She smiled at them mildly.

'We have decided you must come to Norgance very soon,' Saska said.

'Thank you, I shall look forward to it.'

'Next week,' Saska continued. 'Can you ride?'

'A little.' Since she'd been able to walk, she had been led round the palace gardens on her pony twice a week, by an old groom, but she'd never taken command of the reins herself. She had been strapped into a bucket seat, with her legs hanging over to one side. They had taught her to make her spine long, her body erect. All ladies of breeding should know how to sit on a horse correctly, and their horses were without spirit, buffed to a gloss and bedecked with gilded leather.

'It is only a two-hour ride,' said Saska. She glanced at her sister. 'Perhaps Pharinet could bring you. You do not visit us regularly enough, Pharry.'

Varencienne noticed the almost imperceptible grimace that shivered across Dimara's face.

Pharinet, sitting listening to Ligrana, who was curled at her feet, looked up. 'You know why it's difficult for me to come,' she said. 'I hoped you understood.'

The atmosphere in the room immediately condensed. A strange expression crossed Saska's face: pain and collusion. Dimara stared at Pharinet as if she'd uttered an obscenity.

'Your memories will always be there,' Saska said softly.

Pharinet smiled a little, ducked her head. 'Of course I'll bring Ren over.' she said. 'You are almost family, and I'm sure she'll love Norgance.'

Everna then changed the subject and began to talk about people of whom Varencienne had never heard. What had happened in Norgance? Varencienne wondered. She thought of Pharinet, younger, but no wilder than she was now, and there was a shadowy space in the picture where something, or someone, else must fit.

The next day, Pharinet came hunting for Varencienne and found her on the beach. Varencienne was both pleased to see her, and slightly annoyed that her dreams had been interrupted. She had been imagining the lives of the seapeople, who came into the caves at night to make strange worship to a god that lived on neither land nor sea, but had a foot in each element. Something about the fantasy wasn't quite right, and she had been working on it.

'Little Ren, you spend so much time alone,' said Pharinet, her hands on her hips, her eyes looking out past Varencienne to the horizon.

'I like to be alone,' Varencienne replied.

'You are a dreamer!' There was no mockery in Pharinet's voice; her amusement seemed affectionate.

Varencienne felt bold. 'I suppose I am. My head likes making up stories. They seem so much better than real life.'

'So, what kind of story were you just thinking of? You were lost in it. I don't believe you saw me coming.'

Varencienne smiled at this, and for the first time in her life, related her imaginings aloud. 'But I have to work out a detail,' she said. 'Something doesn't feel right.'

'Perhaps you should have a goddess, rather than a god,' Pharinet suggested. 'Or else, a goddess of the sea, who meets in the shore cave with her lover, a god of the land.'

Varencienne studied Pharinet for a moment, searching for irony. 'A goddess, yes,' she said at last, 'but no god. I should have thought of that. Whenever I pray, it is to Mivian, Madragore's granddaughter.' But Mivian did not feel real, not like Madragore with his heavy presence and dour, fanatical priests.

'I can see you praying,' Pharinet said. Perhaps she too had a fecund imagination.

They walked together along the shore, the sea rising and collapsing around them, sneaking up in circular, shallow swathes, cutting them off from the land. Varencienne's skirts were soaked. Her feet were bare.

'You are very much at home here,' Pharinet said. 'Fey little maid. So lonely, and yet not.'

She has been thinking about me, Varencienne realized, and there seemed some threat to her isolation in that. 'Are we going to Norgance?'

'That is why I came to find you,' Pharinet said. 'I know little of you, yet suspect the visit does not inspire a great eagerness within you.'

'Not at all. I would like to go.' She paused. 'Niska is an odd girl, though. Is all well with her?'

'She's a sea child, perhaps the girl you would have been if you'd been born in Caradore. Don't be misled by appearances. She's shy in new company. I think you will like her eventually.'

A friend, Varencienne thought, someone like me. 'Ligrana is like you,' she said. 'Or wants to be.'

Pharinet laughed. 'I am a bad influence. I spent a lot of time in Norgance when Ligrana was younger. She's only a couple of years older than you, whereas Niska is almost twenty-four.'

'Really! I would have thought it the other way round.'

'Niska hasn't grown up. I don't think she wants to.'

Varencienne was silent. They continued their walk, with no discomfort between them. Then Varencienne said, 'What is that on the sand?' They walked towards it, and saw that it was a human arm, bleached by the sea, and rotting.

Varencienne stared at it in wonder. It was a man's arm, and had once flexed upon his body, lifted things, perhaps bore weapons. 'How did it get here?'

'On the deep currents,' Pharinet said, poking the arm with her booted foot. 'There will have been a sea battle further south. I heard a fleet of small, fast ships from Berringey tried to intercept the imperial flotilla. Our admirals had the priests conjure up a red storm, and the invaders all perished in a swell of fire and steam.'

'How do you hear of things like that?' Varencienne asked.

Pharinet studied her for a moment. 'News travels,' she said, 'and is all around you if you want to hear it.'

'I don't know about the wars,' Varencienne said. 'I know so little about my country, really.' She looked around herself, her arms wrapped over her chest, as if shocks of reality might uncover themselves at any moment.

'I'm not surprised,' Pharinet said in a dry voice.

Varencienne looked down at the arm. 'He might have had a wife, or sisters somewhere.'

'And they might even mourn his loss,' added Pharinet.

Varencienne glanced up at her. She sensed censure, but could not offer an argument. 'He might have survived without his arm.'

Pharinet laughed without humour. 'That is probably more of a fantasy than your dreams of the merfolk and their husbandless goddess.' She walked on ahead then, and after a few minutes Varencienne followed her.

Norgance was further inland. If Caradore was like a prancing horse, frozen on the cliffs, the flags of its mane still fluttering, Norgance was a lazy grey lizard lying close to the land, its limbs relaxed and sprawling. It lay in a valley, surrounded by sharp, golden-lichened cliffs. At one end, a waterfall crashed into a deep pool and the slow black wheel of a watermill churned in the sunlight, surrounded by rainbows. From the high road that ribboned over the lip of the cliffs and down to the valley, Norgance and its estates looked like child's toys that Varencienne could pick up and examine. Inside each building would be tiny people, simulacra dashing about their business, speaking in high squeaks.

Varencienne could not ride as well as Pharinet, and the journey had taken longer than anticipated. Pharinet had been patient and willing to instruct her companion. Varencienne enjoyed the freedom. She wanted to control a horse with expertise and gallop about the wild land. She would ride astride, like Pharinet did, and dare to wear the clothes of a boy.

Pharinet had spoken at some length about her brother. She was clearly incapable of understanding that Varencienne did not, and could not, love him like she did herself. 'Val was such a beautiful boy,' she said, her eyes distant with memories. 'Everyone loved him. We were inseparable as children. It breaks my heart we rarely see him now.'

Varencienne sensed a comment was necessary. 'I miss my favourite brother in the same way. It's strange isn't it, that we can have such relationships with our brothers. It's very different to any other kind.'

Pharinet delivered a narrow glance. 'Yes. It has its special qualities.' She sighed. 'Oh, Ren, I wish you knew him as I did, but some part of him is buried so deep now. I have a clear picture of a day we spent together one summer. We were looking for sand crabs down by the shore, and I had just found a really big one with snapping claws. Val was walking towards the sea and I called his name. I shall never forget when he paused and turned, looked back over his shoulder at me. His eyes, his face, were full of secrets and humour. I felt as if an arrow of the sun had pierced my heart. His beauty seemed doomed, somehow.'

Varencienne felt uncomfortable with the intimacy of this story. 'Are you twins? You look very alike.'

She nodded. 'Yes. Our mother succumbed not long after we were born. Apparently the strain of bearing two children was too much for her. Our father was, like Val is now, often away on the emperor's business. We were brought up by Everna. She might as well be our mother.'

'I was a bit afraid of her at first, but she seems very nice.' Everna, though not an effusive woman, often did small things to ensure Varencienne's comfort, but they rarely met other than at mealtimes.

Pharinet laughed a little sadly. 'Poor Evvie! Her heart was broken once, but I expect you've already dreamed up the possibility of that with your love of inventing stories.'

'No!' Varencienne was intrigued. The revelation explained a lot to her. 'Who was it? When did it happen?'

Pharinet's laughter was now more joyous. 'Oh, you love the idea, I knew it. He was quite a plain boy, actually. Val and I were about fifteen when it happened. Everna fell in love and it was so strange to see, because she'd always seemed so old and irredeemably unmarried. We thought it was funny the way she mooned about the place, holding books of poetry over her heart.'

'Did he leave her, or betray her?'

'No,' Pharinet said shortly, and all the joy left her voice. 'He drowned.'

'How terrible!'

'That is the way of things in Caradore. We love, they die.'

Varencienne remembered certain remarks Pharinet had made when the Leckerys had visited the previous week. She contemplated bringing the subject up, but decided against it. Even though Pharinet was outwardly friendly, Varencienne sensed an invisible boundary of familiarity, which she must not attempt to cross. *I wonder if she likes me now. Will a day come when I know all about her?*

They paused above the valley of Norgance, where Pharinet leaned forward in her saddle. 'I spent so many dizzy hours here as a girl.' She sighed. 'How quickly time passes. It was such a luxury then. I thought I had so much of it.'

'You still do!' Varencienne said. She did not want to see shadows about vibrant Pharinet.

'Yes, yes, but some things time steals away from us for ever.' She sighed again, more heavily. *It was not sadness in her*, Varencienne thought, *but wistfulness, and joyful memories.*

'Tell me another memory,' Varencienne said.

Pharinet glanced at her sidelong, one eyebrow raised. 'Well!' She thought in silence for a moment. 'I remember when I was twelve and Niska and Ligrana's brother Merlan was born. I was staying here, and went up the cliff path with my friend . . .' She frowned.

Who was the friend? Varencienne wondered, but kept quiet, her face a mask of enquiry.

'Ellony – Merlan's older sister . . . She is dead now. We went to the Ronduel, a circle of megaliths, on the moor above the cliffs over there. We sang prayers and made a cairn of grass and flowers. I can still smell it. We asked for the things that girls will – a handsome lover, the magic within to bloom. We each had our sights set, even then. And because we believed, those things came to pass, but our prayers could not have been right, because now it is all lost.'

She would not say more, Varencienne knew. Her words had been carefully selected, like light seen through the think of shivering curtains. Now her eyes peered back into the past, and she looked older. *I have no such moments to think of*, Varencienne thought. The most exciting episodes of her past life had been evenings spent with her friends. It had happened almost every night, but sometimes a special spark had come into the gathering and they had somehow laughed more freely, felt strangely excited, almost expectant. Perhaps Pharinet and her friend had felt that way too, but they had been out here in the wild air of Caradore, where dreams were more likely to become reality.

Pharinet gathered up the reins of her horse. 'We must not dwell on the past,' she said. 'We must always look forward, even if only into clouds.' She urged her mount down the steep path and Varencienne followed, her

181

mind high up on the opposite clifftop, where the ghosts of two girls spun around the glistening, silent stones that laid their shadows over them.

It was Niska who suggested they take Varencienne up to the Ronduel. A dainty feast of sweet cakes and honeyed tea had been consumed, and Varencienne's throat was sore from speaking so much. She had been relieved to discover that Saska's sister, Dimara, was not present. If she had been, Varencienne was sure she wouldn't have been able to converse so easily. The Leckerys had interrogated her about her life in Magrast, and Varencienne had been surprised at how much she could remember. 'She has an eye for details,' Pharinet said. 'She has to store them all up so she can reinvent them.'

'Oh?' Saska put her head on one side.

Pharinet should not have said that. What more would she say?

'Our little Ren creates new worlds all the time,' Pharinet continued. 'It is a talent she has.'

Was she being mocking, or had she simply accepted Varencienne's tendency to fantasize as an endearing trait? Varencienne felt some explanation was needed. 'I had so much spare time back home.'

'And you didn't leave the palace much,' Saska said, in apparent sympathy.

Varencienne put down her cup. 'No.' The tea had left a sticky feeling in the back of her mouth. 'But I had a lot of books. Some of them were very old and talked about countries that do not even exist any more.'

Saska shifted on her seat. 'Well, your father might have had a lot to do with that.'

'Now, now,' said Pharinet lightly, then, to Ligrana, 'How about we take Ren for a walk to the mill?'

'No,' said Niska, who had so far uttered no sound. 'To the Ronduel.'

Varencienne thought Pharinet might object to the idea, as she seemed to have intimate memories connected with the place, but Pharinet only smiled slowly. 'Yes, good idea. Ren should see it.'

Varencienne could not walk as quickly as the other women up the cliff path. They were fit and strong, with wide lungs used to inhaling the heady air of Caradore. They were like nimble deer, their legs pumping without effort. No noblewoman of Magrast would have exerted herself so strenuously. It made sweat come – and a lady could not allow such an indignity. Varencienne was conscious of the hot prickle beneath her arms and on her upper lip. Twice she had to pause and press her hand to her side. Would she faint before she reached the top?

'Ren, you have been such a hearthcat,' Pharinet said, grinning. 'You need more than a walk across the shore every day to wake up your body.'

Ligrana laughed rather cruelly, but then Pharinet put her arm around Varencienne's shoulders. 'Come on, I'll give you a ride.' She crouched down, her black hair spilling forward, and then Varencienne was up on Pharinet's back, like she used to climb on to Bayard when she was younger. She could see so much more now, the valley spread out below, the twisting, glittering water, the slow procession of the herds, the dancing branches of the trees. Pharinet's body worked surely beneath her, like a beast of burden, as if she could not feel Varencienne's weight at all. Ligrana had been put in her place. She looked sullen now.

At the top of the cliff a wide expanse of short wiry grass yawned before them, while in the hazy distance, there were more mountains. But they were insignificant compared to the Ronduel; that was at once fragile and monstrous; its gargantuan stones balanced delicately upon one another. They had braved the winds and the fierce rains for perhaps thousands of years.

Varencienne scrambled down from Pharinet's back. 'It's incredible!' she exclaimed, another of those obvious remarks that seemed to fall out of her mouth at times when she wished they wouldn't.

This time, Pharinet did not smirk, and Ligrana seemed not to have heard.

'Strong magic here,' Niska said, slipping a thin, cold hand through Varencienne's elbow. Her touch was disturbing, the tickle of a fish's fin.

The women walked slowly beneath the shadows of the dolmens and Varencienne could not help but feel that once they were enclosed by the stones, the wind could no longer reach them; they had entered a doorway through time. She would not have been surprised to see a twelve-year-old Pharinet squatting on the grass, petals and fragments of grass winnowing through her fingers. But I should be surprised, Varencienne thought. I have never seen a ghost, and surely would be frightened of it. Yet I really expect to see her at any moment, and I would not be afraid at all. It would seem complete, somehow, and natural.

'Make a wish,' Niska murmured. 'Everyone does the first time they come here.'

I can't think. It's too sudden. I should have been warned. The wrong thought will come into my head. Varencienne laughed nervously. She must not squander this moment, yet her mind was empty.

Pharinet and Ligrana were walking together by the furthest stones. They seemed a hundred miles away. I wish to understand, Varencienne thought.

It seemed inadequate, too small. Then she added, don't let him make me have a child. Please. That was firm and definite, a blood-coloured thought in her head. Perhaps she should dare to wish to be a widow.

Then Pharinet was up close to her again. 'Remember wishes might come true,' she said, her voice a thin strand on the wind which had somehow come coursing around their shins once more. Skirts threshed and hair lashed. They were like wild women. Varencienne put her hands against her mouth and laughed. She felt her age, young and full of potential.

'The old magi who built this place will have heard your wish,' Pharinet said. She laid a hand against the nearest stone. 'If you have pleased them, they will grant it.'

'I hope so,' Varencienne said. She too touched the stone, expecting to feel a vibration or strange heat. She felt nothing but the cold grain of the rock beneath her fingers. 'Why did they build this place?'

'It was a kind of church,' Ligrana said. 'Built long before the gods of the empire were born as thoughts in the heads of men.'

Varencienne suspected they were Pharinet's words, secondhand. 'Were there no gods before?'

Ligrana opened her mouth to speak, and Pharinet gave her a sharp look.

'Is it a secret?' Varencienne said into the wind. The women were silent around her, she could feel their complicity. She had stumbled upon something.

'Not really,' Pharinet said at last. 'There are old gods of the land, and old beliefs, and old customs. Times change.'

She has worshipped here, Varencienne thought. She told me so. Who heard her prayers?

'Madragore is the only power now,' said Ligrana. 'Your family have seen to that.'

This was a puzzle. The slightly barbed remarks were becoming ever more frequent. The Palindrakes and the Leckerys gave up their sons, their husbands and fathers to the empire, yet the women seemed to seethe against it. 'It is nothing to do with me,' Varencienne said, wishing at once that she hadn't. Just by saying it, she was making herself a part of what they subtly accused her. Hadn't someone said to her she would be her father's envoy in Caradore? She did not want to be. She was herself, very much herself. Pharinet knew that, didn't she?

As they slithered and jumped back down the cliff path to Norgance, Varencienne pondered what she had learned. She wanted Pharinet and the others to trust her. This feeling was new and raw inside her. Their insinuations made her feel like an unwanted interloper, and urged her to justify herself. This felt wrong, because she knew it did not help. The women of Caradore had secrets and she was flitting around the hidden flames of them, curious and in danger of being scorched. The land pulsed with ancient mysteries that she wanted to penetrate. She belonged here; the others just did not know it.

She and Pharinet rode home long before the sun set. They travelled for a while in silence, Varencienne still smarting from the way she'd been excluded. Pharinet and the Leckerys had a history between them; she was new and she must be patient and not resentful. As a royal princess, she should be above petty feeling, but she felt she must prove herself in some way. Perhaps it could begin with a question. 'Pharinet, are you suspicious of me?'

Pharinet turned round in the saddle, a quizzical expression on her face. 'In what way, little Ren?'

'Because I am the daughter of the emperor. I'm not blind to the feelings in Caradore. There is a problem, I can sense it. I was not sent here as a spy, I was just married off. I am no one really. I have barely met my father.'

Pharinet pulled her horse to a halt and Varencienne's mount came up alongside. 'What's prompted this?'

Varencienne shrugged awkwardly. 'Just a feeling. The Leckerys *are* suspicious of me. I feel I've done something wrong, but know I haven't. There's nothing I can do about who my parents are. It's not my fault.'

Pharinet nodded, her face thoughtful. 'Perhaps I should explain about how people feel. This is an old country and was once independent. People don't forget. They burn inside for freedom.'

'I can't see how you're not free.'

Pharinet laughed. 'Oh Ren, you are so innocent! We are not free because Saska has lost a son and a husband in the campaigns and her remaining son is away in Mewt. We are not free because Valraven has no choice but to be what your father wants him to be. The sacrifice of men guarantees we women still have these splendid old domains to wander around in, but we wander around them alone. That is the price, and it does not give freedom.'

'The empire expands to give people liberty, from oppression and cruelty.' Varencienne was aware of a hateful primness in her voice. Even to her, the comment sounded ridiculous and uninformed.

'You will have been fed that along with your mother's milk,' Pharinet said dryly. 'Empire isn't about liberty, it's about power and the expansion of power. It's about fear, not just of those who cower before the inexorable dark clouds, but the men who hide within them, who are afraid of losing what they have. Maybe the empire believes it fights oppression and cruelty, but it has become the very thing it sought to alleviate. Perhaps it was not always so. Perhaps one time in generations past, an exhausted lord asked some ancestor of yours for aid in securing his lands. Perhaps that was where the hunger started, within a noble cause. Nobody really knows, because history is rewritten by emperors.'

None of this equated with the languorous life Varencienne had known in Magrast. Women sewing and women talking, candlelight and the scent of flowers and incense. Everything had been so slow and simple. 'What you are saying is not my life. I know nothing of it. You should not judge me for what I do not know.'

'I do not judge you, Ren. We are wary, and perhaps you are right in saying we believe you might report back to your family. Can you blame us?'

'I have not even written to my mother. My real family were my friends—' she paused '—except for my brother, Bayard.'

'Ah yes,' said Pharinet, after a pause. 'Bayard.' Her voice made his name sound dark.

Varencienne shuddered inside. 'You know him.' It did not have to be a question. That shocked her. She had accidentally turned over a stone and found another secret.

'Yes, I have met Bayard,' Pharinet said. 'He came to Caradore once.'

'He never told me. When?'

Pharinet shrugged. 'Oh, some years ago now. Val got to know him when he went to Magrast to begin his training.'

Varencienne sensed Pharinet had not liked Bayard. Was this because he had reported back to their father? But what could he have said? It could be the reason, however, why nobody trusted her. 'He never told me,' she said again, as hurt as if he'd told a stranger he despised her.

'Well, no doubt he had his reasons.' Pharinet's face assumed a smile which seemed forced. 'It's all in the past.'

'Did he do something to upset you?'

Pharinet's lips became pursed. 'Not in any way you might think. I'd rather not discuss it.'

Varencienne could not respond to this. She sensed a story, another of Pharinet's memories that she would not share. The subject must be abandoned. 'I want to be here,' she said. 'This is my home now. Let me live in it.'

Pharinet smiled more freely. 'You will have a long life, little Ren. Take each day at a time.'

That night Valraven came to Varencienne's bed. At dinner, he'd told the family he would be leaving for the south in the morning. This nocturnal visit would be his last for now, perhaps for ever. As he knelt between her splayed thighs, unbelting his robe, Varencienne thought of the things Pharinet had told her earlier that day. She tried to imagine the boy who'd gone crabbing on the beach, but if he lived in Valraven now, he was deep in hiding. She let him do as he wished, but as he rose from the bed, she said, 'Do you like going away on campaign? Are you looking forward to going back to it?'

He looked at her with naked surprise. It was, after all, the first time she had ever spoken to him on these occasions. 'My sisters have been filling your head,' he said in the mild way he had that now infuriated her because it was so exclusive.

She sat up in the tangled bed. 'It has nothing to do with that. I just wondered.'

For a while he looked at her, perhaps thinking he did not like this new, talkative aspect, yet he did not leave her immediately as she'd thought he might. 'We all have our duty, Varencienne. I'm sure you understand that.'

His words made her flush. This would not work; she had been mistaken. Her confidence sank, and she lay down again, staring at him. In a strange sort of way, she felt he was now familiar to her, but of course he was not. The image she had of him was Pharinet's, not hers, the image of a boy who no longer existed. Perhaps it would help if she could bring herself to call him 'Val', which was a name his loved ones used, but she could not. She still shrank from addressing him personally.

'You know my brother, Bayard,' she said. 'Pharinet told me he came here once.'

Valraven's eyes seemed to turn to obsidian. She had angered him, clearly. 'Some time ago,' he said.

'Will you see him when you return to your unit?'

'I don't know.' He smiled tightly, showing her that he did not want to smile, and left the room, closing the door quietly behind him. No tender, parting words for the new wife. Not even a polite 'good-bye'. He just used her and left, irritated because she wanted to talk to him. Pharinet did not know him at all. She was in love with a fantasy.

After a few moments, Varencienne hurled herself from the bed, stumbling, striking her knee on the floor. She clawed her way into a dressing-gown and then, with her knee still burning, ran across the room and yanked open the door. Beyond, the corridor was silent and empty, star-shine coming down through the skylights. All was stillness. She imagined Valraven might have folded himself up into a shadow and flown away, the moment the door had closed. What would she had done if she'd found him there? She shivered, but it was not that cold.

187

She found herself downstairs, padding through the great hall. The banners shifted restlessly on the walls, and overhead monstrous candelabra of wood and iron swayed in the invading wind. Particles of sand sifted across the floor. She left footprints in them.

Outside, the wind seemed warm. She walked in a daze, like the ghost she'd always dreamed she could be, out through the castle walls, through the sleeping village around it, towards the sea. Nobody challenged her or tried to stop her, and she could not stop herself. Her heart raged with conflicting feelings; humiliation, anger, injustice. The waves were a roar ahead of her, throwing themselves at the land. It was like someone angry banging their head against a wall, again and again and again. The foam, as it slithered down the sand, would be bloody.

Then, as if the journey had been completed in an instant, she was sitting on the cold, hard shore, watching the grey waves heave and wrestle with the impassive rocks. The tides were senseless, all that energy expended in the endless crash and rise. Why didn't the sea stay calm and temperate, always at the same level, flowing evenly around the rocky spikes and caves? The sound of it filled her head. She stood up and yelled, 'Stop it! Stop it!' but her voice was a tiny, useless squeal. The waves were like the ragged, lacy wings of a swarm of great beasts that battled beneath the surface. She could see their snouts breaking through, blowing out spume. They could march on splayed claws towards her and then they might bow their weed-crowned heads at her feet, or else devour her in fury. Perhaps the choice was hers.

She felt full of tears, but could not weep. Energy raged about her body, so that she had to run down the beach, her nightgown flapping, her hair a pale banner on the wind. Croaking out dry sobs, she began to climb on to the rocks that were continually being drenched in spray. They were a hard, black tongue poking out into the sea that she was driven to walk, scramble and jump along. If she fell, the waves would grab and kill her, but she would not fall. The feelings that raged and crashed within her would keep her safe. Tonight, she felt as strong as the sea itself. It was not calling to her, as before. She felt quite apart from it, even despised it. This was Valraven's beach, the senseless waves were his. They were like a physical expression of all the humanity dammed up inside him; natural feelings that had found a way to wear the obstruction away, so they could pour out and engulf and drown.

Sometimes a greater wave would come pouncing up and collapse upon her, and she would be thrown down on to the sharp wet stone. Her hands and feet were cut, her nightdress and gown heavy and torn about her body. She knew she should feel cold, but her flesh was numb. Eventually she reached the far end of the promontory, where there was a narrow ledge above the tumbling waves. Here she pressed her back against the wet, barnacled rock, her arms spread along it. The tide was going out; she was not in that much danger. She would stand here and watch it leave, show the sea how unafraid she was.

Then she saw it; a wave that was not a wave. It rose up, and did not fall. It continued to rise, spreading itself out in a lacy fan that resolved into tattered wings. There was a long neck like the skeleton of a viper, delicate and coralline. The body was agile and pale as shell, the limbs fragile and clawed. It was ruffled with a frill of white weed, and it uttered a great, honking cry, tossing up its equine head. Ancient fishing nets were caught about its body, hung with curtains of deep-sea weed. There were spars of broken ships caught in them, and pale objects that might be human bones. Soft anemones bulged like jewels from the creature's hide. It was monstrous yet beautiful, like Valraven; full of indifferent power. It had white, cats' eyes, the size of fists. Was this a perigort? It did not look like a bird, yet it had wings. No bird could ever be that big. It lunged towards Varencienne where she stood frozen against the rock. Hovering before her, it thrust out its dripping muzzle and she gagged on a strong stench of brine and fish. The great head turned to the side, examined her through one unblinking eye. Its breath was cold, smoking.

Varencienne could not scream and was beyond feeling terror. The creature hung motionless before her for perhaps only a second and then reeled away with unnatural speed, up into the sky.

Her back was arched against the rock; she felt her thighs hot and damp from the terrified release of urine. Her body ached and blood ran down her arms, the cuts stinging fiercely. She could not get back to the castle. She would die here. A sob bubbled out of her constricted throat. She called out in her mind, 'Pharinet! Pharinet!' The creature might come back, or a different one rise from the insane turbulence around her. But this time, there was no Pharinet to pull her back to safety. She had only herself. Do it, she said aloud through clenched teeth. Move. Quickly. Now. You got here, now get back.

Slowly she edged around the rock, her legs insubstantial beneath her. She crawled back towards the beach, falling and scrabbling, determined not to cry. This was what she'd wanted, wasn't it? Now she must be brave enough to finish the adventure.

When she reached the sand, she collapsed into a ball, pressing her head down between her knees, her arms reaching out ahead of her along the shore. Every muscle in her body was burning with cold and exertion. But she had won. She had faced the power and returned to land alive. She rolled on to her back and lay with her knees arched, her feet planted firmly on the damp sand. A soft ripple of laughter came out of her. She had never felt so strong.

It took some time to find Pharinet's sleeping chamber. She found the sisters' quarters fairly quickly and then she had to open door after door. When she found her quarry, she slunk into the room like a predator, then knelt dripping beside Pharinet's bed. The woman looked vulnerable in sleep, her jaw slack and sagging. Varencienne reached out with icy hands and shook her awake. Pharinet jumped up with a start, her eyes round with terror. She did not seem to recognize who knelt there. 'I saw it,' Varencienne hissed. 'It came up out of the sea.' Her fingers were flexing before her like the bony claws of the beast.

The fear went out of Pharinet's eyes. She wiped sleep-tangled hair from her brow. 'You are a little fool,' she said. 'Hand me my robe.'

CHAPTER FIVE

Dragon Priestess

'What did you think you saw?' Pharinet asked. They were in her small private room, strewn with her clothes, and tea was brewing over the fire.

Varencienne was shivering now, wrapped in a cloak of Pharinet's. 'I'm not sure. A monster.' She rubbed her numb fingers together. 'I've heard it before, I think. At night. What is it? It seemed to know me.' She described as much as she could remember of what had happened. 'I called for you, Pharinet, but knew you could not come to me. I had to rescue myself. It was very important.'

Pharinet sighed and sat down on a couch. 'What you have seen is impossible,' she said, 'yet perhaps not. Can I confide in you, Ren? What I have to say is a secret of Caradorean women.'

'Of course you can confide in me,' Varencienne said. 'I will never speak of it to anyone.'

'Well, what you described sounds like a sea dragon, or the memory of one.'

'A sea dragon.' Varencienne paused, frowning. 'It seemed very real, not a ghost at all.'

'Whether real or not, it came to you, and that in itself is remarkably significant. It looked upon you, Valraven's wife, but did not mark you for good or bad.'

'Mark me?'

'You are what we call the "sea wife", the wife of the dragon heir,' Pharinet said. 'The sea dragons are ancient elemental creatures, but the legends tell us they are banished from this world. Your family was responsible for this, many years ago.'

Varencienne leaned forward. 'Tell me about it.'

At the end of the story, when Pharinet described how she became a priestess of the dragons, Varencienne sensed there was more, but perhaps that would be revealed in time. She reached out with a cold hand and touched Pharinet's fingers, which were laced on her lap. 'Thank you. I know now that you trust me.'

Pharinet smiled uneasily. 'It's not that difficult. I believe your family know more of these legends and their implications than we do.'

'Really? Why do you say that?'

Pharinet shrugged and went to the fire to busy herself with the kettle, which was now puffing steam into the room. 'Just a feeling.'

'I knew from the moment I came here that I would find magic in Caradore,' Varencienne said.

'Don't look so dreamy. The dragons aren't sweet, fairy creatures. They take lives and sanity.'

'You speak as if from experience.'

Pharinet sighed and shrugged. 'You could say that.'

'Will you not tell me about it?'

'It is very late at night, and I'm tempted, because the dark encourages us to speak our hearts, but no, little Ren, don't drag my sad songs from me. Some things are best forgotten.'

Varencienne knew that whatever those things were, Pharinet had far from forgotten them. 'That day, when you took me to the sea, I had a feeling that you knew something about me or recognized something within me. I heard you talking with Everna while you thought I was asleep. Can you at least explain that?'

'Everna and I have slight differences in our beliefs. She is a traditionalist, and is quite happy to keep the old ways alive. But they are just like little plays, meaningless ritual. I think the dragons, and other elemental beasts like them, are symbols for the life of the world. I think humans have become estranged from that power, to their detriment.' She handed Varencienne a hot mug. 'Drink that. You need some warmth in you.'

'You haven't answered my question.'

Pharinet sat down again, and took a sip of her tea. 'These are not the easiest concepts to describe. I believe that my brother, Valraven, still carries a vestige of the original power, and that his wife – you – are, or can be, the channel for that.'

'You're saying you believe I can bring the dragons back.'

'Nothing quite that dramatic. I think between you, you could bring that element alive again in Caradore. Magravandians are fire people, which can be seen as the opposite of water. But both are essential.'

'What effect will that have?'

'I don't know. Maybe a tiny shift in people's hearts, to instigate a greater change.'

'The downfall of the empire?'

'I would not expect you to conspire in that. Maybe we have to look at things on a smaller scale. Valraven needs to come home, in a spiritual sense.'

'What does he think about all this?' Varencienne had a feeling he would not believe such things.

'Val does not know everything,' Pharinet said carefully. 'He does not want to. The little he does know has led him to believe that meddling in ancient magic is dangerous and foolish. He thinks it is all a delusion adhered to by people who are hungry for temporal power.'

'He isn't the man you want him to be,' Varencienne said. 'He is a creature of the imperial army. I can see that. I can sense it. He has no warm feelings for anything or anyone. You cannot shape a person like that into a spiritual leader.'

'He wasn't always that way,' Pharinet said. 'Life has changed him.'

They were silent for a while, then Varencienne said, 'Do you think I was meant to come here?'

Pharinet did not answer immediately. 'I'm not sure that matters. You *are* here, and you obviously have an affinity for the land. I think you love Caradore, because it can give you freedom of a kind you've never experienced before. You seem to me to be a wild and joyous creature, but those aspects are contained. I see the potential for release.'

'I think I *was* meant to come here,' Varencienne said, 'but for myself, not Valraven, or you or an old legend. Part of me was already here.'

Pharinet smiled into her tea. 'It really is very late. Drink up, and go to your bed. We can talk about this again tomorrow.'

Varencienne lay awake, her mind racing. She could not hope to sleep. It was as if she'd somehow stepped through a strange portal into a world very different, yet uncannily similar, to the one she'd left. Things did not make complete sense to her. What were these sea dragons? If they were creatures of water, why did they fly? What had happened in the past that Pharinet did not like to talk about now? Varencienne had a feeling that at one time, perhaps when Pharinet was very young, she had tried to reawaken the dragons. She would have done it for Valraven, whom she worshipped. Had something gone wrong? Varencienne could not dispel the impression that clues lay at Norgance. The Leckerys were involved.

These secrets excited Varencienne. It was as if one of her own fantasies had come to life. She just wished Valraven Palindrake wasn't a part of it. If there had to be a hero, why should it be him?

Varencienne quite expected that now she would be taken into the Sisterhood of the Dragon. What she had not accounted for was the fact that Everna was less enthusiastic about her participation than Pharinet was. Pharinet did not exactly say so, but Varencienne guessed that Everna's response was an emphatic 'no!'. Or perhaps the other women of the group had refused her entry. Everna did not discuss the matter with Varencienne herself and outwardly her manner did not change. But Varencienne sensed something, and it had a flavour of the past about it.

'Will *you* train me as a priestess?' Varencienne asked Pharinet.

'There is little I can teach you,' Pharinet replied. 'We can work together, performing little rituals and singing songs, but the one thing of importance I might give you, you have already experienced for yourself.'

'What I saw on the beach?'

'Exactly. I see that as a kind of initiation. Everna and her friends might choose to exclude you from their practices because of your bloodline, but the dragons themselves make no such distinctions. You are Val's wife. That is the most important thing.'

'Pharry, I do not feel like his wife. If I did, I'm sure I would care more for him.'

Pharinet made no comment on this, but Varencienne sensed that in some way she was pleased. She did not want Varencienne to love Valraven, not really.

Varencienne learned of the legends of Foy and her murderous daughters, Jia, Misk and Thrope. Were there any male dragons? No, there were only Palindrake heirs.

'Surely not!' Varencienne exclaimed, misinterpreting Pharinet's meaning.

'It is a mystical union,' Pharinet said.

'Have you seen the dragons?' Varencienne asked.

'I thought so, once. I also went on a journey in my mind to the underwater city where the dragons sleep. I saw the Ustredi, the merpeople.'

'Can I do that?'

Pharinet eyed her thoughtfully. 'There are dangers attached to it,' she said. 'But perhaps one day, it might be feasible.'

Pharinet showed to Varencienne all the little rituals that Foy reputedly liked. They made pools, not fires, upon the beach, into which certain significant items would be placed: shells, stones, food and liquor.

Varencienne learned how to say, 'Oh Great Foy, take unto yourself that which we offer. Look with gentleness upon us. We keep your waters clear in our hearts.'

Varencienne knew that the dragon queen was a terrible creature. She was old and tattered and cruel. It was perhaps best to keep her sweet.

At the same time, Varencienne noticed more frequently the odd wisps of smoke that seemed to haunt corners of the castle. She told Pharinet about this. 'I smell burning, but there is no fire. I see smoke.'

Pharinet was clearly uncomfortable with this revelation. 'You are a daughter of fire,' she said. 'Perhaps this is what you see.'

'I never did before coming here, and if that was the case, you'd think I'd have seen it at home.'

'You were asleep there. You knew nothing of elements.'

'It seems strange that fire creatures should manifest in Caradore, though.'

'Perhaps you're imagining it.'

'Pharinet, I can't believe you'd say that to me.'

'I don't know what it is, then.'

Pharinet would not be drawn out on this subject, but Varencienne filed it away in her mind with all the other questions and clues she had gathered.

While she and Pharinet rode over to Norgance every couple of weeks, and the Leckery women made reciprocal visits, Varencienne never got the opportunity to speak with any of them alone. Ligrana, she was not particularly bothered about, but she felt sure that Niska was a person she should cultivate, someone who could be induced to talk, reveal things. Varencienne also sensed that Pharinet would not be wholly in favour of that, so one morning, when she knew Pharinet and Everna were going to the market at Mariglen, she rose early and rode over to Norgance on her own.

The day was bright and clear, and a strong wind came off the sea, hectoring the trees in their late summer glory. As her horse cantered along the narrow road, with grasses blowing wildly to either side, Varencienne became conscious of how much she'd changed since the spring. Now she could control a horse with aplomb and thought nothing of making this journey alone. She felt strongly aware of her own character, the way it was shaping and forming. She had opinions about things and her imagination didn't just make her a fantasist, it gave her curiosity and insight. She was so much more self-reliant than before. She had servants, and she had Oltefney, but now she did more for herself. Oltefney, if anything, had become Everna's paid companion more than her own.

*

Saska was surprised to see Varencienne, but quickly hid this reaction with a more welcoming manner. 'The girls are out in the garden. They *will* be pleased to see you.'

Varencienne was not wholly sure this was the truth. Ligrana and Niska sat in an orchard, working on pictures they made from thread and shells. They were as surprised to see her as their mother had been.

'Look who's here,' Saska said.

Varencienne wondered how she could get Niska on her own. But luck was with her because Ligrana was having a music lesson that morning.

'What would you like to do?' Niska asked Varencienne, clearly unsure she could cope with the visit.

'Are there any more places like the Ronduel? I like to look at old places.'

'Well, we could go to the Chair,' Niska responded uncertainly.

'What's that?'

'It's a rock formation, not far from the Ronduel, and it looks remarkably like a big stone chair. In olden times, it was said that if you sat in it, visions would come to you.'

'What kind of visions?'

'I don't know,' said Niska defensively. 'They're just stories.'

Her manner told Varencienne that Niska believed firmly otherwise. 'Let's go there, then.'

Whenever she was with Pharinet, Varencienne always felt awkward with the Leckery girls. Now, alone with Niska, she felt very strong and confident. She could sense that Niska was easily controlled.

They climbed the same cliff path that led to the Ronduel, and this time Varencienne was pleased to note she did not get out of breath or suffer from aching calves. Niska walked ahead, her posture glum.

At the top, they entered among the standing stones, and once again, the wind seemed to drop, as if the menhirs created a special space. The sky looked unnaturally huge above them, its shimmering blue studded with silver-edged white clouds. The sky had never looked so big in Magrast.

Varencienne sat down on the grass and patted the ground beside her. 'Let's sit here a while, Niska. It's so lovely.'

Reluctantly, Niska sat down, folding her skirts about her in a neat, feline way.

'I feel like I've lived in Caradore for years,' Varencienne said, leaning back on stiff arms. 'It's the most beautiful place in the world.'

'But there are beautiful places in Magravandias, too,' Niska said. 'My brother told me about them: the Seven Lakes, Misponia. Haven't you been there?'

Varencienne shook her head. 'To tell the truth, Niska, I haven't been anywhere beyond Magrast before I came here, other than to one or two important churches in nearby towns. Let's just say royal women aren't encouraged to travel.'

'Well, I don't travel much either,' Niska said. 'None of us do. There doesn't seem to be any need.'

Varencienne sighed. 'Sometimes I wonder what other countries are like, though. Don't you?'

Niska wrinkled her nose. 'I don't really think about it. I like to make countries up. In my mind. I think they must be better.'

'I like making things up too, but you know that already.'

'Mmm.' Niska tossed back her head and closed her eyes, as if to sun her face.

Varencienne studied the other girl's face. So far, she had made some remarks that seemed designed to put Varencienne at ease. After a few moment's silence, Varencienne said, 'Can I confide in you, Niska?'

Niska opened her eyes and looked at her, but she didn't say anything. Her expression was guarded.

'All I want is your word you won't tell your mother or Ligrana what I have to say.'

Niska frowned. 'I'm not sure I can promise that. It depends on what you're going to tell me.'

'I know about the sea dragons.'

Some of the wariness fell away from Niska's eyes. 'Oh, well, yes. I know that. Pharinet wanted you to join the Sisterhood, but Everna spoke out to . . . to an important person in the group, and it was decided it wasn't a good idea.' At the end of these words, she looked a little pained. 'We have to go with the majority.'

'You are part of the Sisterhood, then?'

Niska paused, then nodded. 'I suppose there's no harm in you knowing.'

'There isn't. I'm no threat to you. I feel very much in tune with the dragons. I wish everyone would stop looking on me as my father's daughter. I am Valraven's wife. Doesn't that count for anything?'

'Perhaps people will change their minds in time. You should be patient. You've only been here a few months.'

Varencienne sighed. 'You're right. I just want to belong. Is that so bad?'

Niska's face crumpled into a sympathetic expression, as Varencienne had guessed it would. 'No, of course not.' She reached out and lightly touched one of Varencienne's hands. 'It's just because of the history between your family and ours, that's all. Everyone needs to get to know you as an individual. I'm sure that will come.'

This was a delicate moment. Words spun patterns in Varencienne's mind, but she knew she had to be careful. She gazed out through the stones, to the heathland where wiry heathers clustered between swathes of golden lichen. 'I want to go to the Chair. I want to see visions, visions of the truth.' She got to her feet and Niska squinted up at her.

'The truth?'

'Yes,' said Varencienne. 'The things that people won't tell me.' She held out a hand. 'Come on. Take me there.'

They followed a track between the heather, and now Niska was silent again, clearly fretting. Varencienne did not know whether the old site would really show her visions, but one way or another, she intended to learn something that day.

The track led into an old forest. Oak, beech and chestnut clustered together there, greened with the lichen breath of the forest, their trunks contorted by age. Sunlight came down through the canopy to make pools of gold along the dry dirt path. Nodding ferns skirted the trees, and the lush viridian grass around them was close-cropped by deer. Presently, through the trees, a huge spine of rock could be seen, which seemed to extend into the forest for some distance either side. It was like an immense sleeping dragon, with a warty grey skin. The stone was patchworked with moss and ferns, and in places spindly trees grew out of crevices.

'It's so strange,' Varencienne said. 'It looks as if it doesn't belong here. A piece of mountain dropped by a god.'

Niska smiled. 'It's called the Mage Pike. Caradore is full of marvels like this. Wait till you see the view from the top.'

Varencienne eyed the apparently sheer rock face. 'Will it take long? Where's the path?'

'It's quite a climb,' Niska said, 'but not difficult. I hope you're not afraid of heights, though.'

'I don't think so,' Varencienne said.

'To the old magi, this place was sacred,' Niska said. 'They hollowed out the rocks in places to make caves where they enacted their secret rituals. There are simulacra in the stone. A dragon, of course, but others too. An old witch, a sleeping boy. I'll show you.'

Steps had been cut into the rock, leading the way up a narrow channel. They were slippery and damp and often difficult to negotiate because of plants growing on them. The girls climbed for about fifteen minutes before having to squeeze themselves through a slim aperture. Varencienne drew in her breath. They stood upon a wide platform, spongy with moss, beneath which was a sheer drop of several hundred feet. They looked down upon treetops. Caradore was spread out before them, miles upon miles of forest, mountains and heathland, with the occasional smoothed area of habitation. She saw castles, the old domains of the ancient families, clinging to sheer cliffs. She saw hamlets hidden in forest glades. People moved like ants along the roads.

To the right was a rock wall, into which more steps had been cut. 'The Chair's up there,' Niska said, pointing. 'If we go the other way, there are caves and tunnels I could show you.'

Varencienne ventured towards the drop. She had never seen such a vista before. A bird must see the land like this.

'Be careful,' Niska said. 'People who go near the edge often can't control the compulsion to jump.'

For a moment, Varencienne's head spun, and she laughed nervously. 'The feeling is horrible, but strangely pleasant. It would be like flying.'

'I think you'd better come back here.' Niska took hold of her arm. 'I heard about your escapade with the sea. Are you drawn to dangerous actions?'

'I never thought so, but perhaps I am.' Varencienne linked her arm through Niska's. 'Let's go to the Chair.'

'When we get to the top, don't let go of me,' Niska said. 'I don't trust you.'

They entered another narrow stairway, which led to a perilous lookout on which a single dolmen stood. Here the platform was much smaller, and Varencienne felt dizzy.

The Chair was on the face of the Pike itself, approached by another narrow staircase that led downwards. The well of the stairs hid the view of the landscape, but still Varencienne clung on to Niska's hand. The platform on to which they emerged was covered in elderly shrubs with leathery leaves, which made it feel safer. The Chair was in a narrow cave, shaped into a seat, complete with stone arms. Niska guided Varencienne to sit in it. Before her, the land of Caradore stretched out and away. Varencienne felt light-headed and shivery.

Niska settled herself on the bottom step, hugging her knees. 'Is this not the most wonderful view you can imagine?' she said. 'They say the old kings of the land would sit here after they were crowned. They would be given messages for the future.'

Varencienne gripped the stone arms of the Chair. She could understand why people might have visions there. The sense of danger, the fact that you could so easily slip and fall to your death below, conjured a strange state of mind. Niska said nothing more, and stared out at the landscape

199

with a dreamy expression on her face. Varencienne breathed slowly and heavily. Now was her moment. She could use this opportunity to great effect.

After a few moments, Varencienne drew in her breath sharply. Even though her eyes were closed, she knew she had Niska's attention immediately. She breathed heavily for a while, and then expelled a small sigh.

'Ren?' Niska murmured softly. 'Are you all right?'

Varencienne swallowed. 'There are pictures in my mind,' she said in a faint voice. 'It is astounding.'

'What can you see?' Niska asked encouragingly.

Varencienne wrinkled her brow. 'It looks like Norgance. It's as if I'm looking at a painting of it.'

'Look closer,' Niska said.

Varencienne paused for a few seconds, then murmured. 'I can see Pharinet, only she's much younger. She's in the garden, and there's another girl with her. They're playing.'

'What does the girl look like?' Niska asked urgently.

'Like you.' It was the best answer Varencienne could think of.

'Ellony, my sister,' breathed Niska. 'It must be. What else can you see, Ren?'

Varencienne screwed up her face, moved her head slowly from side to side. 'I can't see anything else, but I feel a great sadness.'

'Yes,' said Niska. Her voice had risen in pitch.

Varencienne could almost see the pictures she described. Pharinet would have played in the garden with Niska's dead sister. That was easy. Perhaps she needed to say something else, something which would prompt Niska to tell her everything. She gasped and made her body go rigid against the stone. 'The dragons!'

Niska made a sound of concern and even reached out to touch Varencienne's knee. Varencienne herself was composing what to utter next when a clear, vibrant image splashed across her mind. She saw a woman and a man struggling on a beach. The colours were all wrong: the sky looked like a monstrous bruise, the sea thick and dirty grey like mud. The woman was hideous, her pale face almost green, her eyes staring and dark, fierce yet empty. Her open mouth was shockingly pink against her pallid skin. At first, Varencienne thought the man was trying to harm this woman, but as the scene continued in her mind, she saw that the opposite was true. The woman was dragging the man towards the sea. She was laughing. She meant him harm. There were other shadowy figures around, but she could not quite make out the details. Something evil and gloating seemed to hang invisibly over everything. It filled

Varencienne with a terrible despair. Then she saw Pharinet's face, etched with deep misery. Caradore was on fire and Norgance a dusty ruin. Everything was ended.

Varencienne opened her eyes and expelled a short cry.

'What is it. Ren?' Niska cried. She was kneeling at Varencienne's feet, her face full of worry.

'Something happened on the beach. A woman and a man. She dragged him into the sea. Her face was really strange, almost green.'

'Great Foy,' breathed Niska. 'That was Ellony too.'

Varencienne stared at her in shock. 'What happened?'

Niska looked away. 'Let's go. I feel strange here now.' She stood up.

'Niska,' Varencienne said. 'You must tell me.'

Niska nodded, her expression tight. 'Not here, though. It feels as if something's here. Something's watching us.'

Varencienne shuddered. She felt more disorientated than before and the yawning landscape before her seemed occluded by a dirty mist.

Niska took Varencienne's arm and pulled her from the seat. Varencienne could barely walk. Her limbs shook. 'I feel so cold,' she said.

Niska murmured reassurance and quickly led the way back to the lookout, and from there down on to the wider platform. Here, Varencienne collapsed on to the smooth, sun-warmed stone. Her head was pulsing, not with pain exactly, but a strange pressure. She felt disordered in mind and body. She had been prepared to lie, make up a convincing story. The horrifying, ugly images had been so unexpected. She sat with her head resting on her knees, while Niska stroked her hair.

'What did I see?' Varencienne asked, her voice muffled. 'Did that really happen?'

'Oh yes,' Niska said and there was a hard, uncharacteristic bitterness in her voice. 'I did not witness it myself, but it sounded like you saw the time when Ellony went into the sea. Some people say the dragons took her. She dragged Thomist with her.'

'Thomist?'

'Everna's husband.'

'The one that drowned,' Varencienne said softly, 'yes, Pharinet mentioned that to me once.' She fixed Niska with a steady eye. Now was the time. She could not succumb to weakness or fear, she must pursue her enquiries. 'How did it happen?'

Niska's eyes flicked away from Varencienne's gaze. She shrugged. 'I'm not sure exactly. Ellony wasn't well. She had strange ideas. You should ask Pharinet, perhaps. She was there when it happened.' Niska looked back at her companion. 'How much have you been told about Ellony?'

Varencienne shrugged. 'Very little. Just that she was your sister and Pharinet's friend, and that she died.'

'Not about her and Valraven, then?'

'No, nothing about that.' Varencienne felt herself grow still inside. Part of her did not want to hear what was going to come next.

Niska gazed out anxiously at the landscape. She appeared to be wrestling with an inner dilemma. Her hands bunched into fists, unbunched again. 'They should have told you,' she said, as if to convince herself, 'but then Pharinet wants the past buried. They all do, my mother, Everna, the other women . . .'

'They should have told me what, Niska?' Varencienne queried gently.

Niska hesitated, then said, 'Ellony was Valraven's bride, Ren. She married him in the same year that Pharinet married my brother, Khaster.'

Varencienne shivered, remembering Twissaly's words about always having serviced the 'bride's chambers'. Someone had lived in those rooms before her, but now she was dead. And Pharinet: she too had had a husband. Where was he now? 'This is a shock,' Varencienne said. She did not have to lie. 'Please, tell me all you know about what happened, Niska. It's important to me.'

'I understand that,' Niska said. She reached out and touched Varencienne's hands. 'I like you, Ren, and I don't think it's right things are kept secret from you. Some things, anyway.' She flushed a little, and Varencienne wondered what memory had prompted that.

'I'll be very grateful for whatever you can tell me,' she said.

'Ellony adored Valraven,' Niska said. 'She took her role as his wife very seriously. Perhaps too seriously. She became ill.' Niska rubbed her face with her hands. 'One day, she and . . . she and Val and Pharinet were on the beach one morning, and Ellony went peculiar. She tried to run into the sea. Thomist saw what was happening and came hurrying to try and stop her. She took him with her. No bodies were ever found.'

'Why didn't Valraven and Pharinet stop her? What were they doing?'

Niska looked deeply uncomfortable now. 'I think they did, but it was no use. Ellony was too strong.'

Something about this didn't ring true to Varencienne. For a start, the name 'Ellony' did not suggest a strong woman. Still, that could be deceptive. But Niska had implied through her reactions at the Chair that she resembled Ellony herself. And Niska was not a physically strong creature either. What had *really* happened? Perhaps Niska was right; only Pharinet could tell her, and maybe Pharinet wouldn't want to. This was clearly one of her secret demons, a shameful secret. This tragic event could also be the reason why Valraven was such a cold man. It was possible he grieved for a lost first wife, the light in his world, which had been brutally extinguished. Involuntarily, Varencienne felt a little warmer towards him. 'What of Pharinet's husband, your brother?' she asked. 'Where is he now?'

'Dead too,' said Niska. 'But in battle. It happened very shortly after Ellony and Thomist died. It was a time of great tragedy for both our families. We thought we'd never feel happiness again. But life goes on. You can't stop it.'

Varencienne shook her head. 'It's almost too much to take in,' she said. 'All those deaths so quickly. It must have been terrible.'

Niska nodded. 'It was. We have yet to get over it fully.' She sat back and wrapped her arms about her knees. 'I'm glad to speak of it, because we never do.'

'You can talk to me, Niska. I'm more than happy to listen.'

Niska's eyes had become watery. 'I used to have terrible nightmares about Ellony. She would come to my window and slide through the glass like a mist. She came to steal my breath, an ugly, monstrous seawoman. Her skin was greeny-white, and she had a mouth full of hooked fangs like a predator fish.' Niska shook her head, wiped tears from her cheek. 'I loved her so much, she was so beautiful in life, it seemed unbelievably cruel that I had to become afraid of her. I would wake screaming just as Ellony stooped over me in the bed. She had cold saliva that smelled of fish. It fell on to my face.'

'That's horrible,' Varencienne said. 'You poor thing.'

Niska nodded. 'I missed Pharinet so badly. She used to live with us, you see, when Ellony was alive. She and Ellony had to swap houses to be with their husbands, although Val and Khas were rarely at home. Pharinet moved into Norgance shortly after she married Khaster. Ligrana and I loved having her there. She was such fun. If ever I had a nightmare, Pharinet would always hear me, because her room was close to mine. She'd come to me, wake me up, and hold me in her arms. Then she'd tell me strange and lovely stories that took all the fear away. She used to be good at making up stories. After Ellony and Thomist died, she returned to Caradore to look after Everna. Valraven employed Goldvane as steward at the same time, for obvious reasons. Pharinet was supposed only to stay there for a short while, but then we got the news from Cos that Khaster had been killed, and Pharinet never came back to us. She stayed with her sister. She couldn't comfort me any more, but Ligrana slept in my room for over a year. I think she must have had nightmares too, but she never admitted to it. She likes to appear strong, like Pharinet.'

Pharinet *was* strong, yet she'd not been able, apparently, to prevent her best friend, who was ill, from running into the sea. 'She should have told me all this,' Varencienne said. 'It might have been painful, but she should have told me. It explains so much.'

'I know, but you must understand it is a subject nobody wants to dwell on. Pharinet must believe she could have saved Ellony. I think she punishes herself even now.'

'It does seem odd, given that Ellony was probably quite weak at the time, that three healthy adults could not restrain her.'

'Well, people can find an unnatural strength in certain states of mind, can't they?'

Varencienne nodded. 'I suppose so. What was wrong with your sister, exactly?'

Niska frowned. 'It was a strange illness. It began even before her marriage. I suppose we have to face the fact that she was a little mad. She suffered from delusions.'

'What kind of delusions were they?'

Niska sighed. 'I'm not sure I should be telling you this. It's very personal.'

Varencienne gripped one of Niska's arms. 'Please, Niska. You can trust me.'

'She was afraid of the sea, of the dragons. That day, I think she thought they were calling to her, or something.' Niska's voice rose with distress. 'I can't tell you any more, because I don't know anything. Nobody does. None of us could see into Ellony's mind. She was in torment.'

'Hush,' Varencienne murmured, curling an arm around Niska's shuddering body. 'Don't say any more. You're upsetting yourself.' She sensed she had pushed Niska far enough. The information would come out a bit at a time, from this and other sources, including, it seemed, her own mind. Varencienne had never experienced a waking vision before. Perhaps the magical air of Caradore had drawn the ability out of her. 'I wonder why that terrible time was shown to me?' she said.

'You asked for truth,' Niska replied. 'You got some.'

Varencienne and Niska returned to Norgance in a subdued mood. Varencienne was intrigued by what she'd discovered, but also felt slightly guilty about her manipulation of Niska. It had hurt her. Still, Varencienne felt the ends justified the means. If she were to understand her husband and his family, she had to know the truth. She couldn't wait to tell Pharinet she'd had a vision, although she guessed the subject matter might not invoke a favourable response in her sister-in-law. However, this would have to be faced. Mentally, Varencienne was already squaring her shoulders for the confrontation.

Back at Norgance, they discovered that Saska's sister Dimara had arrived for tea. Varencienne and Niska went into Saska's salon, where Ligrana sat with the other women. 'What is the matter, child?' Saska demanded of Niska. 'You look like you've been crying.'

'A fall,' said Niska. 'We went to the Chair.'

Saska bustled forward. 'Any injuries? Let me see.'

Niska shied away. 'No, it's nothing. Just a knock. I slipped on the steps.'

'You should be more careful,' said Dimara in an expressionless tone. 'One mistake on the Pike and you'd not live to regret it. It is not a place for games.'

Dimara's tone needled Varencienne. 'We were not playing games, Mistress Corey. I asked Niska to take me to the Chair, because I wished to find out whether the legends about it are true.'

Niska expelled an anguished sound.

'And *did* you discover anything?' Dimara asked.

Saska and Ligrana had gone suspiciously quiet, as if deferring to the older woman.

'As a matter of fact, yes,' said Varencienne.

For a moment, the salon was tensely silent. Varencienne sensed she had angered Saska's sister, but couldn't really see how. Perhaps it was simply prejudice: she was Magravandian, a foreigner and an interloper. She held Dimara's gaze fearlessly, challenging her to say something more, but after a few moments, Dimara looked away, like a cat who'd lost a staring contest.

'Come and sit down,' Saska said loudly. 'Ligrana can play us a tune. She learned a new one today.'

Varencienne hurriedly gulped down some bread and ham, a slab of dense pale cake and a cup of tea. Ligrana obligingly played on her spinet, which meant no one had to talk. Niska could barely eat. She looked afraid. Varencienne wanted to leave Norgance now. She wanted to speak to Pharinet. Putting down her empty plate, she said, 'I must go home now. I hadn't planned to stay this long.'

'It's been lovely to see you, dear,' Saska said. 'You must come again.'

Varencienne stood up and inclined her head to Dimara. 'Good day to you, Mistress Corey.'

Dimara inclined her head stiffly. 'Have a safe journey home.'

Niska also got to her feet. 'I'll see you to the yard.'

Once the salon door had closed behind them, Varencienne took hold of Niska's arm. 'I'm sorry about today. I can see it upset you.'

Niska shrugged. 'It's not your fault. These things would have to come out eventually.'

Varencienne kissed Niska's cheek. 'I appreciate you being frank with me. You didn't have to.' She paused. 'I hope I haven't got you into trouble though. Your aunt looked furious to discover you'd taken me to the Chair.'

'Oh, don't worry about Dimara,' Niska said hurriedly. 'She's just very protective.'

'I didn't realize I was so fearsome!' Varencienne said, softening the remark with a laugh.

On their way to the stable-yard, they walked down a gallery, where long windows overlooked a water garden. On the wall opposite hung portraits of Niska's ancestors, some staring grimly, others smiling, surrounded by children. Niska recited their names and little anecdotes about their history. She paused before the portrait of a young man astride a handsome bay horse. 'And this is Khaster,' she said.

Varencienne let go of Niska's arm and approached the painting. 'He's beautiful,' she said, an inadequate response in comparison to the strange lurch she felt in her belly. The eyes of the portrait seemed to stare right into her. 'He looks sad.'

'That was painted just before he went to Magrast for the first time. He wasn't happy about leaving home.'

'Pharinet must have been devastated to lose him,' Varencienne said.

Niska was silent for a moment, then said, 'Yes.'

Varencienne stole a sidelong glance at her. She itched to ask a question, but restrained herself. Niska must not be pushed too far, but the implication in her brief pause was extremely revealing.

CHAPTER SIX

Sisters

A short distance from Caradore, Varencienne came upon Pharinet, who was riding to find her. Pharinet pulled her showy prancing stallion to a halt and demanded, 'Where have you been? We've been worried sick.'

Varencienne could not keep the sharpness from her voice. 'Given that you're on the road to Norgance, you must have some idea. I went to visit Niska. You told me we two should be friends, remember?'

Pharinet inspected her with narrowed eyes for a moment or two. 'You are a minx,' she said. 'What are you up to?'

Varencienne urged her horse past Pharinet's. 'I'm up to nothing. The same cannot be said of you.'

Pharinet trotted her mount alongside. 'Explain!'

Varencienne made a careless gesture with one hand, although her heart was beating fast. Pharinet still had the capacity to intimidate her. 'I know about Ellony and Khaster. Niska told me.'

'So?'

Varencienne could only admire Pharinet's coolness. 'I would have preferred to hear it from you. Something happened here, didn't it, and in some way I think it affects me too. Why won't you tell me? Don't I have a right to know?'

Pharinet shrugged irritably. 'I probably would have told you eventually. Clearly, Niska neglected to mention that those memories hurt me deeply.'

'She did mention that actually. She tried to explain why you'd kept silent.'

'She shouldn't have told you.'

'I made her. We went to the Chair on Mage's Pike. I saw something there.'

207

Pharinet did not hide her surprise. 'Like what?'

Varencienne felt uncomfortable now. Her vision seemed so unlikely. 'I saw Ellony drag Thomist into the sea. It was a horrible sight. She looked like a demoness.'

Pharinet's face took on a furtive expression. 'That's impressive. Only Ellony ever had visions at the Chair before. But I suppose it makes sense that you should share that ability. You are the sea wife, after all.'

'I'm not sure I agree with you. Surely being the sea wife involves rather more than simply being married to Valraven? I share no spiritual connection with him.'

'Neither did Ellony,' Pharinet said, with what Varencienne interpreted as venom. 'What else did you see?'

'I saw you,' Varencienne replied. 'I saw your face. You looked very upset. Then images came to me of Caradore in flames, Norgance in ruins.'

Pharinet hesitated for a moment. 'Nothing else?'

'No.'

'Are you sure?'

'Yes. What do you think I saw?'

Pharinet smiled tightly. 'Let's go home.'

Varencienne pulled her horse to a halt. 'No, we have to talk first. I have questions, I want answers. If you won't tell me, I'll ask Everna.'

Pharinet laughed lightly. 'There's no need for threats, Ren. I agree entirely that we should talk. I would just like our conversation to take place in the privacy of my sitting-room, that's all.'

From the stable-yard of Caradore, Varencienne and Pharinet went directly to Pharinet's chambers. Here Pharinet produced a bottle of wine and two goblets. 'Won't Everna want us to go to dinner?' Varencienne said. The atmosphere between them was like a taut thread.

'We can eat later,' Pharinet said, pouring out the wine. She handed Varencienne a goblet. 'I have come to the conclusion that it doesn't matter if you know the truth.'

'How magnanimous of you. I am more than ready to hear it.'

Pharinet nodded and sat down in an armchair opposite Varencienne. She sat like a man, knees apart, her arms resting on her open thighs, between which she held her goblet. She turned the cup in her hands, the only evidence of nervousness. 'I will tell you first how I hated and loved Ellony in equal measure. It made her death all the harder.'

Varencienne leaned away from Pharinet, her goblet held high to her chest. 'Why did you hate her? She was your best friend, wasn't she?'

Pharinet took a long gulp of wine, then reached to refill her goblet. 'Can't you guess? I thought you had.'

Varencienne shrugged. 'Tell me.'

Pharinet sighed. It took some moments for the words to come. 'Val and I were lovers once.' She took another generous mouthful of wine.

Varencienne could not help but be sympathetic to Pharinet's discomfort. 'Oh, that. Yes, I did have an inkling that was the case. So, you were jealous when Valraven married Ellony?'

Pharinet nodded, smiling bitterly. 'Yes. Isn't that foul?'

Varencienne pulled a wry face. 'You couldn't help your feelings. But what about Khaster? You married him at the same time, didn't you?'

'I went along with arrangements. It was expected of me, as it was expected of Val to marry Ellony. We all grew up together.'

Varencienne hesitated for a moment. 'I saw a portrait of Khaster today in the gallery at Norgance. He was a very attractive man, or did the portrait flatter him?'

Pharinet laughed sadly. 'No, it is a fair likeness. Khaster was a beautiful person. He deserved more than me.'

'It just seems very sad to me that you couldn't be with the man you loved.'

'He was my brother!' Pharinet shook her head. 'I suppose incestuous relationships are commonplace to you.'

Varencienne shrugged. 'In Magrast, the only objection to these relationships between siblings is dynastic. Such unions rarely produce healthy young, but in our country marriage is rarely about love. My knowledge of life beyond the palace is limited, because I led such a sheltered existence, but I do know that fidelity is rarely expected.'

'Things are different here, Ren. And opinions. I am not proud of the things I did because of the feelings I had for Val. I had to watch him marry my best friend, and it killed any love I had for her. I myself married a man who was both good and handsome, but whom I did not love. Khaster always knew that. The whole affair was tragic and it upsets me to remember those times. But perhaps the main reason I have not confided in you about them is because your brother, Bayard, was present at the end. He instigated it.'

Varencienne blinked in surprise. '*Bayard?* how?'

Pharinet leaned over to replenish Varencienne's goblet. 'I will tell you now, tell you everything. Isn't that what you want? But don't interrupt me with questions. Just allow me to get the story out.'

Pharinet conjured perfectly the world in which she grew up, and to

Varencienne it seemed like an idyll. Pharinet, her brother and their friends had been so free. Varencienne could almost smell the herby, salty air and see the children of Caradore and Norgance playing on the wind-scoured moors and in cave-studded coves. Her skin prickled as Pharinet related the story of the night of her initiation with Ellony. She could also see the similarities with her own nocturnal experience on the shore. But Pharinet's narrative really came alive when she spoke about Valraven. Her love for him filled her words and shone from her eyes. When she related how they'd eventually confessed their feelings for one another, it seemed like the ultimate romance. By this time, Varencienne too could not help but perceive Ellony as rather an impediment. It was easy to share Pharinet's conflicting feelings about her childhood friend.

Pharinet stood up. 'I've yet to tell you the worst,' she said. 'I need more wine for that.' She went to a cabinet and took out another bottle, which she uncorked.

Varencienne sat with her legs curled beneath her. She had drunk two large goblets of wine herself, and now felt slightly light-headed. 'Does Niska's aunt, Dimara, know about all this?' she asked. 'I've noticed she's cool with you, and I picked up hostility from her today.'

Pharinet expelled a derisive snort. 'Dimara has pretensions. She is the Merante, the high priestess of the Sisterhood and believes everyone else's business is her own.'

'She's the one who didn't want me to join the Sisterhood, isn't she?'

'Among others.' Pharinet poured more wine into Varencienne's proffered goblet. 'She has made assumptions about me, and probably several good guesses. I don't care. She can think what she likes.' Pharinet settled back into her chair. 'Now I'll tell you about Bayard. You might not like it.'

Varencienne pursed her lips, but made no comment. She did not want to hear Pharinet talk about Bayard in the same tone she'd used to speak of Ellony, but if she wanted the story, she'd have to hold her tongue.

Pharinet leaned back in her seat. 'I'm not the only one to conduct a clandestine affair with Valraven. Bayard did too.'

This remark had the intended effect. Varencienne reared upright in her chair. 'That's impossible. You haven't heard the way Bay speaks of Valraven. He despises him.'

Pharinet shrugged, raising a languid hand. 'The affair did not last, and what you have heard is no doubt the poison that lingers in a broken heart.' She appeared quite drunk now.

'How did you know about this?'

'Khaster told me, and Bayard confirmed it. Later, I saw evidence with my own eyes.'

'Very well. Tell me, then.'

Varencienne listened with rising unease and disbelief. Could Pharinet be exaggerating or fabricating her story? It was impossible to believe Bayard, whom she loved, could have been this dark influence over the Palindrakes. Pharinet spoke bitterly, yet honestly. She seemed to have forgotten to whom she was speaking, for her relation of the sexual encounter she'd had with Bayard in the garden was uncomfortably explicit. Her words were like black fists flying into Varencienne's face and beyond that into her mind, her soul. She wanted to silence Pharinet or walk away, but was equally gripped and intrigued by what she was hearing. She could see her brother on the beach, his hands upon Pharinet's shoulders. She could hear his voice. *Oh Bay*, she thought. *How could you not have warned me? You must have known I'd hear of this, and from a stranger's lips.* Had he lain awake fearing this moment, knowing it would surely come? Pharinet had intimated he was adept at magic. Would part of him now sense that she knew?

Pharinet finished her tale by describing what happened on the beach on the day when Ellony ran into the sea.

'And after that?' Varencienne asked. 'Is that when you all fell out?'

'A falling out? Did I mention that?' Pharinet laughed.

'You are no longer friends with Bayard, that's clear.'

'He left,' Pharinet said. 'He just walked from the beach and rode home to Magrast, to leave us with the disorder he'd left behind.' She grimaced. 'Now can you understand why I said your family know more about the dragons than we do? Even your mother. She wants Bayard to be emperor one day, and I believe she'd do anything to accomplish her aim.' She drained her goblet, picked up the bottle, found it empty and threw it on the floor. 'Now my throat is dry and sore. It's like old tears.'

Varencienne felt as if she were in shock. 'These are not the people I know,' she said, slowly shaking her head. She pressed the heel of one hand against the bridge of her nose. 'It doesn't make sense to me.'

Pharinet yawned. 'You don't know them as well as you think you do. You were kept in ignorance. But now you know.'

'My mother should have spoken of this to me. Some of it, at least. Surely she must have known I would become part of this story the moment I set foot in Caradore?'

'You are clearly just a pawn to them. You must see that. You've never been close to your mother.'

'No, but Bayard . . .' Varencienne shook her head. 'I feel he's betrayed me.' She looked up at Pharinet. 'Do you think he still has an interest in Caradore?'

Pharinet stared at her, although her eyes appeared to be slightly unfocused. 'Who knows? He and Val are no longer close. Val blames him for what happened to Ellony and Thomist.'

Varencienne frowned. Some instinct inside her advised there was rather more to their estrangement than that. But what? The person Pharinet described was not the brother Varencienne knew. He had never seemed cold or cruel to her, but noble and sensitive. Perhaps her mother had sent him to Caradore, forced him to do what he had. Varencienne had to concede she knew little of Tatrini. 'I wonder now whether my mother designed for me to come here,' she said. 'But if she wanted to use me, why not speak of it, give me instructions? She can't be confident enough to leave things to chance. Or . . .' Varencienne could not suppress an inner shudder, 'is she influencing events even now by other means?'

'I don't know what goes on in your mother's mind,' Pharinet said, 'but I suspect that after Bayard tried unsuccessfully to meld the power of fire with water, she lost interest. Valraven is perhaps too damaged for her purposes.'

'Pharinet, what is the future? What do *you* hope to achieve with all this dragon worship?'

'It is not about worship, Ren, but about power. We wait, and keep the old traditions alive, in the hope that, one day, their power will once again be ours. After what happened to you on the beach that night, when you saw a dragon rise, I believe that if anyone has the power to awaken Foy and her daughters, it's you. You are far stronger than Ellony was.'

Varencienne smiled grimly. 'And I have an ally in you, which she did not. How convenient for you that I do not love my husband.'

Pharinet did not flinch. 'It's not the same now. I still love Val, but we are no longer close in that respect. He has no one. He is so alone. What power came through that terrible day affected him badly. I believe he turned to fire, immersed himself in it, but only through war and conquest. He has no spiritual side. He's buried it deep inside himself.'

'I find it hard to believe that Valraven and Bayard were lovers,' Varencienne said. 'Bayard warned me about your brother before I came here, Pharry. He seemed to dislike him.'

'Perhaps he does. Now. After what happened here, Valraven isolated himself from Bayard, from everyone. He doesn't know the truth of what he is, and he has a smattering of fire-drake lore. He should learn more, but he won't. Part of our curse is that should he attempt to commune with the sea dragons once more, Caradore will burn. Like in your vision. Valraven has not been told this, but perhaps he senses it.'

212

Varencienne paused, then said carefully, 'I don't think you can get him back, Pharry.'

She sighed. 'I know *I* can't, but perhaps he can return to Caradore, the son of his father, the man he was. That's all I want now.'

Varencienne knew that was not the whole truth.

CHAPTER SEVEN

Woman of the Land

That night, alone in her bedroom, Varencienne could not help but think of the story Pharinet had told her. There seemed to be echoes of Ellony's agonized cries lingering in the drapery around the bed. If she concentrated hard enough, Varencienne was sure she would see a sad, pale wraith drifting across the floor, wringing its hands, eyes black and wild.

Varencienne sat on top of the bed, clasping her knees. What she'd learned had not changed her feelings for Valraven. The man Pharinet knew could not exist in Varencienne's mind. He was what he was and she felt nothing could alter that now. But the information she'd heard about her mother and brother certainly had changed her feelings. She felt bewildered and betrayed, yet madly curious. The empress of Pharinet's tale was perhaps the kind of mother Varencienne would have liked to have had all along: a priestess, a sorceress, with a forgotten book of secret knowledge. Her own fantasies could not have provided a more perfect history. Yet this Tatrini lived only in Pharinet's words. Varencienne would need proof for herself.

In the morning, she wrote to Bayard, and in covert terms intimated what she had learned. Help me to understand this, she asked him. Tell me what you can.

The post-rider came that day and the letter went into his bag, to be carried through the mountains and across the plains of Magravandias, until it reached wherever her brother was stationed. She tried to imagine him reading it, how he would react. The man Pharinet had met was not the person Varencienne knew. It was the same as for Valraven. How many personalities resided in a single body? Was it possible all aspects of a person could be real?

214

In the afternoon, Varencienne walked upon the beach. The sky was purple with storms, yet the air was hot. A dark pall hung over the sullen ocean. In this place, Ellony had vanished into the waves. Bayard had stood here, his hands upon Pharinet's shoulders, Valraven a smouldering presence behind them. They had been younger then, but not that much younger. Six years ago. In Caradore, that seemed like a lifetime.

Varencienne decided that the dragons and their magical religion were only a backdrop to what had occurred, not the focus. In comparison with the real and tragic human events that had taken place, ostensibly in the dragons' name, Varencienne found her belief in them faltering. The dragons were magic, but human suffering was not. Was it possible that everyone involved had deluded themselves, and the only power humming in the air had been that of human feeling? Perhaps it was the same even now.

Varencienne stared out over the slowly heaving waves. 'Foy, if you're down there, sleeping, your dreams are nightmares,' she murmured. 'And they have touched us with pain. I hope your sleep is restless.'

Bayard did not respond to his sister's letter immediately, but this was only what Varencienne expected. It could take months for mail to reach him. As autumn drew its gaudy banner across the land, the Sisterhood celebrated another festival, which Varencienne, of course, could not attend. Niska told her all about it afterwards. They had begun to spend more time together, and Varencienne rode over to Norgance regularly, often staying overnight. Sometimes, Pharinet would come with her. Niska was not averse to conducting small rituals with Pharinet and Varencienne, which often took place at the Ronduel. They did not attempt communion with the dragons, but the land itself. In that place, they thought about the changing cycles of life, its inexorable surge through time.

Once Niska said that she thought Ellony was sometimes with them in their rites. Varencienne shuddered at the thought and hoped not. She could only picture Ellony as a vengeful, bitter spirit. Perhaps her own imagination conjured strong feelings of anger hanging around the bride's chambers. Smoke wisps still hurried past the edge of her vision, as if driven by an unfelt wind. Caradore was not at rest. Ghosts walked there, unseen: the shade of a younger, innocent Valraven, Ellony, Thomist, Pharinet's parents, and even Khaster, although he had not lived there. His shade would be beautiful, sensitive and mournful. Varencienne found herself thinking about Khaster a lot. Every time she visited Norgance, she went to stand before his portrait. She wished she had been given to such a man. How ironic life was.

Valraven was due home on leave for the winter festival, and during the days before his arrival Varencienne became filled with a compulsion to visit the Chair once more. For some reason, she could not communicate this desire to either Pharinet or Niska. It was a personal feeling, which she must obey in secret. So one morning, an hour before dawn, she rode out alone without telling anyone in Caradore, and took a different route to the moors above Norgance, to avoid the Leckerys and their staff. This was also quicker than riding to Norgance first.

Varencienne and Niska had visited the Chair several times since the first, but although Varencienne sometimes picked up evanescent feelings and impressions, she'd yet to experience a repeat of that initial clear imagery.

She arrived at Mage's Pike an hour after dawn. An autumn mist covered the land, making goblin giants of the trees. The air was hushed and still, as if the fog were an enchantment beneath whose spell the whole world slept. The jangling of the horse's bit seemed too loud; it might awake some elemental creature from its slumber. By the time Varencienne hooked her mount's reins over a tree branch and began to climb the Pike, her spine was crawling with presentiment.

From the platform, she looked down upon a world of cloud. Occasionally, a crow might rattle from the treetops and scrawl an arc across the shifting blanket, but otherwise Caradore lay still, although the air seemed to vibrate with an unheard song. Mist settled on Varencienne's cloak like beads of polished quartz. Her hair was lank around her face, her breath steaming. Leaves fell from the trees and landed silently on the path along the Pike below her. She had walked a carpet of wet gold to reach this place. If she was truly the sea wife, then her predecessors throughout the generations must have come to the Chair seeking knowledge. She felt strongly that she belonged there, which warred with the nagging inner suspicion that she was an interloper. She did not love the dragon heir. Occasionally, she'd wished him dead. She wasn't sure in her heart what she really wanted, or why she was there.

The path to the Chair was slick, but Varencienne's feet were sure upon it. She felt no danger. Moisture dripped from the shrubs about the stone seat itself, sliding from the wads of tight red berries and glossy leaves that enclosed it. The air smelled sickly-sweet, with an undertone of loam. Varencienne had been aware of the fermenting season all the way to the Pike, but at the Chair itself this fecundity seemed to spill over with especial plump ripeness.

She settled herself upon the cold wet stone, which was covered in leaves. Presently the dampness seeped through her clothes to her thighs and buttocks. Her toes and fingers felt stiff and chilled, yet the rest of her body was strangely warm. She gripped the arms of the Chair and closed her eyes, willing visions to come. But she could not shift her awareness from the smells around her. They filled her head, distracting her concentration. Her own desire for answers seemed puny in comparison with the immense surge of life around her, its fruiting, its continuation. Colours boiled behind her eyes: crimson and gold and copper. A quiet inner voice whispered, Here is the message itself.

Varencienne went utterly still. She opened her eyes. The world hadn't changed at all. Within her, a fruit had dropped from the tree of knowledge and broken open. Its seeds had spilled into her mind and were sinking down. It would take time for them to grow, to blossom, but for a single conviction, which was already in bloom.

She felt Valraven was damaged beyond repair. Perhaps it was not his task to reclaim his heritage, but despite this, a possibility existed for the Palindrakes to begin anew. It would mean she must go against all that she had previously felt. She would have to put aside her own preferences for the greater good, and in doing so, would transcend her own being. In this way, she would never again fear she was an interloper. She must conceive with her husband a child.

The idea was so simple and so perfect, Varencienne was awed by it. If she should have a son, she would ensure he matured free of the demons that had plagued his father. She would not surrender him to the empire. She would use whatever influence she possessed with her family in Magravandias to protect him. Something had changed Valraven from the boy Pharinet had grown up with to the passionless warrior he was now. Varencienne had yet to discover the full story, but she had no doubt that one day she'd be successful in this task. Then she would have armour and weapons with which to defend her son.

Varencienne stood up abruptly. The land was showing her the answer, presenting its fruits to her in silent appeal. She could not ignore the message.

Varencienne rode straight home, without visiting the Leckerys as she'd originally intended. By the time she reached Caradore, she'd not been greatly missed because it had become her habit to ride before breakfast, sometimes with Pharinet, but often alone. She went directly to her sister-in-law's chambers, filled with the desire to reveal her decision.

Pharinet listened to Varencienne's impassioned outpourings with an expression of bemusement, but as her enthusiasm ran its course, Varencienne became increasingly aware that Pharinet's expression was forced.

She couldn't be jealous about this, surely? She already knew Varencienne's feelings for Valraven. Still, no spoken response was forthcoming.

'Does this not seem the way forward?' Varencienne demanded. 'Please Pharinet, I feel very strongly about this. I need your support.'

Pharinet expelled a sigh, then nodded. 'Yes, you are right, of course.' She hesitated, picking through the remains of her breakfast. 'At one time, I had hoped that I might have Val's child, but that was not to be. I cannot argue that we need another dragon heir. It is why Val married you, after all – well, one of the reasons.' She looked up at Varencienne. 'But it is really up to nature, isn't it?'

Varencienne shook her head. 'I feel that now I have made this decision, it will happen. It was the message given to me on the Pike.'

Pharinet smiled. 'I can't believe I'm hearing these words from you. You were so against the idea of children. What if you hate having one yourself? How will you cope?'

Varencienne made a dismissive gesture. 'We'll find a nurse to look after him. That's a Magravandian royal tradition I refuse to surrender. I'll just have to endure the pregnancy and birth as best I can.'

Pharinet smile widened into a laugh. 'You are a singular creature, Varencienne.'

'Some things just have to be done.'

Valraven's return happened to coincide with Varencienne's birthday. When he arrived at the castle, he sent a servant to summon her to the stableyard. Here she was surprised to discover Valraven had bought her a gift, a beautiful Mewtish mare, the colour of old silver coins. Did this signify he was still friendly with Bayard? Varencienne doubted anyone else would remind him it was her birthday. When she questioned him about it, he responded, 'I paused in Magrast on my way to Caradore, and the empress invited me to tea. She asked me to bring you a gift from her. The next day, a Mewtish horse dealer was in the yard, and I saw the mare. I thought you'd like her. Pharinet tells me in her letters you have become quite a horsewoman.'

'The mare is very beautiful. Thank you.' Varencienne paused, then opted for bluntness. 'It would please me if you'd visit me tonight. There is something important I wish to discuss with you.'

Valraven examined her curiously for a few moments, then said shortly, 'Very well.'

It was only after Valraven had gone into the castle that Varencienne realized they had just had their first conversation.

The empress had sent her daughter some delicate, ancient jewellery that had once belonged to Tatrini's grandmother. Varencienne was suspicious at once. Why was Tatrini thinking of her now? Perhaps there was a message in the gift. That night, as she waited for Valraven to come to her, Varencienne read the accompanying letter. The empress spoke warmly in it, expressing the hope that Varencienne was happy and well. 'I often think of you,' she wrote, which Varencienne found hard to believe. She had consumed the best part of a decanter of dark red wine, and in a passion, scrawled a reply to her mother. First, she thanked Tatrini for the jewellery, then launched into a tirade. 'You are a stranger to me. Why give me presents now? Did you send me here? Palindrake was Bayard's lover, but you knew this, of course. He failed in whatever you wanted him to do, so you sent me instead. Isn't that so? What plan lies behind your actions?'

She knew it was dangerous to be so open in a letter, but had to purge herself of her feelings. Perhaps, tomorrow, she would burn the evidence.

When Valraven came into her room, Varencienne was drunk and told him bluntly that it was time for them to have a child. He regarded her expressionlessly as she spoke, but this she expected anyway.

'You seem to think I have some control over this,' he said. 'If that was so, surely there would have been a child before now.'

She shrugged. 'Perhaps it is I who have control. In any case, I have made up my mind.'

He smiled a little then. 'You are becoming like your mother,' he said. 'Caradore has made a woman of a little mouse.'

She wanted to tell him what she knew about him, but decided against it. She sensed that any mention of Ellony or Bayard would send him hurrying from the room. Like the other women around him, she would continue to keep him in ignorance. That night, for the first time, she recognized the fragility in him that Pharinet felt so concerned about. He could kill and he could use his cold nature to bully, but if the light of knowledge burst over him, he might crumple. As usual, he instigated a cold and clinical coupling, but to Varencienne this did not matter. She would never to look to him for warmth or affection. However, as she lay back while he knelt between her splayed thighs, she could not help thinking of Khaster. If he was making love to her now, she could open her eyes and see him looking down at her with kindness and adoration. She would reach up to him, drag him down to her embrace. She would curl her limbs about him. A spark of lust ignited within her, but before she could enjoy it, Valraven ejaculated and withdrew from her body. She almost laughed. But even so, at the moment when he'd released his seed, she'd been thinking of love, of closeness. This had to be seen as a good omen.

The letter Varencienne had written to the empress was never sent, although she did compose a more measured reply the following day. She extolled the virtues of Caradore, and spoke warmly of her new female relatives. 'They have taught me so much,' she wrote, and left the allusions at that. What she'd learned about her mother had changed the image Varencienne had of her in her mind. They had never been close, but now Varencienne could see Tatrini as an individual, someone strong, who tweaked strings of power from the shadows. She felt it was time the empress realized her daughter was not a nonentity, but then perhaps Tatrini had suspected it all along. If that was so, Varencienne admired the cool patience of a woman who could move a piece upon the board of life and then wait, without acting, to see what would happen.

Varencienne waited anxiously for a month to see whether she was with child. No blood came the first month, and none the second. Varencienne did not confide in anyone but Pharinet. 'Should I see a physician?' she asked.

Pharinet shook her head. 'I know who you should see.'

That very day they rode out of Caradore to the forest along the cliff, and here Varencienne was introduced to Grandma Plutchen. She supposed this must be a tradition with Palindrake women. The old woman only laughed when Pharinet explained why they were there. 'Have you no eyes, child?' she said, gesturing at Varencienne. 'Look at her. I hardly need to examine the girl.'

Varencienne was quite shocked a commoner could be so forthright with a noblewoman, but Pharinet clearly took no affront. 'Please Grandma, use your art with Ren. We want to be sure all is well. We want her baby to be healthy and strong.'

Grandma Plutchen gave Pharinet a strange, lingering look, then nodded. 'I'll put your mind at rest, though I'll tell you now, you've naught to fear. Also, don't think in terms of one cradle. The lass has two hearts beating in her belly.'

Pharinet laughed in delight, turning to Varencienne. 'That's wonderful! Did you hear that, Ren?'

Varencienne could not be so pleased. She thought only of the heavier pregnancy and longer labour. Grandma Plutchen took her into the back bedroom. 'You're a strong little mare,' Grandma said, as her fingers delved expertly in Varencienne's private places. 'Yes, yes, all is good. It's as it should be.'

'Thank you,' said Varencienne stiffly, pulling down her skirts.

The old woman washed her hands in a basin and then stood with folded arms, watching Varencienne put on her stockings and shoes. 'That family carries pain like a posy,' she said, shaking her head. 'Do none of you know the meaning of joy?'

Varencienne just gave her a hard glance. Had she no respect? She refused to comment. Grandma Plutchen, shook her head once more, grinning, and went back to the kitchen. Varencienne followed.

'Well?' asked Pharinet.

'So it begins,' said Varencienne.

A letter came from Bayard in the cold, dark months of the year before spring comes. The ground was hard, the trees skeletal, and little could be done to warm the draughty corridors of Caradore. Varencienne's stomach was round and taut now. Her breasts pained her, and she often felt ill. These symptoms she refused even to acknowledge. They would pass.

She took her brother's letter to a high room in a turret, where the windows were broken and snow blew in. She needed to be alone to see what he had written.

CHAPTER EIGHT

News

My dearest sister Ren,

I trust you are in good health and find Caradore agreeable. I suppose it was inevitable you should discover my part in the Palindrake history, and I hope it did not make the situation difficult for you. I could not tell you before, although I thought about doing so. It was a great shock to me that you were given to Palindrake, but perhaps no surprise at all. The decision was not solely our mother's, although I suspect she suggested it to our father initially. The official reason, of which you know, still stands. But I think Mother wishes to maintain a presence in Caradore, for she always has an eye on the future. Do not think she will use you in the same way she made use of me. That avenue is forsaken. The book cannot return to Caradore. Do not think even to ask for it.

I can understand why you are angry I did not tell you I knew Valraven Palindrake, but it would not have been easy for me to to do so. You would have asked too many questions. Now there are fewer for me to answer. I loved Valraven from the moment I first saw him, which is a time I can recall in crystal clarity. They brought him into the cathedral to initiate him into the Splendifers and I could tell at once that here was a singular man. His hair was the purple-black of the king crow, and he had the bearing found only in those of royal blood. He was tormented even then, for he had just left his sister after discovering for the first time that she returned his love. Valraven is confused by feeling. It sends him reeling, which is both endearing and exasperating. I talk this way as if he is still the man he was, which of course he is not. I courted him, but he did not recognize this fact. Men of Caradore are uncomfortable with affection among brothers, and with many other kinds of affection too, I feel. They can be rigid in this way. We sent him into the firepits, which I thought would change him, and it did. Perhaps more drastically than I had accounted for. When he returned to Magrast after his wedding, it was clear to me he was disturbed and I realized the time for games was over. I went to his chambers and offered him the hand of friendship. His friend, Leckery, was causing him grief over events that had transpired in Caradore, and he needed a confidant at that time. He told me his wife was gravely ill, though I have always thought he cared less about that than about his dilemma over Pharinet. I was astonished he could surrender his sister to such a man as Leckery and told him so. That was when he confessed his feelings for her. I could take away the pain of that by accepting without question or censure the way he felt about her. In Magrast, of course, such things are commonplace. He was comforted by this and turned to me for reassurance like a young boy. He seemed to me a fascinating mass of contradictions. His calm nature spoke to me of inner strength, yet at times he was vulnerable and afraid. He learned to fight, and then I saw in him a mindless savagery that seemed at odds with his innate nobility. In love, he was passionate and demanding, while also possessing the capacity for an isolating coldness.

We went to Cos, and in that hostile land, Valraven learned the finer points of warfare. He was destined to be a general, far from enemy lines, yet that did not satisfy him. Even before his full promotion, he would lead his men in battle, and soon earned the reputation for invincibility. He was also considered lucky. Whomever served beneath him felt his influence protected them. It was true he lost fewer men than other commanders, and even though his troops feared his often reckless campaigns, they respected and obeyed him utterly. They called him The Dragon, and some claimed they had seen fire burst from his eyes as he fought. The Cossics tried many times to assassinate him, but always failed. To me, at that time, he was like a god. Leckery detested me, and blamed me for the changes he saw in his erstwhile friend. But I was never responsible. What bloomed in Valraven Palindrake had lain hidden inside him since birth.

When I was next in Magrast, our mother sent for me and told me I should go with Valraven to Caradore on his next leave. She said that I was not making full use of my friendship with him. I was puzzled by her words, and then she explained to me about the sea dragons, and the history of the Palindrakes. I discovered Valraven was not called The Dragon for nothing. I did what I did merely to ensure survival in a competitive environment. I need all the support I can get, for on the day that our father passes succession to Gastern, all of our lives could change. Our eldest brother is, as you know, an inflexible man, with ideas of his own about how the empire should be run. We should all ensure we have a place to our liking in this new order when it arrives.

Pharinet, Valraven and I attempted to rewaken the ancient dragons, but failed, in that we provoked a power we could neither control nor were prepared to face. We had the knowledge the empress had given us, we had each other, but the sea wife was weak, perhaps tainted. With hindsight, I can see that Pharinet was the true sea wife. We should not have tried to pass the power to the Leckery girl. You know, of course, what happened to her. I do not feel it was regrettable. The Leckerys are not fit consorts for people such as the Palindrakes, whereas we of the Malagash dynasty eminently are. My fears for you do not concern the family, for whom I have the greatest admiration, but Valraven Palindrake himself. I will explain. After the rite at the shore, I did what I could to re-establish unity between Valraven, Pharinet and I. We arranged to meet in my chambers, so that we could seal our friendship with love and pleasure. But we were not alone. The daughters of Foy possessed us, entered our flesh to experience its pleasures, which they lack. The Palindrakes and I should have come together in perfect balance; physically, mentally and spiritually. The dragon daughters perverted that. They hate living beings, but also envy us. Their cold forms crave our heat. Their passionless hearts hunger for the sensation of emotion. But they are like careless children with these things, which are toys to them. They do not realize how fragile human feeling is, and once they have broken it, they cast it aside.

I cannot, and would not, describe that night in detail to anyone. Suffice to say, I faced the worst of myself and found it pleasing. Only with morning came horror, shame and regret. There is an aspect of Valraven which is troubled and frail, and could not withstand this experience. I did not realize at the time how grievously it would affect him. When we returned to Cos, he was twice the man he was, but the elements that were enhanced were those of savagery, coldness and madness. I saw him commit atrocities that appalled even me. He was full of rage, which I think was the rage of Misk, the dragon daughter who has secured for herself a seat in his soul. She has never left him, whereas Jia and Thrope possessed Pharinet and myself for but a single night. Valraven was not as broken as I'd thought. Misk had fashioned a new toy from him, one more to her liking. After that, Valraven turned from me completely, blaming me for the damage he'd suffered. I believe he has a subconscious inkling of what has happened to him, and denies Misk some of her pleasures deliberately. Ever since the night she first came to him, he has never touched me again in love, or anyone else, to my knowledge. Misk's vicarious indulgences centre solely around war and death.

As for Khaster Leckery, do not believe all that his family tells you. He is not the noble creature they no doubt fondly remember. He took satisfaction from the fact that Valraven Palindrake became estranged from me. He even had the audacity to taunt me, which unfortunately prompted me to reveal the fact that his wife was unfaithful to him with her brother. I also mentioned I had slept with her myself during the visit to Caradore. Leckery was a fop and a hypocrite. He scorned Magrast and all her people. He scorned our ways, and in particular my relationship with Valraven, which he called unnatural. Yet all the while, he kept a boy himself – Tayven Hirandel, a slut of the court, well-used by the majority of our brothers. I doubt Leckery's grieving family are aware of this relationship. Pharinet deserved better than such a man. As I suspected, he could not deal with the information I gave to him. He was a coward, and I find it hard to believe he died in battle. More likely he adorned with his effects a ravaged corpse which was beyond recognition. Then he would have run away. Officers such as he rarely venture into the front line, yet off he went, a man who was supposed to be a reluctant conscript. He will be dead by now. If he did abscond, he was lost in a savage land, and any foreigner would be killed there outright.

If I talked of Valraven Palindrake disparagingly before you went to Caradore as his bride, it was the voice of my pain. Take care, Ren. Do not make the mistake I made, of thinking we have mastery over the elements of Caradore. What came into me on that fateful day we tried to wake the dragons was feeling intense beyond endurance. That is the nature of water. And the cost of my actions was that I lost he whom I loved above all. Bitterness turned that feeling to hate, but I am not deceived. The ghost of what could have been haunts my heart. Do not think you can reach him, because you can't. Enjoy your life with Pharinet and her friends. She is a fine woman. If you are lucky, Palindrake's presence will plague you only rarely. Do not love him, for his ice will extinguish your fire. That is my strongest advice.

     Your loving brother,
     Bayard

CHAPTER NINE

Dragon Queen

Varencienne laid the letter in her lap and leaned back against the cold stones of the window casement. Outside, huge snowflakes fell out of the sky to hiss upon the ground, the walls, the treetops, and blew in to turn to water on her hands. She felt a poignant melancholy, especially for the unfortunate Khaster. Whatever Bayard said about him, Varencienne felt in her heart that Khaster had been a good man. If he had taken a male lover, it was hardly surprising. After hearing of Pharinet's betrayal with two men, he had probably sought solace that would not remind him of his faithless wife. As for Bayard's suspicions concerning Khaster's alleged death, they were undoubtedly impossible to prove one way or another. There would be more to the story, of course, because there always was, but this time Varencienne had little hope of discovering the truth. If it survived at all, it lay deep in the hostile land of Cos. She hoped that Bayard was right in his assumptions, though. She hoped that Khaster was alive, had escaped the anguish of his life and now lived somewhere in Cos, freed from pain. Bayard's revelations to Khaster had been cruel and needless, yet from the tone of his letter her brother clearly thought his actions were justified.

Varencienne went back down to the main area of the castle, but sought to avoid Pharinet. The knowledge Bayard had revealed hung heavily within her. Should she tell Pharinet or not? In her position, Varencienne would want to know, but then the information was hurtful. Pharinet claimed not to have loved Khaster, but Varencienne did not think this was wholly true. She had merely not loved him as much as she loved Valraven. Also, Varencienne felt angry with Pharinet, because she had lied. She'd implied Bayard had left Caradore directly after the rite at the shore. Now

226

Varencienne knew the truth. Pharinet, Valraven and Bayard had been possessed by the dragon daughters, who'd used their flesh as vehicles for their own pleasure. Pharinet had taken part in that act only hours after the ocean had taken her sister-in-law and friend. The carelessness of this unfeeling act, plus the nature of other information Bayard had imparted, made it impossible for Varencienne to approach Pharinet now. Neither could she confide in Niska. Yet the need to unburden herself was great. Ultimately, there was only one person to whom she could whisper these terrible things.

Varencienne put on her thickest cloak of wolf fur and took the slippery path down to the beach. She had to be careful to avoid prying eyes, for she knew that anyone in the castle would prevent her from making this excursion. She carried the future dragon heir in her belly, and the weather outside was foul. People died on more clement days.

The air was thick with soft snowflakes that leached all sound from the world. There was no wind, although the air was bitterly cold. Varencienne's tears turned to ice upon her cheeks. She told herself she felt so upset because of the hormones that now controlled her body, preparing it for motherhood.

The sea was like molten lead, hardly moving, and the sky above it was dirty grey. Varencienne sought the shelter of a rocky arch near Pharinet's sea-cave. It was peaceful there, and so quiet. Varencienne clambered up the rocks, and here there were echoes thrown back from the arch above her: the scrape of her feet, her breath. She found for herself a small niche and sat back into it. From there, she could observe the waves.

Grandma Plutchen's words came back to her: 'That family carries pain like a posy. Do none of you know the meaning of joy?' It was true. A maelstrom of thoughts whirled around Varencienne's mind, mixing into one another.

She should feel love for the new life she carried, yet her heart was numb. She should love her husband, but how could anyone love so cold and cruel a man? The Palindrakes had made mistakes which had ruined and ended lives. But perhaps it was not entirely their fault. They acted in ignorance. What would Caradore have been like if the empire had not consumed it? Foy and her daughters might still be manifest in the land, through their channels, the dragon heir and his sea wife. And, more recently, if Bayard had not come home with Valraven that time, Ellony and Thomist would still be alive, perhaps even Khaster. But if that was so, Varencienne would never have married Valraven and come here. What would she be doing instead?

Did all these separate elements comprise the parts of one big dilemma?

Varencienne sighed and closed her eyes, pressing her head back against the rock.

'Foy, if you sleep out there, let me enter your dreams. Show me a way to bring joy back to Caradore. Give me the knowledge of healing.'

She didn't know what else to say. She rested her head on her raised knee; snowflakes, which had formed a crust on the fur of her hood, melted against her closed eyes. Could Foy ever be an agent of healing? All the legends she'd heard suggested otherwise. Then why bother to plead at all?

You are doing what you can already, Varencienne thought. Surely children would bring joy to the Palindrakes? She was quite sure she'd give birth to a boy and a girl.

But another, darker voice whispered within her. Yes, but they might grow only to suffer the same fate as Valraven and Pharinet. When the Magravands took Caradore, they took more than land or dignity.

The emperor was afraid of the Caradoreans, Varencienne decided. That was why their heritage was kept from them. How could she change that? Despite the fact she could feel no great surge of love for her growing son, she did not want to surrender him to the empire. She felt that allowing him to be lord of Caradore was the only way for the wound in the Palindrakes' collective soul to be healed. But how could she convince her father of this? Could her mother be an ally?

Ideas and imagined conversations spun round in Varencienne's head. None seemed practicable. Maybe she should just give birth to her child and carry on, as Pharinet did, dreaming of a possible future.

She felt it, then, a vibration beneath the rock. For one terrible second, she thought an earthquake had come, or subsidence, and that she would be swallowed whole by cracking stone.

The sound travelled up her spine and settled in her brain. It was then that she recognized it as a cry: despairing, yet defiant. It was a trumpet call that blazed with light and streamed banners of memory. It was the song of Caradore in strength, the song of victory. It was the voice of Foy.

Varencienne braced herself against the rock. Her frozen hands were numb against the stone, their fingernails turning blue. 'I am here,' she said aloud. 'Speak to me, great Foy. Show me.'

She pushed herself back against the sharp icy stone. Her head felt full of pressure, and a needling pain started up behind her eyes. The air pressed down upon her like gloved fists. She felt she must burst.

Without warning, her mind broke free of her body. She felt it tear away, instantly and shockingly. She was shooting up into the sky and, looking down, could see herself slumped among the rocks. She was sprawled like a discarded doll, or as if all her limbs were broken. Her face, her hands, were the white of death. The sea below pulsed with distant blots of light that seemed to rise from some great depth. They were a beacon that called to Varencienne's spirit. Like a diving bird, she swooped down towards them.

The sea closed over her and she was travelling down so fast that she could perceive no details of her surroundings. Nuggets of light shot past her, mere blurs. The experience was having far more effect on her senses than the visions and impressions she'd had at the Chair. This felt so real: as bizarre as a dream, yet she was awake. She could feel the cold water rushing past her, smell its fishy saltiness. Bubbles crackled in her ears.

Her descent was so speedy, it took only a few minutes, but perhaps it was difficult to judge the passing of time in this state. Gradually Varencienne became aware of being surrounded by a weak green radiance, which grew increasingly brighter. Her plunge began to slow. She passed through an immense soft tangle of iridescent weed and, beyond it, a scene revealed itself to her.

She found herself on the edge of a precipice, looking down on what could only be the place Pharinet had once described to her: the sunken kingdom of the Ustredi. It must be a dream, yet it clearly was not. She was really there, hanging in the water above the astounding ruins. They were so big they dwarfed Magrast. Giants must have built the city and lived there – or dragons. Pharinet thought that, at one time, it must have been above sea level, but Varencienne did not agree with that. This was a sea kingdom. It had always been so. The gigantic buildings were dark and deserted. All light came from the sea bed itself. There were no merpeople twisting in and out of the cyclopean doorways.

Varencienne no longer felt completely human. She had a body of silver light. Had she created this herself? She was still unsure how much control she had over this vision, but twisted her ethereal body and discovered she could move like a fish. Whatever this form was, and however she had come to possess it, it was lissom and quick. She launched herself over the precipice and undulated swiftly towards one of the great black openings in the stone. The buildings could have been temples or palaces. They exuded an aura of sacred power that was both dangerous and holy. The walls were covered in strange inscriptions and carvings, their fine detail blurred, smudged with weed and colonies of tiny black molluscs.

Varencienne entered the nearest building, a minnow swimming into a drowned cathedral. Inside, it was lit dimly by the unearthly greenish radiance. She found herself in an immense domed chamber whose walls were ribbed like the interior of a sea creature's shell and covered with strange lumpish projections that suggested ornamentation. The floor was littered with cubes of stone of various sizes, some as small as dice, others the size of houses. Varencienne could not discern their purpose. The floor was also ribbed and blended seamlessly with the walls. There were several doorways leading off the chamber, and from some of them came disturbing vibrations. Varencienne hovered, tiny in the immensity of this underwater space. She was so small that if anything did still occupy the building, she was sure it would not even notice her.

She was drawn towards one of the doorways and swam through it. Beyond was a triangular corridor. Varencienne darted down it. Colossal statues with the mouths of fish lurked in the weedy shadows. Between them were openings into other, smaller chambers, whose floors were draped in carpets of fluorescent green sea-foliage. Shifting veils of weed obscured the walls, in which fishes swam and crustaceans crawled. Otherwise there was no sign of life.

Varencienne explored the building for what felt like several hours. She became lost within a labyrinth of passageways and chambers, yet felt no fear. She was here for a purpose and sensed strongly that once she had fulfilled that purpose, she would find her way out very easily. The vibrations she had perceived earlier were louder now. It was almost as if a choir of very deep voices sang somewhere nearby, and she was drawing closer to it all the time.

She came at last to a gargantuan pointed archway. Streamers of rotting black weed hung down from its apex and slow-moving, slug-like molluscs oozed through them, emitting a wan light. Varencienne shivered through the gently waving ribbons.

Beyond was a chamber so vast she could barely comprehend it. The floor was heaped with sea-treasure. Sunken ships lay on their sides like discarded toys. She saw the pale glint of gold and the seductive shimmer of jewels. Torn sails drifted on the gentle current, the garments of drowned giants. Varencienne swam slowly across the chamber, between the clawed spars of the ships. She expected to see skulls grinning at her from the wrecks, but there were none. The vibrating sound was a constant hum now and the meagre light began to grow dimmer around her.

She entered a realm of shadows, and here something pale moved. It was huge, a shifting mass of detritus: weed, wooden spars, rocks and netting. Varencienne swam closer and a long narrow head snaked out of the mass, fixing her with a yellow feline eye.

'Foy,' murmured Varencienne, and the name came out of her in a stream of glittering bubbles.

The dragon queen heaved her great mass upon the floor, splintering galleons beneath her bleached claws. Each movement seemed to pain her. She was old and decaying. Her bat-like wings were spread out across her haul, full of holes. Here there were bones aplenty, but they could also have been part of the queen's body.

'Speak to me,' Varencienne said. 'Tell me my purpose. Tell me what should be done.'

The dragon could not speak. She was a creature without a voice, an elemental force reduced to stagnation. But looking at her, Varencienne became aware of knowledge. She saw in her mind the figure of a man, young and straight-limbed, his hair blowing about his shoulders. This image Foy gave to her as an aged grandparent might impart a jewel of her youth to her daughter's child.

'Is this my son?' Varencienne asked. 'Is this what you show me?'

But no, she knew this man. It was Khaster Leckery. Did this mean he was alive? Did he have some part in her future? A scene revealed itself to her as if a magical mirror was held before her eyes. It was like looking out of a window. She saw a mill next to a dark pool, and a boy diving into it. When he emerged, he was a man, and he held a shining chalice in his hands. She did not know this person. Could he be her son? As if her mind conjured the image, she saw him then in battle, red darkness all around him, smoke and blood. She could hear terrible screams of agony. Then the image shifted and she saw herself with this man, running away from Caradore. She saw Valraven in the castle, looking more like a demon than ever, his face ugly with rage. Then the man she thought might be her son was standing like a gigantic god above a city in flames. He had the chalice in his hands again and poured its waters over the fire, extinguishing it completely.

The images ceased abruptly. The whole sequence had perhaps taken no more than a few seconds to play itself before Varencienne's inner eye.

The dragon laid her long snout down between her front claws. Her massive sides heaved in a sigh and bubbles trickled out of her splayed nostrils. Her eyes closed, as if by showing the images she had exhausted herself.

Varencienne swam closer right up to one of the wrinkled eyelids. When that eye opened again, she would be engulfed in its light. 'Poor Foy,' she said, but had no hands to reach out and touch. How could this dragon be summoned to rise in strength? She had no strength. She could not rise.

'What is your strength?' Varencienne said. 'How can I help you?'

The eye did not open. Foy expelled a lamenting groan.

Varencienne filled with emotion: despair, sadness and resignation. She had made demands and they had hurt Foy. She was so weak. Varencienne experienced a fleeting impression of a younger Foy, flying through the sea, swimming through the sky. Her daughters were with her, creatures of light. Now they were something else, hideous sirens full of hate and lustful revenge, over which their mother had no control. They were not confined to the underwater realm, because human greed had loosed them into the land. Foy's sorrow engulfed Varencienne's entire being. The dragon queen did not want resurrection; she wanted release.

Varencienne was jerked back into her body with a nauseating jolt. Someone was shaking her, calling her name. She opened her eyes and saw Pharinet's face hanging over her.

'By Madragore, I thought you were dead!' Pharinet hissed. 'What are you doing out here? Are you mad?'

Varencienne groped towards her with numb stiff fingers. 'Pharry,' she said in a croak. 'I saw Foy. I've been down there.'

'What?' Pharinet's voice was the cold hiss of falling snow.

'It's true. I travelled in my mind. I met Foy. I had to do it.'

Pharinet seemed frozen, then knelt down and put her arms around the girl. 'Why, Ren? Why now? You shouldn't take risks.'

'I wasn't,' Varencienne said. She shook her head painfully. 'It was terrible, Pharry. Foy wants only to die. She cannot live, she cannot die. We help keep her in that state.'

'You're raving,' said Pharinet. 'Can you stand up?'

'Listen to me! It's important.'

Pharinet sighed. 'We can't talk here.'

'We must, because I will never speak of it again. It's so clear to me now. There are no dragons, Pharry, not in the way that the Sisterhood want. There is only ourselves. We have the solutions for the future, not fabled beasts. Foy is a captive of human desire. It is cruel.'

Pharinet examined her for a few moments. 'I understand what you're saying, but I can swear to you that the power of the dragons is very real. I have felt it in my flesh.'

'I know,' Varencienne answered. 'They possessed you, along with Valraven and my brother. He did not ride home directly after Ellony disappeared. I know what happened afterwards. He told me.'

Pharinet went very still. 'How?'

'A letter,' Varencienne said. 'Didn't you consider I'd write to him, given what I've learned recently?' She gripped one of Pharinet's hands. 'What you experienced was the bitterness of the dragon daughters, not Foy's presence. You must expel any remnant of it from your heart.'

'Dispel it?' Pharinet snatched her hand away from Varencienne's hold. 'You can't comment or give me advice about that time, Ren, because you weren't there. You don't know what you're talking about. It was hideous. Valraven, Bayard and I, we came together like monsters. I hated myself for it. Ellony and Thomist were not even cold in their sea-grave. Our coupling was like dancing on their tomb. Yet I could not resist. Can I blame Jia for that? I felt her presence within me, yet part of me knows the desire was utterly mine, the selfishness, the heartlessnes, the lack of care. Jia smelled it out, perhaps, and attached herself to it, but I will not blame an elemental force for what took control of me that night. It would be too convenient.'

Varencienne stared at Pharinet, unable to speak. She could almost see the steam of raw emotion pouring from Pharinet's body.

Pharinet put her head in her hands. 'I vowed never to speak of that night again, not to anyone, least of all you. Look what you have done to me.'

'You needed to speak,' Varencienne said. 'I did not make you do it.'

Pharinet stared up at the sky, blinking away tears. Varencienne could see her trying to control what she felt, the need to weep with abandon until the grief was purged. But perhaps it never could be. An ocean of tears would not be enough.

'I want to go home now,' Varencienne said.

Varencienne kept her silence. She did not tell Pharinet, or anyone else, about the visions she'd experienced in the city beneath the sea. Only time would reveal if there was any truth in them. The meeting with Foy affected her deeply. She felt it had shown her only human weakness, greed and stupidity. The rituals the Sisterhood conducted meant nothing; they were selfish. What they really perpetuated was the continuing, if distant, reign of the dragon daughters, whose influence hung like a depressing miasma over the land. Varencienne wanted to deny this influence and felt that the only way to do that was to allow Foy to die, to look to the future in terms of taking responsibility for it. For too long, the Caradoreans had relied on a myth.

In the autumn of that year, Varencienne gave birth to twins, a boy and a girl. The boy was named Valraven for his father, but the girl she felt driven to name Ellony, for the daughter that Niska's sister would never have.

PART THREE

Revenant

CHAPTER ONE

Homecoming

Three Years Later: Caradore

Everna and Varencienne sat with the children in the garden at Norgance. Saska was picking apples with her daughters nearby, helped by Oltefney, who was now virtually a member of the Palindrake family. Dimara wasn't there, but then she always shunned the house when Varencienne came to call. The sun shone gently over the late summer scene, casting a golden glow over the walls of the great house. The air smelled of ripening fruit.

Everna pursed her lips and said, 'I thought young Rav would have the Palindrake colouring. It seems strange to see a son of our house so fair.'

Everna did not wholly approve of this departure from tradition, Varencienne realized, and probably blamed her, the mother. 'Perhaps he will have more of the sun in him when he becomes a man,' she said, with a placatory smile. 'We need light in our lives.'

This was a careful criticism of Valraven the father, but Everna chose not to recognize it.

Much had changed over the last three years. The Sisterhood had finally asked Varencienne to join their ranks, an invitation that she took pleasure in declining. This did nothing to improve her relationship with Dimara Corey, but her opinion was irrelevant to Varencienne. She knew the truth now. Foy would never rise. Whatever the Malagash dynasty had done to the dragons, and the Palindrakes, the damage had been too thorough. What remained was a fragile memory, sustained by the Sisterhood's ignorant worship. Varencienne could only despise the way Foy was kept alive in a wretched, powerless state.

Valraven had seemed pleased with his children, although, like his wife,

237

he was not given to displays of affection. Everna had once again assumed a mothering role, as she had when her brother and sister had been born. This slightly surprised Varencienne, given the speech Everna had given her on the battlements when she'd arrived as a new bride in Caradore. Pharinet adored Rav, and he spent nearly every day with her, sitting in front of her horse's saddle as she rode about the estate, exploring the land with her. However, it was blindingly clear that Pharinet shied away from Rav's sister, Ellony.

Varencienne herself had found the whole birth process foul and had no desire to think about it ever again. The only time she'd consider having more children would be if the boy died. She hoped this would not be necessary. Now that Valraven had an heir, he no longer visited Varencienne's room on the rare occasions he came home on leave. This suited both of them fine. Everna might shake her head and make a disapproving sound, but Varencienne knew that Valraven did not desire warmth or contact from any living person, and she herself did not want to endure intimacy with a man who felt that way. Now they were able to be cordial with one another. She sensed he was grateful for the way she behaved and regarded him. She was, in fact, his perfect wife. Varencienne knew she herself had the potential to be a passionate creature, but there was no one in Caradore to ignite her feelings. The closest she came to it was when she thought about Khaster Leckery. Even now, she still liked to walk the long gallery in Norgance, savouring the moment when she could pause before the portrait. Khaster inhabited her fantasies, but even if he wasn't dead, he might as well be. This situation was entirely to Varencienne's liking. Ghosts could be whatever she wanted them to be, whereas real men were problematical. They had to control and demand.

Varencienne felt far older than her years. She liked life in Caradore, and had resigned herself to the fact that magic resided only in the past. When she'd arrived here, she'd awakened memories, but it seemed that once she had learned the tragic history of her new family, and the sad truth about the dragons, that immediate sense of magic had faded. If she ever thought she saw wisps of smoke in corners of Caradore, she now convinced herself it was a trick of the light. It disappointed her a little that her imagination had become less active than in the past. Some part of her had been lost, but she felt that in many ways this had to be seen as a blessing.

She wrote to Bayard and her mother regularly, but had not seen either of them since she'd followed her new husband to his home. There was never any mention of the past in their correspondence, and Bayard skirted the subject of Valraven. When the twins had been born, Leonid, her father the emperor, had sent gifts, but neither of Varencienne's parents seemed interested in actually seeing their grandchildren.

The empire's purge through Cossic territory now meant that corner of her father's domain was secure. The armies waited on the borders, perhaps wondering when the order would come for them to march onwards. Casualties had been great and supplies were low. It was believed the empire would rest and re-arm itself before making any further moves.

These events, of course, barely touched the lives of the women in Caradore. Their men were still absent, but recently there had been no fatalities among them. Local families all breathed a sigh of relief to think that, for a while at least, their menfolk were off active duty. Varencienne knew Valraven was on leave in Magrast, but he had not come home.

Now she lay in the caressing sunshine, and it was as if her life was complete. She had somehow got her own way. She wondered then about her old friends, Mavenna and Carmia. They had exchanged a few letters early in Varencienne's marriage, but this had petered out. Everna's words had come true, she had other friends now to occupy her mind, and the children had come.

Little Ellony ran to where her mother sat beneath the shade of the trees. In her cupped hands she held a captive butterfly, which she presented proudly to Everna. Ellony was a careful, sensitive child. If Rav caught a butterfly he'd no doubt kill it accidentally. The insect lay with outspread wings across Ellony's tiny palms, and then flew up into the branches. The girl laughed in delight. 'Pretty!'

Everna reached out to stroke her hair. Ellony always went to Everna.

'You are her real mother,' Varencienne said.

Everna glanced at her, perhaps seeking irony or bitterness in her face, but Varencienne knew she would find none. 'I sometimes wonder whether it is my fault,' Everna said. 'Those things I once said to you. They affected you, didn't they?'

Varencienne sighed, blinking up at the leaves. 'Perhaps they did, but it is irrelevant. I have performed my duty, and everyone is happy.'

Everna shook her head. 'You are like an old woman sometimes, Ren.'

Varencienne laughed softly, but said nothing.

Everna stared at her, clearly formulating another remark, but it was never spoken. A servant ran out from the house, screaming, 'Lady Saska!'

The sense of urgency was immediate, and with it came a thrill of dread.

'What is it?' Saska hurried forward, knocking over a basket of apples with her skirts.

'Sir Merlan!' gasped the servant, hands flapping.

Saska let out a dreadful moan, her hands flying to her face.

Niska and Ligrana were frozen in the act of rising from the grass, their hair hanging forward. Oltefney was frowning; curious and apprensive. 'What is it?' she asked.

'No,' breathed Everna.

Varencienne felt estranged from it all. It seemed another tragedy was about to befall the house of Norgance. She was slightly impatient with it.

Then a male voice called, 'Mother!'

The moment cracked and splintered. The sunlight came back in. Suddenly the garden was full of delighted squeals and Ligrana and Niska were scampering forward. Oltefney got to her feet behind them, her face wreathed in a relieved smile.

Varencienne turned in her seat. A young man had come into the garden. Not dead, then, but returned. A sense of recognition flooded through her; felt her flesh grow hot. It was Khaster. She nearly choked, but after only a moment, she realized it was someone else, someone who looked like him, who'd stolen his brother's face.

'Thank Foy,' said Everna, grinning. She got up and summoned the children. 'Uncle Merlan,' she said to them. They came forward, shy.

Varencienne also felt impatient with the way all the women immediately fawned over the newcomer. Reluctantly she got to her feet and went to stand at the edge of the group surrounding Saska's eldest surviving son. Close to, he looked uncannily like the portrait of Khaster that hung in the long gallery. But the resemblance was only physical, Varencienne felt. Merlan was neither melancholy nor despairing, but quite the opposite. There was also a certain slyness to his expression. Light brown hair fell over his face, which was corded with muscle as if his features were in constant motion. Varencienne had heard all the stories about Merlan; he now held quite a prestigious position as Assistant to the Governor of Mewt. He was not a soldier but an administrator, safe from combat. His skin had been tanned dark brown by the hot sun of Mewt, and gold highlights shone in his hair. He wore gold Mewtish earrings in his ears, hoops wound with tiny enamelled snakes.

After some moments of effusive greeting and hugging, Saska took her son's arm and indicated Varencienne. 'This is Valraven's wife, the emperor's daughter.'

Merlan looked her over. 'Of course, the Princess Varencienne.'

Varencienne inclined her head.

'I saw Val while I was in Magrast,' he said. 'I have a package for you.'

'Thank you,' Varencienne said. 'I trust you will visit Caradore while you are here?'

Merlan glanced at Everna. 'I expect I shall. Where's Pharry?'

'She's not with us today,' Everna said, 'but she'll be sorry to have missed this homecoming.'

Varencienne wondered about that.

Later it became clear to Varencienne that Pharinet felt uncomfortable around Merlan. Perhaps this was because he looked so much like Khaster. It seemed an instinct had made her decline to accompany her relatives to Norgance that day. Varencienne watched Pharinet's face as Everna described the afternoon's events. 'He has changed a lot now,' she said. 'He is quite dashing. You'll be surprised.'

Varencienne knew she was not the only person present to detect a subtext to that remark. Merlan was around twenty years old, twelve years younger than Pharinet. Would such a match be permissible in Caradore?

Pharinet merely gibbered a laughing response, which illustrated her discomfort, then said, 'He's a boy, Evvie!'

'He's done very well for himself. Seems so mature.'

Men were worshipped in Caradore. Varencienne was sickened by it.

Two days later, Merlan rode over to Caradore, accompanied by his sisters and his little brother, Foylen. Varencienne, watching from an upper window of the castle that overlooked the courtyard, realized with some despair that a happy get-together of young people had been planned. She only hoped Pharinet would elect to be part of it, but she had her doubts.

Slowly Varencienne descended to the hall, where the Leckery women were talking loudly with Everna. The twins waddled about, making high-pitched noises. Wincing, Varencienne attempted to arrange her face into an agreeable expression.

'Ren!' Niska called. 'We have ordered a picnic from the kitchens. We shall all ride out somewhere nice together.'

'Actually,' said Varencienne, 'I feel a slight headache coming on.' The noise of the children would be hard to bear, because the Leckerys always encouraged them to be loud, but it would be worse to endure the sycophantic pawing of Merlan.

The Leckerys seemed oblivious to her mood, however, and ignored her arguments. Within the hour the company clattered out of Caradore, Foylen driving a cart in which sat Niska, Ligrana and the twins. Everna and Pharinet, predictably, were absent. Varencienne rode her own horse, as did Merlan. In the event, they did not ride far, just some distance along the cliff path in the direction of the Rock Village. Partway there was a grove of ash trees, their drooping branches fluttering nervously in the wind off the sea. Here Ligrana and Niska set about laying out the picnic among the wild lavender. Varencienne was not in the mood for this. Not even bothering to offer to help the other women, she sat down on the grass and clasped her hands round her knees. Merlan stood beside her. 'Your children are beautiful. I suppose one of us Leckerys should start breeding soon so we can carry on the interfamily marriage tradition that began with Valraven and Pharinet.'

Varencienne considered that remark in poor taste. Or had it been a jibe? 'Is that why you're home, to secure a bride?' she asked. 'It seems the obsession here.'

'I'm in no rush.' He sat down. 'Though I expect my mother will have coach-loads of local nubiles parading around for my benefit while I'm home.'

'You're lucky to have a choice.' Something about Merlan made her feel defensive.

He narrowed his eyes at her but made no comment. 'So, what do you do with yourself here? It must be boring for you after Magrast.'

'Not at all. I love Caradore. It has a lot of history. The ancient sites interest me very much.'

'And I expect everyone has drummed into you how the history is mostly the fault of your family.'

She smiled tightly. 'At first. I think they realize now I'm my own person. I'm very interested in history. The sites tell you a lot about the past.'

'And they approve of you poking round old Caradore?'

'Excuse me? I don't have to "poke" around my own home.'

'I wasn't referring to that. I meant the *old* Caradore, the one the Palindrakes left when the empire moved in.'

She frowned. 'I didn't realize there was one.'

He reclined on the grass, resting his head on one hand. 'Then you've missed the most important site, surely.'

'Where is it?' Varencienne asked. She was finding it increasingly difficult to dispel the illusion she was speaking to Khaster. Merlan was someone else; she must be careful.

He jerked his head in the direction of the Rock Village. 'That way. It's quite a ride.'

'Have you been there?'

'Yes. When I was much younger. Some friends and I ran away for a couple of days. We were looking for ghosts.'

'And did you find any?'

He wrinkled his nose. 'Not exactly. But it's a bleak spot.'

'Is it very ruined?'

'Most of it is still standing, but I would say it's unsafe. Not that we cared about that as boys.'

Varencienne examined him carefully. 'I would like to see it, but somehow I can't imagine anyone wanting to take me there. I scent bad memories and fear.'

Merlan smiled slowly. 'I can take you.'

Varencienne realized that he had made her a conspirator in making him feel special, like the other women did. He had led the conversation, created its conclusion. Perhaps she should decline the invitation. However, she had to admit that this male attention intrigued her; she'd experienced so little of it. What were his motives? She was sure it couldn't be simple friendship. Strangely enough, the idea did not displease her. Was she seeking to realize one of her fantasies? It would be easy to imagine that Merlan was Khaster, far more so than pretending that Valraven was. This reaction, though shocking, also amused her. It made her feel reckless and alive. 'That's very kind of you,' she said. 'When can we go?'

He grinned at her. 'Tomorrow?'

Back at Caradore, Varencienne went looking for Pharinet and found her in one of the worksheds of the village that surrounded the castle. The shed was long, low and dark, the heavy air almost unbreathable in the afternoon heat. It smelled of tar, fish and rotting vegetation. Here sea plants were processed, turned into soap, fibres and animal feed. Pharinet was taking her pick of the latest crop for her servants to transform into cosmetic potions.

Varencienne told Pharinet about the picnic, and then mentioned Merlan's offer. 'I didn't know there was another castle. This, I suppose, was one of your secrets.'

Pharinet frowned. 'No, not really. It's a ruin, dead. I just didn't think to mention it. Why do you want to see it?'

'There may be answers there.'

'You already have your answers. You've made up your mind that the dragons are lost to us for ever.'

Varencienne shrugged. 'I just want to see it. I really do.'

Pharinet shrugged. 'Then go.'

'You don't mind?'

Pharinet began to sort through a mottled hank of dried weed. 'Why should I? It's just a ruin.' There was a tight tone to her voice.

'Pharry . . .?'

'What?'

243

'Is Merlan *very* like Khaster?'

Pharinet threw down the dry tangle and fixed Varencienne with a stare. It was not enough to deter her. 'Well, is he?'

Pharinet looked away, rubbed a piece of weed between her fingers. 'A bit. But they're different people. I don't know Merlan very well. He left Caradore before you came here, and I've not seen him since. He left here a boy and came back a man, as they all do.' She pursed her lips. 'But Merlan is not scarred, because he has an easy life. He comes bounding back to Caradore, oozing his good fortune.' She shook out some stinking fibres. 'He seems fond of himself, but that is not unusual in a man.'

'He intrigues me.'

Pharinet looked up and narrowed her eyes. 'You didn't know Khaster, Ren.'

Varencienne wandered around the work table, trailing her fingers across the surface. 'I feel I do. He seemed very . . . heroic . . . a tragic sort of person.'

'All that was tragic was that he was forced to leave his home and take up a life he hated. Ultimately, it killed him.'

Varencienne looked up slowly and met Pharinet's eyes. *Did it?* she asked without words.

Pharinet dropped her gaze, and Varencienne noticed the pulse of colour rising up her neck. 'You have no right to judge. In some ways, you're in the same position I was: married to a man you cannot love.'

Varencienne shrugged. 'True.' She smiled and tapped her fingers against the table. 'Still, I shall go to Old Caradore and see if I can awaken a few ghosts.'

Pharinet shook her head. 'Be careful, Ren. You are accepted here, but it's taken time. Don't do anything to jeopardize that.'

'What *are* you suggesting?'

'I think you know,' said Pharinet quietly.

That evening Varencienne's excursion to Old Caradore with Merlan was treated with what she felt was an undue amount of comment and excitement. Niska appeared to think she was being very daring, while Ligrana couldn't resist the odd sniping remark, clearly believing Varencienne just wanted to impress her brother. Everna, predictably, advised against it, backed up by Oltefney. 'There's nothing good left there,' Everna said. 'It should be left to lie.'

'My family destroyed it,' Varencienne replied. 'Don't you think I should consider it my duty to see what they did?'

'You have expended considerable effort convincing us you have separated

244

yourself from your family,' Everna said waspishly. 'If that is the case, you should shun the place as we do. Also, it may be dangerous.'

Varencienne cast a glance at Merlan. 'I'm sure I will be well looked after.'

'Valraven would not like it,' Everna said.

'Valraven is not here, and he need never know.' Varencienne stretched in her chair. 'It will be an adventure.'

'Too much of one,' said Everna. 'You'd be hard-pressed to ride there and back in a day.'

'Perhaps we could stay overnight.'

Oltefney expelled a disgusted snort. 'Is this really the pampered young princess of the Magrastian court speaking? Only a couple of years ago, you could barely dress yourself. Now you are thinking of camping rough in a ruin.'

Pharinet was grinning now, having clearly got over her earlier reaction. 'Oh, I think Ren will be fine,' she said. 'She has a belief in herself that creates an aura of safety.'

'I assure you she will be in safe hands,' said Merlan.

'I am responsible for my own safety,' Varencienne retorted.

Merlan raised an eyebrow at her. 'Should we encounter wolves or vagabonds, I will watch with interest as you deal with the situation.'

Varencienne found it uncomfortable to meet his glance. In the firelight, he looked more like his older brother than ever. 'Is that likely?'

He shrugged. 'Probably not, actually. As in all good legends, Old Caradore is a lonely, empty place. It is said both animals and humans avoid it, and no birds sing.'

'But of course. I would expect nothing less.' The tension between them intrigued and excited her.

Everna muscled in on their exchange. 'If you insist on this escapade, at least take some of our own guard with you,' she said. 'Legends aside, we have no way of knowing who or what might have made the old castle its home.'

'I suppose so,' said Varencienne. She quite liked the idea of leading a troupe of men into the unknown. *How quiet my imagination has been,* she thought. *Foy killed it. She showed me too much and destroyed my capacity to dream.*

CHAPTER TWO

Old Caradore

At dawn Varencienne rose from her bed and dressed herself in the garments Pharinet had lent her: soft suede trousers and shirt and high leather boots. Admiring herself in the mirror, Varencienne decided she should have adopted this sort of garb before. It made her feel competent and powerful. Were men's clothes part of what made them what they were? Oltefney had ordered the maids to leave out a cold breakfast in the small dining-room. The castle was so quiet, and it was still dark. No one was awake, except for herself, Merlan, and the guards who would accompany them. It seemed to Varencienne that this journey she would make was somehow preordained, because she'd got her own way so easily. She hoped to learn something at Old Caradore, or at least to feel something again. Then there was Merlan himself. Was something destined to occur between them? Only a day or so ago, her life had seemed settled and ordinary. She had felt old and unimaginative. Now everything had changed.

Shortly after she'd eaten, there was a soft knock at the door. She did not speak, but went to open it. Merlan stood at the threshold. She still felt a shock of recognition when she saw him. He had stepped from a portrait, from another world. Perhaps he was the man Khaster should have been. 'Are you ready?' he asked.

'Yes. I'll just get my cloak.'

He ventured into the room behind her. 'A coat would be better. It's a cold morning. Also, cloaks flapping about when you're climbing over old stones are not ideal.'

'I do not possess a coat. Pharinet has not provided me with one.'

'Perhaps one of the men might have something you could borrow.'

They went down to the guardhouse, where horses waited outside, huffing the chill air. 'It's kind of you to take me to the old castle,' Varencienne said, 'but I suspect this is mainly because you want to go there again yourself. Why?'

'It's a journey I've been meaning to make for a long time. I just haven't been home.'

They entered the stableyard. 'Old Caradore isn't your family home,' Varencienne said. 'What's the attraction?'

Merlan closed the gates behind them. 'You are either intrinsically curious or have a suspicious mind. What are my motives to you?'

She shrugged. 'I'm just curious, as you said. How long will the journey take?'

'About four hours if we keep up a good pace.'

Four horses stood in yard, being tacked up by a young guard Varencienne knew as Dray. A middle-aged man supervised the operation. This was Hamsin, one of the Palindrakes' most trusted officers, known to Merlan from his childhood. 'Excuse for a day out,' he said, as the older man examined the girth of his saddle.

Hamsin did not smile. 'Lady Everna requested I come with you.'

Varencienne could see he did not want to. What was he expecting? Was it just superstition, or did Old Caradore really lie under a curse?

'Could you find a good coat that will fit the Lady Varencienne?' Merlan said.

Hamsin looked Varencienne up and down. His expression was not exactly approving. 'See what I can find,' he said.

The coat he produced smelled musty and felt slightly damp, for which he apologized, but Varencienne did not complain.

The company left the castle and presently were cantering along the cliff path leading north-east. High tide washed the rocks below and perigorts hung impossibly huge, on outspread wings above it.

Varencienne had thought the travelling would be difficult; up tiny, twisting trails between mountain crags and through trackless forests. But soon after leaving Caradore's immediate territory, the party crossed the heath and joined the old Lord's Road, which had been built in the time of Valraven's great-great-great-grandfather. The road was constructed of huge slabs of yellowish stone, in which the sun picked out stars of quartz, and it was in surprisingly good condition. Varencienne commented on this, and Hamsin told her that traders passing into the north of Caradore always used this route.

'What is in the north?' Varencienne asked.

'A great wilderness full of animals, trees and plants of great value,' Hamsin answered.

'The people there have changed little in hundreds of years,' Merlan said. 'Perhaps some of them are not even aware of the empire, tucked away in their high eyries.'

'What sort of people are they?'

Hamsin laughed. 'You wouldn't like them, my lady.'

'Rather rough,' added Merlan. 'But before you start worrying about them, I can assure you they have no interest in Old Caradore. If anyone lives there, it won't be stray northerners.'

'I am not disposed to worry,' Varencienne said tartly. 'I was just curious.'

Along the way, they passed through villages and skirted the borders of other great estates. Merlan told Varencienne the names of the families who lived there: Galingale, Shieling, Ignitante and Doomes, many of whom Varencienne had already met. Some of them she had visited. But the further away from Caradore they went, so the families became only romantic names. Varencienne imagined that each of these great dynasties would have histories and scandals equal to the Palindrakes. The very sound of their names conjured images of great antiquity: Darthenate, Quiribellin, Gegadour.

They rode through a sparse wood, in whose centre they came upon a standing stone, carved with curling symbols. 'In this place,' said Varencienne in a dramatic voice, 'I feel that a daughter of the house of Darthenate met with the heir of Gegadour. It was a tragic match, and ended with her brothers slaughtering her lover against that stone.'

Merlan laughed. 'Not bad. The families were Darthenate and Rook, actually, and the Darthenate girl was burned there.'

'I knew it! I have a gift for these things.'

The men thought this was very amusing, but Varencienne was only half-joking.

Around midday they rode down a wide avenue of soaring poplars. Fields spread away to either side, in which shaggy cattle grazed. The hills beyond were crowned with follies: arches and mock ruins. Perhaps they were not follies at all, but had once been whole temples and summerhouses. Immense clouds boiled across the intensely blue sky, occasionally obscuring the sun. The air smelled of fallen fruit and damp earth.

'Whose domain is this?' Varencienne asked.

'No one's,' Merlan answered. 'We ride now upon Palindrake soil, of course, but I'd wager you're the first Palindrake to come here for generations. Local farmers use the land. Valraven's family has always charged them a small rent for the privilege.'

'We are close, then, to the castle?'

'It's not far.'

This was not at all how Varencienne had imagined the place. She'd thought the old domain would have been reclaimed completely by the forest. It was clear that at one time the land they rode in had once been part of a great estate. Lodge houses punctuated the road and some of them were still lived in.

'Why did the Palindrakes abandon this place?' Varencienne asked.

'By order of the emperor, Casillin, who took Caradore,' he replied. 'It was one of the conditions he set down. This was the seat of the Palindrakes' power. You will see. We have come very close to the ocean again. Listen, you will hear it.'

They drew their horses to a halt and Varencienne strained her ears to catch the whispering crash of far surf. It was there, faint, muffled by the tall trees. 'I can't believe Pharinet never came here,' she said. 'It seems her sort of place.'

'Superstition, fear, distaste,' said Merlan. 'Any of these sentiments might have prevented her.'

'From what I know of Pharinet, I'd have said such things would have encouraged her,' Varencienne said.

The road twisted round between the ancient trunks of an oak forest. Sunlight made coins of gold upon the road. Leaves and branches were strewn across it as if a storm had recently taken place. The company passed beneath a grey arch, atop which reared the broken effigies of dragons, surrounded by sentinel Ustredi. A wall snaked away into the trees to either side. This was the main entrance, although the gates had long gone. Varencienne learned that her ancestor, Casillin, had ordered this to be so. Old Caradore could never be a sanctuary again. Her inner lands lay open to whoever wished to walk there.

Beyond the arch, the road continued in much the same manner for some miles. Varencienne looked for broken turrets above the tree line, but saw nothing. The sound of the sea, though, was louder now. Sometimes she felt as if it was crashing into underground caverns beneath the horses' feet, because its roar seemed to come from every direction at once.

Then the ruins were before them. For a few moments Varencienne did not even recognize them for what they were. They looked like cliffs, covered with thyme and grass tufts and young birch trees. The company rode over a stone bridge, beneath which was a dizzying drop to a road far below. It was then Varencienne realized they had arrived at the Palindrakes' former home.

Rocks swarmed up the castle's side as if trying to reclaim and transmute it into a natural form. The domain had been built amid the living rock, sprawling over acres of ground. It was difficult to see where rocks ended and castle walls began. The stone was gilded with lichen and garbed in swarming growths of an evergreen shrub Varencienne had never seen before. The leaves were tiny and polished, like green fairy coins.

Varencienne drew her horse to a standstill. The men did likewise, looking back at her. 'I have *never* seen anything so beautiful,' she said.

The men said nothing. Varencienne urged her horse onwards, mindless of her companions' presence. The bridge led to an overgrown road where pale stone cobbles barely poked through the grass and apple green moss. Varencienne cantered along the road, driving her mount to go faster and faster. She wanted to find the main gate, for at this angle there was no way in to the castle. The land on the right side of the road dropped down hundreds of feet to a maelstrom of thrashing waves. Wind blew strongly off the sea and seemed filled with whispering voices. Varencienne clawed her hair from her face. She expected to hear the crack of flags in the wind, but there was just the whistle and moan of the raw elements that quested through the immense pile of stone.

Varencienne slowed her horse to a trot. She gazed up at the walls. They seemed to be mostly intact, punctuated by narrow arched windows, but the glass had gone. Perhaps they'd never had glass. It was so old. Battlements glowered down at her, possibly hiding observant eyes. She was not afraid and, conscious of the men riding behind her, wished she was alone to enjoy this communion with the past. She did not want human voices to intrude with inane comments or warnings. She wanted only the song of the sea and the wind, so that Old Caradore might reveal its ghosts to her. If anyone should be there with her at all, it should be Pharinet.

The castle was situated on a rounded promontory; the sea surrounded it on two sides, the right and the front. The front wall was the most badly damaged, which gave Varencienne a shock when she came upon it. She thought of Magravandian hordes battering at the main gate, but then realized that the elements were probably mostly responsible for the decay. She dismounted, staring at the huge jumble of stones and rocks that blocked the entrance. She had to get in somehow.

Merlan and the guards arrived alongside her and Merlan jumped down from his horse. She appreciated the fact that at first he did not speak. He allowed her to break their silence.

'The Palindrakes should live *here*,' she said.

'Might be a bit draughty,' Merlan suggested.

She glanced at him, realizing that levity was probably the best approach. The sight of this place was overpowering, simply because it was abandoned. It had not been just a noble family who had lived here, but a dynasty of great rulers. The Palindrakes had been reduced horribly. 'Can we get in?'

'If you're agile.'

Varencienne put her hands on her hips, already looking for the best route. 'Drag me, if necessary.'

Dray would stay with the horses, while Varencienne, Merlan and Hamsin negotiated their way inside.

'There are other entrances,' Hamsin said. 'From the lower road, which leads to the sea. You saw it beneath the bridge. I expect the paths down there will be more dangerous, though, if not impassable.'

The immense tumbled stones were firm beneath their feet. They must have lain that way for hundreds of years. Plants and trees grew among them, and bright green lizards skittered away, wriggling their tails between the climbers' feet. Bright gold lichen crumbled beneath Varencienne's fingers, releasing a strong, herby scent. Merlan helped her up, offering a hand and hauling her over the most perilous places, but in fact the climb was not that difficult. Soon they could see into a wide area that was more like a town square than a yard. Buildings had tumbled into it, but ahead, rearing from within a protective wall, was the main keep itself.

'This must have been a town in its own right,' Varencienne said, rubbing her hands on her trouser legs. Her palms smarted a little from the scrapes she'd received on the way in.

'Old Caradore Town lies a couple of miles to the west along the old road,' Hamsin said, 'but the Palindrakes had most amenities on hand: blacksmith, brewery, clothmakers and herbalists, that sort of thing.'

The emperor Casillin must really have feared the Palindrakes to let this place fall to ruin, Varencienne thought. Surely this should be jewel of the empire, with the wide road from the south busy with traffic from Magravandias. There should be towns along the way, richness and opulence. As it was, New Caradore lay closer to the border, with all the panorama of its mother country spreading away to the north.

'This was the gateway to the north,' Hamsin said, as if reading her thoughts. 'The Lord's Road runs right up into the mountains.'

'I want to see the keep itself,' Varencienne said.

As they walked towards it, Merlan said, 'I'm quite impressed by the way you have such feeling for Caradore. I did not expect it.'

Varencienne glanced up at him. 'Neither did I. I was married off without realizing what that entailed, but I found myself in a fairytale. This land is beautiful, as if I dreamed it up in my head. But then, you must have seen many lands.'

251

'Some. I'm stationed in Mewt.'

'I know. That must be wonderful for a different reason. So exotic.'

Merlan nodded. 'It has immense history, like Caradore does, and it's also full of magic, but as you said, a different kind. The gods of Mewt are still very much alive, and not even the emperor would attempt to destroy them.'

Varencienne hesitated, then said, 'You know about the old gods of Caradore, then?'

He smiled. 'I give them more credence than most, and Mewt may be responsible for that. I sometimes wonder . . .' He paused and shook his head.

'Wonder what?'

Merlan glanced at Hamsin, who was strolling behind them, his easy posture hiding a professional alertness. 'Well, perhaps you are the wrong person to confide in.'

Varencienne snorted. 'You think I'm going to run to my father shrieking, "Papa, Papa, those naughty people in Caradore say bad things"?'

He grinned more widely. 'No. I don't think that. And what I have to say isn't heretical against your father.'

'Oh? I'm intrigued. Still, you can rely on my silence, if it's needed. I can be discreet.' She placed a hand over her heart. 'You have my word, on my children's life.'

'Very well. I sometimes wonder whether the people of Caradore surrendered their gods rather than had them taken away. It was as if once the empire became involved, the Caradoreans wouldn't play the game any more. I think that Casillin wanted the old ways to continue, but for his benefit. The Palindrakes, led by the redoubtable Ilcretia, wouldn't let him have it. And young Valraven was never more than a pawn. Ilcretia was the one who decided the male Palindrakes should be kept from their heritage. The old legends say that the Magravandian mages worked sorcery so that no Palindrake heir could ever invoke the old gods again without risking destruction, but what they meant was that the Caradoreans should not try to use the ancient magic against *the empire*. I don't think they were against indigenous belief systems, per se, as long as their own god was acknowledged the leader of the pack. They consider Madragore to be lord of all gods, but his church does not actually deny the existence of other gods. He is an emperor, like your father, always pushing his way into other belief systems, taking them over, making their deities his vassals, but he does not remove them from history.'

'I have never thought of it like that.'

'I have, because, as you say, I've visited other lands. I've seen the temples and cathedrals of Madragore, with his subject local deities, like appointed governors, skulking in their little shrines. They are his generals, much like the Caradorean nobility have become your father's generals.'

'You don't see any Caradorean gods in shrines,' Varencienne said.

'No, you don't. I think that is partly because Valraven himself, as spiritual leader of this land – whether acknowledged or not – has no truck with them. If he did, perhaps they wouldn't be dead.'

Varencienne fell silent, thinking of the Sisterhood. 'Are gods really that important, though?'

'They are if we accept they are invented by us. They are part of us, aren't they? And if we deny them, we deny part of ourselves. In Caradore, this is a stubborn act, I feel.'

Varencienne laughed. 'You have strange ideas, Merlan Leckery.'

'That is why I am so valued by my employer.'

Varencienne wanted to ask about his employer then, and learn what his duties actually entailed, but they had come to the gate of the keep, or what was left of it. The top of the arch had gone, but beyond it could be seen the wild remains of a former garden. The walls had hidden a far more elegant building than could be imagined from the outer gate. The castle was built in a square around a central court. A wide road led through the walls, and the entrance to the keep itself stood above a sweeping flight of steps. The walls were carbuncled with turrets and balconies, and ivy hung down in swags. The atmosphere in the courtyard was still. The wind did not intrude there.

Varencienne led the way to the main entrance. Her heart was beating fast now, her breath shallow. She felt slightly light-headed, as if the weight of centuries pressed down upon her, filled with tragedies and celebrations. The Palindrakes had left their history here, all of it.

Inside, the building was quite light, because all the windows were uncovered. There was remarkably little structural damage. Overhead, floors were intact, although Hamsin suggested it might be dangerous to try and walk across them. Varencienne was conscious that they might fall upon her at any moment. Perhaps they were held aloft only by a delicate balance, and the fact that no busy human presences had intruded there for so long. Merlan had been right about birds shunning the place. None roosted in the outer courtyard, or ventured into the keep itself. All was utterly silent. Varencienne doubted even a mouse scurried here. She went to touch the walls, which were constructed of the same creamy stone as the newer castle further south. She wanted vibrations to stream up her arms, for impressions to come, but none did. The history of the Palindrakes kept itself to itself. She imagined it gusting away from her to find a dark corner in which to hide. Perhaps it smelled her Magravandian blood and fled from it, frightened.

'We must stay here tonight,' Varencienne said.

'We have no provisions, we'll freeze,' Merlan said. 'Be sensible. We've got time to take a good look around.'

'I want to see it in moonlight, feel it.'

He sighed. 'I should not have talked of ancient gods. Now you want to invoke them.'

'The only thing I want to invoke is life,' she said. 'The Palindrakes left it here.'

'Lord Palindrake was butchered in the yard out there. As were most of his men. His wife and daughters were raped, along with some of his sons. Other women and children, wretched with grief and shock, were taken into captivity and shipped to Magrast. Palindrake's heir was subjected to a brutal ritual that stripped him of his heritage. That is only a part of it, greatly sanitized. There is nothing here you should wish to awake, Varencienne.'

She glanced at him archly. 'The past is not all gilded memories of summer, Merlan. If some aspects of it are uncomfortable, it doesn't mean they shouldn't be confronted.'

He shrugged. 'You think what you like, but I'm not staying here overnight.'

'Are you afraid?'

He shook his head at her in apparent exasperation, but said nothing.

'There's no one here,' Varencienne said, gazing up at the blackened roof 'No one ever came here again. It's like an enchanted place.'

They passed through the main hall and came across a great stone staircase cut into the wall that led upwards. Varencienne walked up it, one hand on the wall. Merlan and Hamsin kept close behind her. 'Wait at the top,' Hamsin said. 'Don't go charging off, my lady. You could take a tumble through the floor.'

Varencienne could not see how. A stone gallery led around the hall, with dark openings leading off it. The gallery looked sound, although the men insisted they couldn't be sure.

'I want to find Ilcretia's rooms,' Varencienne said.

'How?' said Merlan, the tightness in his voice suggesting he now thought this trip hadn't been such a good idea after all. He clearly hadn't counted on Varencienne's enthusiasm. 'There will be no sign left to tell which rooms were hers.'

'Oh yes there will,' said Varencienne firmly. She stepped off the stairs and went towards an archway ahead.

Hamsin sprinted past her. 'Let me go first, my lady.'

Sighing, Varencienne allowed him to do so. He paused at the entrance to a corridor and looked to left and right. Presently he ventured inside. Varencienne went to peer after him, ignoring Merlan's hissed command not to. The passageway was very dark, but light came down through the ceiling, suggesting that somewhere floors and roofs had called in. She could see doorways, all shut up. Sconces on the walls were dripping drifts of webs and dust and the floor was covered in broken stone. She wanted to see a shadowy figure walking away from her, trailing robes in the dust, but leaving no mark. She wanted to hear a soft sound, a sob or a smothered laugh. Everything was silent and still, but for Hamsin's burly figure feeling his way gingerly up the left of the passage.

'Can we come yet?' Varencienne asked in a loud whisper. 'Try one of the doors, Hamsin.'

He looked back at her, his face set in an expression of weary patience. Obligingly, he reached for one of the door rings. Varencienne laughed at his expression of shock when the door opened easily beneath his hand and he nearly fell into the room beyond. Varencienne went after him, Merlan following.

The room was a disappointment, but then she shouldn't expect treasures to be revealed behind the first door. A huge fireplace was set into the wall, streaks of soot rising up like frozen flames against the crumbling plaster. There was a wide casement, where someone might sit, looking out over the garden. Varencienne went to lean upon it. She imagined what it would be like if this room was restored and thick furs were draped over the windowseat. A fire would burn in the great hearth, smelling of sap. Outside, she imagined late autumn, the beginning of chill. This would be a comfortable room. There'd be thick tapestries upon the walls, woven of jewel-coloured yarn. She wondered what it had been used for, but couldn't dispel the idea that it had been a sitting-room of some kind. 'Did they take all the furniture to the new castle?' she asked.

'I expect so,' said Merlan. He came to stand beside her. 'You're obsessed.' He grinned at her.

She stretched her mouth into a grimace. 'Haven't you got any imagination? Just think what this place must have been like in its prime.'

Merlan looked around himself 'Clearly your imagination is more fecund than mine is. Any ghosts yet?'

She ignored the remark. 'We should look in other rooms. Perhaps the family's private chambers were on the next floor.'

'First we have to find the stairs,' Merlan said.

'They must be near where we alighted on this floor,' Varencienne said. 'It's obvious.'

'I wouldn't count on it. This is a huge place, added to by generation after generation of Palindrakes. Originally it would just have comprised the ground floor and this one. There could be another staircase somewhere other than the main hall.'

'Well, let's go and look.'

Varencienne marched out of the door, and Hamsin ran to overtake her.

They looked in other rooms on the way back down the passage, but they too were empty. Varencienne didn't really know what she was looking for. It was clear that Ilcretia would have taken all her effects with her when she moved south. The place had been ransacked. No doubt anything she'd left behind had been pilfered by the invading army. Varencienne thought then of the book in her mother's possession. How had Casillin got his hands on that? Why had her family known about it, but not the Palindrakes? These things mystified her. She had to know.

Eventually, after roaming through several passageways, they emerged into the well of another, smaller, galleried hall. The great wooden staircase that reared up to meet them looked intact; its surface was dull, almost petrified. It swept up to a floor above, where some of its banisters were missing.

Hamsin was uncomfortable about venturing on to the next floor. Varencienne's heart had begun to beat faster; it hadn't been sluggish before. The shadows that massed on the gallery above them seethed with significance. She became aware, for the first time, of *presence*. Something was up there. A pang went through her that took a few moments for her to identify as fear.

'Varencienne,' murmured Merlan, and his voice seemed to come from far away. 'You've gone pale.'

'Up there,' she answered, equally softly.

He followed her gaze, and she heard him swallow thickly. He was afraid, although she doubted he'd admit it. 'When I was a boy, we wouldn't go up to the top,' he said, in a voice she guessed was designed to break the tension in the air. 'In fact, I don't think any of us went beyond the ground floor. I certainly didn't.'

'Did you sense something?'

'We spooked ourselves, as children will. It's hardly surprising.'

'We have to go up there, Merlan. It's very important. I can't explain how much so.'

He sighed through his nose. 'What's this all about? Why are you here – the real reason?'

She glanced at him. 'One day I might explain, but trust me when I say this is the right thing to do. For me, anyway. Are you still my escort?'

He hesitated, then nodded.

'Then come on.'

'Let Hamsin go first.'

Hamsin, now, did not seem so keen. Varencienne guessed he would prefer his master's mad wife to go up to that haunted realm by herself. Huffing, he shouldered past them, and made a great show of testing the first stair. 'You have to be careful with these old staircases,' he said. Then, slowly, he began to climb, his companions following.

Varencienne could tell that the staircase was firm and sound. It neither creaked nor wobbled, sharing the invulnerable immensity of Old Caradore itself. She realized the place really was indestructible. It had been sacked and abandoned, yet even though its surrounding buildings had crumbled and the walls had fallen, the keep still stood. It seemed defiant somehow, or suggestive of unfinished business. Perhaps, it was waiting to be reborn.

At the top of the stairs, the atmosphere clung to Varencienne's face like wet cobwebs. She found it hard to draw breath, and the feeling of light-headedness had returned. The unseen presences were watching her now. What did they see: Magravandian blood or the wife of Valraven, who loved this place? Would her love allow them to forgive her ancestry? She had a brief, petrifying vision of being pushed by invisible hands over the banisters. Instinctively, she moved closer to the wall. She could sense Merlan watching her closely, beginning to worry how strongly she was affected by the atmosphere. He wouldn't say anything yet, because to say something aloud would confirm his fear, Hamsin's fear, and her own. They might freeze in terror, panic or die.

You are making this worse, she told herself. Stop panicking. It's only memories, filling the air, pressing down on you. Fight it, or go back down the stairs. The men will be led by you. You have to be strong and show it.

She straightened her spine and willed the massing shadows to draw back. She pushed them from her, but not with hostility or aggression. In her mind she told them she knew she was trespassing in their domain, but that she meant only good. They must let her pass; they must let her see. She sensed, or perhaps imagined, that the atmosphere lightened a little, but it still took all her courage to venture into one of the passageways leading from the gallery. Hamsin and Merlan now followed her. No one suggested that one of them should lead.

She put her hand upon the cold stone of the archway and peered round the corner. It wasn't dark. The roof had come away and filled the corridor with rubble. Above the sky was a shimmering blue, skimmed by thin clouds. Seeing that made Varencienne feel better. The castle did not have total sway here. The outside had got in. 'It's all right,' she said, looking round. It was hard not to laugh at the others; they looked like scared boys. Merlan's shoulders relaxed a little. He came forward.

'Now, you must agree this bit looks unstable,' he said in a light, yet ragged tone.

Varencienne nodded. She couldn't disagree. At the end of the passage-way was an enormous round opening that she thought would once have contained stained glass. Perhaps there'd been a picture of the dragons there. 'This is it,' she said. 'This is where Ilcretia lived with her children.'

'How do you know?'

'I just do.' She looked back at him, then down the passage to the right. Here it was darker, and the ceiling was mostly intact, with the occasional tongue of hairy plaster hanging down. She knew she had to go down there, but was also aware that the ceiling might fall on her. 'Wait here,' she said.

'No!' Merlan was emphatic. 'We must go back, Ren.'

It was the first time he'd used the affectionate form of her name. She smiled at him. 'I'll be fine. I'm meant to be here. Also, if you great males come tramping down here, there's more chance of the roof caving in. I'm a delicate little thing. I'll just scamper like a mouse.'

'Be careful,' he said. Hamsin said nothing.

Keeping her hand on the wall, Varencienne ventured slowly up the passageway. She wanted this to be over and wondered why she was so driven. Was it her desire that was pushing her, or something that remained here drawing her in? She couldn't be sure. Glancing back, Merlan's stern face seemed a hundred miles away. She couldn't stop now. Her hand slipped into a recess. She had found a door. Relieved, she opened it and stepped forward.

She had to suppress a scream. The floor had nearly gone. Before her was a terrifying drop to the next floor. The space was like a vortex of time, sucking her forward. She took a step back, her head spinning. No. No.

Back in the passageway, the shadows crowded round her again, finding her vulnerable and afraid. She pressed her hands against her eyes. Stop it. Stop it. Be strong.

Groping, she pressed forward. She passed other doors, but did not want to look beyond them. She was drawn to the end of the passageway, and here she found a door hanging open.

Inside were some narrow steps, spiralling up. A turret. There would be a room at the top. The steps were of stone. They'd be safe. Rubble covered them and Varencienne had to pick her way carefully. Her chest was full of pain, as if her blood had become thicker. A great weight pressed down upon her head. At the top was another door. This she stared at before opening it. Beyond it, something would be shown to her.

Be kind to me, she said. Look upon me with gentleness. It was a prayer to Foy, but also to the spirit of Old Caradore.

With one hand, Varencienne pushed against the wood. The door opened smoothly, as had all the doors they had tried in this place. There was no sense of being kept out, quite the opposite, but what reason the lingering presences might have to draw living souls to them could not be guessed.

Varencienne held her breath. The turret room was dark, even though slivers of light came down through holes in the roof. She heard a sound, the first since they'd entered the keep; a rustle in the far shadows. Varencienne took a step into the room and then it was too late.

A woman crouched in the corner, clutching to her a group of wild-eyed children. Her face was terrible: too white, like a corpse, with dull black eyes.

Varencienne could not scream. She could not even draw breath.

The woman squatted malevolently before her; a hideous revenant. She must be a gypsy creature, a vagabond, not anything else, please, not anything else. Malnutrition and disease could do that to a face, couldn't they?

Varencienne sucked a painful breath into her lungs. She would speak and say, 'It's all right,' in a soothing voice. Then she realized there was no woman, no children. She was looking only at a jumble of old rags; grey and white, covered in dust. Splintered rafters looked liked the thin arms of children. Spots of mildew looked like hollow eyes. Varencienne laughed to herself, seeking comfort and normality. She put her hands against her face, found it gritty. What had happened here?

Varencienne no longer felt afraid. She walked into the room and stood in a beam of light that came in from the sky. She sensed melancholy, but also resolve and a kind of ferocity. With a clench in her belly, she became certain that this must have been the place where Ilcretia and her family had been captured by the soldiers. It was so clear now. The top room of the castle, perhaps a place where they'd be overlooked until the battle was over and the victors lay drunk in their spoils. But the dragon heir had meant too much to Casillin. It was essential the boy be found. So they'd searched every corner, every cellar, every sewer, until eventually they'd come here. The vision Varencienne had had at the threshold was what the invaders must have seen. A desperate woman, haggard and spent, but full of hatred.

259

She sat down on the floor, her hands dangling between her knees. 'Tell me, Ilcretia,' she said aloud. 'What are your secrets? Is it true you trapped and changed the dragons, by caging them in your bitterness?' She could not appeal to ghosts with desires from the present, because surely that would mean nothing to them. Ghosts existed only in the past, caught up in their melodramas, reliving and reliving them. Selfish they were, selfish and blind. She rested her cheek on her knees and closed her eyes. She had to attune with the place, penetrate the spongy membrane of awareness that separated her from the memories that still clung to every stone of Old Caradore. The feelings she'd had here were very similar to those she'd experienced at the Chair with Niska: the light-headness and disorientation, the shortness of breath. She willed herself backward in time, imagining how Ilcretia must have felt, hiding here, and knowing that her hope for non-discovery was scant. Outside were the sounds of fighting: the cries of men, the hack of steel against stone and bone, the serpent hiss of arrows. Horses neighed hysterically, children sobbed in despair, loyal hounds bayed and whined, and women shrieked in a terrible, high-pitched way. Ilcretia could do nothing. She was lady of this realm, in more ways than one, yet she was powerless. Her people were being slaughtered around her, yet here she was, trembling in a corner, in wait and in dread. Had she put her hands over her ears? No. Her arms were about her children. Her neck was stiff with pain, her jaw clenched tight.

Varencienne felt chilled. Her nose and fingers were numb with cold. Ilcretia knew what Casillin would want: the dragon heir, his priestess and her knowledge. She felt guilty because in some way this certainty gave her relief. Magravandias might take prisoners, and force them to utter vows, but what lived in the soul could never be touched. Ilcretia would never let Casillin have the dragons and their secrets. She knew she would survive and that Valraven would also. Guilt warred with principle. Her son should die rather than become the means whereby the fire king gained control of the great waters. She should summon up a storm, call out to the winds to lash the castle with killing whips of rain and lightning. But she hadn't the strength. Nor the true will. She must weave her art and hide her eldest son. A little ensorcelment. Just a glamour. It might work.

She rocked her body back and forth, waiting for the heart's pierce that would tell her that her husband was dead. There was a moment's stillness, and fragments of dust, ash and straw sifted down from the ruined ceiling. Then came the baying roar from the enemy, the irrepressible caw of triumph. She felt it in her heart, felt the light go out. It doesn't matter, she told herself, it doesn't matter.

Varencienne expelled a gut-deep moan of weariness and despair. There were no phantoms before her eyes, no horrific scenes replayed upon the shadows. Just feelings. Ilcretia had planned to play a long game, but somewhere along the way, her intentions had become diluted or perverted. The Sisterhood of the Dragon didn't keep her plan alive; they had ossified it, made it into a pageant, a myth. Who had been responsible? Was it simply the distance of time from the event that weakened the impact of her ancient rituals?

Varencienne raised her head weakly. The sun had moved position and now streamed down through a wide hole above her head, burning her hair. Trials upon rocks in the night were one thing, but she felt that any true initiation into the Sisterhood should be a night spent here, in this room, soaking up the past. It had to be faced and accepted. Only then would it be possible to cast it off and move forward. Foy was Ilcretia, of this Varencienne was sure. There had never been a living dragon queen to summon, but only elemental spirits. If anything slumbered restlessly beneath the sea, it was Ilcretia's essence, disempowered and vengeful.

She heard a male voice calling her name and got to her feet. She felt neither dizzy nor disorientated. This was just an old room: empty. For now.

Varencienne went back down the stairs. Merlan had been brave enough to venture up the corridor. She saw his pale face looking up at her as she descended the winding steps.

'We can go now,' she said.

CHAPTER THREE

Seductions

The party arrived back at Caradore long after dark. Everna and Oltefney had gone to bed and there was no sign of Pharinet in the family chambers. Goldvane, however, was still up, and slightly disgruntled. Presumably, Everna had ordered him to wait for her before retiring. Varencienne felt languorously tired. She asked Goldvane to order a hot meal from the kitchens for herself and Merlan. 'Is there a fire in the main family room?' she asked.

Goldvane nodded. 'I have kept it stoked for you.'

'We'll eat there then.'

In the sitting-room, Merlan sat in a chair by the fire, while Varencienne curled up on the couch. 'Thank you for today,' she said. 'I appreciate it.'

He raised his hands expressively. 'It was a pleasure.'

'Don't lie. You thought I was tiresome.'

'Rash, maybe, but not tiresome.'

Varencienne paused and then spoke. 'I felt Ilcretia strongly in that turret room.' She had not yet spoken to Merlan about her experience.

He nodded. 'You were determined to find her somewhere.'

'I didn't imagine it, Merlan.'

He shrugged. 'I wasn't there. All I know is that old place is full of the echoes of screams. It isn't good.'

'I love it. I think the Palindrakes should restore it.'

'Your family removed them from it in the first place. Don't you think your father might not approve?'

'I'm sure he wouldn't care. Why should he? Valraven is firmly his creature. He has no secret yearning to break free of the empire, I'm quite sure of that.'

'You speak with little affection for your husband.'

'That is because I have none for him.'

He studied her. 'Are you attempting to shock me?'

Varencienne thought carefully before she answered. 'Only if you're shocked by truth. I answered your question. I had no say in my marriage to Valraven. I was given to him. Why should such an arrangement breed love?'

Merlan did not appear surprised by her words. 'Oh, I don't know. Valraven is a handsome man, very dashing and courteous. I thought you might have grown to love him.'

Varencienne snorted. 'Clearly you know little of him. It's a cold courtesy he has.' She leaned forward in her seat. 'Do you know what he is, Merlan?'

'He is the dragon heir. Is that what you mean?'

'Not just that.'

'They call him the hand of fire, the eye of the emperor. It is said that as he slays in your father's name, so your father witnesses the event. Valraven pledged himself to the fire. Yes, I know what he is, Varencienne. A traitor to his land, his gods.' He stared at her without blinking, perhaps unsure of whether he should have been so blunt.

'He's possessed,' Varencienne said.

'By fire?' Merlan put his head on one side.

Varencienne looked away. 'Yes, by fire.' She found she couldn't confide in Merlan about everything.

'But it is not our concern,' Merlan said. 'Or is it? Do you care about the world?'

She thought about it. 'No. Why should I? I have no control over it, and to care seems a needless burden.'

He laughed. 'Today, in that desolate old place, you were full of care.'

She leaned back against the cushions. 'That's different again.' She frowned. 'I have become wrapped up in this land, Merlan. I love it very much, but perhaps that isn't care in the way you see it. Some things simply *are*; we cannot change them. We can only live our lives in our small corners of the world. The rest might not exist.'

'But it does,' Merlan said.

'You say that because you've seen more of it.'

'One day the world might come to you. Have you ever thought of that?'

'What do you mean?'

He shrugged. 'Nothing remains static. The world changes constantly; tides ebb and flow. The Magravandian star has reached its ascendant. What will happen next?'

'Are you suggesting a fall?'

He paused for a moment. 'Let's just say that Mewt makes you reflective. I sit out in the hot nights, beneath a million stars. The dust of Mewt is filled with the past. It was once a great kingdom, an empire in its own right, but it was vanquished by Cos. The great line of Mewtish kings, and their spiritual heritage, was lost. The country became part of the Cossic empire. But eventually that too was destroyed. There have been many empires. None last for ever.'

'I do not think Magravandias will fall in our lifetime. It is still expanding.'

Merlan raised his eyebrows. 'Why do you think that?'

'What I've heard suggests as much.'

'The Cossics are troublesome. Theirs is a large country, and they have always been men of war. Magravandias might believe it has quelled the enemy, but it hasn't. Cossic terrorists snap at the heels of Valraven's army. They have an exiled king who inspires them to fight on. The Cossic rebels will never win, but neither can they be beaten. They are a constant worry, a drain on resources. Valraven's troops cannot press eastwards, because they have to deal constantly with trouble in Cos.'

'If Valraven were to die, it would be a great blow to my father's army, wouldn't it?'

Merlan nodded. 'Of course. He is their heart. But he will not die.'

'How can you be so sure? If I was a Cossic terrorist, I'd be planning assassinations continually.'

Merlan shook his head. 'They have tried it, and will continue to do so, but Valraven will not die. Not in that way. Don't ask me how I know, because there is no rational basis for it. He is charmed, Ren. He is deadly.'

Varencienne shifted uncomfortably in her seat. 'And yet you considered I might have grown to love him. What kind of creature would that make me?'

He paused meaningfully. 'The deadliest of beasts are often the most attractive.'

'Perhaps I find different things attractive.'

He narrowed his eyes. 'I look at you, and I'm unsure what I see. Your image seems to flicker and waver, as if you are a hundred different women. My opinion of you changes constantly. Are you a fey and imaginative creature, or a bitter, jaded woman? Are you full of joy or resentment? It seems as if all these might be true.'

'The same could be said for Pharinet. I'm no more complex than anyone else.'

'But you are your father's daughter, and that inescapable heritage gives you a certain something, which smells deliciously of danger. I feel there's something indestructible within you, and it is as cold as Valraven.'

Varencienne sensed these remarks were designed to flatter her. She wanted to tell him he needn't bother. She'd already made up her mind she desired him. The flattery was now superfluous.

Servants brought in the meal, and Varencienne told them to go to bed. They could clear away in the morning. She and Merlan went to sit at a table by the window and began to eat. Varencienne discovered that the devouring of food could be transformed into an act of sensuality. Every time she licked her fingers, or ripped meat from a bone, she was aware of Merlan's tense scrutiny. He wanted to see her as mysterious, aloof, challenging but conquerable. He had built up this multi-faceted image of her in his head. He didn't know her. He had made assumptions. She didn't care. He could think what he liked, as long as it excited him.

Outside the night prowled around the turrets of Caradore. The air was still, but there was a strange, restless sound. 'Listen to that,' Varencienne said, pausing with a chicken bone halfway to her mouth. 'It is the voice of the sea. It is singing upon the shore. Soon a storm will come.'

'And the storm will not abate until the sea has purged itself of its dead.'

Varencienne smiled. 'I love the old legends. At one time, I think their magic must have been very much alive.'

'Perhaps it still is. It depends on your view.'

Varencienne wrinkled her nose and bit into the tender meat. 'I used to believe in magic,' she said, chewing, 'but when I looked for it, I found that it was dead.'

Merlan laughed. 'How can you say that? You found it today. It watches us from the shadows.'

'You are a contradiction. If you'd spoken this way earlier, maybe we could have made old Ilcretia manifest before us.'

'Perhaps I did not suggest it, because I believed that we could.'

Varencienne tossed the bone on to her plate. 'I feel you are trying to communicate something. Speak plainly. The day has been a game of words.'

'Perhaps I'm trying to find your measure.'

'Oh, and by that you mean what?'

He leaned forward across the table. 'My employer, Lord Maycarpe, he talks to me a lot.'

Varencienne folded her arms and leaned away from him. She raised a single eyebrow.

'He talks to me about your family, about your mother, your brothers, and now and again, you.'

'How can he? He's never met me. I've never even heard of him.'

Merlan shrugged. 'People talk. They love to do it. And what they don't know, they speculate about.'

'Please get to the point.'

'Be patient. First, I must tell you about Maycarpe. He fancies himself as an esoteric scholar, and has embraced the culture of Mewt like a native. Magic hangs thick in the air in Mewt. Its capital, Akahana, where we have our governmental building, is extremely ancient. Maycarpe went there as a young man. It sucked him in with its secret perfumes, its irresistible song. Ghosts walk by daylight in Akahana. I myself saw something inexplicable at the tomb of Harakte, a king who died a thousand years ago. Imagine it, Varencienne.' He raised his hands and gazed at the shadowed ceiling. 'It is nighttime, but the air is hotter than a summer's day, full of exotic and pungent aromas: spiced meat, sweat, dung, unbearably sweet perfume, clouds of incense. The stars are so bright and so clear, they hang like clusters of iridescent doves' eggs over the land. There is always music, just a thread of it, undulating like a snake through the narrow streets. Lamps burn dimly and sometimes, in one of the windows, the shadow of a woman passes across the light.'

Merlan paused, tapping his lips with a taut finger. Varencienne shivered. The crack of the fire in the hearth seemed to intrude on the image he conjured for her. 'Go on,' she said softly. 'Tell me the story.'

'When I first went to Mewt, I was very young, as Maycarpe had been. I wasn't sure what I was meant to feel there. I am Caradorean after all, and Mewt too is a conquered country. The people there exclude you from everything. They walk in mystery, slowly and with grace. Their history lives for them. They worship it. Nothing ever dies there. One night, I went for a walk feeling dizzy from the heat and uncomfortable in every bone of my body. The world felt so uncertain to me; I was afraid. I found myself in the plaza outside the Harakteon, which is a great complex that functions both as a tomb and a temple. I stood there for a while, marvelling at the great pylons, soaking up the atmosphere. Moonlight made the stones very white, and the shadows deep and blue. I saw a man emerge from the inner precincts. He was not dressed as a priest, but in the ceremonial garb of a warrior. I thought he must be one of the palace guards, who had come to pray in the temple. The old imperial army of Mewt is no more, but Magravandias has allowed Prince Mefer to retain a small company of élite soldiers as a personal bodyguard. I nodded to him, thinking perhaps that two men alone in the night might pass some pleasantries, whatever politics might separate them during the day. He inclined his head also, and came towards me. "The night is beautiful," I said in what I can only presume was tolerable Mewtish. He halted a few feet away from me and nodded. His expression was intense, as if his mind was thinking of ponderous things. I sat down on a broken column and took out my pipe, thinking to share a smoke with him.

'"I am a stranger to this land," I said. "I have come to work here."

'He looked at me, half smiling, but still said nothing. I offered him the pipe and he shook his head. Despite his silence, I did not think at any time that he meant me harm. If anything, I felt very easy in his company. I talked for a while, in my language and his own, and he appeared to listen. I told him about Caradore, and how my people, like his, had a great history. I told him how different my country was, but that I hoped to acclimatize to Mewt, because I felt it had much to teach me.

'I suppose I could have rambled on all night, because he was the first person I'd spoken to since arriving in Akahana who wasn't Magravandian. But suddenly, he put his hand upon my arm and fixed me with an intent gaze. "You should never forget," he said. "Don't make that mistake. Remember everything, for it is the curse of men that they forget."

'I opened my mouth to respond, but realised I was alone. The man had gone.' Merlan frowned. 'This is very hard to explain, but he didn't just disappear. It was so natural. He just went, as if he'd never been there at all. Also, I'm not sure what language he spoke in, only that I understood it.'

Varencienne had wrapped her arms about her chest. She felt she might begin to shake at any moment. 'A ghost,' she said. 'Was it?'

Merlan stuck out his lower lip. 'I suppose it must have been. I went back to my quarters and had to pass Maycarpe's office, which we also use as a sitting-room a lot of the time. Maycarpe was in there and called out to me to share a nightcap with him. He could see at once how rattled I was, and made me tell him what had happened. I did so without hesitation, even though until that evening I had regarded him as something of a tyrant. I also knew that what I had to say might sound disturbingly political. I had taken it as a criticism of the empire. But Maycarpe didn't appear concerned about that. He was delighted with my tale. "What you saw, my boy, was Harakte himself," he said. I wanted to know why he should think that and he said it was obvious. In me, Harakte's spirit had recognized a kindred soul, a member of a race who had been vanquished.

'Maycarpe's remarks disturbed me. Surely none of us, Caradoreans in particular, should harbour any such thoughts. We are Magravandian now, and are supposed to be happy about it.'

Merlan shook his head. 'That night, I first began to get to know Lord Maycarpe. He had delved deep into Mewt's history. He had tracked down forgotten temples in wild corners of the desert, where old priests keep the most ancient of traditions alive. He had persuaded them to teach him. He is a magician, Varencienne, and saw in me a prospective pupil. What I had seen that night convinced him. "Your countrymen are soldiers," he said, "but right from the start, those buffoons in Magrast could tell your talents lay in a different direction, which is why you are here with me. There are no coincidences, my boy. Look upon your destiny, for it has found you."'

Varencienne drew in her breath. 'That is amazing. So now you are telling me you're a magician like your mentor?'

Merlan laughed, a hint of embarrassment in his voice. 'I would not go so far as to say that. Maycarpe has not taught me *what* to think, but *how* to think, perhaps. It was he who first made me realize that humanity creates gods rather than the other way around.'

Varencienne nodded slowly. 'I think I agree with that. The sea dragons, for instance. How much do you know of their legends?'

'Quite a lot, and I'm ashamed to say that most of that information came from Maycarpe. He's an authority on Caradorean myth.'

'I came to a conclusion about the dragons,' Varencienne said. 'I just don't think they were ever real creatures. They represent the Caradoreans' hopes and desires, and their fears. If what you said about Ilcretia today was true, then they have become stale and decayed because the hopes of the people have been quashed.'

'How do you know they're stale and decayed?'

Varencienne shrugged carelessly, but nonetheless took gratification from her reply. 'Because I've seen Foy. Not once, but twice.'

Merlan looked at her with surprise. Varencienne took a pale yellow apple from a dish on the table, and shrugged. 'It's true.'

'When did you see her?'

Varencienne turned the apple in her hands. 'Once, not long after I came here, I went to the beach and something rose out of the water. I didn't know what it was until Pharinet explained the legends to me. Then later, when I was heavily pregnant, I journeyed in my mind to an undersea domain and there saw what was left of Foy. She is a rotting carcass.'

'A moment ago you said you didn't believe in the dragons.'

'I said I thought they represented Caradore's hopes and fears. That is what I saw decaying in the depths of the ocean. My mind saw it, but now I wonder about how real it was. What I saw killed the idea of magic for me, because it was so pathetic, so final. Magic *is* optimism and hope, isn't it? The desire for more than what is mundane to exist.'

Merlan nodded. 'I agree with some of what you say, but I also think that when a race, or even a community of people, pour their faith and feelings into an idea, it can become real. The Caradoreans could invoke the dragons because they believed they could.'

'Now, they don't. Now Valraven is the lapdog of another god.' Varencienne bit into the apple, chewed and swallowed. 'So, tell me what Lord Maycarpe had to say about me.'

'He thinks it was no coincidence you were sent here.'

Varencienne laughed. 'Aha, I see. The conspiracies at court.'

'You know, of course, about your brother Bayard's visit to Caradore?' He clearly thought she didn't.

'Yes, I know of that.'

'Maycarpe told me Bayard wanted to reawaken the dragons, reveal their presence to Valraven.'

'I think that maybe Bayard was inspired by simple human lust rather than a penchant for magic and gods.'

Merlan shook his head. 'Perhaps you don't know Bayard as well as you think you do. He has been taught by the most accomplished adept at court: your mother. She wants him to become emperor, you know.'

'Yes, I've heard that from Pharinet. You can't shock me with revelations, Merlan. I've heard most of them before. But somehow this intrigue about my mother and Bayard doesn't measure up to what I know of them. If Tatrini had a reason for me coming here, why didn't she speak to me about it, why hasn't she since? I know that people, especially people like my family, can be prepared to play a long game, but I would have thought the second move would have occurred by now.'

'Perhaps it already has. Neither of us can know if or how Tatrini works to influence events here. Perhaps she was waiting for you to find Old Caradore. Perhaps she has nudged you that way.'

Varencienne laughed again. 'Oh, Merlan. It is late at night. Fanciful ideas sound reasonable in the dark, but I cannot believe this.'

'Tatrini is no fool. She will know, as I do, how empires rise and fall like waves in the ocean. Whatever plans she has for Bayard will involve uniting countries in belief. Religion is a stronger weapon than guns or blades. It can cut deep into the soul, that which endures beyond life. She wants to revive the dragons, Varencienne, and soon you will have evidence of this for yourself. Remember my words. Foy is not just a goddess, she is a symbol of elemental force. You know the strength of water, its power to destroy, but in the higher realms, it is also the element of the emotions. It has the power to create. Fire alone does not have that potential. Control

269

water and you control feeling. That is power indeed. Think about it: having the authority to inspire fierce loyalty, patriotism, the worship of a single man.'

Varencienne examined him through narrowed eyes. 'Maycarpe told you this?'

Merlan nodded. 'Some of it. The rest I realized for myself.'

'Your employer does not sound a particularly loyal member of my father's staff.'

'You are wrong. He does his job well enough, and accepts what is. He is not a secret rebel, but a thinker, an individual. Neither of these things is encouraged in an oppressive regime. Maycarpe likes to understand how things work, empires included. He has infected me with this desire.'

Varencienne put down her apple core; the remains of the white flesh were already tinged with brown. 'Do you think I must act in some way, Merlan? Is this what our conversation has been leading to?'

'I think you should cast off the pessimism and scepticism you have built around yourself. You want to believe in ghosts, but not in gods. You obviously have a link with the dragons, yet you will not work with it.'

Varencienne was silent for a while. 'But what good can come of it? If I do it, surely it will comply with my mother's wishes, and I'm not sure I want what she wants.'

'As you said to me earlier, we each have our own small corner of the world. Live in yours. Tatrini may not have counted on one thing: your awareness.'

Varencienne stood up and went to stand in the window. She could see the pale breakers pouncing on the beach far below. The sky was overcast, yet the sea looked luminous. 'If only it was possible to swim down to that underwater kingdom in the flesh,' she said, 'but it lies too deep.'

She heard Merlan's chair scrape back against the carpet, then his soft footfalls. He walked like a thief. Her body became sensitive and alert even before he laid his hands upon her shoulders. She did not turn round. His breath was a damp burn on her neck.

'If there should be an emperor,' Merlan murmured, 'it should be someone in whose blood magic runs strong.'

'You?' Varencienne snapped. She had begun to tremble. His hands moved down her arms, his fingertips brushing the side of her breasts.

'No.' He kissed her lightly on the back of the neck. 'Valraven.'

She turned round to him then, enabling him to wrap her in an embrace. 'Is this what you've been leading to? You want me to conspire in a rebellion?'

He shook his head. 'Not in any way you think. The sea wife has always

270

been the power behind the dragon heir. It is time for change, Ren. It is time for sense.'

'Sense? What on earth is sensible about your suggestion? You know what Valraven is. How can you believe he'd make a better emperor than Gastern, or even Bayard?'

'Val is a bitter man,' he replied, 'but bitterness can be healed. He should be allowed to be what he was meant to be, not just a puppet of the Malagashes. You can help him, Ren, whatever your feelings are for him.'

'You think power interests me?' She shook her head, but her arms involuntarily went around his neck. 'I would be setting myself up in direct opposition to my mother.

Merlan shook his head. 'Don't think of that. There are many factions, all competing with one another. Nobody really knows what someone else is thinking or planning.'

'You said my mother is an adept. Surely she'd guess, or sense it?'

'She is adept, yet she is proud. Most of her energy is expended keeping the fire-mages, the priesthood of Madragore, in the dark about her activities. They are Gastern's allies and always will be. They too are powerful and will certainly be opposed to any idea of Bayard becoming emperor. You can be sure they're aware, to some degree, of whatever Tatrini is planning. She will know this and will be taking care to cover her tracks. I don't think she'd consider you a threat to her. It will give us a secret avenue.'

'You can't be sure of these things, Merlan. As you said, my mother is no fool.'

He shrugged and pulled her close. 'I would love to show you the cities of Mewt. Then you would feel what I'm saying. You'd know I'm right. You wouldn't even have to understand it.'

'And what is your position with regard to the fire-mages?' she asked. 'Are they aware of your desires?'

'I am hidden in Mewt, my plans occluded by its very nature as a country. I don't take unnecessary risks.'

'Couldn't confiding in me so frankly be seen as a risk?'

He grinned. 'I am a good judge of character.'

Varencienne sensed there was rather more to it than this. Should she trust Merlan? She wanted to, not because of his plans for Valraven, but because she wanted to be close to him. She could go along with his ideas for now, if only for a single night. Ultimately, the only thing that felt real to her was the fact she was experiencing new and pleasurable feelings. In the dim light, Merlan was not himself but his vanished elder brother. Another ghost. She shuddered. Was it possible Khaster had come back for this one night? The man before her now, his body pressed against hers, did not seem like the one who had ridden to Old Caradore with her earlier that day. They talked of destiny, yet their bodies communicated on a much baser level. She must make him forget about conspiracies for a while.

'Well,' he murmured, close to her ear. 'What do you think?'

She kissed his neck. 'I think that tonight we should concentrate upon other, more immediate concerns.'

He laughed softly. 'As you wish, although this matter cannot rest for long.'

He pulled her closer, kissed her slowly. Varencienne suddenly became conscious of the window behind them, the wide beach that lay below, where anyone, looking up, might see them limned against the light.

'Come away from the window,' she said.

CHAPTER FOUR

Ghosts

In the early morning, Varencienne went down to the beach. It was barely dawn, and seabirds flew low over the ocean. The storm had come in the night and gone. She had lain beneath Merlan in his bed while the wind had shaken the stones of Caradore. They had conjured the storm. It raged inside them. Now Varencienne felt drained, but the feeling was languorous. As she walked upon the weed-strewn sand, she decided she must return with Merlan to Norgance. She needed to focus her thoughts and believed that a visit to the Chair might help. She would go there alone, whatever objections anyone else might try to put in her way. Merlan had given her much to think about. She was torn between thinking that his ambitions were unrealistic and selfish and the certainty that there was sense in his words. Valraven as emperor? Was that possible or even desirable? Her father was a comparatively young man. Was Merlan talking about some far future event, or something more sinister? Valraven as emperor.

Varencienne sat down upon a low rock, her chin in her hands, gazing out to sea. What Merlan was talking about of course was Caradore as emperor. Valraven would just be a convenient figurehead, a glamorous icon to use as a focus. Was Maycarpe in on this, and other high-ranking Magravandians? Merlan had implied that some of her father's trusted staff felt he was stretching resources too far. Cos was a burden and a worry; it should be resolved around a table, not on the battlefield. Poor Mewt; conquered first by Cos, then by Magravandias. Mewt was not a worry to the empire. It had learned to look inwards, to remove itself from the world of politics and war. Strangers might believe they controlled the land, but they did not know what they controlled. Merlan had said to her that

Magravandias ruled the flies that skittered over the surface of the pond. Because the sun made a mirror of the water, no one could see beneath it, so they believed the mirrored surface was all there was to rule. They were ignorant of the huge dark fish sliding in the darkness beneath, quick slippery predators that could rise to the surface for a single second and devour a hundred flies.

Caradore and Mewt were just two lands. Varencienne knew there were many others, both big and small. Madragore had once revealed to the Malagashes that he was the god of the world, and therefore his general would be king of the world. Her father must still believe this. It was ingrained into the blood of her family.

Varencienne knew that at some point she would have to speak to Pharinet about this matter, but for the time being her sister-in-law seemed to be avoiding her. The previous night, Varencienne had been certain Pharinet would have waited up for her, or would at least have come to her room first thing in the morning. But there had been no sign of her. Perhaps instinct had advised her Varencienne had spent the night in Merlan's bed in the guest wing. Varencienne was unsure exactly of why Pharinet should mind about this. Could it simply be jealousy? Surely not. Pharinet would have done the same thing when she'd been Varencienne's age.

After breakfast, at which Pharinet did not make an appearance, Varencienne informed Everna and Oltefney that she intended to ride back to Norgance with Merlan and spend the afternoon there. His sisters had returned home the previous evening. Everna did not question this, nor did she enquire about the previous day's trip to Old Caradore. But her mien did not suggest a mood that Varencienne would have to deal with later. Oltefney was more curious, and asked questions. Varencienne was careful with her answers, aware that Everna might easily be upset. Merlan was quite a sombre presence at the table. Did he regret the previous night? He would not meet Varencienne's eyes.

Later, as they began the journey to Norgance, Varencienne wondered if this tension and discomfort would persist, but once they were away from prying Palindrake eyes Merlan became easy in her company again. His earlier reticence had obviously been because he didn't want anyone to know how intimate they'd been. Now it was as if they'd been together for years. As their horses galloped along the road to Norgance, with the sun cutting through the morning chill and burning away the mist, Varencienne imagined what it would be like if she were married to Merlan instead of Valraven. He would be a companion and a lover. They would do things together, talk.

Halfway there, they turned off the main track on to a twisting pathway through the woods. Here, they dismounted and made love again, among the ferns. Varencienne had never felt this way for, or with, a man, and she could tell that pleased Merlan. What his feelings for Valraven were, she could not tell. He spoke about him as if he didn't really know him, yet was prepared to serve beneath him. There was no liking in his voice, not even admiration, just a businesslike acceptance of what the dragon heir represented. Perhaps he hated Valraven for what he'd done to Khaster.

As they lay together in the breathing green of the forest, Varencienne said, 'Here is the light of day, pure and radiant. What of your subversive plans now?'

'I meant what I said,' he replied. 'Don't believe it was my intention to say or do any of these things before I came here. It was only once I'd met you and spent a little time in your company that I knew I could be honest with you.'

'Why? You don't really know me.'

'I feel I do. I know you are Valraven's wife, and the daughter of the emperor, yet you are still yourself, first and foremost.'

He covered any responding remark from her with a kiss. She sensed this was mainly to silence her. Why did he trust her so much?

At Norgance, Niska came out to meet them, eager to hear about their trip to Old Caradore. None of the other Leckery women were present, perhaps to make a point.

'Something happened to you there, didn't it?' Niska said excitedly. 'I can tell. What was it?'

'I will tell you all about it later,' Varencienne replied. 'First, I need to visit the Chair again.'

Niska's eyes were round. 'You received information, saw something at Old Caradore? I must come with you to the Chair!'

'No!' Varencienne made an effort to smile. 'I really need to be alone, Niska. Please respect this.'

'Of course.' Niska tucked her hand through her brother's arm. 'Merlan can tell me what he saw while we're waiting for you.'

'I saw nothing,' Merlan said, laughing. 'Just a ruined castle.'

Niska pulled a face. 'Then make something up!' She rolled her eyes and led him into the house.

Varencienne watched them go. Suddenly she felt as if she was on the outside, looking in.

*

275

The bright day had been occluded by blue-grey cloud, against which the summer trees burned like green flames. By the time Varencienne entered the forest above Norgance, rain was coming down in warm swathes, making a familiar, comforting patter against the leaves. Climbing to the Chair, Varencienne was sheltered by the canopy. The rain invoked rich smells from the earth beneath her feet; it almost steamed with perfume. Once out of the protection of the branches, Varencienne's hair and cloak quickly became soaked. The rock was slippery beneath her feet, and in the distance thunder boomed among the mountains. She climbed to the perilous seat, taking care to press herself against the lichened wall of rock. It would be so easy in these conditions to slip and fall hundreds of feet to the treetops below.

I do not want visions, Varencienne thought, as if addressing whatever agency haunted the Chair. I want a clear mind.

She settled herself on the wet stone, pushing her spine against it, and laid her forearms on the arms of the chair. For a while she just sat and listened to the rain. It trickled in a runnel from the rock overhead, creating a waterfall before her face. She was behind a veil of water, gazing out at the land. How many people had sat here in the past seeking answers? She could feel their presence all around her – and the questions: Why? How? Who? Where? When?

I don't even know what I want to learn, she thought. When I first came here, I wanted to know about the dragons, about magic and about the past. The seeds were sown and the shoots came up, but then they withered. The history of Caradore is about people, not magic. But that is wrong. The two are intertwined.

Varencienne closed her eyes, willing herself to see something, or at least realize something, but in the darkness all that existed was the patter of rain and the chuckle of the water running off the rock. She admitted it was difficult for her to look at the political situation in a serious light. She had made her life small, and greater concerns seemed no part of her world. Caradore dreamed on in her mantle of green and mist. Whatever business scurrying humans conducted on the land meant nothing to its great eternal spirit. Sitting there, at one with the rock, as if her own arms were petrifying into the stone, Varencienne could only feel the same way. Yet Merlan was right. Everything changed continually, like the seasons. The actions of humans seemed so trivial and petulant. She would like to see Mewt. She thought that it had more in common with Caradore than Merlan realized. It had its own personality. The only difference was that the Mewts tolerated the presence of conquerors through negation. It did not matter to them about the possession of land and power, because ultimately nobody could possess them anyway. Lifetimes were too short. Men wanted to stamp their feet and make a loud noise to be remembered, but once you were dead, what was the point?

Magravandias was teetering on the brink of change, and Merlan thought that Valraven should be made a figurehead of that change. It made sense. He had the looks for it. If the pain of the past and its fierce legacy could be taken from him, he could make a good emperor. Varencienne could see him in costly robes, with impassive face, meting out wise judgements. But she could not imagine herself in this picture. She could not see herself back at Magrast, or in any image that contained both her and her husband. The most she aspired to was one day to be mistress of Caradore. Should that happen, she would send people north to reclaim the old castle. Even if she could not live there, she could have a small part of it made habitable, so that she could go there alone. I am such an isolated creature, she thought. I have children, but there is no overwhelming feeling of love for them that mothers are supposed to have. I would defend them, and protect them, but what else? They should enrich my life, but there is an empty place inside me they cannot reach. Perhaps I have inherited that from my mother. Yet she cares deeply for some of the boys, Bayard in particular. Maybe, if I had a child with someone like Merlan, I would feel differently, but that would be unfair on little Rav and Ellony. They are innocent. They are part of me.

Varencienne sighed and opened her eyes. On the horizon above the purple mountains she could see a dark column extending down from the bruised clouds. It looked like a tornado. She had never seen such a thing, but once, as a child, Bayard had told her about them. He said a whole village had been taken from the coast by a spiralling column of wind. Nothing had been left behind at all. What if such a savage elemental force came whirling over Caradore? Would the castle be dismantled, dragged up into the sky? She shuddered. It could be an omen.

She heard a noise and turned her head to see a figure descending the narrow stairs cut into the rock on her right. 'Merlan, you followed me.'

He came towards her in a mist of rain, pausing on the bottom step, half hidden in shadow. 'It will happen, regardless of what you think or do,' he said.

'I thought you needed my complicity. I came here to think about it.'

He was silent for a moment, and although she couldn't see his face properly, she could tell he was staring at her intently. Eventually, he slapped the stone with one hand and turned round. 'Someone's waiting for you at Caradore. You'd better go back.'

'Merlan?' She could hear his footsteps as he ascended the stairs. Quickly she rose from the seat and made to follow him. For one sickening, dizzy moment, her feet slipped and she slithered on her knees towards the lip of the ledge. Her stockings ripped, and the flesh of her knees. Her feet hung over the edge. Desperately, she grasped at the tough ferns that grew out of crevices. 'Merlan!' He did not come back. Gradually, she hauled herself back to safety, her heart beating wildly in her breast. How could he leave her like that?

Her knees throbbed with pain; the grazes were quite deep. Despite this, Varencienne managed to run up the steps, her heart full of confusion and disappointment. But when she emerged on to the lookout above, there was no sign of Merlan. He must have darted off really quickly. Why was he angry with her? Only a short time ago, they'd been making love.

Her knees were bleeding through her torn stockings. The palms of her hands were cut too, and her gown was badly ripped. She must get home. Someone was waiting there. But who? Was the answer to that the reason why Merlan had been angry?

Once she reached the forest floor once more, Varencienne felt completely disorientated, realizing how close to death she'd been. What if she'd fallen? She expected that Merlan would be waiting somewhere nearby for her to come down from the rock. She would demand an explanation, act hurt and aloof. Merlan did not appear.

Varencienne walked into Saska's sitting room, aware she must look like a drowned corpse who'd come back to seek revenge on the living. The whole family was gathered there, including the dark-countenanced Dimara. They all looked up at Varencienne in surprise.

Varencienne did not even utter a greeting, but marched across the room to loom over Merlan. It took all her will not to slap his face. 'How could you leave me like that? I nearly fell!'

His expression was that of genuine perplexity, while around him his relatives uttered shocked retorts. 'Leave you?' he said. 'What do mean?'

'At the Chair,' Varencienne answered. 'You know.'

Merlan glanced round at his mother, clearly seeking support.

'He has not left my side,' said Saska, rather coldly. 'You must have been mistaken, dear.

Varencienne shook her head. 'That's impossible. He spoke to me.'

Merlan raised his hands to her. 'No. I swear to you, Ren. I didn't come to the Chair.'

'You had a vision,' said Niska eagerly. 'That must be it.'

'He spoke to me,' Varencienne repeated, sitting down on a chair. Her hands dangled between her knees.

The atmosphere in the room seethed with embarrassment and also hostility, which emanated mainly from Dimara. Varencienne would not look at the woman. She despised her and the sanctimonious expression that she knew without looking wreathed Dimara's face.

Saska broke the awkward silence. 'You're soaked,' she said, standing up. 'Go up to Niska's room and dry yourself off. You can borrow a gown from her. I'll get the kitchen to prepare you some hot soup.'

Varencienne clawed tendrils of hair from her face. 'No! I have to go home. Now. He told me. There's someone waiting for me at Caradore.'

The room became stiffly silent once more. Varencienne could hear the echo of her own manic words through its stillness.

'I think you should dry off first,' Saska said. 'It's pouring down out there.'

'Who's waiting for you?' Ligrana asked sharply. 'Is Valraven home?'

'I don't know,' Varencienne replied. 'He just said . . .'

'Who did?'

Varencienne was silent for a moment, then raised her head. Every face was looking at her in consternation and, in most cases, concern. She knew the answer, but was afraid to speak it.

'If it wasn't Merlan, who was it?' Ligrana insisted.

Varencienne had to unclench her jaw to speak. 'It was Khaster.'

Everyone was staring at her as if she'd uttered an obscenity. Saska's hands flew to her face.

Then Niska spoke. 'She was at the Chair. Perhaps she did see something. Perhaps Khas came to her there.' Niska's expression was of desperate appeal: Please don't hate my friend. Varencienne's heart clenched at the sight of it.

'What exactly did this person say to you?' Merlan asked, trying to appear academic.

'Are you sure it wasn't just a stranger?' Ligrana added, before Varencienne could respond.

Varencienne shook her head. 'It was difficult to tell. The rain was coming down. I assumed it was Merlan because it looked like him. It *sounded* like him.' She did not want to repeat exactly what had been said to her, not in front of the women. 'He just said I should go home, because someone was waiting for me. I tried to follow him, but I slipped. I nearly fell over the edge. I called Merlan's name, but nobody came back. He left me.' She raised her hands, noticing how grubby and bloody they were. She must look like a madwoman. 'I'm telling the truth. It was no stranger. He knew me. And if it wasn't Merlan, who else could it have been?'

279

'Strange Khas should appear to you when he's never been seen by any of his own family,' Ligrana said.

Varencienne shrugged. 'I can't explain it.'

'What were you doing there anyway?' Dimara demanded. She rarely spoke, but when she did, it was always in tones of impending doom.

'I often visit the Chair,' Varencienne responded icily. 'I find it inspiring, and I sometimes receive messages there concerning the welfare of my loved ones.' The mere sound of Dimara's voice was enough to banish the panic and bewilderment she felt. Varencienne always rose to a challenge. It was in her blood.

Dimara raised her heavy eyebrows. 'Is that so, Princess?'

Varencienne smiled. 'How strange. No one has called me Princess for years. I thought everyone had forgotten I was one.'

'I never forget anything,' said Dimara.

Least of all a grudge, Varencienne thought, but decided it was better left unsaid.

'Dry yourself off upstairs,' Saska said firmly, in a clear attempt to defuse the situation. 'And put some ointment on those grazes. Have something to eat, then Merlan can accompany you home. If someone *is* waiting there, they can wait a little longer.'

Come on,' said Niska, getting to her feet. 'I'll take you up.'

'Thank you.' Varencienne directed one penetrating glance at Dimara before taking Niska's offered hand and walking out.

Once the door had closed behind them, Varencienne had to vent her feeling. 'That woman! How dare she speak to me like that. She's just a dried-up old spinster, obsessed by myths, yet she acts like she's Foy herself. Stupid old mare!'

Niska, who liked everyone to get along, made a worried sound. 'Don't mind her, Ren. She's just oldfashioned. She'll come round in time.'

'I have no desire for such a circumstance,' said Varencienne. 'There's no love lost between us.'

They went into Niska's sea-coloured bedroom, where Varencienne stripped off her gown and ruined stockings. Niska fetched a basin of water from the bathroom and some ointment. While Varencienne sat on the bed, Niska knelt before her and bathed her wounds.

'I wouldn't mind if I'd done something bad,' Varencienne said, still smarting over Dimara's treatment of her, 'or if I'd swanned around Caradore full of pretensions. But I never have. All I wanted was to find a home here and that miserable dry mare does everything she can – which admittedly isn't much – to make things uncomfortable for me.

'Just ignore it,' Niska pleaded. 'Don't get angry.' She wrung out her bloodied cloth in the water. 'Tell me about Khaster. It's more important.'

Varencienne paused, then risked a potentially dangerous question. 'Do you think he's dead, Nish?'

Niska looked up at her sharply, but there was a hint of craftiness in her eyes. 'Why do you say that? Do you think it was a real person you saw today, not a ghost?'

Varencienne shook her head. 'Not, not that. What I saw was a fetch, but whether of a dead or living person, I couldn't tell. I've just had a strong feeling that your brother is alive and living somewhere else, that's all. Have you never had that feeling?'

Niska dropped her eyes, began dabbing at Varencienne's knees again.

Varencienne winced. 'Be careful!'

'Sorry,' Niska said. She sat back with her hands clasped between her thighs. 'Yes, I have had that feeling, Ren. But I would never speak of it, because if Khas is alive, it means he ran away. It would mean dishonour for our family.'

'But you do *hope* he's alive, don't you?' Varencienne asked carefully.

Niska nodded. 'Of course. I loved him very much. He was the most beautiful man alive.'

Varencienne was just about to ask Niska to expand on this statement, hungry as she was for facts about Khaster, when the bedroom door opened. Dimara stood at the threshold, her face like that of a vengeful goddess on the brink of casting a curse.

She pointed at Niska and said, 'Out!'

Niska began to rise, but Varencienne placed a firm hand on her friend's shoulder. 'Don't go, Nish.'

'You don't want her to hear what I have to say,' Dimara said.

Varencienne was conscious of sitting there wearing only her undergarments, and then decided she should draw power from the situation. She was a beautiful young woman. She must use this as part of her defence. She patted Niska's shoulder and got to her feet, shaking out her damp hair. 'There is no truth you can utter that I would not wish Niska to hear,' she said. 'Please, spit forth your venom, mistress snake.'

Niska uttered a shocked sound and put her fingers to her mouth, gazing up at Varencienne with surprise and more than a little admiration.

Dimara came forward. 'Keep out of our affairs,' she said. 'Khaster was ruined by your murderous family. He would not appear to you. I know you lie. You do it all the time.' She pointed at Niska. 'You lie to get information out of her.'

Varencienne laughed. 'You want to believe that, of course. Please do. It is of no consequence to me.'

Dimara narrowed her eyes. 'Don't think I'm not aware of what you're up to, you and that polluted bitch at Caradore. She's a Malagash creature and always has been, since your corrupt brother put his mark on her.'

Varencienne turned to Niska. 'She is speaking of Pharinet, although you might not recognize her from the description.' She turned back to Dimara. 'You have a fecund imagination, Mistress Corey. Please explain to me what it is you think I'm up to.'

'You refused to join the Sisterhood because you are working with the bitch to inflame Madragorian influences in this land. It is what your brother tried before you, and you were sent here to carry on his work.'

Again Varencienne laughed. Her humour was genuine. 'I am astounded! To begin with, it was you who initially refused me entry to the Sisterhood. I wanted to be part of it, but your little clique kept me out. Why should I be grateful when you changed your minds? It was too late. You want to swap truths? Swallow this one. You deify your dead. Khaster is a god to you, and as his high priestess, you can't bear the thought of him appearing to anyone but you. What about Ellony? Does it gall you a girl with my blood shares her name?'

'It is an abomination!'

'Quite. A little girl is an abomination. Do you hear this, Niska?' Varencienne turned her back on Dimara and lifted the gown from the bed that Niska had laid out for her. Niska was utterly still and silent, clearly hoping her aunt would not extend her attack.

'You have to blame someone for Ellony and Khaster's deaths,' Varencienne said, pulling the gown over her head. 'Pharinet is your scapegoat. You're the only one who feels that way about her. No one else does. Admit it. Would your sister condone the accusations you've made?' She turned her back to Niska. 'Fasten the hooks, would you?'

Niska stood up and began to fumble with the fastenings.

Dimara's expression had taken on a furtive cast. 'There are those of us among the Sisterhood who share each other's beliefs. This is a secret not widely known.'

'Cabals within cabals.' Varencienne sighed theatrically. 'I have no interest in it. Why are you here? Just to try and frighten me or to achieve a result?'

'I'm here to tell you that some of us are aware of what you are, and your purpose. Don't think we're all easily duped. You're being watched.'

'How flattering.'

Dimara shook her head. 'Confident, aren't you. Think you're so power-ful. Remember this, Princess. You're far from Magrast here. If you attempt your necromancy again, I swear to Foy I'll wring the life from your body myself.'

'Necromancy?' Varencienne grinned involuntarily. 'What evidence have you for this? Have I been seen digging around in graveyards?'

'Don't be so pleased with yourself,' Dimara said. 'You can't intimidate me that way. You know very well what I mean by necromancy. You summoned the shade of Khaster today, for your own vile purposes. If you attempt it again, I will know. Also, keep your dirty paws off Merlan.'

'It is Merlan's choice to befriend me. I suggest you advise him of your objections and let him make up his own mind.'

'You are using him,' Dimara said. 'I know why you persuaded him to take you to Old Caradore. You wanted to work your necromantic mischief there, too.'

'Then, I was amazingly successful,' Varencienne said. 'I saw Ilcretia there.' She knew this information would goad Dimara.

'She would not manifest to you, a daughter of her oppressors,' Dimara said, 'not unless you used dark sorcery.'

Varencienne sighed. 'This little chat has been entertaining,' she said, 'but I'm growing bored of it. You live in a world of fantasy, Mistress Corey. I don't believe in your sorcery, magic, necromancy, whatever. I live in a world of human concerns, that of my children and my husband, my family and my friends. Believe me an evil witch if you like, I cannot stop you. But I want you to know that I think you're a deluded fool, you and your bunch of meddling crones.'

Dimara drew herself up to her full height. 'You are a liar,' she said. 'It matters not to me what glib words come out of your mouth. I know your measure, and you know that I know. That is all that's important.' With a final sneer, she swept out of the room.

There was silence for a moment, then Niska said, 'I'm sorry, Ren. I'm really . . .'

'Hush,' said Varencienne. Now that Dimara had gone, she felt shaky. The hostility from the woman had hit her like a physical assault. She sat down on the bed. 'It's not your fault. It's because I'm Magravandian. She and her friends want to believe those things she said about me are true. I hope you know they're not.'

Niska knelt before her and wrapped her arms around Varencienne's waist, pressing her head against her body. 'Of course, of course!' She looked up. 'But do you really not believe in magic?'

Varencienne stroked Niska's face. 'There are many kinds of magic,' she said.

When Varencienne and Niska returned to the sitting-room, Dimara had gone. Varencienne doubted she'd returned to report the argument to her family.

Saska escorted Merlan and Varencienne to the stable-yard. 'Please don't think I doubt what you saw today, Ren,' she said. 'You must realize our reaction is based on the fact that we lost someone very dear to us. It was actually quite hurtful to hear that you might have seen his ghost.'

'I must apologize,' Varencienne said. 'I spoke without thinking. I was just upset because of my fall. Normally, I would have been more tactful.'

'I understand,' Saska said. They had come to the portrait of Khaster in the gallery and here they paused. Saska touched her son's shoulder. 'You really are very like him, Merlan.'

Merlan leaned over to kiss his mother's cheek. 'No I'm not. You mustn't think that. We have a slight physical resemblance because we're brothers, but that's the end of it.'

'Is he still here?' Saska murmured. 'I wish he'd come to me, tell me he's all right.'

'Khas is gone,' Merlan said gently. 'Don't live in the past, Mama.'

Saska smiled weakly. 'It does keep coming back though, doesn't it.'

'Only if you let it,' Merlan replied.

Varencienne could tell Merlan was annoyed with her for what had happened. There was a tight silence between them as they began to the journey back to Caradore. Varencienne shrank from justifying her actions. She'd apologized to his mother. What more did he want? Foy take these Leckerys. They were a difficult bunch. Varencienne spurred her horse to a gallop and Merlan followed. It was impossible for them to talk at that pace. Tree branches lashed Varencienne's face as they pelted down the forest road. She drove her mount into a lather and then had to slow her down. The animal was panting heavily. Merlan rode some distance behind.

It wasn't until the turrets of Caradore could be seen above the trees that Merlan brought his horse up alongside Varencienne's mare and broke the silence. 'I regard you as your own person,' he said, 'not your father's daughter or Val's wife. Please extend to me the same courtesy.'

'What do you mean?'

He sighed. 'I'm not Khaster,' he said. 'And I'm more than just his little brother.'

Varencienne was pleased he'd made the first approach. Her annoyance ebbed immediately. 'I know that.' She smiled at him. 'Really I do. You're the best man I've ever met.'

'You haven't met many.'

She laughed. 'Perhaps not, but I like to think I'm a good judge of character. You've brought me alive in a completely new way.'

She could tell he was flattered. 'My pleasure.'

'I'm sorry about today,' Varencienne said. 'I was in an emotional state.'

He smiled. 'Apology accepted. Now that you're calm, do you really think you saw a ghost at the Chair?'

'I saw someone,' Varencienne said, 'and it looked like you. I just drew a conclusion, perhaps wrongly, I don't know. He said to me, "It will happen, regardless of what you think or do". What do you think that means?'

Merlan thought for a moment, then said, 'Life. '

Varencienne smiled ruefully. 'Perhaps. Your aunt thinks I'm a necromancer.'

He laughed. 'What?'

Varencienne related the story of the argument, making it more humorous than it had been at the time. She and Merlan rode up to Caradore in high spirits. Their closeness had been restored. Varencienne had forgotten about the second part of the message she'd received.

When she and Merlan entered the castle courtyard, the first thing they saw was an immense imperial carriage decked out in scarlet and gold. It was surrounded by horses of the guard, immense black creatures, caparisoned in crimson. Soldiers moved among them, removing saddles. Servants were running between them, unloading luggage, and shouting at one another. Excitement and tension hung heavily in the air.

'My father,' Varencienne said, jumping down from her horse.

'Or Bayard?' Merlan suggested.

Leaving Merlan to see to the animals, Varencienne ran up the steps into the castle. Inside, it was clear from the atmosphere of panicked bustle that someone important had arrived. It couldn't be Valraven. He would never travel by such a carriage.

Everna was striding through the hall as Varencienne entered it. 'Evvie!' Varencienne called, untying her cloak as she hurried forward. 'Is my father here?

Everna looked dazed. 'No. It's the empress. Tatrini.'

'My *mother*?' Varencienne asked. 'Why?'

'She has come to see her daughter, I expect.' Everna took stock. 'What have you been doing? You had better tidy yourself up before you meet her.'

'Where is she?'

'Well, of course we were totally unprepared for the visit, so there are no rooms ready. Pharinet has taken her to the solarium. If the weather wasn't so bad, we could have shown her round the gardens.'

Was this the tornado that had been approaching Caradore? Varencienne headed for the stairs. 'I'll be down as soon as I can. Where's Oltefney?'

'In your chambers, laying out garments, and hoping you'll show your face.'

Everna glanced at Merlan, her expression strangely guarded. 'Perhaps you'd better go and join Pharinet and the others in the solarium,' she said. 'You seem to be spending more time here than at Norgance at the moment.'

Merlan smiled blandly and bowed to her. 'It will be extremely interesting to meet the empress. I shall go at once.'

Everna nodded shortly. 'And you, Ren, get changed quickly.'

'I'll be as quick as I can.' Varencienne hurried towards the stairs. She could not imagine Pharinet conversing comfortably with her mother in the solarium. Tatrini had always seemed to her daughter like a great elemental force, moving slowly, inexorable, and without much to communicate in the way of small talk. But then Varencienne had never really known her. As a child, the whispered conversations of the adult women had meant nothing to her, and once she was of an age to be tutored, she'd spent the bulk of her time with the daughters of other noble families, being taught how to walk, dance, sew and flap a fan. Tatrini had never had an intimate conversation with her, nor held her close. Now she was here. It had to be connected with all that Merlan had intimated the day before. Varencienne had unwittingly catalysed something at the old domain, but then her mother must have been well on her way to Caradore by then. Something had started movement in events even before Merlan had returned home.

Upstairs, a flustered Oltefney fell upon Varencienne with famished squawks. She was clearly delighted about Tatrini's visit. 'We were just about to send a messenger to Norgance,' she said. 'The empress arrived only a short time ago. Thank Madragore you've returned.'

'Why is she here? Do you know?' Varencienne asked, hurriedly stripping herself of her borrowed clothes.

'She *is* your mother, my lady. Valraven must have invited her.'

'That seems unlikely.' She held out her arms for Oltefney to slip a fresh gown over her head.

'But he is with her.'

'Valraven? Everna didn't mention that.'

'Not the best time of year to bring Her Mightiness to Caradore, what with the rains and fog, but I'm sure she'll love it as much as your father does.'

'Who has not set foot in the place since Valraven's father died.'

Oltefney ignored this remark. 'Let me brush out your hair and braid it. The wet won't show as much then.'

Varencienne sat down at her dressing table and adorned her fingers with rings. Her lips looked unusually pale. Perhaps she should use some cosmetics. Valraven had not written to any of the family to inform them he would be home. This was a surprise visit, which was unheard of. Something was afoot, something big. All it would need was Bayard to complete the picture, and then chaos might hit the castle in entirety.

As Oltefney tugged at her tangled hair, Varencienne stared at herself in the glass. You have to be strong now, she thought. You have to show how much you've changed. You're not a child to be pushed around any more. Perhaps this gown is the wrong colour. Should I dress in something more sombre?

CHAPTER FIVE

Sorceress

Before entering the solarium, Varencienne paused at the threshold. She could hear the tones of cultured conversation, the occasional polite laugh. Men's voices mumbled sonorously. Straightening her spine, Varencienne advanced into the room.

Tatrini sat regally in a cane chair, her dark gold robes spilling about her in tapestried folds. A high collar framed her sculpted face and her hair was piled high on her head, strewn with pearls. She did not look as if she'd been travelling, but as if she'd had a restful night in a guest room of the castle and had spent several hours preparing herself before coming down to meet everybody. She had with her a single lady-in-waiting, who stood arrogantly behind her chair. Pharinet, clearly caught totally unawares, looked like a stable-hand, her hair loose about her shoulders, her body swathed in close-fitting brushed leather. Valraven was, as usual, a gaunt dark presence. Merlan looked young beside him, but displayed no sense of awkwardness. Variencienne could only admire his sang-froid; only hours before he'd been making love passionately to her, yet now sat easily in her husband's company. Everna was composed, issuing commands to servants. The children sat quietly and obediently on stools before their grand-mother. The gathering looked entirely uncomfortable.

The empress turned and saw her daughter. 'Varencienne,' she said. '*There* you are.'

Varencienne glided over to her mother's seat and kissed lightly the proffered cheek. 'Mother, this is a surprise. You should have warned us.'

'I have been told that already,' the empress said, 'but I have assured everyone that I did not seek to make an official imperial visit. We are

288

family, and it should be informal. I wanted to surprise you to make sure of that.'

Does she want me to behave as if we've always been close? Varencienne wondered, staring at this stranger. Out of the environment of the palace, Tatrini looked completely different. She had an animation that Varencienne had not seen before. 'I have been at Norgance,' she said. 'It's a wonderful estate, a couple of hours' ride from here. We have friends there.'

'Yes, I have already made the acquaintance of this young man.' Clearly Tatrini had forgotten Merlan's name. She indicated her grandchildren. 'What lovely children you have. So well-behaved.'

The children both looked at Varencienne, and she saw with a pang their expressions of uncertainty. She smiled at them, realizing in that moment she must be little more than a stranger to them. So it had been in her own childhood, with her own mother. 'Yes, Valraven and I are very fortunate.' She could not go and muss their hair or hug them, because it would confuse them. They were not used to gestures like that from her.

'Three years old. My, how time flies,' said the empress. 'It seems only a few minutes ago when you were that age.'

Varencienne smiled stiffly. 'I feel as if I've lived here all my life.'

The empress looked around herself. 'It is a charming place. Very quaint. And the countryside is beautiful, of course. Your father and Bayard have always sung Caradore's praises.'

Varencienne winced, and was sure that at least two other people in the room did so also. Was Tatrini ignorant of Bayard's history with the Palindrakes, or had her remark been intentionally discomforting?

'How is Bayard?' Varencienne said. 'I have not heard from him for some months.'

'He is very well,' Tatrini replied. 'Happily, he is no longer stationed in Cos. Almorante is thinking of taking a wife. We despair of finding one for Gastern. He is so picky. Leo has earned a certificate at college. Everyone is doing fine.'

A troupe of servants came in bearing refreshments, supervised by Goldvane at his most officious. The kitchen staff had clearly worked hard to produce a spread fit for an empress, while at the same time making it appear that the Palindrakes must have late afternoon snacks of this nature every day.

Everyone sat down, obviously relieved to have the distraction of food.

'If it will please you, we could arrange for some of the local families to visit,' Everna said.

The empress raised a hand. 'No, I absolutely forbid it. This time is for family. I wish to make your acquaintance.'

Varencienne and Merlan exchanged a glance. Varencienne thought it quite extraordinary that she did not feel any guilt about her relationship with Merlan, even though Valraven was sitting nearby. She wondered whether anyone could perceive a difference about her, a special shine. Pharinet seemed so distant. She *must* have guessed. Where were the languid yet sharp comments that she'd usually utter? The Pharinet whom Varencienne thought she knew would not let that remark from the empress about family go unchallenged.

'What has prompted this visit?' Varencienne asked, conscious of everyone's eyes focusing upon her, even though she did not let her gaze stray from her mother's face. 'When I lived at home I never knew you to leave the palace.'

The woman who looked back at her was indeed a stranger, posing as an intimate. 'My dear, I can assure you I had a life full of social engagements you never witnessed. It is true I should have come here before, but events have kept me at home.' She smiled at Valraven. 'You have your husband to thank for this visit. It was he who persuaded me.'

'I shall thank him in due course,' Varencienne said. 'Would you care for another muffin?'

The empress shook her head. Her eyes strayed to the white statue that grimaced out of the greenery behind Valraven's chair. 'What an unusual ornament,' she said.

Valraven turned. 'That is an ancestor of ours. Her name was Ilcretia.'

'She looks as if she is about to pounce.' Tatrini laughed. 'Right on to your neck, Lord Palindrake.'

Presently a maid servant came into the solarium to announce that the empress's rooms were ready for her and that her luggage had been unpacked. 'I think I shall change,' said Tatrini.

She fixed Pharinet with a stare. 'Perhaps you could show me the way.'

Pharinet stood up awkwardly. 'Of course.'

They left the room, followed by the silent lady-in-waiting.

'If that is what your mother wears for travelling, how does she dress herself for an official function?' said Merlan, clearly attempting to crack the ice in the atmosphere.

Varencienne smiled. 'She is a singular creature.' She turned her attention to Valraven. 'I have to admit I'm surprised you invited her here.'

'Don't be misled,' Valraven replied. 'It was mainly her idea. I'm sure she wanted to see the children.'

'They are three years old. She has taken a long time to make up her mind about this.'

He shrugged. 'Perhaps now she has the time.'

Varencienne shook her head. 'One thing my mother always seemed to have an abundance of was time. She never did anything except gossip and sew.'

'Perhaps that is what she wanted you to see,' said Merlan.

Valraven looked at him speculatively. Varencienne wondered if he was thinking about Merlan's strong resemblance to his older brother. 'That is true,' she said. 'Still, before she leaves, I intend to find out what she wants.' She stood up. 'And now is the time to start.'

Varencienne was tempted to enter her mother's room without knocking, wishing to catch her unawares, but in the event felt unable to do so. She was surprised to discover that Pharinet was still present, sitting on a window seat, appearing strangely at ease, while at the same time very uneasy. Tatrini herself was composed on a couch, still attired in her gilded gown and making no attempt to change it.

'Mother, I would like to talk to you,' Varencienne said.

Tatrini smothered her reaction, although Varencienne perceived it was there: a degree of surprise. 'Well, of course we shall talk,' the empress said. 'It is the main reason I am here.'

Varencienne directed a glance at Pharinet. 'Pharry, would you mind?'

Pharinet hesitated, then stood up. 'Not at all. I should go and make myself more presentable for an empress anyway.'

Tatrini laughed. 'You are as charming as Bayard told me you were.'

Pharinet's smile was hardly more than a grimace. She left the room. The lady-in-waiting also stole out discreetly, leaving mother and daughter alone. Varencienne had never been alone with Tatrini before. The last time they'd spoken at any length – and the longest conversation they'd ever had amounted to only a few sentences – had been on Varencienne's wedding day. 'Why are you here?' Varencienne asked. She did not feel frightened at all, only curious and suspicious.

Tatrini settled back against the couch, one arm flung carelessly along its back. She appraised her daughter for a few moments before speaking. 'It was time I saw you. You are my only female child, and now you have children of your own.'

'You had no interest in me before, none at all. I cannot help wondering what has changed that.'

'You are wrong to say I wasn't interested,' said the empress, peering at the sofa back where her hand plucked idly at a loose thread. She looked as if she was posing for a painting. 'I am not the kind of person who abandons themselves to displays of affection. I do not say I am a good mother, but neither am I a bad one. I have thought about you, Varencienne, hidden away out here in a corner of the world. I liked receiving your letters. I was surprised to get them, but gratified nonetheless. Bayard talks of you often. He is curious about Caradore, of course.'

'Of course. Considering what he did here.' Should she have said that? How much did the empress know? Merlan seemed to think she knew everything.

Tatrini nodded distractedly, clearly not at all discomposed by her daughter's remark. 'He was an impulsive boy, but now he is older, and wiser.'

'Why are you here?' Varencienne repeated, more grimly. 'Do you seek to use me as a substitute for Bayard?'

Tatrini studied her. 'Is that what you think?'

The question unnerved her. 'I have yet to make up my mind. It's why I'm here now, asking you about it.'

Tatrini sighed. 'You think you know everything, but life is more complex than you imagine. There is work for you here, I won't deny that.'

'*Your* work! I've done mine. I've produced Rav and Ellony.'

'I like to think there's more to your life than that, wonderful though your children are.'

Varencienne bristled. 'It was all you ever seemed to do, breed sons.'

Tatrini expelled a dry laugh. 'You have made so many assumptions, haven't you?'

'Then what *did* you do?'

The empress breathed in through her nose. 'We live in a man's world, child, or perhaps I should say the men in this world believe it is theirs. But they perceive only half of what is there. They have their functions, as do we. Those of us who are clever play the game, for men believe they have written the rules. But in reality, it is we who command the moves. Some of us, at least.'

'Did you choose my father as emperor, then?'

Tatrini shook her head. 'No, but his mother did.'

'He was the eldest son. There was no choice involved. That is a man's law.'

Tatrini blinked slowly at her daughter, like a predator considering its maimed prey. 'He was certainly not the eldest son. You had an uncle, who was sickly.'

Varencienne digested this remark. Its poisonous implications spilled through her brain. 'Bayard has three elder brothers, none of whom are sickly.'

Tatrini continued to stare at her, perhaps wondering how much she should say to this female stranger. But no, she wouldn't wonder that at all. 'You have inherited my astuteness,' she said. 'Do not look on me as an enemy, Varencienne. We are, in fact, allies. I know you love Bayard above all your other brothers. You want the best for him, as I do.'

'Is it true, then. You want Bayard to inherit?'

Tatrini sighed, averting her eyes once more. 'Your father has been unwell. I do not think it is a serious concern, but he cannot shoulder the burden of power for ever. We have to look to the future, to secure it for our own sons and daughters, and those who will rely upon them.'

'What makes you think Bayard will be the best choice, other than your personal preference?'

'I think it in everyone's best interest that he assumes the role of emperor. Magravandias is a vast, unstable entity. It is held together by belief more than anything else. It is a human drive to want power, and so many are striving for it. The empire is very fragile. Might alone will not sustain it.'

'Perhaps nothing can. Perhaps it is doomed to fall as every other empire has.'

Tatrini narrowed her eyes. 'This should concern you. Imagine what might come after. Some other power might covet Caradore, and then neither you nor your children will be safe. People need to think they are all striving for the same thing. This has nothing to do with war, which only creates division. Unity will come through the other eternal tool of control: religion. The ruling dynasty of Magravandias has always seen itself as the seat of divine kingship, with Madragore as its crown and the power behind the crown. But there are many kinds of divine kingship. People need to feel inspired, not repressed. Bayard can and will inspire people. His brothers are only dark smoke and the faintest gleam of smouldering embers. Bayard is the gilded one. He shines with the divine light.'

'Tell that to the rebels of Cos.'

Tatrini smiled. 'The Cossics are proud. It is possible to control them, but not in any way that's yet been attempted. Their king should be released from exile and brought to Magrast. He should be honoured and married to a Magravandian. He should be given back his throne, and convinced of the benefits of alliance with our realm.'

'Are you speaking of allowing Cos independence?'

'I'm speaking of manipulation. Men, especially kings, are ultimately vain. They see power in land and riches and feel secure once they have those things. I know differently, and so should you.'

Varencienne sat down on the seat vacated by Pharinet. 'What do you want of me, Mother?'

'When you came here, you felt inspiration. The land spoke to you,

293

because it is in your blood. But now you've lost your faith. Not in the magic you so dearly wanted to believe in, but in yourself. You were shown something very important and misinterpreted it. Perhaps the path seemed too hard, and you thought you lacked the strength to climb it.'

'How do you know what I've experienced and felt? Who is making assumptions now?'

Tatrini laughed quietly. 'Oh, *I know*, Varencienne. Be sure of that. It is important to have an efficient intelligence network.'

'Who told you? Valraven?' Was it possible Pharinet had confided in him, told him everything? Surely not. The Caradorean women took great pains to keep Valraven excluded from the rites of the Dragon.

'Valraven knows very little, a fact of which you're already aware. You must work it out for yourself, my dear.'

'You still haven't told me what you want.'

Tatrini considered. 'I want you to assume your rightful role, that's all. The sea wife.'

'You need Valraven, don't you. What do you need him for if Bayard is your gilded king?'

'When you came here,' Tatrini said patiently, 'you rightfully believed the old magic of Caradore could be revived. You felt it stir inside you. You were right. Valraven must be reinstated as the Dragon Lord of this province.'

'Why? What good will that do you, or Bayard? He and Valraven have become estranged.'

Tatrini nodded. 'I know. I will tell you what I want. I want to end war. It is wasteful and far from the true path to power.'

'But how can you use Valraven?' Varencienne asked. 'Casillin put a curse upon the Palindrakes. You know that. They cannot invoke the dragons. In fact, I strongly believe now that there are no dragons, only bitter memories.'

'Oh, there *are* dragons, my dear,' said Tatrini 'They are the faces we put upon forces we cannot otherwise imagine.' She rustled upon her couch. 'The spirit of Foy rots fretfully in her bower of slime. The women here sing songs to her and occasionally disturb her sleep, but they lack the power that Ilcretia and her kind had. Ilcretia made sure of that.'

'The book,' said Varencienne. She frowned. 'How *did* you acquire it?

'That is quite simple,' the empress replied. 'It was given to her daughter, Ahrenia, who married into your father's family.'

'Ilcretia sent the book to Magravandias.' Varencienne shook her head. 'For safe-keeping? She surely couldn't have wanted us to have it.'

'She was a very clever woman,' Tatrini said. 'She knew that one day the tide would turn, and that it would most likely come from the part of her family that was closest to the heart of power. Ahrenia. As the women of Caradore have kept alive certain traditions, so have the women of your father's family. The emperors generally marry cousins and so on. Leonid's own mother instructed me in the matter, after she chose me for him as a bride. She had no daughters of her own.'

'And this book contains the knowledge to power?'

Tatrini shook her head. 'Don't be ridiculous. A book is a book.' She bunched her fist and tapped it against her chest. 'This is where the knowledge resides. It passes from heart to heart, beyond language. With that book, which was a relic of the beliefs of these people, Ilcretia passed a torch to her daughter. It was just a symbol for a greater act. She knew Ahrenia was travelling into the land of fire, to the very core of it. If the dragon tide should rise again, it would be from there, not from the ragged shores of Caradore.'

'Then perhaps Valraven should be emperor,' Varencienne said lightly, as if she'd just thought of it.

Tatrini sneered. 'No, that is not his function. He does not have the divine blood. He is what he is; a general. But he is a general fighting with one hand tied behind his back, and his eyes blindfolded. I want him restored, for us, for Bayard.'

'What makes you think he would comply? I can think of a dozen reasons why he wouldn't.'

'That is your job,' said Tatrini.

Varencienne laughed. 'Mine? I don't think so. Valraven and I are not close, mother. At best we have a polite, if distant, friendship.'

'The best kind of marriage, the least complicated,' said Tatrini. 'He is just a boy at heart, Varencienne. He's hurt and confused over what Bayard tried to do. He saw people die. He lost his wife and ultimately his friend, Khaster Leckery. Nobody ever really explained why this happened, so he blames himself. His hard exterior conceals a swamp of fear. Now, listen to me. The time for change has come. While I am here, we will give back to Valraven some of what was taken from him.'

'Just tell him the truth, then,' Varencienne said. 'And pray he doesn't also rediscover a sense of national pride. Otherwise you might have an uprising on your hands.'

'With the majority of Caradorean men away in Cos? I hardly think so. No, Valraven won't be so stupid. Anyway, a lot depends on how information is presented to him . . .'

'And what is withheld,' said Varencienne.

'Precisely. I shall offer a lure to him, which will be that he may be a king in his own land. The sons of Caradore will no longer be squandered on the battlefield. All I will ask is that he regards Bayard as his spiritual lord, that Caradore ally willingly with Magravandias, economically, politically and spiritually. In this way, we can create an empire beyond the most ambitious dreams of men. Think of it!'

Varencienne pulled a scornful face.

'And what of Gastern's allies, the priesthood? Do you really think you can defeat them?'

Tatrini recoiled a little, then spoke coldly. 'They have the power of the fire-drakes, I know that. I share that power, but unlike the priesthood, I lack strength in numbers. However, I intend to harness the power of the sea dragons, which will give me the advantage. The mages are my problem, you do not have to worry about them.'

Variencienne sighed through her nose. 'It will give me great pleasure not to. But there's something else you should think about. Despite your noble aims, there are those in Caradore who will oppose what you wish to do. They want no truck with Magravandias, and dream only of Magrast and all her people perishing in flames.'

Tatrini lifted a disdainful lip. 'The women, with their little Sisterhood? That does not concern me. They are just Valraven's potential handmaidens, his channels and his source to power. If any of them should actually behold Foy or her daughters with their own eyes, they would most likely expire in terror. They have no power, and are no threat to me.'

'They believe their work to be so secret,' Varencienne said. 'They wouldn't even allow me into their ranks at first.'

'I know. Foolish of them. Now they have lost out. You would have been an inspiration to them.'

'Mother, just how do you know? Who is it who tells you things?'

'The person you would least suspect.' She paused. 'Incidentally, how did you know about Ilcretia's book?'

'From a source you would *never* expect,' said Varencienne.

The empress smiled. 'Good girl,' she said. 'It seems I have less to teach you than I thought.'

'What will you teach me, then? The contents of Ilcretia's book?'

Tatrini nodded. 'You will learn that in time. It is only a history book. First, I need your complicity. Do you agree to work with me on this?'

Varencienne shifted uncomfortably on her seat. 'I don't know. I need to think about it.'

'There is no time. We must act at once.'

'Act in what way?'

'You have already begun the process unwittingly. Very soon, a select party will travel north to Old Caradore, the place where this drama began. There, in the presence of your husband, you will conjure the dragons. That is the strongest magic. Believe it.' Tatrini leaned forward in her seat. Her passionless mask appeared to have dropped. Varencienne could perceive her mother's eagerness. 'Tonight, you must persuade Valraven to take us to the old domain. He must lead us. Use whatever wiles you can. He will balk, because memories of the day he lost his first wife are still raw in his mind. His buried instincts will alert him to what is afoot. You must allay his fears, lull his anxieties. Be inventive.'

'This is no small request,' Varencienne said, unable to imagine accomplishing such a thing. 'Perhaps Pharinet is the woman for the job.'

Tatrini shook her head. 'No. The actions of our ritual have already begun and must proceed in a certain way. You are the sea wife. Your siren song must lure the dragon heir to the ancient altar.'

'Who else will be part of it?'

Tatrini laughed. 'Everyone, my dear, everyone. But I shall compose our little party for the trip north. You need not concern yourself with that.' She sighed. 'Now I should like to rest myself. I have a lot of work to do tonight. I shall see you later, my dear. Think about what I have said, but never doubt you are part of this drama. It is your destiny. You cannot escape it.'

Varencienne stood up. 'You have waited a long time for this, haven't you?

Tatrini smiled, an inward private smile. 'We all have,' she said.

CHAPTER SIX

Enticement

During the evening, while Tatrini made a show of entertaining and ultimately seducing the female Palindrakes, Varencienne managed to exchange a few private words with Merlan.

'You must come to my chambers later,' she said.

Merlan smothered his surprise with a laugh, as if she'd just made an innocent witticism. 'Valraven is home,' he murmured. 'It would hardly be appropriate or tasteful.'

'The last place you'll ever find *him* in is my quarters. I might speak to him later, but first I must speak to you. It is vital.'

'People might observe us. What about your lady-in-waiting?'

Varencienne frowned. 'Use the servants' door.' She described quickly how to find this. 'The stairs open on to the little kitchen in my chambers. Twissaly won't be there. Her room is nearby, but she's a heavy sleeper. You'll have only to walk down the servants' run on the right of the kitchen to reach the maid's door to my bedroom. I will leave it ajar. It is concealed behind a curtain. If anyone should be with me, I'll make sure to talk loudly, then you can wait behind the curtain till they leave.'

Merlan smiled. 'I smell conspiracy. Am I right in thinking you are preparing to tell me something I dearly want to hear?'

Varencienne smiled back. 'We must talk.'

She spent the rest of the evening tense with nerves and excitement. Part of her welcomed her mother's ideas, while another part of her still felt suspicious and uneasy. Bayard had come to Caradore full of plans to wake the dragons, but they had ended in tragedy. Could the same thing happen again? Varencienne wanted to discuss this with Merlan before proceeding. This alone was strange. Normally, her instincts would be to go to Pharinet

298

for discussion, but for some reason she found the idea of this difficult. Was her new-found lust perverting her common sense? She hardly knew Merlan really.

Before midnight, Tatrini invited all the women to her chamber for a hot liqueur before bedtime. She claimed she had brought the best merlac with her from home. 'It is a tradition in Magrast for womenfolk to toast the night together,' she said. 'Please come. All of you.'

Everna, Oltefney and Pharinet could hardly decline, but Varencienne said, 'Mother, would you mind terribly if I didn't come? I'm really tired.'

'No, of course not,' said Tatrini. 'You do look rather haggard. You've been gadding around too much! Off to bed with you at once. I shall expect to see you for a nightcap tomorrow evening though.'

Varencienne inclined her head and bobbed a polite curtsey. 'I'll look forward to it.'

In her room, Varencienne did not undress, but paced the floor nervously. How long would it be until Merlan could sneak away from the gathering downstairs undetected? Would Valraven try to keep him up? Presently she heard a rustle by the maid's door and the curtain lifted. Merlan came into the room, gingerly, as if the floor was hot beneath his feet. Varencienne went to him swiftly and they embraced, but he was the first to pull away. 'What's this about?'

'My mother,' Varencienne said. 'She has come here full of schemes.'

'Now there's a surprise,' he said dryly.

Briefly, Varencienne related the earlier conversation she'd had with the empress. 'She has the same aims as you, but perhaps not the same motives.'

Merlan snorted derisively. 'Hardly the same aims. She wants to instate her son as tyrant. That is hardly my cherished goal.'

Varencienne took hold of his hands. 'But will that matter? You said yourself that my mother is the most adept magician at court. With her participation, won't some of your desires be realized? She will not know this, of course, but I think there is a poetic grace in that. Why should she know everything?'

Merlan regarded her contemplatively. 'You are right, of course. But this is too sudden. Perhaps not a good idea. I don't know.' He looked perplexed.

Coldness stole through Varencienne's body to settle in her heart. She drew away from him. 'You need instructions, don't you?' she said in a dull voice. 'This isn't part of the plan.'

He glanced at her sharply. 'There is no plan,' he said. 'Just ideas.'

'Whom do you need to consult? Maycarpe?'

Merlan was visibly discomforted. 'That would be impossible. It would take too long.'

Varencienne expelled a wordless sound of disgust and turned away from him. 'You're as bad as she is. All that talk of trusting me instinctively! It was a lie, wasn't it? You came here brimming with your mentor's instructions to get at me, to seduce me.'

'Ren . . .'

She could feel him moving towards her and wriggled away before he made contact. 'No, I've hit on the truth, haven't I?'

'You're overreacting. Of course Maycarpe and I talked of this situation, and even possible strategies, but I never planned to seduce you.'

'Careful words. What about the rest? Did you hope to find me stupid and gullible?'

You are a Malagash. There was no chance I'd ever think that.'

Varencienne clenched her fists and snarled beneath her breath. 'Right, that's it. I'll be no part of this. Get out.'

'Ren!' He took her by the shoulders, turned her round to face him. 'Think about what you're saying. There's more to this than our feelings. I never intended to hurt or insult you. You are a remarkable woman. If Valraven was king in this land, you'd have power too, and you are the right person to wield it.'

'Oh, so now you've changed your mind and think I should go along with my mother's plan? What about Maycarpe?'

Merlan closed his eyes and shook his head. 'Forget Maycarpe. I'm thinking of you. Of us.'

'Us?' She laughed coldly. 'And what are we? Thieves in the night stealing ephemeral pleasures. There is no "us" beyond this visit. You know it. I'm Valraven's wife, and if you had your way, he'd be living here all the time as lord of Caradore. Would you sleep with his wife beneath his nose? This is just a brief affair.'

Merlan pulled her to him, but she remained stiff and unyielding against his body. 'Don't you think I know that? It grieves me. I will never meet anyone like you again.' He took her face in his hands. 'But we have a chance to help initiate a great change. Caradore can be restored. Our feelings are irrelevant in comparison to that. If you won't do this thing for yourself, for me, for your mother, or Valraven, do it for Rav and Ellony. Think of their futures.'

Varencienne pushed him away from. 'Don't use my children to get at me!'

He raised his arms in exasperation. 'Ren, please!'

The main door to the bedroom opened. Varencienne froze in a posture of horror, while Merlan jumped backward towards the maid's entrance.

At the threshold stood the empress's lady-in-waiting.

'What are you doing here?' Varencienne demanded.

The woman grimaced. 'Forgive my abrupt intrusion, Your Highness, but your mother requested that I station myself here for your service. I have to inform you that Lord Palindrake has just arrived and now waits in your sitting room.'

'Tell him I will visit his chambers shortly.'

The woman's face remained expressionless. 'He was most insistent he should see you now, even though I told him you had gone to bed. May I conduct him here?' Her glance flicked towards Merlan at the hidden doorway.

Varencienne recovered her composure 'Yes, yes, of course. Allow me a moment to ready myself.'

'I shall do my best,' said the woman and departed.

Varencienne turned round, but Merlan had already gone. She sat down on the bed and pressed her fingers against her face. Valraven would not be pleased to have been intercepted by the empress's woman and prevented from seeing his wife immediately. He was used to walking into these rooms whenever he wanted to, even if that was only rarely. Would he be suspicious? Varencienne attempted to compose herself. Why was he here? She heard footsteps in the corridor beyond her door. He was coming. A deep shiver passed through her, and she was compelled to turn quickly and look behind her. There was no one there – no one she could see – but she sensed she was being watched. Merlan must still be hiding just beyond the maid's entrance. He wanted to hear this interview. Varencienne wasn't comfortable with this, but she had no time to order him away now. The door was opening.

Valraven came into the room and closed the door behind him. Varencienne perceived immediately an unusual air about him. He was agitated about something.

'My lord?' Varencienne said, rising from the bed. She realized that she was still fully dressed, which hardly complied with the lady-in-waiting's assertion that she had gone to bed. Valraven did not appear to notice this discrepancy.

'There is a matter I wish to discuss with you,' he said.

For a brief, chilling moment, Varencienne thought he knew about her affair with Merlan. He would not be jealous, but he would chastise her nonetheless, because she was his wife, his property. 'And what matter is that?' she asked.

'A dangerous matter. It is my belief that we must both take great care at this time.'

Varencienne felt a slump of relief within her. This wasn't about Merlan. But what was it about? 'I don't understand. What danger is this?'

'It is to do with your family,' he said. 'Your mother is here for a reason.'

'What reason?' Varencienne could almost see the fear hanging about Valraven like a dark smoke. This was the man celebrated for his fearlessness, who was rumoured to be supernaturally invulnerable to attacks. He had lived through a hundred battles, perhaps taken a thousand lives. He had ordered executions and torturings. What could make such a man afraid?

'Varencienne, I feel you already know some of what I wish to tell you. Let us speak plainly. Your family has a penchant for sorcery. You know as well as I do what has been attempted here before. You also know the consequences of that. When your mother asked me to escort her here, a feeling came to me. It was the same strange feeling I had on the morning when your brother performed a ritual on the beach below the castle. It has a smell to it I recognize. It is the smell of danger and evil.'

Varencienne stood up and walked slowly around him, although she took care not to touch. 'Danger and evil? Valraven, you are an incarnation of that, aren't you? What makes you so afraid? Is it knowledge of yourself, a terrible truth?'

'I know all the truths about myself. I do not fear them. I do not fear for myself at all, but for my family, my children.'

'What was it Bayard tried to do, and that you fear my mother wants to attempt again?' Varencienne had to know the answer to this question before anything else. How much was Valraven aware of his heritage? Had the women been wrong about him all along?

'You know the answer already,' he said.

'Do I? Perhaps I do, perhaps I don't. I wasn't there. All I know is what I've been told. Now I want to hear it from you.'

'I won't play games with you, Varencienne. Don't take me for a fool.'

She saw the hardness creep back into his eyes. She must not push too far. He didn't want to speak of that day, and probably attempted to repress all memory of it, so she must coax the story out of him. 'It's not a game. It's important. I need to know what you think happened.'

'Why?'

She drew in her breath. 'We are not lovers, Valraven, or even friends. You have come to me seeking an ally. Please indulge me. My question is not without portent. Now tell me. What did Bayard try to do?'

'He called something out of the sea, something ancient. It was something our ancestors threw in there, to hide it. Bayard wants it, and so does your mother. I believe they need Palindrakes, me in particular, to gain possession of it, but I have felt it, and never want to feel it again. It is an ungovernable power. We have lost the knowledge of how to control it. Now, it can only wreak destruction.'

Varencienne nodded. 'You are correct in your assumptions. But what if I tell you that I know why Bayard's procedure went wrong? What if I say that you can wield that power again, and that I know how?'

He looked at her with fierce black eyes. 'I would say you are your mother's creature, and I have wasted my time coming here.'

She shook her head. 'You would be wrong. I am my own creature, Valraven, no one else's. Any action I take will be selfish, to preserve myself and that part of myself that lives in the children. When Bayard performed that ritual, Ellony Leckery was the weak link. Pharinet warned Bayard, but he didn't listen. That would not happen again.'

'It wasn't just Ellony,' Valraven said. 'Something entered into me, into all of us. It would have happened whether Ellony had been stronger or not. I cannot begin to describe to you what it felt like.' He sat down on the bed, his eyes unfocused as he remembered. 'I have witnessed the most terrible things. I have seen the worst of human nature. I have seen despair beyond imagination, and pain and grief. I have inflicted those things on people.' He glanced up at her. 'You are right. I am an incarnation of evil, for I can do those things without feeling, without caring. But the reason I am like this is because of what happened that day on the beach. It needs what I do to exist. I have to feed it. It lives deep within me. I had to fight it, push it down deep into my soul. If it is evoked fully again, I will be lost. I will become destruction.' His hands clenched upon his thighs. 'Don't think I fear for myself. I don't care what happens to me. But I don't want to destroy what is left of Palindrake. And I will. I can sense it.' He closed his eyes briefly. 'When I am here, at Caradore, I am completely aware of what I am, what I've become. I remember the boy I was, his innocence. He looks out from a cage behind my eyes. He is the witness. What lives in me now is an engine of war. To win territory, to conquer men: these things give me temporary respite from an urge I can neither understand nor describe.' He looked up at her. 'There is no remorse inside me for what I do. It is my duty for the empire. I want to feel something, but I can't. That, perhaps, is the worst of it.'

He shook his head. 'That day, when Bayard took us to the shore, I believed he would show me something wonderful. We would all be changed. What arrogance!'

Varencienne was silenced. She would never have believed Valraven could speak to her in this way. He was showing to her his inner self, or what remained of it. She could not doubt his sincerity. She sat down beside him and took his hands in her own. He did not flinch or pull away, but neither did he relax or move towards her. 'I understand your fear,' she said softly, 'because I know the nature of what took control of you that day. You are right, my family knows of sorcery. But what my mother seeks to do is erase all Bayard's mistakes. That power you felt, it could be yours, as a force of creation, not destruction. You are from a water family, Valraven, despite your current affinity for fire. Fire can only destroy, but water has the potential for both destruction and creation. It can erode and smash, but it is also a medium for life. Peace can never come from fire or, if it does, it is the peace of silence when all is burned away. Peace *can* come from water. Think about it.'

He was looking at her with curiosity and a faint glimmer of hope. How hagridden he was, how desperate inside to be free of what rode him. 'I am a Splendifer,' he said, 'given to the fire of Madragore. I feel it is the only thing that tempers the force inside me. Whatever it was, it came from the sea. It *is* water.'

Varencienne nodded. 'I understand your feelings. Your perspective is skewed, that's all. You are right, I *do* know why my mother is here, and you are also correct in assuming she wishes to reopen this matter from the past. But she seeks to heal it, to make changes for the better. Val . . .' Varencienne leaned closer towards him, 'you must believe that I have the means to save our son, and all the other sons of Caradore, from a life in the imperial army. I can make you King of Caradore.'

He became suspicious again, pulled away from her. 'You sound like Bayard.'

'Don't make that mistake,' she said. 'I am very different.' She paused. 'You should know that Bayard still loves you. He is not a perfect creature, but he has the potential to be great, just as you do.' Why am I saying these things? she thought. Do I believe them?

Valraven sighed, his expression grim. 'Bayard still loves me. Of course. That's why he did all he did.' He laughed bitterly.

'He did it for love.'

Valraven stood up, expelling an exasperated snort. 'Love? You don't know what you're talking about. You don't know what happened to Khaster, to Tayven.'

She went cold. 'What did happen?'

'I could have prevented it, but I didn't. When I acted, it was too late. All was lost.'

'What do you mean?' she said. 'Tell me.'

He shook his head vehemently. 'No. Almorante made me vow to keep silent and I will. It is a shame upon your family.'

Varencienne stood up beside him. 'You must tell me, you must.'

'I can't,' he said. 'But it assures me no good can come of anything Bayard tried to do here. I don't know what your family has told you, but I can never be king here, Varencienne. Nobody wants that. They just want the power they think is mine.' He laughed coldly. 'And I do not even know what that is. I have no name for it.'

'I do,' Varencienne said softly.

He turned away. 'I don't want to hear it. I came here to seek your aid in preventing your mother from doing anything. If you do not share that desire, I must leave. I must stand against her alone.'

'Then you have nothing to fear. She cannot act without you. She needs your co-operation. You must do this of your own free will.'

Valraven regarded her for a few moments. 'I cannot believe Tatrini's intentions are benign.'

'They are,' Varencienne said. 'I have spoken to her at length. I have not lied to you. She too has asked for my help, which is why I said I could make you king. She requires complicity from both of us. Oh, Valraven, think about this matter! Nobody wants Gastern to inherit. He is a fanatical ascetic. It is time for change. People realize that, many people. You are part of that change, and so am I. It is not just about sorcery, but politics.'

He was silent for a moment. She knew her words had shocked him. 'Is Almorante behind this?'

'No.'

'Bayard?'

'No. Tatrini. She is trying to retain control of something that is very unstable.'

'But if Gastern doesn't inherit, who will? It will mean assassination. Is this what your mother really wants? Is this the reason behind everything?' He shook his head in disbelief. 'She will give me Caradore if I give her Gastern. She thinks I have the capability to sway the military's loyalty.'

'I don't think it's that simple.'

'Who is it, Varencienne? Who does your mother want on the throne?'

'Oh, who do you think?' she said fiercely.

He grimaced. 'Bayard, the most unsuitable candidate. Even little Leo would be a better choice. I can't condone that. Bayard's a maniac. He's no Leonid. Your father believes in what he does. He is a man of Madragore, fighting for what he sees as a holy cause. Gastern might not share his father's nobility, but Bayard cares only about indulgence of the senses.'

'Mother thinks otherwise. She sees potential in Bayard. He may be damaged, as you are, but that damage can be reversed.'

Valraven shook his head again. 'It's as if Leonid has already gone, or doesn't exist. He's in the prime of his life. Where has all this come from? Are we speaking of a revolution here?'

'Mother is concerned for my father's health.'

'Really? I would imagine she's the primary threat to it.' He growled through his teeth. 'The Malagashes are a demon tribe. I want nothing to do with their conniving.'

'We must think about ourselves. What will happen will happen . . .' she paused, in wonderment, and then spoke slowly, 'regardless of what we think or do.' She sat down. 'That was the message. Great Foy.' She put her hands against her face, suddenly breathless.

'What message?'

She looked up at him. 'From Khaster.'

'What?'

'I don't know whether he's alive or dead, Val, but I saw him at the Chair on Mage's Pike. He said, "It will happen regardless of what you think or do". I just spoke those words without thinking.'

'Khaster *is* dead,' Valraven said softly

'He spoke to me.'

Valraven turned away, clawing a hand through his hair 'What is all this? How many strands are there to this weave?'

Varencienne stood up again, went to her husband. 'Val, we have to do it. We have to follow our destiny. I know I'm right. Trust me. We must go to Old Caradore.'

'What? Why?'

'It is the only place. We must turn back time there, make things right.'

'You are deluding yourself.'

'No! You must believe me. I have seen and heard things since I've lived in Caradore that you would not imagine. I am in touch with this land. I sense what it needs. What will happen in Magravandias may be beyond our control, but we have our own corner of the world to take care of. Let us take this opportunity when it's offered.' She believed it herself now. 'Khaster, or his spirit, will take care of you. He is present among us.'

'No one, alive or dead, could have that much capacity for forgiveness,' Valraven said.

'Perhaps he doesn't forgive you. Perhaps he just knows what should be.'

Valraven was silent for a moment. One day, Varencienne would wrest all his stories from him, but not yet. Tonight, he had shown her he was just a man. He had given her power.

'What is it you think we have to do?' he said.

She spoke quietly. 'Go to Old Caradore. It is where Bayard's ritual should have taken place.'

'Must we do the same thing again?'

'Not exactly. Our intention must be to expel this dark influence you feel. It must be remade in its true form.'

'Which is?'

She felt inspired. 'The spirit of this land, free from bitterness and fear. Knowledge will be given to you there. I cannot give it to you, you have to find it for yourself.'

'You do not know how much I want to believe you.'

'I know. I will not ask you to trust me. All I ask is that you dare to dream.'

He stared at her for a moment. 'If you are wrong, all is lost.'

She nodded. 'I know, but I'm confident I am right. Go to my mother. Tell her you will lead us to the old domain.'

He hesitated. 'You surprise me. You are a contradiction.'

She laughed coldly. 'How do you know that? We are virtually strangers to one another.'

Again, a pause. 'Are you implying you want that to change?'

She stared back at him. 'No. I believe we function perfectly well as we are. I can never be the queen of your heart, Valraven. You know that.'

He looked away from her. 'I'll go to your mother, but never forget that the consequences of this night will lie mainly in your hands. Can you accept that responsibility?'

She inclined her head stiffly. 'I have already done so.'

Valraven bowed curtly to her and left the room.

For a few moments, Varencienne stood motionless in the middle of the room, her face pressed into her hands. What had she done? A change had been initiated. Were her actions right, or had she simply fulfilled her mother's desires? Her mind was in turmoil.

A noise from across the room prompted her to raise her head. Merlan stood against the door curtain, his arms folded. 'I am greatly impressed with you,' he said.

'Well, I'm not with you.' Varencienne rubbed her forehead. A needling pain had started up behind her eyes. 'You had no right to eavesdrop on my conversation.'

He laughed and came forward to embrace her. 'Don't be angry. You were incredible. I could almost believe you were inspired by genuine feeling.'

Varencienne uttered a wordless noise of annoyance and pulled away from him. 'Maybe the feeling *was* genuine,' she said.

'Despite everything, he fascinates you, doesn't he?' Merlan remarked. He sounded curious rather than affronted or jealous.

Varencienne remembered the day she had first seen Valraven Palindrake, the brief flutter of excitement that meeting had kindled. 'It is pointless for anyone to feel that way,' she said. 'My marriage to Valraven can never be anything more than it is.'

Merlan made no comment. He sat down beside her, took her hands in his own. 'You must make sure I'm included in the party to Old Caradore.'

'Must I?' She examined him stonily. What had happened to their feelings for one another? Only the day before they had been lovers. Now, it felt different.

He squeezed her hands. 'Ren, don't be bitter. I know it must seem as if I've used you, but . . .'

'And haven't you?' she snapped.

He sighed. 'Used is not the right word. I'm not that callous.' He pressed the backs of her hands briefly to her lips. 'Our affair might only be brief, because of circumstances, but even if you weren't Valraven's wife or Leonid's daughter, I would still have wanted you. Please believe that.'

She couldn't resist laughing. 'You are trying to be gracious, I know. You have a glib tongue. Is this why Maycarpe thinks so highly of you?'

He looked uncertain and his grip upon her hands became loose.

She drew her fingers away and patted his hands. 'It's all right, Merlan. I understand. I'm not angry, just resigned.' She leaned over and kissed him and he pulled her body against him.

'Ren . . .'

'Hush. I want to ask you something.

'What?'

'Do you know what happened to your brother Khaster?'

She felt his body stiffen against her. He let her go and briefly pressed a hand to his mouth. 'What do you mean?'

'You heard what Valraven said. You must know what he was referring to, otherwise surely you'd have commented on it the moment you walked back into this room.'

He closed his eyes for a moment, then nodded. 'I know some of it, although it's not a subject I ever mention in Caradore.'

'Is he alive?'

Merlan sighed. 'I really don't know. Bayard hated Khaster. He was jealous of him, for many different reasons. Khaster didn't help himself. He couldn't resist making the odd jibe at Bayard whenever the opportunity presented itself. It was a dangerous game, and he lost.'

'In what way?'

'I heard all this second-, maybe third-hand. I don't know how much of it is true. Once Khaster returned to Magrast after Ellony's death, he was in a poor state. Almorante took pity on him. He always had a high regard for Khaster. I heard that Almorante engineered a situation between Khaster and a boy named Tayven Hirandel. The lad came from a very high-anking Magrastian family. He was a creature of Almorante's, no doubt sent into a rather dubious royal service by his parents. In Magrast, that would be seen as an honour. It's said that Tayven helped Khaster get over what had happened in Caradore. I really don't know the extent of their relationship, because information of that kind cannot be trusted from a Magravandian. They would always assume such a friendship was sexual in nature. Knowing Khaster, I find that difficult to believe, but even so, Tayven was a good friend to him. Unfortunately, it gave Bayard a weapon to use against my brother.' He frowned, shook his head. 'The details are muddled, but something happened in Cos. As far as I can gather, Bayard had his cronies murder Tayven in a way only a mind like his could devise.'

'No!' Varencienne said. 'That's my brother you're speaking of. I'm sick of Caradoreans saying these terrible things about him.'

Merlan stared at her for a moment. 'I'm sorry, Ren, but it happened. That part of the story, at least, I know is true. Almorante himself had to deal with the situation afterwards. It was all covered up, but I know it happened.'

'How did Bayard allegedly kill this boy? Perhaps it was an accident.'

Merlan laughed. 'I can assure you it wasn't. I don't want to describe it to you.'

'I'm not squeamish. Tell me.'

'No. Suffice to say, it took a long time for Tayven to die. Someone told Khaster what was going on and he went to Valraven for help.' Merlan broke off and pressed his fingers hard against his eyes, shaking his head. 'I have lived that moment for Khas a thousand times. What must he have felt like, pleading with his oldest friend to save the life of someone he loved, when he knew what Tayven was going through at that very moment?'

'What did Valraven do?'

'Nothing,' Merlan said bitterly. 'He alone could have dealt with the situation, but he refused even to listen to Khaster's pleas. Almorante was in Magrast. Khaster was effectively alone. He could do nothing.'

'But why wouldn't Valraven help?' Varencienne asked, perplexed.

Merlan shook his head. 'Who knows how his mind works? People said that his behaviour in Cos had been strange and erratic. He used to cut himself with his own blade, apparently. Whatever happened here in Caradore badly affected his mind. The kindest thing I can say is that he wasn't himself. You heard tonight that he would not speak of it.'

'What happened to Khaster then?'

'The next day, a skirmish occurred in the hills nearby. I heard that Khaster was like a man of stone. He led his men into battle, and in the chaos, they lost sight of him. Later, a body was found that was said to be Khaster's, but not everyone believed it was. A lot of the men felt he'd lost his mind and simply run far into enemy territory. I really don't know, Ren.'

Varencienne felt chilled. She could not speak.

Merlan took her hand again. 'Promise me you will never speak of this to my mother and sisters.'

She nodded. 'You have my word,' she said in a dull voice. 'It would kill them, especially your mother.'

'Nor Pharinet and Everna. Nobody. Promise!'

His urgency shook her from her numbed lethargy. 'I do. I do. I just needed to know, that's all.'

'You can't be glad to hear it.'

'I'm not.' She sighed heavily. 'Can't you look for your brother, Merlan? Can't someone try to find out the truth?'

'People did look. Later, when Almorante heard what had happened, he sent people into the hills, some of his most skilled trackers. They searched for many months. There was no sign of Khaster. If he is still alive, he wants to remain hidden.'

'Perhaps he's forgotten his life, who he is,' Varencienne suggested.

Merlan shook his head. 'Let it go, Ren.' He paused and then stared at her knowingly. 'I think you've spent too much time in the portrait gallery at Norgance.'

She ignored this. 'I can't believe you can just let it rest. If your mother knew, she'd do everything in her power to find Khaster. She'd never stop looking.' She realized at once the implications of her words. 'I'm sorry. That was vile of me. I didn't mean to insult you. You lost a brother.'

'I went through my grief years ago,' Merlan said. 'I've had to reconcile myself to the fact that Khaster is lost to us. To you, it must seem like a recent event. I'm not insulted.'

'Do you hate Valraven for what he did, or rather didn't do?'

Merlan sighed. 'No, not really. You can't hate someone who's so damaged. Bayard was responsible. And one day he will pay for his actions.'

'He is my brother,' Varencienne said defensively. 'And I love him. You said yourself you don't know how much of that story is true.'

'Ren, I'm afraid you're going to have to face up to the fact that, painful though it may be, your brother is not the person you want him to be.'

Varencienne drew her fingers over her face, her shoulders slumped. 'Very few people are, it seems.'

'You must forget about this. Think about what's important now.'

She nodded. 'I will. I'll make sure you are included in the party going to Old Caradore. That's what you want, isn't it? I owe you something for what you've told me.'

'You owe me nothing for that,' he said, then paused. 'Perhaps I'd better go now.'

She smiled wearily at him. 'No. Stay. I won't be disturbed again tonight.'

'Are you sure?'

'Yes. I want to feel something now, something physical. You can give me that.' She reached out to touch his face. 'We are all selfish creatures, Merlan, every one of us.'

Merlan left her bedchamber before dawn. Varencienne could not sleep. She lay in bed, mulling over the previous night's revelations. If what Merlan had told her was true, then Bayard should never be emperor. Bayard. She saw his face in her mind's eye. Could he really be this monster the Caradoreans believed him to be? Merlan's story had changed things. She knew now she must retain control over this situation. If she was to go along with her mother's plans, it must be for Valraven's sake, not Bayard's. 'Oh, Bay,' she said aloud to the cold room. 'Who are you?'

Shortly before breakfast, Pharinet came to Varencienne's chambers. 'Your mother kept us up very late last night,' she said, and Varencienne sensed at once that Tatrini had already spoken to the Palindrake women about her plans.

'You seem to get on quite well with her,' Varencienne replied.

Pharinet frowned. 'Yes, but . . . What is it, Ren? You look distracted. What's wrong?'

Varencienne yawned. 'Nothing. I slept badly. So what do you think of my mother now?'

Pharinet pulled a grimacing face. 'Strangely enough, she surprised me. She appears to talk sense.'

'In what respect?'

'You don't have to skirt the issue. We discussed the visit to Old Caradore.'

'And what are your thoughts on the matter?'

Pharinet shrugged. 'Her arguments were persuasive.'

Varencienne laughed coldly. 'By Foy, this doesn't sound like you. I can't believe you'd ally yourself so quickly with her.'

Pharinet fixed her with a burning stare. 'You know, more than anyone, how much I want Val to be what he was, more than what he was. If Tatrini can help accomplish it, she has my full support.'

'You trust her, then?'

'Don't you? I know she's talked to you about it.'

'I think trust is a priceless commodity. However, I am not wholly against her ideas. It is whether we will retain control that bothers me. Also, although she speaks of Valraven being king in Caradore, she will still need him in Magrast. The two situations are not particularly compatible. That leads me to wonder whether we're being given the whole truth.' Ideas were taking on clearer shape in Varencienne's mind. 'After all, my mother wants to attempt something that failed before, with tragic consequences. We have to be aware of that.'

'But you are not Ellony. Tatrini is not Bayard.'

'True, but are they the components that caused the failure before? We don't really know, do we? It might have been Valraven himself, or even you. It might be the nature of the dragon daughters.'

Pharinet sighed through her nose impatiently. 'I can see the sense of your arguments, but Ren, I really want to try this thing. It's very important to me. I've waited a long time.' She flung up her arms. 'What else do we have? The Sisterhood? They are ineffective. We need something more, and we may not be offered this chance again.'

Varencienne snorted. 'I doubt that. It is very important to Tatrini as well. She won't give up without a fight. She needs us. Therefore we have time to make measured decisions and to take precautions.'

Pharinet nodded. 'You're right, I suppose.' She paused. 'Have you spoken to Valraven?'

'So my mother informed you of that proposal, did she?'

'Of course. We cannot lead him to the rite in ignorance, as we did before. *Did* you speak to him?'

'Yes.' Varencienne gave Pharinet a brief description of the conversation she'd had with her husband the previous night, omitting all mention of Khaster.

Pharinet looked wistful by the end of it. 'Val has never spoken to me about that day on the beach. Never. I had no idea what he thought and felt about it.'

'He wants help,' Varencienne said, 'and may take risks to get it, but he is also afraid. I understand his fears and respect them. He may well be right. We have no way of knowing what will happen when we perform the ritual. We may end up with a monster on our hands, a dragon daughter incarnate.'

'I don't think that will happen,' Pharinet said, 'not if you're involved. You're no simpering weakling. You're strong, and very aware.'

'Don't pin all your hopes on me. I'm a novice at this.'

Pharinet put her hands upon Varencienne's shoulders. 'I have no doubts about you. I am sure this is your destiny.'

Uncomfortable, Varencienne pulled away. 'What about Everna? I can't imagine she was so easily swayed by my mother's talk.'

'She was very much for the idea, actually.'

'That amazes me. Why?'

'Everna has a secret hope, I think. She hopes Thomist might be restored to her.'

'That is a dangerous hope, because it won't happen.'

'We don't know that.'

'We do,' Varencienne said quietly. 'Pharry, if we perform the ritual, and we are successful, we won't see dragons rising from the waves. We won't see dead people walking from the ocean. The effect will be subtle, something that occurs within us. You know that. You're not stuffed with delusions like the Sisterhood. Just who does my mother think should take part in the rite?'

'You, me, Everna, Val and herself.'

Varencienne frowned. 'That's not enough. We need more of a male presence.'

'Merlan?' Pharinet suggested archly.

'Why not?' Varencienne demanded. 'He has knowledge of magic.'

'He is not a Palindrake.'

'Neither is Tatrini. My Palindrake blood is also somewhat thin.'

'Your mother was emphatic that she should select the participants for the ritual.'

'I can deal with her.'

Pharinet waved a languid hand at her. 'Oh, do what you think is right. All I ask is that you take your part.'

After Pharinet had gone, Varencienne felt swamped with depression. Talking about the ritual and expressing hopes was all very well, but the reality was a great unknown. What would Foy want? If she could be given the strength to rise, would she come in joy or resentment? Perhaps a lot of that depended on the state of mind of those who performed the ritual. And that was something that failed to inspire confidence in Varencienne's heart. The Palindrakes would not be able to focus their thoughts dispassionately, and surely that would be an essential requirement if the ritual was to succeed. Everna wanted a dead man to walk from the sea back into her arms; Valraven was full of fear and uncertainty; Pharinet was fired by unrequited love, shame and guilt. These were dangerous ingredients. Varencienne realized she would feel happier if it was just herself, her mother, Merlan and Valraven who performed the rite. That way there would be fewer hidden factors and rogue emotions.

Tatrini, however, when Varencienne spoke to her later, was very much against the idea. 'The Palindrake women must be part of this. They are the dragon priestesses.'

'They are unstable,' Varencienne argued. 'We have to protect ourselves. Also, I'm still half certain that Foy wants only to be left in peace. What you propose may be wrong.'

'Varencienne,' said the empress, 'an elemental force does not have feelings. It just *is*. Whatever emotions might churn through Palindrake hearts, it matters not what kind they are. The dragons need our energy to revive. Emotion is energy, whatever type it is. Foy will rise in strength, have no fear. She will claim back what is hers.'

'You speak with confidence,' Varencienne said, 'but it does not wholly convince me.'

Tatrini laughed. 'Believe me, I have performed a hundred rituals more perilous than this. I never put myself at unnecessary risk.'

'What of Merlan Leckery? Do you agree to him participating?'

She nodded thoughtfully. 'Yes, I suppose so. I can see the sense of including him, because in a way, this will mirror certain aspects of the last ritual. It would have been better to have Bayard present, but of course that would have caused problems.'

For a moment, Varencienne considered saying something to her mother about Bayard, then decided against it. Tatrini must not know her daughter had doubts about him. She moved closer to her mother. 'If we do this thing, you must promise to take every precaution.'

'If?' Tatrini said, leaning away fastidiously. 'There is no if, my dear, only a when. And of course, I shall invoke the strongest possible protection.'

Varencienne shuddered. She realized then her mother wasn't afraid at all.

CHAPTER SEVEN

Home

On this road, Varencienne thought, as the stone ribbon to Old Caradore unfurled before her, Ilcretia had ridden towards the castle as a new bride. Her wedding to the Palindrake heir would recently have taken place in the domain of her parents. Varencienne was sure that Ilcretia had first come to Caradore in the same season that now spread its pageant over the land. Her path too would have been strewn with forest gold. Caradore had been a land unconquered then. The sight of the old castle's towers and turrets through the ancient trees would have inspired wonder and excitement, with no hint of fear and sinister secrets. .

The company crossed the old bridge to the mossy road that surrounded the castle. Everna and the empress travelled in the imperial carriage, flanked by guards, while Varencienne and the others rode their horses ahead of them. Varencienne felt strangely pulled between two times, that of Ilcretia's first homecoming and Valraven's return to his ancestral domain. She wondered, briefly, if Ilcretia had once felt the same wrench. Perhaps, as she'd crossed this bridge, a taint of sorrow to come had brushed her skin like an unseasonal breeze, full of frost. She would have shuddered, felt momentarily afraid, then pushed it from her mind. Varencienne, violated by knowledge, could not push anything from her mind.

Her companions were silent, each cocooned in their own thoughts, although she could hear the whisper of words coming from behind the veiled window of the carriage. The ritual would take place at the hour of sunset, rather than that of dawn, as Bayard had tried before. Tatrini had explained that dusk was the time when, traditionally, the ancient Palindrakes had communed with the denizens of the sea. However, this meant

315

that there would be a few hours to spend in each other's company as they waited for sunfall – a few hours of tension and awkwardness.

Neither Tatrini nor Everna were enthusiastic about climbing over the rubble that blocked the castle's entrance, so guards erected a pavilion outside the walls, where later the ladies would sleep. The empress, dressed in a dark green gown, sat with Everna drinking tea, which one of the guards had prepared for them. The wind made a wing of her high collar and pinched strands of hair from Everna's careful coif. Merlan and Valraven had gone off with Pharinet to look at the keep. Varencienne, shunning company, decided to find a path down to the beach. She found the atmosphere bizarre. It was almost as if they were all enjoying a simple day trip out together, yet in just a few hours, all their lives could be changed irrevocably. It didn't seem possible.

As she descended an overgrown path, she heard a movement behind her. Turning, she saw the silhouette of one of the guards standing at the clifftop. 'I will be fine, go away,' she said. The man took a step back, although she knew he'd continue to watch. Did the empress know of dangers she hadn't mentioned to her companions?

The beach was of fine white sand, with a swathe of black shingle near the water's edge. The tide was out. Immense rocks gowned with thick dark weed rose from shallow moats of trapped sea water. Gulls squabbled on the guano-smeared summits. Behind her, the pleated cliffs were pored with caves. The surroundings were physically similar to the coastal landscape at New Caradore, but the ambience here was very different. Edges were blurred somehow, and a sense of antiquity hung heavily in the air. The trees that leaned over the cliff tops were huge and ancient, their salt-twisted limbs like those of tortured spirits. Mature wild shrubs threw swags of flowers down the rocky face, and descending creepers created billowing green curtains, thrusting out tendrils of leaves. Varencienne was swamped with a feeling of nostalgia for events that had never occurred. History lived on in this place. She was sure that if she let her mind drift, she would hear voices from those times, and figures would flicker across her vision.

Varencienne sat down on a low rock and hugged her knees, resting her cheek upon them. She closed her eyes, listening to the soporific hiss and crash of the far waves. It would be easy to fall asleep here.

She sensed rather than heard footsteps on the sand behind her, and for a while did not raise her head. Whose ghostly feet approached her? Would they show themselves to her?

'Varencienne.' The sound of her name, uttered by an unmistakably human voice, shattered the moment.

'Mother!' She sat up straight. 'I thought you were a ghost.'

The empress picked her way carefully across the shifting sand to the rock and there sat down beside her daughter. 'I am not surprised. The spirit of the place is very strong here. It drugs you like an opiate.'

Varencienne felt uncomfortable with this close proximity, unsure of her mother's motives for seeking her out. She doubted it was a simple desire for her company. 'Is everything ready for tonight?'

'All that needs to be ready is the hearts and minds of those who will participate. That is really beyond my control.' She clasped her hands neatly in her lap. 'We must trust in fate.'

Varencienne rubbed her arms. 'I feel nervous.'

'To be expected.' The empress did not extend a hand to comfort, or even turn her eyes to her daughter. 'I have come here to teach you. There are things you should know before tonight.'

'What things?'

'Some of what was in Ilcretia's book. It was mainly a storybook, you know. But the stories are rooted in history. They concern the ancient contract between the Palindrakes and the Ustredi.'

'What kind of contract?'

Tatrini sighed, narrowing her eyes. 'A potent one. Cassilin Malagash was very much afraid of the ancient sea people. The dragon heir could command them, you see. That link had to be severed, otherwise Magravandias could never control Caradore. Cassilin would have had another Cos on his hands. In the night, the Ustredi would come and wreak their vengeance against the invaders. He could not risk such a thing happening. When Valraven's ancestor uttered his vow to Madragore, thus banishing the sea dragons, he also closed the portal whereby the Ustredi could commune with the land. The contract was broken.'

'I have not heard the Sisterhood mention any of this.'

Tatrini made a scornful sound. 'I am not surprised. They do not know it. Ilcretia made sure the knowledge was never passed on. If anyone cursed this place, it was she. She didn't want anyone coming back here, poking around. At least, not until the time was right.'

'I have thought about Ilcretia along those lines,' Varencienne said. 'But what exactly was the contract the Palindrakes had with the sea people? I presume it was of a spiritual nature.'

Tatrini gave her daughter a considering look. 'You are something of a sceptic, aren't you. Never doubt that the Ustredi are real. They exist in their own realm as we do in ours. As humans, we should not presume to know all the secrets of the world.'

Varencienne laughed in incredulity. 'You're telling me the city I saw in my visions is a real place? How is that possible?'

'The city you saw does not exist at New Caradore.' The empress pointed out towards the east. 'It lies that way, in the murk of a deep crevasse. It is called Pelagra, which is how the Palindrakes got their name. It was originally Peladrake, which means sea dragon. The family was a priesthood to the dragons. There are tunnels beneath the castle that lead down to sunken lagoons. In such places were the rites of the contract observed.'

'How did such a situation come about?' Varencienne asked carefully. She could not believe her mother placed any credence in the old stories.

'I will tell you the legend. Long ago, twin Ustredi, a brother and sister, desired knowledge of the other realms of the world. They hungered to explore the dry land and the sky domain above it. They craved to have dominion over the fire-pits and their denizens. In the book, they are remembered as Mera and Merin, but I think the true form of their names would be incomprehensible to us. They went to the court of Foy and told her that she too, as a mighty elemental queen, should not be confined to the depths of the ocean. In those days, Foy was a serpent and her daughters were tusked fishes. Foy agreed to give the twins a pearl of her power, so that they might be able to survive in elements alien to their own. In return, they would secure for her new territory. Once the peoples of the land turned to her in worship, she would be able to rise from her domain.

'Many of the Ustredi bewailed the twins' plan. They anticipated disastrous results, but they were wrong. Mera and Merin swam to the surface, and as they rose towards the air, they took on a new form. Legs grew from their tails, like the legs of developing frogs or newts. By the time they reached the shore, their tails dropped off completely. Their gills closed up and they took their first painful gulps of air. You can be sure it burned their throats like fire. At first, they could only lie upon the beach, unable to move their weak new limbs, gasping for breath. And so it was that a local girl came upon them. She called for the men of her family who were hunting crabs nearby, and between them, they carried the twins back to their village. The people of the village knew that these were sea people, because their legs were so weak and small, like the legs of babies. I should imagine it was a gruesome sight. Their eyes were very round, like fishes' eyes, and their fingers were webbed. They found it difficult to move in air, because it did not support their bodies in the manner to which they were accustomed. And they could not speak, they could only sing. The people recognized it as the song that fishermen sometimes heard in the night, when their boats were becalmed upon the ocean. Despite living close to the sea, the villagers were worshippers of earth, whose gods were basilisks or earth dragons. Basilisks are green creatures, who can look like thorny bushes. They are small and quick. The people regularly petitioned them to bargain with the sea dragons, so that fishermen's ships might pass unharmed across the ocean's surface. Humans did not attempt to commune with the sea creatures themselves.

'At first, the villagers were afraid of the twins, thinking some terrifying sea beast would come to claim them and perhaps wreak havoc, but as time passed, nothing like that occurred. Mera and Merin's limbs grew strong and true. They learned to speak as humans do, and their faces lost some of their fishy cast. They spoke of the realm beneath the sea, and the Ustredi who lived there. They told of Foy, who was far stronger than the shy basilisks. "Worship Foy," they said, "and the riches of the sea will be yours." Their words and their eyes were persuasive. The people smelled magic on them, and yearned for the promised rewards. So they built shrines to the sea dragons and worshipped there. Foy gained dominion upon the land. She could now walk upon it if she wished. The twins created for themselves a home on the clifftops some distance from the village. They each took a lover from the local community and married them. They had children whose blood, we can be sure, was saltier than most.

'Years passed. The twins remembered their promise to Foy and went travelling. They ventured high into the northern mountains, where the eyries of the sky people were hidden. These were the worshippers of air, and their deities were the cockatrices, winged creatures as befitting their element. Mera and Merin were now very beautiful to behold, and magic shone from them. They brought Foy to the sky people, and had them build temples beneath the crashing veils of waterfalls and beside mountain lakes. Foy's dominion expanded. She could fly now, if she wished.

'Mera and Merin travelled south into the land that is now Magravandias, and here they met resistance. The fire worshippers there wanted none of Foy. Their fire-drakes were strong and immanent in the land. It is common knowledge that fire and water each possesses the capability to destroy the other. They cannot exist side by side together, and this caused a war.

'As people fought on land, Foy rose from the sea, and her form was changed. No longer a serpent, she had aspects of earth and sky. She had wings to fly and feet to walk the land. Terrified of her magnificence and ferocity, the shy basilisks and airy cockatrices fled this earthly plane, and it was left to Foy and her daughters to take on the fire-drakes. Neither side could win, because neither fire nor water can be totally banished from the world, but Foy expelled the fire-drakes from Caradore, and they did not return for many thousands of years.

'The twins created the tribe of Palindrake, who are the intermediaries between the people of the land and the sea. Over the centuries, their humble home expanded into a mighty domain. Beneath it, secret caves and tunnels were constructed, and here, once a year, the Ustredi would rise from their city and visit their hybrid relatives. It is said that strange marriages took place. Sons and daughters of the earth would be given to the Ustredi, who had a great fascination for humankind. They also liked to eat the animals of the land, and these too were given to them. In return, the sea people would bring to the landdwellers riches from the depths. These riches took many forms: not just the treasures from sunken ships, but marine life that could be used as medicines, and visionary philtres. They brought baskets of pearls and living coral and green gems. Foy ruled over all, and it was a time of plenty. Her cold breath kept the fire-drakes of the south at bay. This situation persisted for several thousand years, but then the fire-drakes created for themselves a god on earth. Cassilin Malagash, the Lord of Fire, came to Caradore and took the dragon heir for himself. The contract was broken, and Foy was banished back to the depths of the ocean.'

After Tatrini had finished, Varencienne was silent for a while. Eventually, she said, 'It is a wonderful legend, but surely only that. Don't you think the old stories are really disguises for truth? Perhaps seafaring people interacted with the original inhabitants of Caradore, but I do not think they were merfolk.'

Tatrini nodded. 'I understand your view, and it is healthy. We should not believe in anything too readily, but neither should we dismiss it out of hand.'

'Tonight, perhaps we shall see,' said Varencienne.

'I hope so. I also hope you understand why the sea dragons must return. We should have command over both water and fire.'

'What about air and earth?' Varencienne asked.

'Foy embodies those elements also.'

'The legends say she banished the cockatrices and the basilisks. Surely that's as bad as the fire-drakes banishing her?'

'I think the other elemental creatures were never properly developed by those who conceived their forms. Foy is perfect. There is no need for anything else.'

'Even so . . .'

'Accept what is,' said the empress. 'Now, I think we should return to the others and begin to prepare ourselves.'

The Palindrakes hoped to turn back time – not that of several centuries, but simply six years. Standing with them on the beach, Varencienne realized that for her new family, this wasn't really about tradition, or even about the land itself; it was about personal needs, shame and grief. Their desire for this ritual to make everything right pulsed out of them as a palpable force.

Varencienne herself felt very little inside. Now that the moment was upon her, she did not feel afraid, yet neither could she believe something life-changing was about to happen. Valraven still didn't know his heritage. Would this knowledge be given to him in trance?

At the end of the day, the group gathered in a semicircle on the beach, where the water crept towards them. Varencienne was extremely conscious of Merlan's near presence. Even though they had met secretly over the past couple of days, they had barely exchanged a glance all the way to Old Caradore. She wished they could have had a few moments to talk before the ritual. Tatrini was in control, organizing everyone, instructing them how to breathe deeply and conjure the required physical and mental state. Everna and Pharinet exuded tension like smoke, while Valraven was a motionless and emotionless statue beside them. Varencienne found herself thinking of Bayard, of he and Valraven together. She couldn't imagine it. People had secret lives. They were never really themselves.

Sunset had bloodied the world, and a vast untidy flock of seabirds wheeled against the darkening sky, crying mournfully.

'That is the siren song,' murmured Tatrini. She stood in the centre of the group. 'Varencienne, that is the song you must sing. Listen to them. Call forth the dragon daughters.'

Varencienne opened her mouth and expelled a croak. It was an ugly, rasping sound, the greedy carrion-eater's demand for food. The sound of it struck her as absurdly comical. Was this the way to conduct a rite of such importance? Smothering laughter, she uttered squawks and squeals, imagining herself like the birds above, selfish and mindless, driven by the simple instinct to survive. Around her, the Palindrakes shifted uncomfortably, although she was aware of Tatrini and Merlan being as still as stone. The cries coming from her mouth were changing. As she listened to the gulls, it was possible to perceive a strange melody within their raucous calls. Sounds she could not before have imagined began to emerge from her throat. The atmosphere around them all was transforming. The song came easier now, echoing out over the waves. The seabirds dipped and lifted to its rhythm like musical notes upon the sky of dusk.

Tatrini took one of Valraven's hands in hers, and one of Varencienne's. She stepped towards the encroaching tide, taking them with her. 'Dragon queen, dragon daughters, come forth from the cold darkness,' she called.

'The siren song of the sea wife calls unto you. Come now to the dragon heir, who is your avatar on earth. We await your presence.'

Varencienne continued to sing, and now her voice seemed small upon the night. The seabirds were silent, wheeling around her, the only sound the whirr of their wings. The ocean appeared sullen, heaving towards the land. Strange lights pulsed within it, some distance from the shore. Varencienne's voice faltered.

· 'Sing on,' murmured the empress, gripping Varencienne's hand tightly. 'They come.'

They come, thought Varencienne. Yet isn't one of them here already in Valraven? What are we drawing to us? Where is the protection my mother spoke of?

Varencienne suddenly felt vulnerable and was overwhelmed by an urge to flee. She pulled against her mother's grip, but the empress would not let go. 'Do not give in to fear,' she said. 'It is an animal instinct. Rise above it.'

A silvery green smoke hovered above the waves. Within it, Varencienne could perceive indistinct shapes. 'Can you see that?' she cried. 'Can you all see it?' She glanced around at the others.

'There is a mist,' said Pharinet, narrowing her eyes.

'Something,' Everna agreed in a strangely slurred voice.

Merlan said nothing, although his eyes looked wild.

Varencienne glanced at Valraven. 'I see two shapes,' she said. He smiled at her. In the twilight, his skin looked greenish. Varencienne shuddered. The smile was not Valraven's smile. *She* was in him. 'Who are you?' Varencienne murmured.

'Summon them!' ordered the empress, apparently oblivious of what was taking place beside her.

'Who *are* you?' Varencienne cried

The answer echoed in her mind. *Missssk.* She thought she saw Valraven lick his lips with a thin, forked tongue. The dragon daughter had risen within him. Her presence hung around his body like a second skin. Varencienne swallowed painfully, for her throat was utterly dry. 'Come forth,' she said slowly. 'Come forth, Misk, and join your sisters.'

Valraven hissed. *No. This is my skin.*

'It is the skin of the dragon heir,' Varencienne said. 'You must leave it. Behold, your sisters are waiting.'

With her free hand, Varencienne gestured at the sea. Two sinuous female forms now undulated within the sparkling green smoke. They preened themselves with clawed hands. They writhed and sighed, wrapped in shifting cloaks of green hair. Their eyes were serpents' eyes. Beyond them, Varencienne could see dark shapes bobbing upon the waves. Sleek backs broke the surface of the water. Seals or Ustredi?

'Come forth,' Varencienne said again. 'Misk, take us to the ancient realm. The contract will be revived and your mother will rise again. But you must come forth.'

Again, a hiss. *The dragon heir must be restrained. If he speaks the old words of power, the land will fall to flame. Such is the will of the fire lord.*

'No,' Varencienne said. 'That will not happen. I am a daughter of fire. I am Cassilin's daughter. I am here to remake his word.'

She could see a misty face superimposed over Valraven's features. Misk had resided for six years in a human body. She would not relinquish it willingly.

Between Varencienne and Valraven, the empress was now silent, although encouraging her daughter with her eyes. *You know what to do. Go with your instincts.*

'Misk, come into me,' said Varencienne. 'Experience a woman's heart, a woman's body. Isn't that more what you desire?'

'Yes,' breathed Tatrini.

A sly expression flickered across Valraven's features. Then a leaping force almost knocked Varencienne from her feet. The impact forced the breath from her body. She could not breathe. An alien, smothering presence was inside her, too active, too forceful. 'Misk!' she cried.

Valraven looked dazed. He stared at her in horror.

This is what Ellony felt, Varencienne thought. I have to go into the waves. I can't resist it. I have to go.

She pulled away from her mother's hold and began to run the short distance to the lip of the incoming tide. She heard voices cry out her name behind her in fear and despair. She laughed. She did not care. Her sisters were there, beckoning to her, eager to embrace her once more. *I bring you flesh, dear ones. Sweet human flesh.*

We have been waiting, beloved.

The water swirled around Varencienne's ankles, snatching at her skirts. No one could stop her. No one.

Then she felt hands upon her arms, pulling her back. She snarled and wriggled. No human could restrain her. She was too powerful for their feeble strength to match hers.

'Leave her! I command you!' Valraven's shout was close to her ear.

A jolt passed through her body. Misk was listening; she could not disobey. The dragon heir's function was to command the denizens of the

323

sea. Varencienne could hear Merlan's voice calling out to her, but it seemed to come from very far away. Valraven was close to her. He was all that existed.

'Get out,' he said, in a low voice. 'Get out, Misk. I command you.'

Varencienne experienced a terrible, wrenching pain throughout her entire body. It felt as if her guts were being torn out of her. She uttered a shuddering cry. Misk streamed out of her, trailing silvery green smoke. Jia and Thrope rose up as columns of twisting water, drawing her in.

Valraven pulled Varencienne back towards the sand. She was retching uncontrollably, vomiting seawater that was filled with tiny crabs and fishes.

'Tatrini!' Valraven cried, his voice full of fear. 'What is this?'

The empress came forward. 'It's all right,' she said. 'You did what was right. In your heart, you knew instinctively what to do. It is your function, Valraven.'

Varencienne straightened up, wiping her mouth. The spasm had passed. Everna, Pharinet and Merlan crowded round her, uttering words of concern.

Tatrini ushered them back. 'We have summoned the daughters,' she said. 'Control yourselves. Valraven and Varencienne must complete the process.'

'Complete it how?' Varencienne asked.

She looked to Merlan for support, but he merely shrugged helplessly. He could not help her. He could only observe, for to offer suggestions now would alert the empress to the fact he had more knowledge than she imagined.

The empress, however, clearly needed no advice. She faced Valraven. 'Command the dragon daughters to take you both to Foy,' she said. 'Not as sacrifices to the sea, but as guests of the underwater realm. They must sing the song to call your souls from your bodies.'

The misty shapes still hovered over the waves, as if awaiting Valraven's orders. He shook his head. 'I saw her,' he said. 'Her name was Misk. She was in me.'

'Yes,' said Tatrini. 'She is a daughter of Foy, the dragon queen. She is yours to command, Valraven. This is the knowledge that has been kept from you.'

Unexpectedly, Pharinet uttered a moan. 'Great Foy, our beloved Caradore,' she said, her fingers pressed to her face. 'He must never know the truth. It will destroy us.'

'Silence!' Tatrini grabbed Pharinet's arm. 'You have awaited this moment for years. Banish the fear.'

Pharinet shook her head. 'I cannot. The time has come, yet I'm afraid.'

'Fear of that ancient vow is in our blood,' Everna said.

'Perhaps that is what gives it power,' Merlan suggested. 'Her Mightiness is right – you must ignore or banish it. Fear is what keeps you in chains.'

'It would be foolish and dangerous for us to ignore it,' Everna said. 'Varencienne and Valraven must question the dragon daughters. We must be sure of . . .'

'Oh, be quiet!' Tatrini snapped. 'We have no time for leisurely interviews. The deed must be done, the link to the past broken. I have more knowledge of this matter than you.'

'I hardly think . . .' Everna began.

Varencienne turned away from them all. Valraven was standing at the water's edge, oblivious of the argument, staring at the place where the eerie mist roiled above the sullen sea. Varencienne went to him. 'Do you understand?' she asked.

He nodded vaguely. Looking at him, Varencienne could see the boy that Pharinet mourned for. He was not himself, she decided, but then reconsidered. Perhaps the man she had known until now, the one so beloved of the emperor, had really been Misk. It would be easy to try and absolve Valraven for his actions, but that would be too convenient. Behind her, Merlan argued in a cool voice with the women. At that moment, it seemed inconceivable she was close to him. He was just another voice on the outside, while she seemed cocooned in a separate world, with Valraven at her side. She could no longer understand what the others were saying to one another. The sounds they made were merely the petty squabble of seagulls over carrion on the beach.

Valraven pointed towards the hovering mist. 'They are diminishing,' he said softly, 'fading away.'

Varencienne nodded. 'Then perhaps we should go with them.'

'Will it mean the end for Caradore, Ren?'

She shrugged. 'I don't know. I really don't. But we're here, and we came with the intention to revive your power. We must do it, or for ever torment ourselves with thoughts of what might have been.'

Valraven glanced down at her. 'I cannot give this power to your mother,' he said. 'Of all things that is the one I am most sure about.'

Varencienne sighed. 'I know. I don't think she *could* have it. Ask the daughters to sing the song, Val. You don't have to invoke the curse. Just learn what you are.'

Valraven stared at her for a moment, then faced the dragon daughters. He did not speak aloud. From far away, came the rushing of an approaching storm. A wind whipped up the waves. Valraven took Varencienne's

325

hand. The song stole into her mind, spun around inside her head as if it was an empty cave. She had a yearning to leave the prison of flesh, and the sensation of being pulled from her body grew stronger and stronger.

They were in an underwater cavern, lit by flickering torchlight. Around its edge was a rocky shore and here a number of people had gathered. Dark, glossy shapes broke through the surface of the oily water. Ustredi. The people were singing to them. Baskets and carts were arranged upon the damp sand, filled with joints of meat, cheeses, hams, fruit. Young people, decked in flowers and shells stood among this produce.

Varencienne and Valraven stood some distance back from the group, although Varencienne knew they were in no danger of being seen. She and her husband were invisible ghosts in this world. They were far below Old Caradore. 'These are your ancestors,' she said. 'They are honouring the contract between the people of the land and the people of the sea.'

'I remember,' Valraven said, 'but these are not my memories.'

'They are the memories of your blood,' Varencienne said.

A sheet of water seemed to fall before her eyes. The world rippled. Varencienne realized her attire had changed. She was now wearing a loose, ill-fitting robe of coarse green cloth, as was Valraven beside her. They must have become part of this time. She gripped his hand more tightly. He began to walk towards the water, taking her with him. As they approached the shore, people turned to stare and their ranks parted. They bowed as Varencienne and Valraven walked between them. Women threw their skirts up over their faces to hide them, while men placed their hands over their eyes.

Are we so hideous to them? Varencienne wondered

At their approach, the sleek shapes in the water became agitated. The surface boiled with their movement and haunting cries filled the air. Valraven released Varencienne's hand and raised both his arms. At this gesture, the youths and maidens bedecked with flowers ran forward, uttering ululating shrieks, and threw themselves in among the restless Ustredi. The sea cries became more predatory. Now the Ustredi reared up from the water, beauteous creatures, hideous creatures. They flexed the claws of their long-fingered webbed hands. They shook their weed curtains of hair. Fish-lipped mouths gobbled at the dry air. They fell upon the willing sacrifices, pawing at their bodies, dragging them down. The farm produce was left ignored on the cold wet sand. The Ustredi wanted living tribute. The victims made no sound, and on the shore, the waiting company murmured soft prayers to Foy.

Varencienne observed these proceedings impassively. It was the way of things. She knew the time had come for her to cast off her loose robe and dive into the water. Her body craved this element. Her skin itched uncomfortably. Only the cool salt tide would soothe her. She and Valraven must join the Ustredi, who would soon return to their city beneath the sea. She pulled the robe over her head, while Valraven tore the cloth from his body. His skin was hairless and greeny-white in the dim light; his facial features had become more blunt. When he turned to Varencienne and smiled, she saw that his teeth were pointed like a shark's. Despite these strange changes, he possessed a stark, alien beauty. From his expression, she could tell that her appearance was similarly changed. They had become Mera and Merin, the first of the Palindrakes.

Once again joining hands, they dove into the water, following the Ustredi who had now begun to retreat from the cave. Varencienne could see their lissom shapes below her, trailing a wake of shining bubbles. She could just make out the floating gowns of the sacrificial girls, the limp limbs of the youths. Crushed flowers broke free from their bodies and drifted up past her like flakes of perfumed skin. She swam with her arms pressed close to her sides, using the muscles of her belly, torso and thighs to undulate through the dark water. Her desire to breathe ripped open the seals of the long unused gills at her throat.

The Ustredi were joyous in their return to Pelagra. They had brought their prodigal siblings with them. Varencienne was caressed by the swift bodies that darted over and under hers. The sea was filled with the sound of their fluting purrs. And then the great crevasse was before them. The city below exuded a strong acid green radiance. Varencienne and Valraven plunged over the abyss amid their brethren. They felt the cold burn of that subaquatic light, the life-giving properties of its rays.

Down they swam to the great triangular entrance of the temple of Foy. They had come to report to her, to tell her of their great victories over the people of the earth. The Ustredi swam away, carrying the drowned bodies of the sacrifices among them. Valraven and Varencienne went into the temple. They did not have to swim down miles of labyrinthine corridors as Varencienne had done the last time she'd made this astral journey. On this occasion, Foy was vigorous and strong, curled upon a vast dais in the cathedral vault of the first hall. Her appearance was clearly serpentine and her wings resembled elaborate fins or the floating tails of great fishes. When Foy noticed her visitors, her head snaked upwards on a sinuous neck, and a long black tongue flicked out of her mouth to take morsels from a passing shoal of tiny bright fish. Varencienne could feel the immense slow tide of the dragon queen's feelings. They were not like human emotions, nor even the cold instincts of the Ustredi. This was truly elemental, the primal form of every existing feeling. Mera and Merin's interaction with the people of the land had changed Foy. She was becoming more human, because of the human faith that poured into her. The land people were reshaping her with their thoughts.

Foy's voice resounded inside Varencienne's head. There were no words, but symbols and colours that formed a language she could understand. 'Show to my daughters the wonders of the world you have explored.'

'It is our pleasure, great queen, to bring you this tribute,' Varencienne replied.

A gout of acidic radiance engulfed the dragon queen, and from this emerged the etheric forms of Jia, Misk and Thrope. Like Foy, their appearance was very different to what Varencienne had seen before. They were primitive mermaidens, with neckless fishes' heads. Their eyes were devoid of any feeling, but a cold passionless intelligence lurked in their glassy depths. The daughters came weaving out from the shadow of their mother, their dead eyes fixed upon the changed forms of the beings they perceived as Mera and Merin. So the emotion of envy was born in the collective soul of the seapeople. Jia, Misk and Thrope gazed upon these semihuman forms and found them beautiful.

'Give this to us,' they said in unison. 'Give us your shape.'

'This shape comes from living on the bare land,' said Valraven. 'It involved sacrifice to attain.'

'We would do that,' said the daughters, sidling closer. 'Oh Merin, you are fine to look upon. Let us taste this shape.' They sniffed around Valraven and Varencienne's bodies. 'Oh, Mera and Merin, let us eat of these strange tides that move through your bodies. We want to experience these clenches of the heart, these cataracts of intention.'

'These are feelings you describe,' said Valraven. 'They come from living upon the land, among human folk.'

'We could do that,' said the dragon daughters.

Unexpectedly, Foy expelled a rumbling gust of disapproval, making the water roil. From the wild splashes of colour that flashed across her mind, Varencienne sensed the dragon queen perceived the hunger in her daughters and detested it. 'No!' she roared. 'These tastes are for me alone, for only I have the wisdom to use them. You are wild, daughters. You are hungry. Move back.'

Jia, Misk and Thrope ignored their mother. Without further words, and with a callous precision, their essence slid into the bodies of Valraven and Varencienne, crossing from one to the other in rapid succession. Varencienne reeled beneath this violating assault. She sensed the icy inquisitiveness of the dragon daughters, the surge of lust they experienced to wear human flesh. It was a hunger that would never leave them.

'We shall linger, yes we shall,' they sang, squirming their dark essence through Varencienne's flesh.

'No,' said Varencienne, though she was powerless to prevent them.

Beside her, Valraven's face was stretched into a rictus of agony. His body swayed as the daughters investigated it.

'Enough!' boomed Foy, lashing out with her tail. This action sent both Varencienne and Valraven flying, but was enough to expel the curious daughters from their bodies.

'Mother, what is yours is ours to share,' they sang. 'For are we not of your being, your presence?'

'You are the dreams I have had in the dark,' replied Foy. 'Know your place.'

The dragon queen's head thrust forward towards her visitors. 'You have not come here alone,' she said, 'but draped with ghosts. They think of fire.' She lashed her great head. 'What is their purpose? What calamity do they portend?'

'I have come to learn the history of my people,' Valraven said.

The dragon queen regarded him with one of her round eyes, cocking her head to the side. She sniffed him and recoiled. 'You have carried a taint to me.'

She began to twist and writhe upon her dais, uttering audible sounds of distress. Her daughters wheeled around her, crying out in fear.

Varencienne reached for Valraven. The boiling water made it difficult to see what was happening, or to control their own movement. They were in danger of being expelled from the temple on a current of Foy's feeling. Valraven was torn from Varencienne's grasp. She was helpless to prevent it, and saw his body twisting away from a her, a pale shape in the greenish murk.

Images slapped across Varencienne's inner eye. She saw the human followers of Foy carrying the dragon banners into the land of fire. She saw the battles, which were bloody and protracted. The representations of the fire-drakes and the court of Foy flapped, ripped and tattered, in the hot smoky wind. She saw the evolution of Foy, from sea serpent to a creature embodying other elements. She saw Foy rise in splendour from the ocean on wings of immense span that were like intricate carvings of coral. Delicate spines adorned her head like a crown. Her claws were of mother-of-pearl. This was Foy in her prime, full of vigour to beat back the onslaught of the smaller, quicker fire-drakes. The Palindrake family were the guardians of the land, interbreeding with pure humans down the millennia until virtually all the aspects of the Ustredi had vanished within them. All that remained was the ability to commune with the seapeople and with the sea dragons themselves. Jia, Misk and Thrope, covetous of human shape, but nevertheless still within their mother's control, transformed into the sirens, creatures who were imagined in a variety of forms. They were beautiful seamaidens, they were smaller versions of their great mother who could fly in sea or sky, and they were sail-like predator fish, attended by a court of manta rays. The dragon daughters were feared and respected, for the land people knew their ways were capricious, but they could still be petitioned to grant boons and to exact revenge on enemies. The song of the dragon daughters could be captured in great shells and used as an allure by the lovesick.

Varencienne experienced this pageant of images. She saw the generations of Palindrakes, enacting rituals beside the sea, ensuring the prosperity of the land. But then a dark and bloody smoke came encroaching from the south. Within it was concealed the army of Cassilin Malagash. Old Caradore fell before them, and the dragon heir was forced to swear fealty to Madragore, the lord of fire. The Ustredi fled from this influence, and no longer came to the cool caverns beneath the castle. No one remained there to greet them in any case.

Foy sank down to the furthest reaches of Pelagra. The wounds inflicted on the slaughtered dragon heir manifested as injuries on her own body. Her essence leaked from her as a black stream. She lay in pain, tortured by the strong emotions of those who had previously worshipped her. The dragon daughters, free of their mother's influence, became dark hags to harass the living souls they so envied. The dragon heir was lost to Foy. She could no longer commune with him, the sea wife, and their cabal of priests and priestesses, for all had been disbanded. Ilcretia Palindrake, fearful of the consequences of the Malagash dynasty having recourse to the ancient sea magic, made sure this would never occur. She sacrificed her son to the fire, let the fire-drakes cast their ember wings over him. The secret history remained in the book her daughter took to Magrast, but the rituals themselves were never recorded. It was up to Ahrenia to instruct her own daughters and other female relatives in this lore.

For a moment, Varencienne thought the story had ended, for the sight of her inner eye went dark, then a flash of light made her wince. She felt wind against her body and saw the beach of Caradore, illuminated by a dull green light. Valraven was there, and Pharinet and Bayard. Varencienne could see spiky colours of lust emanating from all three of them, a mutual need and hunger. Then she saw Ellony. It was the moment before the dragon daughters took her. Ellony was looking right at her, as if Varencienne was hovering above the sand some feet away from her. Varencienne saw the overwhelming fear in Ellony's eyes, the hideous awareness of all that would happen to her. She saw the rushing formless shapes of the dragon daughters fly past her and force themselves cruelly into Ellony's frail body. She saw the ghastly transformation, the thousand different expressions of terror, lust, greed, hunger, despair, misery and glee that crossed Ellony's face. Can I help you? Varencienne thought. She felt strangely serene, even though what she saw appalled her. She sensed Ellony reaching out to her through time, desperate for someone to save her, someone strong. Varencienne almost felt as if she could reach out and pluck Ellony from her fate, hold her close, shield her. But then a dark figure came running across the sand, a man. It must be Thomist. The dragon daughters were delighted. They wrenched Ellony's body into fearsome contortions as Thomist sought to control them. Varencienne could hear their laughter. Then it was too late. Ellony and Thomist were dragged into the sea, taken down beneath the waves.

The images in Varencienne's head turned to mist and blew away. She found herself hanging as a blade of silver light, like an etheric eel, before the present form of Foy. Insubstantial luminous forms hung from the dragon queen's ragged body like sucker fish. They were attenuated and gaseous, but Varencienne was still able to recognize two of them as Ellony and Thomist. Here their spirits must have clung for six years, prisoners of the underwater realm. Varencienne sensed that Foy was unaware of their presence. The spirits clung to her, because there they were safe from the predations of the dragon daughters, but they needed release.

Something swam past Varencienne, a spined half-human creature with a long, sinuous tail and taloned hands. Black hair streamed from its head and all the way down its spine. It was Valraven. He glided up to Foy and hung before her in the water.

The dragon queen examined him through a tired eye. She could barely lift her head. Varencienne became tense. Could he raise the dragon queen now? Could he restore her glory?

Valraven swam close to Foy and caressed her gently heaving flank with waving fins. Varencienne could see his life force shooting out from his body in spiked rays of light. If anyone, or anything, had the power to heal Foy, it was he.

The dragon queen raised her snout a little and blinked her enormous eyes. Was there hope in her expression, or fear?

Valraven hovered before her, his fins spiralling blurs along his flanks. 'Great queen, do you hear me?' he asked.

'I hear you,' Foy replied.

'Then accept my command.'

'I hear you,' said Foy.

'Sleep,' said Valraven. 'Be at rest. The hurt will leave your body. The torment will leave your mind.'

Foy exhaled a plume of bubbles in an immense sigh. Her eyes closed and the life seemed gradually to leave her body, until all that lay before Valraven was a monstrous heap of bleached bones, broken coral and waving weed, whose shape barely suggested the form of a sleeping dragon. The untidy pile shifted and collapsed, and at the same moment, all the captive souls began to stream upwards like a shoal of shining fish.

Varencienne opened her eyes and found herself standing upon the shore beneath the shadow of Old Caradore. Time seemed not to have passed, for the setting sun was still visible in the sky. Tatrini and the others still appeared to be arguing over what should be done, but they appeared, strangely, to have increased in numbers. A large crowd of shadowy shapes gesticulated angrily at one another. Varencienne could pay no attention to them and turned away. Over the water hung the vague shifting shapes that could be sea-mist or dragon daughters.

Valraven sighed deeply and rubbed his face with his hands. Then he raised his arms. 'Go forth,' he said. 'Jia, Misk, Thrope. Go forth. Return to your realm.'

Varencienne watched him curiously. When she glanced back at the sea, there was no sign of the mist, but standing on the water, appearing as solid as herself, were Ellony and Thomist. They were smiling, but did not speak. Ellony raised one hand towards Valraven and Varencienne felt a wave of energy wash over her. It was the ultimate compassion and forgiveness. She blinked, and in that moment, Ellony and Thomist disappeared.

Varencienne became conscious she was still holding on to Valraven's hand. He stared at the water with an unreadable expression on his face. 'They're safe now,' Varencienne murmured. 'They've gone to their proper place.'

Valraven closed his eyes briefly. 'I know.' He turned to Varencienne. 'I could have raised Foy,' he said. 'I nearly did.'

'I realized that,' Varencienne replied. 'I could feel it. Why didn't you?'

He shook his head. 'It was not for me.' He withdrew his hand from Varencienne's shoulder. 'I am what I am. It is too late, but perhaps those who come after me will have their chance.'

Varencienne nodded slowly, cradling her own cold hand, which had held him. 'It is why I wanted children.'

Valraven breathed in through his nose as if summoning courage and resolve. 'Tatrini must make me King of Caradore as she promised. It is the only way. We have to embroil ourselves in this matter. But I have no power to give her.'

'She doesn't know that,' said Varencienne. 'That may be our best hope.' She paused. 'However, the dragon daughters still appear able to manifest in this world, and you commanded them, so perhaps you're not as impotent in this situation as you think.'

He pulled a sour face. 'Give Tatrini the dragon daughters? Is that wise?'

'Did I say that?' Varencienne replied. 'If a person has never tasted the whole feast, they are content with the savoury crumbs that fall from the table.'

Valraven sighed again. 'There could be a bloody conflict ahead of us. Am I right to ally myself with this faction? My loyalty is to Leonid.'

'We must do what we can to survive. I am sure nothing will occur immediately.'

'And in the meantime, Magravandias marches upon the world.'

Varencienne narrowed her eyes. 'Do you feel different now that Misk has left you?'

'I feel awake,' he said.

Varencienne squeezed his hand. 'We must go to the others. Stop their squabbling.' She paused, looking at the group further up the beach, which was now clearly visible to her. It had increased in numbers; Varencienne's eyes had not deceived her. The Leckerys were there, accompanied by Dimara and a couple of her cronies. They must have followed the empress's party out of Caradore. 'Oh,' Varencienne said. 'This looks like trouble.' How had they learned of Tatrini's plans?

'What is it?' Valraven said. 'What are *they* doing here?'

'It is the Sisterhood of the Dragon,' Varencienne said dryly. 'Your secret priestesshood. No doubt they have come to lend their strength to yours.'

Valraven raised an eyebrow at her.

'I'm sure they mean well,' she said.

Voices were raised in anger. The empress and Dimara exchanged insults, while Saska wrung her hands, comforted by Everna. Niska and Ligrana stood uncertainly by Pharinet, their expressions tense. Merlan stood back from the situation, his expression half amused, half furious. Whatever else might have occurred while Varencienne and Valraven had experienced their visionary journey, it was clear the group on the beach had not seen

Ellony and Thomist rise from Pelagra. They had been too busy arguing for that. Varencienne despised them. They were so blind.

Valraven marched up to them and for some moments stood with folded arms watching the altercation. Merlan was first to notice Valraven was there and moved closer to the others, observing the dragon heir carefully.

Dimara's face was pushed near to Tatrini's. Both women had shed their dignity and clearly didn't care. 'You have no right to place your taint in this place!' Dimara was saying, arms waving.

'You are nothings,' Tatrini responded coldly, a withering sneer on her face. 'Get back to your hearths and your gossip.'

'You thief, you mother of thieves!' yelled Dimara.

'Silence!' Valraven cried, and everyone froze at once.

Then Dimara recovered her composure and her voice. 'My lord, we are here as your servants and your priestesses. Once we heard what this woman was planning, we came here at once.'

'How did you hear of this?' Varencienne demanded.

Dimara examined her with contempt. 'You Magravandians believe you have us all dancing like little puppets to your tune. Well, you are wrong.'

'They had to know,' said Everna, betraying herself.

Tatrini laughed. 'We all have our *sources*.'

'And who exactly is yours, mother?' Varencienne said. 'Everna as well? That would make everything neat and tidy, wouldn't it?'

'It isn't Everna,' Valraven said. 'The Empress Tatrini has eyes and ears everywhere.' He turned to Pharinet. 'Hasn't she, sister?'

'Pharinet?' Varencienne exclaimed. The implication of this accusation made her flesh chill. Pharinet, she had trusted.

'Val,' Pharinet said, in a low voice. 'You didn't have to . . .'

'Oh don't judge her,' he said. 'We are both Magrast's creatures. Bayard made sure of that.'

'La la la,' trilled the empress sarcastically. 'How wonderful these revelations are. What will come next, I wonder?' She cast a knowing eye at Merlan. 'Have *you* any dark secrets, young man?'

'Enough of this,' said Dimara impatiently. 'Nothing I, or my sisters, hear concerning Pharinet Palindrake surprises us, but our family are above reproach. I suggest we return our attention to the matter at·hand.' She bowed slightly to Valraven. 'My lord, forgive us. We demean your actions with this pointless debate. I know what you have been driven to attempt. Now, you must tell us, is all well with you?'

'I am in good health,' Valraven said.

'Then . . . what happened?' Dimara asked.

Valraven shook his head. 'There will be time for that. First of all, you tell me what all the shouting was about.'

Dimara pulled herself to her full height. 'The Malagashes are in possession of hallowed Caradorean property. We demand that it be returned to us.'

Valraven frowned. 'I don't know what you mean.'

'The sacred book,' said Dimara. 'It was stolen by the oppressors.

Valraven glanced at Varencienne.

'It was a history book,' she said, 'full of ancient tales. Ilcretia's daughter, Ahrenia, took it with her to Magrast when she married.'

Valraven nodded shortly. 'I see.'

'No you don't,' said Dimara. 'She twists the truth. The book belongs to us. These thieving vermin have no right . . .'

Valraven interrupted her. 'Mistress Corey, whatever your feelings, I should remind you that you are referring to the Empress of Magravandias and her family. Keep a civil tongue in your head.'

'Quite right,' said Tatrini. 'I could have you thrown into a Magrastian dungeon, or your tongue cut out '

Valraven narrowed his eyes at Tatrini. 'As for you, madam, your behaviour here is unseemly. Have you no pride?'

Tatrini closed her eyes briefly and shook her head, her lips pursed. 'It is inconsequential. While these interlopers have been yelling at us, we've been unable to assist you in your task. We must begin the process again . . .'

'No,' said Valraven. 'It is complete.'

Tatrini frowned. 'Complete?'

'Yes.' Valraven folded his arms. 'I understand so much now. For too long others have born the weight of my own fear, shame and guilt. But no longer.'

'Foy, did she speak to you?' Tatrini asked. 'You must tell us.'

'Foy will not rise,' Valraven said.

'You must try again, as I suggested,' Tatrini began, but Valraven silenced her with a raised hand.

'Foy will not rise, because I have given her peace. She sleeps restfully now, and you will attempt to raise her at your peril.'

'Then the Ustredi . . .'

'No,' Valraven said. 'I will not revive the contract, especially for you. I am your servant, Your Mightiness, but I also know that you, and any of your blood, cannot treat human sacrifice with the proper reverence such selfless acts deserve.'

Tatrini laughed. 'My lord Palindrake. How bravely you speak, and yet if it wasn't for me, you wouldn't have this new awareness. You cannot refuse me my requests. Have you no honour?'

'You have what you came for,' Valraven said. 'As I said, I am your servant, and more use to you now than before. It is my duty to serve those who come after me in this world, and if you treat them well, you will have my unswerving loyalty. This I swear.'

Dimara raised her arms. 'All hail Valraven, Dragon Lord of Caradore.'

'Save your praises,' Valraven said. 'None of us are divine or righteous. We are all motivated by small concerns and undeserving of communing with elemental powers like Foy. All we can aspire to is the greed of the dragon daughters.' He smiled coldly at Tatrini. '*They* are yours, madam, for they are all I can give you.'

Tatrini addressed her daughter. 'Is this true?'

Varencienne shrugged. 'I saw Foy given rest. I saw Ellony and Thomist freed to travel to the next world.' At this point, Saska and Everna both uttered soft cries, but Varencienne ignored them. 'I know that Valraven is right. We cannot raise Foy. She is damaged and no longer the power that she was. The Palindrakes have changed. Their blood has mingled with the people of the fire-drakes. We cannot look to the past to solve current dilemmas. In my opinion, we should work together to form new strategies for the future.'

Tatrini raised bunched fists. 'But the elemental power, Varencienne. You have seen it, felt it. It must be ours.'

Varencienne shook her head. 'It is my belief that human drive and human reason are all that we need to make a new world for ourselves. To think otherwise is a delusion. Our very existence, and all that we are, is magic.' She smiled at Merlan. 'We have intelligence, we have passion, we have creative thought. We are the stars of the universe, each glowing brightly. All we require is selflessness, to think carefully about the world we might create for our children.'

Valraven put his hand upon her shoulder. 'She speaks sense. Let us leave this place.'

Night had fallen upon the beach of Old Caradore. As the party began to move back towards the cliff path, Varencienne paused and turned back to the sea. She did not know, could not imagine, how her life would progress from here. There were so many possibilities. Valraven called to her, but she did not turn round. She sensed that a circle had been completed, but which one? That which had begun six years ago, or that which had started with Cassilin's conquest of Caradore? Had she merely taken the first few steps upon a new circle, one that she, Valraven and their families had initiated and therefore must complete? On the horizon, the sky was dark with oppressive clouds, which threatened the moon. Those clouds could so easily eclipse the light of the stars. Varencienne hugged herself. She felt afraid.

EPILOGUE

The young man, wrapped in a sand-coloured cloak that hid all but his eyes, moved silently through the hot dark streets of Akahana. The perfume of musk, of ambergris and of frankincense filled the air. The paving stones of the narrow alleys were still hot, even though it was well past midnight, and from the high windows, lit by flickering orange lamps, threads of music stole out towards the stars.

The palace of the imperial governor dominated the square now known as Leonid Place. Flags hung limply in the still air, garlanded only by swift tiny bats that, at sundown, had swarmed out of the tombs in the nearby desert. The young man moved silently up the wide steps towards the columned portico. His feet made no sound upon the stone. He moved like a phantom. The official on duty at the booth in the hallway opened up the door. The young man came inside. 'I am expected,' he said.

The official inclined his head curtly. 'This way, if you please.' He led the way along a high-ceilinged corridor, which was lit by hanging lamps of dull brass. At the end, a door, standing open. The room beyond contained a variety of Mewtish and Magravandian appointments. Ancient statues stood upon a plush carpet that had come from the court at Magrast. A delicately wrought coffeepot reposed upon a heavy table of black wood, the feet of which were clawed. Light and darkness, thought the young man, and unwound his cloak from his face, letting his long pale hair fall forward on to his chest.

'The agent from Cos, my lord,' said the official and departed.

In the middle of the room, a divan stood beneath a lamp of bronze on a long metal pole. Dim, honeyed light fell on to the man who sat there. He had just put down a book and now laced his long-fingered hands before his face. His expression was wry, upon a lean tanned face. He was of middle years, though his alert posture and bright eyes suggested a fit and youthful body and mind. He wore Mewtish attire, a long, soft pleated robe, belted with gold. 'You are late,' he said to his visitor. 'I expected you for dinner. Yours was spoiled.'

'An unavoidable delay at the port, Lord Maycarpe,' the visitor replied. 'I regret any inconvenience.'

'The inconvenience is yours. You must be hungry.'

The visitor made no comment, but sat down opposite his host.

'Thank you for making this journey,' said Lord Maycarpe. 'I have looked forward to meeting you. I am quite sure this land will delight you, especially after the rather barbaric climate of Cos. I insist that you stay here for a month or so.'

'You are gracious,' said the visitor. 'I have often wondered what Mewt is like.' A slight ironic tone in his voice suggested he had no interest in this introductory small talk. He smiled, an expression of enquiry on his face. *Tell me why I'm here.*

Lord Maycarpe straightened up in his chair. 'Word has come from Caradore,' he said, lifting a narrow fragile decanter from the table beside him. 'It may interest you.'

The young man's left foot moved slightly. That was all.

Maycarpe looked up at him from beneath his arched silver-black brows. 'Drink?' he enquired, gesturing with the decanter.

The young man nodded and held out a hand, into which Maycarpe placed a small ceramic tumbler, no bigger than an eggcup, which he filled with a dark brown liquor. The scent of honey and myrrh filled the room.

'Word has come that the Dragon Lord, Valraven Palindrake, has returned to the old domain,' said Maycarpe.

'Good,' said the visitor and drained his cup. 'What do you want of me?'

Maycarpe sighed. 'Ah, what a question! How many times you must have asked it. And what a variety of replies you must have received.'

The young man's face remained expressionless. 'What do you want of me?'

Maycarpe gestured widely. 'Your dedicated bitterness,' he said. 'What else?'

'Then send me to Magravandias. Send me with a crock of poison, with a dart, with a knife. This I will do. You know that. You could have sent word to me in Cos. Why summon me here?'

Maycarpe smiled. 'Because I wanted to see you. You are a legend, you know. I am curious.'

'Now you have seen me. Tell me what you want.'

Maycarpe shook his head. 'I am not disappointed. You are still beautiful. There are many functions for a man such as yourself in the destiny of the world. People love beauty. They worship it. Can't you see how useful you could be?'

The young man appeared slightly confused by these remarks. He frowned. 'My purpose is to kill, to purge the world of the taint of Malagash. There is nothing beyond it. I am nothing but this purpose. And it is the only thing I can give you.'

Maycarpe nodded. 'Mmm. I can see you'd never opt for public life again, which is a shame.'

'You are correct. A man came to me in Cos and told me it is your aim to instate Palindrake as emperor. I was made to swear in blood I would never speak of this to anyone but yourself. This is an ambitious aim. Does it still stand?'

Maycarpe pulled a face. 'I am not entirely sure. There are so many variables to the situation. I prefer to take the least action possible, for I have found fate itself generally resolves most dilemmas.'

'That and the art of Mewtish priests,' said the young man. He held out his tiny cup and Lord Maycarpe refilled it. 'Will you send me to Magravandias?'

'No. It took me too long to find you, too long to rehabilitate you. I will not squander you now, for that is what would happen. You are too fragile, my friend, to face the fire dragon in its lair.'

'You underestimate me.'

Maycarpe shook his head. 'I assure you I do not. I am aware of your qualities, all of them. I would like to explain how you might help me. The families of Caradore are of the sacred blood. They are a resource. And there are plenty of them, not just Palindrake, though they are of course the ruling faction, or will be. The time will come when I, and my colleagues, will need this resource. We have spent many years studying the multitude of possible futures, through the stars, the demon smoke of alchemical fires and the minds of sleeping men. We have ascertained who will be the most important figures in the coming conflict.'

'I cannot see how this relates to me. I am not Caradorean.'

'Listen to me. There is one, a man who is known to you. It is essential he is brought into our circle, because he has great knowledge, but also, unfortunately, the potential to be a danger, or perhaps just a nuisance. He has no love for the Malagash dynasty, but little for Palindrake either. He will oppose us, whatever strategy we adopt. He has his own plans, formulated mainly through confusion, fear, pain and grief. He must be tamed, educated, seduced.'

The young man put down his tumbler on Maycarpe's table. There was a weary, bitter resignation to his expression. 'I know I am not a warrior of the field, but in one skill I excel, for those who took me in taught me well. I have been educated by the most adept Cossic assassins, as well as by your agents. I can move unseen through the night, or the shadows of a shuttered house. I make no sound. I can kill and be away before a single drop of blood seeps from the wound. This is my function now. It is not seduction.'

'Of course. I meant no insult, but when I reveal the name of this man to you, I feel sure you will understand.'

The young man shrugged. 'Well?'

'Khaster Leckery,' said Lord Maycarpe, fixing his visitor with a stare.

The young man did not react. He merely said, 'That is the name of a dead man.'

'Yes,' drawled Maycarpe distractedly. 'In one sense, he is dead. In a very real sense. In another, he is not.'

The young man stood up. 'I cannot help you. I am no necromancer.'

'Sit down,' said Maycarpe. 'I appreciate this news must trouble you, but please do not run away and hide. You have done enough of that.'

The young man hesitated, but did not sit down. 'I cannot help you, even if I wanted to.'

'Not yet, perhaps. Our prey is clever. He is invisible in the world. All I know is his shadow, his presence, hanging like smoke at the boundary of my perception. I can smell him. I sense his determination, which is partly insane, but therefore all the more potent. I, and my colleagues, have searched for him, but all we can divine is a name. Khaster Leckery, a minor scion of a minor Caradorean house. Not at all an important or powerful individual, you might think. The man he was knew nothing of sorcery and little of life. But the name is there upon the tongues of our seers. Why? One day, we will find this man. It is inevitable. The reason I am revealing your future mission to you now is so that, when we do, you will have had time to formulate an efficient strategy to deal with him.'

'I will not do it.'

Maycarpe frowned quizzically, gazed up at the ceiling. 'Ah,' he said, 'you have come so far. You were forged in a fire of suffering, but like a good sword, you had to be pulled from the fire at the right time, otherwise your blade would have become nothing but a formless, molten mass. It was I who pulled you from the flame.'

'I did not ask for it.'

'No, and I do not expect gratitude, but please accept that by conspiring with me in continuing to live and thrive, you took on a responsibility.

You could have cut open your veins, starved yourself. You did not. You wanted to live. I presume you still do so.'

'I have worked well for you in Cos. You know I have.'

'Indeed, and I am pleased with you for it. Ready yourself for what will come. That is all. You have no choice in the matter.'

The young man stared hard at Maycarpe, who stared back. There was no sound in the room, but for the faint sizzle of the lamp. Eventually, the young man said, 'You want me to find Khaster Leckery for you? Is that it?'

Maycarpe smiled. 'How generous of you to offer, but no. You couldn't do that.'

'Does he really still live?'

Maycarpe grimaced. 'Well, I assume so. Some part of him. Somewhere.'

'Cossic agents told me his body was found on the battlefield.'

'The evidence was never conclusive.'

The young man made a small, agitated gesture with one hand. 'The man I knew would want no part of what you're involved in. He would never have been a danger or a nuisance to someone like you.'

'People change,' Maycarpe said. 'Look at you.'

The young man was again silent for a while. Maycarpe picked up his book once more, leafed through it idly, but really he was looking at his visitor, perhaps perceiving the conflicting thoughts that raged in his mind. Maycarpe did not interrupt the process. He licked a finger, turned a page.

After some minutes, the young man made an abrupt movement, hardly more than a shiver. He raked his fingers through his shining hair. 'There is something I can give to you,' he said. 'It may facilitate your task.'

Maycarpe closed the book carefully, laid it on his lap.

'You are a great magus,' said the young man.

Maycarpe nodded. 'People call me that.'

'Then this might be of use to you.' The young man held out his hands and took from one of his fingers a ring.

Maycarpe took it and examined it. 'The Leckery crest,' he said, turning the shining object in his fingers. 'Khaster's?'

The young man nodded.

'Hmm,' said Maycarpe. 'I have had in my possession other personal effects of his. None of them, not even the most intimate, have given me a window on to his whereabouts.'

'That is a window on to his pain,' said the young man. 'It may be more informative.'

Maycarpe examined his visitor for a few moments, and his wary expression suggested he thought he might have misjudged the young man after all. 'Thank you,' he said and put the ring into a pocket of his robe.

Sounds came from the hallway, those of someone entering the building and walking along the corridor. Footsteps approaching. Lord Maycarpe became alert and spoke urgently, yet softly. 'When you see the man who is about to enter this room, his appearance may be a shock to you. Please do not react. He is a protégé of mine, for whom I have great hopes, but at this time, I do not wish him to know your identity. Is that clear?'

The young man nodded, frowning slightly, and sat down again. Behind him, the door opened. Maycarpe's face took on a warm expression of greeting. 'Merlan!' he cried. 'Good to see you back. We have much to speak of, much indeed.'

The story continues in

CROWN OF SILENCE